The Dragon Charmer

By Jan Siegel

Prospero's Children
The Dragon Charmer

The Dragon Charmer

◆

Jan Siegel

DEL REY *THE BALLANTINE PUBLISHING GROUP*
NEW YORK

www.delreydigital.com

LIBRARY OF CONGRESS CATALOGING-IN-PUBLICATION DATA
Siegel, Jan.
The dragon charmer / Jan Siegel.—1st ed.
p.   cm
"A Del Rey book"
ISBN 0-345-43902-3
I. Title
PR6069.I32 D7 2001
823'.914—dc21   2001025188

Manufactured in the United States of America

First American Edition: August 2001

10   9   8   7   6   5   4   3   2   1

Acknowledgments

Thanks to all at Voyager for their support, their confidence in me, and their editorial endurance, most notably Jane Johnson, Lucas LoBlack, Kelly Edgson-Wright, and publicist Susan Ford, who went to such lengths to avoid working with me again that she actually had a baby. My special thanks to Chris Smith, whom I telephone whenever I'm bored, frustrated, or simply in need of instant communication, in the sure and certain knowledge that he will be at his desk and willing, if not happy, to talk to me. My gratitude and affection to you all.

After Blake: DRAGON

We dreamed a dream of fire made flesh—
we gave it wings to soar on high—
an earthquake tread, and burning breath—
a thunderbolt that clove the sky—
its belly seethed with ancient bile;
its brain was forged in *human* guile
and *human* strength with Vulcan's art
beat out the hammer of its heart.

We dreamed a dream of hide and horn—
the wonder of a thousand tales—
we built from prehistoric bones—
we armored it in iron scales—
and all our rage, ambition, greed
reshaped our dream into our need
with mortal hands to seize the fire—
to more-than-mortal power aspire.

And when the heav'n threw down the sun
and seared whole cities from the earth,
when silence fell of endless death
and wail of demons brought to birth—
when far above the shattered skies
the angels hid their rainbow eyes—
did *we* smile our work to see?
Did Man, who made the gods, make Thee?

Prologue

Fernanda

That night, she dreamed she was back in the city. It was not the first such dream: she had had many in the weeks since she left, some blurred, beyond the reach of memory, some clearer; but this was the most painfully vivid. She was standing on the mountainside wrapped in the warm southern dusk, in a blue garden musky with the ghosts of daytime flower scents. Here were the villas and palaces of the aristocracy, set among their terraced lawns and well-watered shrubberies. There was a house nearby: she could see the golden arch of door or window floating somewhere behind a filigree of netted stems. Its light drew her; and then she was close by, staring inside.

There were three people in the room: a woman, a young man, and a girl. They were sitting close together, deep in talk. She knew them all—she knew them well, so well that it hurt to look at them—the youth with his averted profile, just as he had appeared the first time she saw him properly, and the woman with silver glints in her long hair, though she was not very old, and the girl with her back to the window. Herself. She wore the veil she had been given on the last day, hiding her cropped head, but the colors and patterns that had always seemed so dim and elusive poured down her back like some inscrutable liquid script, tinted in rainbows. It had the power of protection, she had been told. Her unspecified anguish crystallized into the horror of imminent doom; she saw herself marked out by the veil, designated for a future in which the others had no part. She tried to enter through the glassless window, but an invisible barrier held her back; she cried out—*Take it off! Take off the veil!*—but her voice made no sound. The whorls and sigils of the design detached themselves from the material and drifted toward her, swirling together into a maelstrom, and she was rushing into it, sucked down and down into deep water.

And now the blue that engulfed her was the ultramarine of an undersea world. Great weeds arose in front of her, billowing like curtains in the currents of the wide ocean. They divided, and she passed through into a coral kingdom. But beyond the branching fans of white and scarlet and the groping tentacles of hungry flowerets she saw isolated pillars, roofless walls, broken towers. She floated over gaping rooms where tiny fish played at hide-and-seek with larger predators, and the spotted eel and giant octopus laired in cellar and well shaft. And ahead, in the shallows, the sun turned the water all to golden green, and she made out the gleaming spire of a minaret, the curve of a fractured dome. Then at last she found what she knew she had been seeking. He lay in a dim hollow beyond the reach of the sun, and stones weighted the rags of his clothing, and his dark hair moved like filmy weed in the current, and white shells covered his eyes. She lifted the stones that pinned him down, and removed the white shells, and kissed his cold, cold lips—a witch's kiss, to break the spell—and his eyes opened, and gazed at her. The water receded like waves from a beach, and he was lying on an apricot shore under a sky of bronze, and his arms were reaching for her . . .

The dream faded toward awakening, and, as always, there was

a moment in between, a moment of unknowing, when the past lingered and the present was void, a waking to hope and the brightness of a new day. Then realization returned, and all that she had gained, and all that she had lost, rushed over her in a flood of suffering reborn, so she thought her spirit was too frail a thing to endure so much pain. And it was the same every day, every waking. She remembered that it was her birthday, her seventeenth. Tomorrow she would return to London, to school, to study, to the slow inexorable unrolling of her predictable life. She was a diligent student: she would take exams and go to university and succeed in a suitable career. And one day perhaps she would marry, because that was what you did, and have children, and live to be forty, fifty, ninety, until, unimaginable though it seemed, she was old and tired, and the dream came from which there was no awakening. A life sentence. Maybe eventually the acuteness of her loss would dull to an ache, and the routine of her daily existence would numb her feelings and deaden her heart; but in the morning of her youth she knew that this moment, this emptiness was relentless and forever. She had been told she had the Gift, setting her apart from other mortals—that if she willed it she might live ageless and long—but that fantasy had gone with the city, if indeed it had ever been real. And why should she wish to lengthen the time of her suffering?

When she got up she found the veil discarded on a chair—the veil that was all she had left—its patterns dimmed to shadows, its colors too subtle for the human eye. For a minute she held it, letting its airy substance slide through her fingers; then her grip tightened, and she pulled with sudden violence, trying to tear it apart, but the gossamer was too strong for her. She made a sound somewhere between a laugh and a cry, looked in vain for scissors, not knowing whether to be relieved or angry when none came to hand. Finally, she folded it up small—she was always methodical—and thrust it into the back of a drawer, willing it to be gone with her dreams, back into the otherworld from whence it came.

Downstairs there was melon for breakfast—her favorite—and presents from her father and brother. "What do you want to do for your birthday?" they asked.

"Go back to London," she said. "For good."

Part One

Witchcraft

♦

✦ I ✦

I have known many battles, many defeats. I have been a fugitive, hiding in the hollow hills, spinning the blood-magic only in the dark. The children of the north ruled my kingdom, and the Oldest Spirit hunted me with the Hounds of Arawn, and I fled from them riding on a giant owl, over the edge of being, out of the world, out of Time, to this place that was in the very beginning. Only the great birds come here, and a few other strays who crossed the boundary in the days when the barrier between worlds was thinner, and have never returned. But the witchkind may find the way, in desperation or need, and then there is no going back, and no going forward. So I dwell here, in the cave beneath the Tree, I and another who eluded persecution or senility, beyond the reach of the past. Awaiting a new future.

This is the Ancient of Trees, older than history, older than memory—the Tree of Life, whose branches uphold Middle-Earth and whose roots reach down into the deeps of the Underworld. And maybe once it grew in an orchard behind a high wall, and the apples of Good and Evil hung from its bough. No apples hang there now, but in due season it bears other fruit. The heads of the dead, which swell and ripen on their stems until the eyes open and the lips writhe, and sap drips from each truncated gorge. We can hear them muttering sometimes, louder than the wind. And then a storm will come and shake the Tree until they fall, pounding the earth like hail, and the wild hog will follow, rooting in the heaps with its tusks, glutting itself on windfalls, and the sound of its crunching carries even to the cave below. Perhaps apples fell there, once upon a time, but the wild hog does not notice the difference, or care. All who have done evil in their lives must hang a season on that Tree, or so they say; yet who among us has *not* done evil, some time or other? Tell me that!

You may think this is all mere fancy, the delusions of a mind warped with age and power. Come walk with me then, under the Tree, and you will see the uneaten heads rotting on the ground, and the white grubs that crawl into each open ear and lay their eggs in the shelter of the skull, and the mouths that twitch and gape until the last of the brain has been nibbled away. I saw my sister once, hanging on a low branch. Oh, not my sister Sysselore—my sister in power, my sister in kind—I mean my blood-sister, my rival, my twin. Morgun. She ripened into beauty like a pale fruit, milky skinned, raven haired, but when her eyes opened they were cold, and bitterness dragged at her features. "You will hang here, too," she said to me, "one day." The heads often talk to you, whether they know you or not. I suppose talk is all they can manage. I saw another that I recognized, not so long ago. We had had great hopes of her once, but she would not listen. A famine devoured her from within. I remember she had bewitched her hair so that it grew unnaturally long, and it brushed against my brow like some clinging creeper. It was wet not with sap but with water, though we had had no rain, and her budding face, still only half-formed, had a waxy gleam like the faces of the drowned. I meant to pass by again when her eyes had opened, but I was watching the smoke to see what went on in the world, and it slipped my mind.

Time is not, where we are. I may have spent centuries staring into the spellfire, seeing the tide of life sweeping by, but there are no years to measure here: only the slow unrelenting heartbeat of the Tree. Sysselore and I grate one another with words, recycling old arguments, great debates that have long degenerated into pettiness, sharp exchanges whose edges are blunted with use. We know the pattern of every dispute. She has grown thin with wear, a skeleton scantily clad in flesh; the skin that was formerly peach-golden is pallid and threaded with visible veins, a blue webbing over her arms and throat. When she sulks, as she often does, you can see the grinning lines of her skull mocking her tight mouth. She has come a long way from that enchanted island set in the sapphire seas of her youth. Syrcé they named her then, Seersay the Wise, since Wise is an epithet more courteous than others they might have chosen, and it is always prudent to flatter the Gifted. She used to turn men into pigs, by way of amusement.

"Why pigs?" I asked her, listening to the wild hog grunting and snorting around the bole of the Tree.

"Laziness," she said. "That was their true nature, so it took very little effort."

She is worn thin while I have swollen with my stored-up powers like the queen of a termite mound. I save my Gift, hoarding it like misers' gold, watching in the smoke for my time to come round again. We are two who must be three, the magic number, the coven number. Someday she will be there, the *she* for whom we wait, and we will steal her soul away and bind her to us, versing her in our ways, casting her in our mold, and then we will return, over the borderland into reality, and the long-lost kingdom of Logrèz will be mine at last.

She felt it only for an instant, like a cold prickling on the back of her neck: the awareness that she was being watched. Not watched in the ordinary sense or even spied on, but surveyed through occult eyes, her image dancing in a flame or refracted through a crystal prism. She didn't know *how* she knew, only that it was one of many instincts lurking in the substratum of her mind, waiting their moment to nudge at her thought. Her hands tightened on the steering wheel. The sensation was gone so quickly she almost believed she might have imagined it, but her pleasure in the drive was over. For her, Yorkshire would always be haunted. "Fern—" her companion was talking to her, but she had not registered a word "—Fern, are you listening to me?"

"Yes. Sorry. What did you say?"

"If you'd been listening, you wouldn't have to ask. I never saw you so abstracted. I was just wondering why you should want to do the deed in Yarrowdale, when you don't even like the place."

"I don't dislike it: it isn't that. It's a tiny village miles from any-where: short stroll to a windswept beach, short scramble to a windswept moor. You can freeze your bum off in the North Sea or go for bracing walks in frightful weather. The countryside is scenic—if you like the countryside. I'm a city girl."

"I know. So *why*—?"

"Marcus, of course. He thinks Yarrowdale is quaint. Charac-terful village church, friendly local vicar. Anyway, it's a good ex-cuse not to have so many guests. You tell people you're doing it quietly, in the country, and they aren't offended not to be invited. And of those you *do* invite, lots of them won't come. It's too far to trek just to stay in a drafty pub and drink champagne in the rain."

"Sounds like a song," said Gaynor Mobberley. "Champagne in the rain." And: "Why do you always do what Marcus wants?"

"I'm going to marry him," Fern retorted. "I want to please him. Naturally."

"If you were in love with him," said Gaynor, "you wouldn't be half so conscientious about pleasing him all the time."

"That's a horrible thing to say."

"Maybe. Best friends have a special license to say horrible things, if it's really necessary."

"I like him," Fern said after a long pause. "That's much more important than love."

"I like him, too. He's clever and witty and very good company and quite attractive considering he's going a bit thin on top. That doesn't mean I want to marry him. Besides, he's twenty years older than you."

"Eighteen. I prefer older men. With the young ones you don't know what they'll look like when they hit forty. It could be a nasty shock. The older men have passed the danger point so you know the worst already."

"Now you're being frivolous. I just don't understand why you can't wait until you fall in love with someone."

Fern gave a shivery laugh. "That's like . . . oh, waiting for a shooting star to fall in your lap, or looking for the pot of gold at the foot of the rainbow."

"Cynic."

"No. I'm not a cynic. It's simply that I accept the impossibility of romantic idealism."

"Do you remember that time in Wales?" said her friend, harking back unfairly to college days. "Morwenna Rhys gave that party at her parents' house on the bay, and we all got totally drunk, and you rushed down the beach in your best dress straight into the sea. I can still see you running through the waves, and the moonlight on the foam, and your skirt flying. You looked so wild, almost eldritch. Not my cool, sophisticated Fern."

"Everyone has to act out of character sometimes. It's like taking your clothes off: you feel free without your character but very naked, unprotected. Unfinished. So you get dressed again—you put on your*self*—and then you know who you are."

Gaynor appeared unconvinced, but an approaching road junction caused a diversion. Fern had forgotten the way, and they stopped to consult a map. "Who'll be there?" Gaynor enquired when they resumed their route. "When we arrive, I mean."

"Only my brother. I asked Abby to keep Dad in London until the day before the wedding. He'd only worry about details and get fussed, and I don't think I could take it. I can deal with any last minute hitches. Will never fusses."

"What's he doing now? I haven't seen him for years."

"Postgrad at York. Some aspect of art history. He spends a lot of time at the house, painting weird surreal pictures and collecting even weirder friends. He loves it there. He grows marijuana in the garden and litters the place with beer cans and plays pop music full blast; our dour Yorkshire housekeeper pretends to disapprove but actually she dotes on him and cossets him to death. We still call her Mrs. Wicklow although her Christian name is Dorothy. She's really too old to housekeep but she refuses to retire so we pay a succession of helpers for her to find fault with."

"The old family retainer," suggested Gaynor.

"Well . . . in a way."

"What's the house like?"

"Sort of gray and off-putting. Victorian architecture at its most unattractively solid. We've added a few mod cons but there's only one bathroom and no central heating. We've always meant to sell it but somehow we never got around to it. It's not at all comfortable."

"Is it haunted?"

There was an appreciable pause before Fern answered.

"Not exactly," she said.

The battle was over, and now Nature was moving in to clean up. The early evening air was not cold enough to deter the flies that gathered around the hummocks of the dead; tiny crawling things invaded the chinks between jerkin and hauberk; rats, foxes, and wolves skirted the open ground, scenting a free feast. The smaller scavengers were bolder, the larger ones stayed under cover, where the fighting had spilled into the wood and bodies sprawled on the residue of last year's autumn. Overhead, the birds arrived in force: red kites, ravens, carrion crows, wheeling and swooping in to settle thickly on the huddled mounds. And here and there a living human scuttled from corpse to corpse, more furtive than bird or beast, plucking rings from fingers, daggers from wounds, groping among rent clothing for hidden purse or love locket.

But one figure was not furtive. She came down from the crag where she had stood to view the battle, black cloaked, head covered, long snakes of hair, raven dark, escaping from the confines of her hood. Swiftly she moved across the killing ground, pausing occasionally to peer more closely at the dead, seeking a familiar face or faces among the silent horde. Her own face remained unseen but her height, her rapid stride, her evident indifference to any lurking threat told their own tale. The looters shrank from her, skulking out of sight until she passed; a carrion crow raised its head and gave a single harsh cry, as if in greeting. The setting sun, falling beneath the cloud canopy of the afternoon, flung long shadows across the land, touching pallid brow and empty eye with reflected fire, like an illusion of life returning. And so she found one that she sought, under the first of the trees, his helmet knocked awry to leave his black curls tumbling free, his beautiful features limned with the day's last gold. A deep thrust, probably from a broadsword, had pierced his armor and opened his belly, a side swipe had half severed his neck. She brushed his cheek with the white smooth fingertips of one who has never spun, nor cooked, nor washed her clothes. "You were impatient, as always," she said, and if there was regret in her voice, it was without tears. "You acted too soon. Folly. Folly and waste! If you had waited, all Britain would be under my hand." There was no one nearby to hear her, yet the birds ceased their gorging at her words, and the very buzzing of the flies was stilled.

Then she straightened up, and moved away into the wood.

The lake lay ahead of her, gleaming between the trees. The rocky slopes beyond and the molten chasm of sunset between cloud and hill were reflected without a quiver in its unwrinkled surface. She paced the shore, searching. Presently she found a cushion of moss darkly stained, as if something had lain and bled there; a torn cloak was abandoned nearby, a dented shield, a crowned helm. The woman picked up the crown, twisting and turning it in her hands. Then she went to the lake's edge and peered down, muttering secret words in an ancient tongue. A shape appeared in the water mirror, inverted, a reflection where there was nothing to reflect. A boat, moving slowly, whose doleful burden she could not see, though she could guess, and sitting in the bow a woman with hair as dark as her own. The woman smiled at her from the depths of the illusion, a sweet, triumphant smile. "He is mine now," she said. "Dead or dying, he is mine forever." The words were not spoken aloud, but simply arrived in the Watcher's mind, clearer than any sound. She made a brusque gesture as if brushing something away, and the chimera vanished, leaving the lake as before.

"What of the sword?" she asked of the air and the trees; but no one answered. "Was it returned whence it came?" She gave a mirthless laugh, hollow within the hood, and lifting the crown, flung it far out across the water. It broke the smooth surface into widening ripples, and was gone.

She walked off through the wood, searching no longer, driven by some other purpose. Now the standing hills had swallowed the sunset, and dusk was snared in the branches of the trees. The shadows ran together, becoming one shadow, a darkness through which the woman strode without trip or stumble, unhesitating and unafraid. She came to a place where three trees met, tangling overhead, twig locked with twig in a wrestling match as long and slow as growth. It was a place at the heart of all wildness, deep in the wood, black with more than the nightfall. She stopped there, seeing a thickening in the darkness, the gleam of eyes without a face. "Morgus," whispered a voice that might have been the wind in the leaves, yet the night was windless, and "Morgus" hollow as the earth's groaning.

"What do *you* want of me?" she said, and even then, her tone was without fear.

"You have lost," said the voice at the heart of the wood. "Ships are coming on the wings of storm, and the northmen with their ice-gray eyes and their snow-blond hair will sweep like winter over this island that you love. The king might have resisted them, but through your machinations he is overthrown, and the kingdom for which you schemed and murdered is broken. Your time is over. You must pass the Gate or linger in vain, clinging to old revenges, until your body withers and only your spirit remains, a thin gray ghost wailing in loneliness. I did not even have to lift my hand: you have given Britain to me."

"I have lost a battle," she said, "in a long war. I am not yet ready to die."

"Then live." The voice was gentled, a murmur that seemed to come from every corner of the wood, and the night was like velvet. "Am I not Oldest and mightiest? Am I not a god in the dark? Give me your destiny and I will remold it to your heart's desire. You will be numbered among the Serafain, the Fellangels who shadow the world with their black wings. Only submit yourself to me, and all that you dream of shall be yours."

"He who offers to treat with the loser has won no victory," she retorted. "I will have no truck with demon or god. Begone from this place, Old One, or try your strength against the Gift of Men. *Vardé!* Go back to the abyss where you were spawned! *Néhaman! Envarré!*"

The darkness heaved and shrank; the eye gleams slid away

from her, will-o'-the-wisps that separated and flickered among the trees. She sensed an anger that flared and faded, heard an echo of cold laughter. "I do not need to destroy you, Morgus. I will leave you to destroy yourself." And then the wood was empty, and she went on alone.

Emerging from the trees, she came to an open space where the few survivors of the conflict had begun to gather the bodies for burial, and dug a pit to accommodate them. But the grave diggers had gone, postponing their somber task till morning. A couple of torches had been left behind, thrust into the loose soil piled up by their labors; the quavering flames cast a red light that hovered uncertainly over the neighboring corpses, some shrouded in cloaks too tattered for reuse, others exposed. These were ordinary soldiers, serfs and peasants: what little armor they might have worn had been taken, even their boots were gone. Their bare feet showed the blotches of posthumous bruising. The pit itself was filled with a trembling shadow as black as ink.

Just beyond the range of the torches a figure waited, still as an animal crouched to spring. It might have been monstrous or simply grotesque; in the dark, little could be distinguished. The glancing flamelight caught a curled horn, a clawed foot, a human arm. The woman halted, staring at it, and her sudden fury was palpable.

"Are you looking for your brother? He lies elsewhere. Go sniff him out; you may get there before the ravens and the wolves have done with him. Perhaps there will be a bone or two left for you to gnaw, if it pleases you. Or do you merely wish to gloat?"

"Both," the creature snarled. "Why not? He and his friends hunted *me*—when it amused them. Now he hunts with the pack of Arawn in the Gray Plains. I only hope it is *his* turn to play the quarry."

"Your nature matches your face," said she.

"As yours does not. I am as you made me, as you named me. You wanted a weapon, not a son."

"I named you when you were unborn, when the power was great in me." Her bitterness rasped the air like a jagged knife. "I wanted to shape your spirit into something fierce and shining, deadly as Caliburn. A vain intent. I did not get a weapon, only a burden; no warrior, but a beast. Do not tempt me with your insolence! I made you, and I may destroy you, if I choose."

"I am flesh of your flesh," the creature said, and the menace transformed his voice into a growl.

"You are my failure," she snapped, "and I obliterate failure." She raised her hand, crying a word of Command, and a lash of darkness uncoiled from her grasp and licked about the monster's flank like a whip. He gave a howl of rage and pain, and vanished into the night.

The torches flinched and guttered. For an instant the red light danced over the cloaked shape and plunged within the cavern of the hood, and the face that sprang to life there was the face of the woman in the boat, but without the smile. Pale skinned, dark browed, with lips bitten into blood from the tension of the battle and eyes black as the Pit. For a few seconds the face hung there, glimmering in the torchlight. Then the flames died, and face and woman were gone.

They had been friends since their days at college, but Gaynor sometimes felt that for all their closeness she knew little of her companion. Outwardly Fern Capel was smart, successful, self-assured, with a poise that more than compensated for her lack of inches, a sort of compact neatness that implied *I am the right height; it is everyone else who is too tall*. She had style without flamboyance, generosity without extravagance, an undramatic beauty, a demure sense of humor. A colleague had once said she "excelled at moderation"; yet Gaynor had witnessed Fern, on rare occasions, behaving in a way that was immoderate, even rash, her slight piquancy of feature sharpened into a disturbing wildness, an alien glitter in her eyes. At twenty-eight, she had already risen close to the top in the PR consultancy where she worked. Her fiancé, Marcus Greig, was a well-known figure of academe who had published several books and regularly aired both his knowledge and his wit in the newspapers and on television. "I plan my life," she had told her friend, and to date everything seemed to be proceeding accordingly, smooth-running and efficient as a computer program. Or had it been "I planned my life"? Gaynor wondered, chilling at the thought, as if, in a moment of unimaginable panic and rejection, Fern had turned her back on natural disorder, on haphazard emotions, stray adventure, and had dispassionately laid down the terms for her future. Gaynor's very soul shrank from such an idea. But on the road to Yorkshire, with the top of the car down, the citified sophisticate had blown away, leaving a girl who looked younger than her years and potentially vulnerable, and whose mood was almost fey. She doesn't want to marry him, Gaynor concluded, seeking a simple explanation for a complex problem, but she hasn't the courage to back out. Yet Fern had never lacked courage.

The house was a disappointment: solidly, stolidly Victorian, watching them from shadowed windows and under frowning lintels, its stoic façade apparently braced to withstand both storm and siege. "This is a house that thinks it's a castle," Fern said. "One of these days, I'll have to change its mind."

Gaynor, who assumed she was referring to some kind of designer face-lift, tried to visualize hessian curtains and terra-cotta urns, and failed.

Inside, there were notes of untidiness, a through draft from too many open windows, the incongruous blare of a radio, the clatter of approaching feet. She was introduced to Mrs. Wicklow, who appeared as grim as the house she kept, and her latest assistant, Trisha, a dumpy teenager in magenta leggings wielding a dismembered portion of a hoover. Will appeared last, lounging out of the drawing room that he had converted into a studio. The radio had evidently been turned down in his wake and the closing door suppressed its beat to a rumor. Gaynor had remembered him tall and whiplash thin but she decided his shoulders had squared, his face matured. Once he had resembled an angel with the spirit of an urchin; now she saw choirboy innocence and carnal knowledge, an imp of charm, the morality of a thief. There was a smudge of paint on his cheek that she almost fancied might have been deliberate, the conscious stigma of an artist. His summer tan turned gray eyes to blue; there were sun streaks in his hair. He greeted her as if they knew each other much better than was in fact the case, gave his sister an idle peck, and offered to help with the luggage.

"We've put you on the top floor," he told Gaynor. "I hope you won't mind. The first floor's rather full up. If you're lonely I'll come and keep you company."

"Not Alison's room?" Fern's voice was unexpectedly sharp.

"Of course not."

"Who's Alison?" Gaynor asked, but in the confusion of arrival no one found time to answer.

Her bedroom bore the unmistakable stamp of a room that had not been used in a couple of generations. It was shabbily carpeted, ruthlessly aired, the bed linen crackling with cleanliness, the ancient brocades of curtain and upholstery worn to the consistency of lichen. There was a basin and ewer on the dresser and an ugly slipware vase containing a hand-picked bunch of flowers both garden and wild. A huge mirror, bleared with recent scouring, reflected her face among the spots, and on a low table beside the bed was a large and gleaming television set. Fern surveyed it as if it were a monstrosity. "For God's sake remove that thing," she said to her brother. "You know it's broken."

"Got it fixed." Will flashed Gaynor a grin. "This is five-star ac-commodation. Every modern convenience."

"I can see that."

But Fern still seemed inexplicably dissatisfied. As they left her to unpack, Gaynor heard her say: "You've put Alison's mirror in there."

"It's not *Alison's* mirror: it's ours. It was just in her room."

"She tampered with it . . ."

Gaynor left her bags on the bed and went to examine it more closely. It was the kind of mirror that makes everything look slightly gray. In it, her skin lost its color, her brown eyes were dulled, the long dark hair that was her principal glory was drained of sheen and splendor. And behind her in the depths of the glass the room appeared dim and remote, almost as if she were looking back into the past, a past beyond warmth and daylight, dingy as an unopened attic. Turning away, her attention was drawn to a charcoal sketch hanging on the wall: a woman with an Edwardian hairstyle, gazing soulfully at the flower she held in her hand. On an impulse Gaynor unhooked it, peering at the scrawl of writing across the bottom of the picture. There was an illegible signature and a name of which all she could decipher was the initial E. Not Alison, then. She put the picture back in its place and resumed her unpacking. In a miniature cabinet at her bedside she came across a pair of handker-chiefs, also embroidered with that tantalizing E. "Who was E?" she asked at dinner later on.

"Must have been one of Great-Cousin Ned's sisters," said Will, attacking Mrs. Wicklow's cooking with an appetite that be-lied his thinness.

"Great-*Cousin*—?"

"He left us this house," Fern explained. "His relationship to Daddy was so obscure we christened him Great-Cousin. It seemed logical at the time. Anyway, he had several sisters who

preceded him into this world and out of it: I'm sure the youngest
was an E. Esme . . . no. No. Eithne."

"I don't suppose there's a romantic mystery attached to her?"
Gaynor said, half-ironic, half-wistful. "Since I've got her room, you
know."

"No," Fern said baldly. "There isn't. As far as we know, she
was a fluttery young girl who became a fluttery old woman, with
nothing much in between. The only definite information we have
is that she made seedcake that tasted of sand."

"She must have had a lover," Will speculated. "The family
wouldn't permit it, because he was too low class. They used to
meet on the moor, like Heathcliff and Cathy only rather more re-
strained. He wrote bad poems for her—you'll probably find one in
your room—and she pressed the wildflower he gave her in her
prayer book. That'll be around somewhere, too. One day they
were separated in a mist, she called and called to him but he did
not come—he strayed too far, went over a cliff, and was lost."

"Taken by boggarts," Fern suggested.

"So she never married," Will concluded, "but spent the next
eighty years gradually pining away. Her sad specter still haunts
the upper story, searching for whichever book it was in which she
pressed that bloody flower."

Gaynor laughed. She had been meaning to ask about Alison
again, but Will's fancy diverted her, and it slipped her mind.

It was gone midnight when they went up to bed. Gaynor slept
unevenly, troubled by the country quiet, listening in her waking moments to the rumor of the wind on its way to the sea and the hooting
of an owl somewhere nearby. The owl cry invaded her dreams, filling
them with the noiseless flight of pale wings and the glimpse of a sad
ghost face looming briefly out of the dark. She awoke before dawn,
hearing the gentleness of rain on roof and windowpane. Perhaps she
was still half dreaming, but it seemed to her that her window stood

high in a castle wall, and outside the rain was falling softly into the dim waters of a loch, and faint and far away someone was playing the bagpipes.

In her room on the floor below, Fern, too, had heard the owl. Its eerie call drew her back from that fatal world on the other side of sleep, the world that was always waiting for her when she let go of mind and memory, leaving her spirit to roam where it would. In London she worked too hard to think and slept too deeply to dream, filling the intervals of her leisure with a busy social life and the thousand distractions of the metropolis; but here on the edge of the moor there was no job, few distractions, and something in her stirred that would not be suppressed. It was here that it had all started, nearly twelve years ago. Sleep was the gateway, dream the key. She remembered a stair, a stair in a picture, and climbing the stair as it wound its way from Nowhere into Somewhere, and the tiny bright vista far ahead of a city where even the dust was golden. And then it was too late, and she was ensnared in the dream, and she could smell the heat and taste the dust, and the beat of her heart was the boom of the temple drums and the roar of the waves on the shore. "I must go back!" she cried out, trapped and desperate, but there was only one way back and her guide would not come. Never again. She had forfeited his affection, for he was of those who love jealously and will not share. Nevermore the cool smoothness of his cloud-patterned flank, nevermore the deadly luster of his horn. She ran along the empty sands looking for the sea, and then the beach turned from gold to silver and the stars crisped into foam about her feet, and she was a creature with no name to bind her and no flesh to weigh her down, the spirit that breathes in every creation and at the nucleus of all being. An emotion flowed into her that was as vivid as excitement and as deep as peace. She wanted to hold on to that moment forever, but there was a voice calling, calling her without words, dragging her back into her body and her bed, until at last she knew she was lying in the dark, and the owl's hoot was a cry of loneliness and pain for all that she had lost.

An hour or so later she got up, took two aspirin (she would not use sleeping pills), tried to read for a while. It was a long, long time before exhaustion mastered her, and she slipped into oblivion.

Will slumbered undisturbed, accustomed to the nocturnal small talk of his nonhuman neighbors. When the bagpipes began, he merely rolled over, smiling in his sleep.

· II ·

The smoke thickens, pouring upward into a cloud that hangs above the fire. The cloud expands in erratic spurts and billows, stretching its wings to right and left, arching against the cave roof as it seeks a way of escape. But the flue is closed and it can only hover beneath the vaulted roots, trapped here until we choose to release it. More and more vapor is drawn into its heart till the heaviness of it seems to crush any remaining air from the chamber. I see flecks of light shifting in its depths, whorls of darkness spinning into a maelstrom, throwing out brief sparks of noise: a rapid chittering, an unfinished snarl, a bass growl that shrills into a cackle. Then both sound and light are sucked inward and swallowed, and the smoke opens out into a picture.

The moon, thin and curved as a bull's horn, caught on a hook of cloud. It is suspended in a splinter of midnight sky between mountain ranges higher than any mountains of earth, and its dead-white glow streams down into a valley so deep and narrow that neither moon nor sun should penetrate there. The valley is dry, so dry that I can taste its aridity, shriveling my tongue. Everything is in monochrome. I see lakes of some opaque liquid that is not water, shrunken in their stony depressions; luminous steams shimmer on the air above them. At the bottom of the valley there is a garden of petrified vegetation: brittle knots of stems, the black filigree of leaf skeletons, writhen stumps of tree and shrub. A breath of wind would blow it all to powder, but no wind comes there. Beyond looms the temple: the moon reaches in through the broken roof with probing rays, touching the face of an idol whose nose has long eroded and whose lip crumbles. The hearth at its feet is empty even of ash.

"He has gone," says Sysselore, and her voice croaks on a whisper. "He has gone at last."

"He will be back." I know him too well, the god in the dark. "The others may fade or fall into slumber, but *he* is always persistent. He believes that even Time is on his side. He will be back."

For a moment the moonlight falters, then the shadow of the mountains sweeps across the valley, and in that shadow the shapes of things are changed, and there is a rustle among the vanished leaves, and a stirring like an infinitesimal breeze in that place where no breeze ever blew.

He will be back.

And then the darkness turns to smoke, and the picture is lost.

There are changing landscapes, cities and villages, hovels, temples, castles. Ruins sprout new walls, which crumble and fall in their turn. Weeds grow over all. Mountains melt into plains, hills heave upward like waves. The picture falters, pausing on a lonely needle of rock jutting into a flawless sky. For a moment I hear music, a silvery tinkling without a tune, as if the wind is thrumming on forgotten harp strings. I inhale a whiff of air that is both cold and thin: we must be very high up. There are voices chanting, though I see no one. And then I realize that the needle

of rock is a tower, a tower that seems to have grown from the jaw-
bone of the mountain like a tooth, and below it gray walls inter-
face with the cliff, and window slots open as chinks in the stone,
and the rumor of the liturgy carries from within. The chant grows
louder, but the wind takes it and bears it away, and the scene
shivers into other peaks, other skies. Rain sweeps over a grim
northern castle and pockmarks the lake below. The shell of the
building is old but inside everything is new: carpets lap the floors,
flames dance around logs that are never consumed, heat glazes
the windowpanes. Briefly I glimpse a small figure slipping through
a postern, too small to be human. It moves with a swift limping
gait, like a spider with a leg too few. There is a bundle on its back
and something that might be a spear over one shoulder. The spear
is far too long in the shaft and too heavy for its carrier, yet the
pygmy manages without difficulty. It hurries down the path by
the lake and vanishes into the rain. A man walking his dog along
the shore passes by without seeing it.

"A *goblin!*" Sysselore is contemptuous. "What do we want
with such dross? The spell is wandering; we do not need this
trivia." She moves to extinguish the fire, hesitating, awaiting my
word. She knows my temper too well to act alone.

I nod. "It is enough. For now."

We open the flue and the smoke streams out, seeking to coil
around the Tree and make its way up to the clouds, but the wind
cheats it and it disperses and is gone. This is not the season of the
heads, this is the season of nesting birds. The smallest build their
nests in the lower branches: the insect pickers, the nibblers of
worms and stealers of crumbs. Higher up there are the lesser
predators that prey on mice and lizards and their weaker neighbors. Close to the great trunk woodpeckers drill, tree creepers
creep, tiny throats, insatiable as the abyss, gape in every hollow.
But in the topmost boughs, so they say, live the giant raptors, ea-
gles larger than a man, featherless fliers from the dawn of history,

and other creatures, botched misfits of the avian kingdom, which are not birds at all. So they say. Yet who has ever climbed up to look? The Tree is unassailable, immeasurable. It keeps its secrets. It may be taller than a whole mountain range, piercing the cloud canopy, puncturing the very roof of the cosmos: I do not wish to find out. There are ideas too large for the mind to accept, spaces too wide to contemplate. I know when to leave alone. I found an egg on the ground once, dislodged from somewhere far above: the half shell that remained intact was as big as a skull. The thing that lay beside it was naked, with clawlike wings and taloned feet and the head of a human fetus. I did not touch it. That night, I heard the pig rooting there, and when I looked again it was gone.

The birds make a lot of noise when they are nesting: they scold, and squabble, and screech. I prefer the murmuring of the heads. It is a gentler sound.

The next day was spent mostly on wedding preparations. The girls having brought the Dress with them, Mrs. Wicklow exercised her royal prerogative and took charge of it, relegating Trisha to the sidelines, personally pressing it into creaseless perfection and arraying it in state in one of the spare bedrooms. Will had unearthed a rather decrepit tailor's dummy from the attic, formerly the property of a long-deceased Miss Capel, and they hung the Dress on it, arranging the train in a classic swirl on the carpet, tweaking the empty sleeves into place. He even stuck a knitting needle in the vacancy of the neck and suspended the veil from its point, draping it in misty folds that fell almost to the floor. Fern found something oddly disquieting in that faceless, limbless shell of a bride; she even wondered if Will was trying to make a subtle point, but he was so helpful, so pleased with his and Mrs. Wicklow's handiwork, that she was forced to acquit him of deviousness. It was left to Gaynor to offer comment. "It looks very beautiful," she said. "It'll walk down the aisle all by itself."

"*Up* the aisle," said Fern. "It's *up*."

They met the vicar, Gus Dinsdale, in the church that after-noon and retired to the vicarage for tea. Gus in his forties looked very much as he had in his thirties, save that his hair was receding out of existence and his somewhat boyish expression had been vividly caricatured by usage and time. On learning that Gaynor's work was researching and restoring old books and manuscripts, he begged to show her some of his acquisitions, and when Will and Fern left he took her into his study. Gaynor duly admired the books, but her mind was elsewhere. She hovered on the verge of asking questions but drew back, afraid of appearing vulgarly in-quisitive, a busybody prying into the affairs of her friend. And then, on their return to the drawing room, chance offered her an opening. "You have lovely hair, dear," Gus's wife Maggie re-marked. "I haven't seen hair that long since Alison—and I was never sure hers was natural. Of course, I don't think they had ex-tensions in those days, but—"

"Alison?" Gaynor nearly jumped. "Will mentioned her. So did Fern. Who was she?"

"She was a friend of Robin's," Maggie replied. "She stayed at Dale House for a while, more than a decade ago now. We didn't like her very much."

"*You* didn't like her," Gus corrected, smiling faintly. "She was a very glamorous young woman. Not all that young really, and not at all beautiful, but . . . well, she had It. As they say."

"She looked like a succubus," Maggie said.

"You've never *seen* a succubus."

"Maybe not," Maggie retorted with spirit, "but I'd know one if I did. It would look like Alison."

"My wife is prejudiced," Gus said. "Alison wasn't the kind of woman to be popular with her own sex. Alison Redmond, that was her full name. Still, we shouldn't speak harshly of her. Her death was a terrible tragedy. Fern was completely overset by it."

"She *died?*"

"Didn't you know?" Gus sighed. "She drowned. Some kind of freak flood, but no one ever really knew how it happened. Fern was saved, caught on a tree, but Alison was swept away. They found her in the river. Dreadful business. I've always wondered—" He broke off, shaking his head as if to disperse an invisible cobweb. Gaynor regarded him expectantly.

"There was that story she told us," said Maggie. "I know it was nonsense, but it's not as if she was a habitual liar. She must have been suffering from some kind of post-traumatic shock. That's what the doctors said about her illness later on, wasn't it?" She turned to Gaynor. "But you're her best friend; you must know more about that than we do."

What illness? The query leapt to Gaynor's lips, but she suppressed it. Instead she said—with a grimace at her conscience for the half-truth—"Fern doesn't discuss it much."

"Oh dear." Now it was Maggie's turn to sigh. "That isn't good, is it? You're supposed to talk through your problems: it's essential therapy."

"That's the theory, anyway," said Gus. "I'm not entirely convinced by it. Not in this case, anyway. There was one thing that really bothered me about that explanation of Fern's."

"What was that?" asked Maggie.

"Nobody ever came up with a better one."

Gaynor walked back to Dale House very slowly, lost in a whirl of thought. She had refrained from asking further questions, reluctant to betray the extent of her ignorance and still wary of showing excessive curiosity. Fern had never spoken of any illness, and although there was no particular reason why she should have done, the omission, coupled with her distaste for Yorkshire, was beginning to take on an unexplained significance. If this were a Gothic novel, Gaynor reflected fancifully, say, a Daphne du Maurier, Fern would probably have murdered Alison Redmond. But that's ridiculous. Fern's a very moral person, she's totally against capital punishment—and anyway, how could you arrange a freak flood? It ought to be impossible in an area like this, even for Nature. I have to ask *her* about it. She's my best friend. I should be able to ask her anything . . .

But somehow when she reached the house and found Fern in the kitchen preparing supper, hindered rather than helped by Mrs. Wicklow's assertion of culinary bylaws, Gaynor couldn't. She decided it was not the right moment. Will took her into the studio drawing room, retrieved a bottle of wine from the same shelf as the paint thinner, and poured some into a couple of bleared glasses. Bravely Gaynor drank. "Are you going to show me your paintings?" she enquired.

"You won't understand them," he warned her. "Which is a euphemism for 'you won't like them'."

"Let me see," said Gaynor.

In fact, he was right. They were complex compositions in various styles: superficial abstractions where a subliminal image lurked just beyond the borders of realization, or representational scenes—landscapes and figures—distorted into abstract concepts. A darkness permeated them, part menace, part fantasy. There were occasional excursions into sensuality—a half-formed nude, a flower molded into lips, kissing or sucking—but overall there was nothing she could connect with the little she knew or guessed of Will. The execution was inconsistent: some had a smooth finish almost equal to the gloss of airbrushing, others showed caked oils and the scrapings of a knife. Evidently the artist was still at the experimental stage. She found them fascinating, vaguely horrible, slightly immature. "I *don't* like them," she admitted, "in the sense that they're uncomfortable, disturbing: I couldn't live with them. They'd give me nightmares. And I don't understand them because they don't seem to me to come from you. Unless you have a dark side—a *very* dark side—that you never let anyone see."

"All my sides are light," Will said.

Gaynor was still concentrating on the pictures. "You've got something, though," she said. "I'm no judge, but . . . you've definitely got something. I just hope it isn't contagious."

As they talked she considered asking him some of the questions that were pent up inside her head, but she dithered too long, torn between a doubt and a doubt, and they were interrupted.

Later, after an unsuccessful session with the plastic shower attachment jammed onto the bath taps, Gaynor retired to her room, shivering in a towel, and switched on both bars of the electric fire and the television. She was not particularly addicted to the small screen, but she had not seen a daily paper, and at twenty past six she hoped for some news and a weather report. There seemed to be only the four main channels on offer, with reception that varied from poor to unwatchable. The best picture was on BBC 1. She left it on, paying only cursory attention to the final news items, while trying to warm her body lotion in front of the fire before applying it to the gooseflesh of her legs. Afterward, she could never recall exactly what happened, or at which precise moment the picture changed. There came a point when she noticed the bad reception had ceased. She found herself staring at an image that looked no longer flat but three-dimensional, as real as a view through a window—but a window without glass. Her gaze was caught and held as if she were mesmerized; she could not look away. She saw a valley of rock opening out between immeasurable cliffs, many-colored lakes or pools, blue and emerald and blood-scarlet, and a garden mazy with shadows where she could hear a faint drumming like dancing feet and the sound of eerie piping, though she could see no one. She did not know when she began to be afraid. The fear was like fear in a dream, huge and illogical, aggravated by every meaningless detail. A fat yellow moth flew out of the picture and looped the room, pursued by a gleaming dragonfly. For an instant, impossibly, she thought its head was that of an actual dragon, snapping jaws bristling with miniature teeth, but the chase had passed too swiftly for her to be sure, vanishing back into the garden. Then there were pillars, stone pillars so old that they exuded ancientry like an odor. They huddled together in a circle, and spiky tree shadows twitched to and fro across their gray trunks. But as she drew nearer they appeared to swell and grow, opening out until they ringed a great space, and she could see thread-fine scratchings on them like the graffiti of spiders, and sunlight slanting in between. The shadows fled from her path as she passed through the entrance and into the circle, beneath the skeleton of a dome whose curving ribs segmented a fiery sky. "The light only falls here at sunset," said a voice that seemed to be inside her head. "Wait for the dark. Then we will make our own light out of darkness, and by that darklight you will see another world. We do not need the sun." *No!* she thought, resisting she knew not what. She had forgotten it was only a picture on television; she was inside the image, a part of it, and the idol leaned over her, gigantesque and terrible, its head almost featureless against the yellow sky. It was a statue, just a statue, yet in a minute, she knew, she would see it move. There would be a flexing of stiffened fingers, a stretching of rigid lips. Suddenly she saw the eye cracks, slowly widening, filled with a glimmer that was not the sun. She screamed . . . and screamed . . .

Somehow, she must have pressed the remote control. She was in the bedroom, shivering by the inadequate fire, and the television was blank and dark. Will and Fern could be heard running up the stairs toward her, with Mrs. Wicklow faint but pursuing. Will put his arms around her, which was embarrassing since she was losing her towel; Fern scanned her surroundings with unexpected intensity. "I had a nightmare," Gaynor said, fishing for explanations. "I must have dropped off, just sitting here. Maybe it was something on the news. Or those bizarre pictures of yours," she added, glancing up at Will.

"You had the television on?" Fern queried sharply. She picked up the remote and pressed On: the screen flicked to a vista of a fire in an industrial plant in Leeds. Behind the commentator, ash flakes swirled under an ugly sky.

"That was it," said Gaynor with real relief. "It must have been that." And: "I can't think why I'm so tired . . ."

"It's the Yorkshire air," said Will. "Bracing."

"You don't want to go watching t'news," opined Mrs. Wicklow. "It's all murders and disasters—when it isn't sex. Enough to give anyone nightmares."

Will grinned half a grin for Gaynor's exclusive benefit. Fern switched off the television again, still not quite satisfied.

"Have you had any other strange dreams here?" she asked abruptly when Mrs. Wicklow had left.

"Oh no," said Gaynor. "Well . . . only the bagpipes. I thought I heard them last night, but that must have been a dream, too."

"Of course."

Fern and Will followed the housekeeper, leaving Gaynor to dress, but as the door closed behind them she was sure she caught Fern's whisper: "If you don't get that little monster to shut up, I'm going to winkle him out and stuff his bloody pipes down his throat . . ."

At supper, thought Gaynor, at supper I'm going to ask her what she's talking about.

But at supper the argument began. It was an argument that had been in preparation, Gaynor suspected, since they arrived, simmering on a low heat until a chance word—a half-joking allusion to premarital nerves—made it boil over. Without the subject ever having been discussed between them, she sensed that Will, like her, was unenthusiastic about his sister's marriage and doubted her motives. Yet he had said nothing and seemed reluctant to criticize; it was Fern, uncharacteristically belligerent, who pushed him into caustic comment, almost compelling him toward an open quarrel. On the journey up she had listened without resentment to her friend's light-worded protest, but with Will she was white faced and bitter with rage. Maybe she wanted to clear the air, Gaynor speculated; but she did not really believe it. What Fern wanted was a fight, the kind of dirty, no-holds-barred fight, full of below-the-belt jabs and incomprehensible allusions, that can occur only between siblings or people who have known each other too long and too well. It struck Gaynor later that what Fern had sought was not to hurt but to be hurt, as if to blot out some other feeling with that easy pain. She herself had tried to avoid taking sides.

"I'm sorry about that," Fern said afterward, on their way up to bed. "I shouldn't have let Will provoke me. I must be more strung up than I thought."

"He didn't provoke you," Gaynor said uncertainly. "*You* provoked him."

Fern shut her bedroom door with something of a snap.

· III ·

The spellfire burns anew, the smoke blurs. Among the shifting images I see the tower again, nearer this time: I can make out the rhythms of the liturgy, and the silver tinkling of the chimes has grown to a clamor. I sense this is a place where the wind is never still. The air is too thin to impede its progress. Later, the castle by the lake. A scene from long ago. I see shaggily bearded men dressed in fur and leather and blood with strange spiked weapons, short swords, long knives. There is fighting on the battlements and in the uncarpeted passageways and in the Great Hall. The goblin moves to and fro among the intruders, slashing at hamstrings with an unseen dagger. Those thus injured stumble and are swiftly killed. Surprise alerts me: it is rare for a goblin to be so bold. On the hearth a whole pine tree is burning: a giant of a man, red of face and hair, lifts it by the base of the trunk and incredibly, impossibly, swings it around like a huge club, mowing down his foes in an arc of fire. A couple of warriors from his own band are also laid low, but this is a detail he ignores. His surviving supporters give vent to a cry of triumph so loud that the castle walls burst asunder, and the picture is lost.

It re-forms into the shape of a house. A dour, gray-faced

house with the moorland rising steeply behind it. The goblin is descending a footpath toward the garden gate. He is tall for his kind, over three feet, and unusually hirsute, with tufted eyebrows and ear tips and a fleecelike growth matting his head. His body is covered in fragments of worn pelts, patches of cloth and hide, and his own fur: it is difficult to distinguish the native hair from that which has been attached. His feet are bare, prehensile, with a dozen or more toes apiece that grasp the earth as he walks. His skin is very brown and his eyes are very bright, the eyes of the werefolk, which are brighter than those of humankind. They show no whites, only long slits of hazel luster. He pauses, skimming hillside, house, and garden with a gaze that misses nothing, sniffing the air with nostrils that flare individually. Then he continues on down the slope.

"Why do we see him so clearly?" Sysselore is easily irritated: she takes umbrage where she can find it. "He's a goblin. A *house-goblin*. He cannot possibly be important."

"Something is important," I retort.

More people follow, a succession of faces, overlapping, intermingling, many too dim to make out. Some are familiar, some not. There is a man in a cloak and a pointed hood, trading a potion in an unlabeled bottle for a bag whose contents are muffled so they will not chink. And the same man, older, poorer, though he retains his distinctive garb, striding across an empty landscape under the sweeping wings of clouds. Once he was called Gabbandolfo, in the country of his origin, meaning Elvincape, though he had other names. But he lost his power and his titles and now he roams the world on a mission that can never be achieved, going nowhere. Nonetheless, when his image intrudes I am wary: it is a strange paradox that since his impotence his presence has become more ominous, grim as an indefinite warning. He stalks the smoke scenes like a carrion crow, watching the field for a battle of which only he has foreknowledge. "I don't like it," I assert. "*We should be the sole watchers. What has he seen that we missed? What does he know?*"

Outside, night lies beneath the Tree. I hear the whistling calls of nocturnal birds, the death squeal of a tiny rodent. In the smoke, a new face emerges, growing into darkness. It belongs to no known race of men, yet it *is* mortal—sculpted in ebony, its bone structure refined to a point somewhere on the other side of beauty, emphasized with little hollowings and sudden lines, its hair of a black so deep it is green, its eyes like blue diamonds. For all its delicacy, it is obviously, ruthlessly masculine. It stares straight at me out of the picture, almost as if the observer has somehow become the observed, and he watches us in our turn. For the first time that I can remember I speak the word to obliterate it, though normally I leave the pictures to fade and alter of their own accord. The face dwindles until only a smile remains, dimming into vapor.

"*He saw us,*" says my coven sister.

"Illusion. A trick of the smoke. You sound afraid. Are you afraid of smoke, of a *picture?*"

As our concentration wavers, the billows thin and spread. I spit at the fire with a curse word, a power word to recall the magic, sucking the fumes back into the core of the cloud. The nucleus darkens: for a moment the same image seems to hover there, the face or its shadow, but it is gone before it can come into focus. A succession of tableaux follow, unclear or unfinished, nothing distinguishable. At the last we return to the gray house, and the goblin climbing in through an open window. In the room beyond a boy somewhere in his teens is reading a book, one leg hooked over the arm of his chair. His hair shows more fair than dark; there are sun freckles on his nose. When he looks up his gaze is clear and much too candid—the candor of the naturally devious who know how to exploit their own youth. He stares directly at the intruder, interested and undisturbed. He can *see* the goblin. He has no Gift, no aura of power. But he can see it.

He says: "I suppose you've come about the vacancy."

The goblin halts abruptly, halfway over the sill. Unnerved.

"The vacancy," the boy reiterates. "For a house-goblin. You *are* a house-goblin, aren't you?"

"Ye see me, then." The goblin has an accent too ancient to identify, perhaps a forgotten brogue spoken by tribes long extinct. His voice sounds rusty, as if it has not been used for many centuries.

"I was looking," the boy says matter-of-factly. "When you look, you see. Incidentally, you really shouldn't come in uninvited. It isn't allowed."

"The hoose wants a boggan, or so I hairrd. I came."

"Where from?"

"Ye ask a wheen o' questions."

"It's my hoose," says the boy. "I'm entitled."

"It was another put out the word."

"He's a friend of mine: he was helping me out. *I'm* the one who has to invite you in."

"Folks hae changed since I was last in the worrld," says the goblin, his tufted brows twitching restlessly from shock to frown. "In the auld days, e'en the lairrd couldna see me unless I wisht it. The castle was a guid place then. But the lairrds are all gone and the last o' his kin is a spineless vratch who sauld his hame for a handful o' siller. And now they are putting in baths—baths!—and the pipes are a-hissing and a-gurgling all the time, and there's heat without fires, and fires without heat, and clacking picture boxes, and invisible bells skirling, and things that gae bleep in the nicht. It's nae place for a goblin anymore."

"We have only the one bathroom," says the boy, by way of encouragement.

"Guid. It isna healthy, all these baths. Dirt keeps ye warm."

"Seals the pores," nods the boy. "I'm afraid we do have a telephone, and two television sets, but one's broken, and the microwave goes bleep in the night if we need to heat something up, but that's all."

The goblin grunts, though what the grunt imports is unclear. "Are ye alone here?"

"Of course not. There's my father and my sister and Abby—Dad's girlfriend. We live in London but we use this place for weekends and holidays. And Mrs. Wicklow the housekeeper who comes in most days and Lucy from the village doing the actual housework and Gus—the vicar—who keeps an eye on things when we're not here. Oh, and there's a dog—a sort of dog—who's around now and then. She won't bother you—if she likes you."

"What sort o' dog wid that be?" asks the goblin. "One o' thae small pet dogs that canna barrk above a yap or chase a rabbit but sits on a lady's knee all day waiting tae be fed?"

"Oh, no," says the boy. "She's not a lapdog or a pet. She's her own mistress. You'll see."

"I hairrd," says the goblin, after a pause, "ye'd had Trouble here, not sae long ago."

"Yes."

"And mayhap it was the kind o' Trouble that might open your eyes tae things ordinary folk are nae meant to see?"

"Mayhap." The boy's candor has glazed over; his expression is effortlessly blank.

"Sae what came tae the hoose-boggan was here afore me?"

"How did you know there was one?" Genuine surprise breaks through his impassivity.

"Ye can smell it. What came tae yon?"

"Trouble," says the boy. "He was the timid sort, too frightened to fight back. In a way, his fear killed him."

"Aye, weel," says the goblin, "fear is deadlier than knife wound or spear wound, and I hae taken both. It's been long awhile since I kent Trouble. Do ye expect more?"

"It's possible," the boy replies. "Nothing is ever really over, is it?"

"True worrds. I wouldnae be averse to meeting Trouble again. Belike I've been missing him. Are ye going tae invite me in?"

The boy allows a pause, for concentration or effect. "All right. You may come in."

The goblin springs down from the windowsill, hefting his antique spear with the bundle tied to the shaft.

"By the way," says the boy, "what's your name?"

"Bradachin."

"Bradachin." He struggles to imitate the pronunciation. "Mine's Will. Oh, and . . . one more thing."

"What thing is that?"

"A warning. My sister. She's at university now and she doesn't come here very much, but when she does, stay out of her way. She's being a little difficult at the moment."

"Will *she* see me?" the goblin enquires.

"I expect so," says the boy.

The goblin moves toward the door with his uneven stride, vanishing as he reaches the panels. The boy stares after him for a few minutes, his young face, with no betraying lines, no well-trodden imprint of habitual expressions, as inscrutable as an unwritten page. Then he and the room recede, and there is only the smoke.

The owl woke Gaynor, calling in its half-human voice right outside her window. She had started up and pulled back the curtains before she really knew what she was doing and there it was, its ghost face very close to her own, apparently magnified by the glass so that its enormous eyes filled her vision. Its talons scrabbled on the sill; its wings were beating against the panes. Then somehow the window was open and she was straddling the sill, presumably still in her pajamas, and then she was astride the owl, her hands buried in its neck ruff, and it was huge, huger than a great eagle, and silent as the phantom it resembled. They were flying over the moors, and she glimpsed the loop of a road below, and the twin shafts of headlights, and the roofs of houses folded as if in sleep, and a single window gleaming like a watchful eye. But most of the landscape was dark, lit only by the moon that kept pace with their flight, speeding between the clouds. Above the gray drift of cirrus the sky was a black vault; the few stars looked remote and cold. They crossed a cliff and she saw the sea wheeling beneath her, flecked with moon glitter, and then all detail was lost in the boom of wings and the roar of the wind, and Time rolled over her like waves, maybe months, maybe years, and she did not know if she woke or slept, if she lived or dreamed. At one point another face rushed toward her, a pale expanse of a face with a wide hungry mouth and eyes black as the Pit. There was a hint of smoke in the air and a smell of something rotting. "This is not the one," said a voice. *"Not the one . . ."* The unpleasant smell was gone and she felt the plumage of the owl once more, and the wind and the cloud wisps and the dying moon flowed over her, and sleep came after, closing the window against the night.

She woke fully just before moonset, when its last ray stole across the bed and slipped under her eyelids. She got up to shut the curtains, and was back between the sheets when it occurred to her she had done so already before she went to bed.

Fern, too, was dreaming. Not the dreams she longed for and dreaded—fragments of the past, intimations of an alternative future—dreams from which she would wrench herself back to a painful awakening. This dream appeared random, unconnected with her. Curious, she dreamed on. She was gazing down on a village, a village of long ago, with thatched roofs and dung heaps.

There were chickens bobbing in farmyard and backyard, goats wandering the single street. People in peasant clothing were going about their business. A quickfire sunset sent the shadows stretching across the valley until it was all shadow. One red star shone low over the horizon. It seemed to be pulsing, expanding—now it was a fireball rushing toward them—a comet whose tail scorched the treetops into a blaze. Then, as it drew nearer, she *saw*. Bony pinions that cut up the sky, pitted scales aglow from the furnace within, blood-dark eyes where ancient thoughts writhed like slow vapor. A dragon.

Not the dragon of fantasy and storyland, a creature with whom you might bandy words or hitch a ride. This was a real dragon, and it was terrible. It stank like a volcanic swamp. Its breath was a pyroclastic cloud. She could sense its personality, enormous, overwhelming, a force all hunger and rage. Children, goats, people ran, but not fast enough; against the onset of the dragon they might almost have been running backward. Houses exploded from the heat. Flesh shriveled like paper. Fern jerked into waking to find she was soaked in sweat and trembling with a mixture of excitement and horror. Special effects, she told herself: nothing more. She took a drink of water from the glass by her bed and lay down again. Her thoughts meandered into a familiar litany. There are no dragons, no demons . . . no countries in wardrobes, no kingdoms behind the North Wind. And Atlantis, first and fairest of cities, Atlantis where such things might have been, was buried under the passing millennia, drowned in a billion tides, leaving not a fossilized footprint or a solitary shard of pottery to baffle the archaeologists.

But she would not think of Atlantis . . .

Drifting into sleep again she dreamed of wedding presents, and a white dress that walked up the aisle all by itself.

The images wax and wane like dreams, crystallizing into glimpses of solidity, then merging, melting, lost in a drift of vapor.

Sometimes it seems as if it is the cave that drifts, its hollows and shadows vacillating in the penumbra of existence, while at its heart the smoke visions focus all the available reality, like a bright eye on the world. We, too, are as shadows, Sysselore and I, watching the light, hungering for it. But I have more substance than any shadow—I wrap myself in darkness as in a cocoon, preserving my strength while my power slumbers. This bloated body is a larval stage in which my future Self is nourished and grows, ready to hatch when the hour is ripe—a new Morgus, radiant with youth revived, potent with ancientry. It is a nature spell, old as evolution: I learned it from a maggot. You can learn much from those who batten on decay. It is their kind who will inherit the earth.

Pictures deceive. The smoke screen opens like a crack in the wall of Being, and through it you may see immeasurable horizons and unnavigable seas, you may breathe the perfume of forgotten gardens, taste the rains on their passage to the thirsty plain—but the true power is here in the dark. With me. I *am* the dark, I am the heartbeat of the night. The spellfire may show you things far away, but I am *here*, and for now, Here is all there is.

The dark is always waiting. Behind the light, beyond reality, behind the visions in the smoke. Look now, look at the egg. It glows with cold, its white shell sheened like clouded ice, the velvet that wraps it crackling with frost. It is secreted in a casket of ebony bound with iron, but the metal is chilled into brittleness, the lock snaps even as the lid is shut, tampering fingers are frozen into a blue numbness. It has lain there for many centuries, a sacred charge on its caretakers, or so they believe, having no knowledge of what it is they cherish, or for Whom. The image returns often, its mystery still unrevealed. Maybe it is a symbol: the deepest, truest magic frequently manifests itself through symbols. Maybe it is just what it appears to be. An egg. If so, then we at least can guess what lies curled within, unhatching, sleeping the bottomless sleep of a seed in midwinter. The men who watch over it have gentle hands and slender, otherworldly features. They do not suspect the germ of darkness that incubates within the egg.

The picture shifts, pulling back, showing us for the first time that the casket stands on an altar of stone, and the altar is in a circular chamber, and the chamber . . . the chamber is at the top of a lonely tower, jutting like a tooth into the blue mountain air. A few pieces of the pattern fall into place. Others drift, disembodied, like jigsaw fragments from the wrong puzzle.

"Why *there*?" asks Sysselore, forever scathing. "A monastery, I suppose, remote, almost inaccessible—but *almost* is never enough. Why not hide it outside the world?"

"Magic finds out magic. Who would look for such an object in the hands of Men? It has been safe in ignorant hands, hidden in plain view, one of a thousand holy relics guarded by monks in a thousand mountain retreats. They will have cradled it in their own legends, endowed it with a dozen meanings. No one has ever sought it there."

Somewhere in the tower a bell is struck, drowning out the rumor of the wind in the chimes and the rise and fall of the chant. The swelling of its single note fills the cave; the walls seem to shake; flakes of earth drop from above. The tower trembles in its sky gulf. Or perhaps it is the smoke that trembles, unbalancing the picture. We see the egg again, but it is no longer cold. Heat pulses from within, turning the thick shell to translucency. Bent over it is a dark face among the golden ones, dark as the wood of the casket, a face subtle as poison, sharp as a blade. The gaze is lowered: it does not seek concealed watchers now. Its whole attention is focused on the egg. The throb of the bell is a long time dying. And then comes another sound, a tiny crack, echoless, all but inaudible, yet the aftershock of that minute noise makes the very floor vibrate. The shell fractures, seamed by countless thread lines that glow with a red light as if from a fire in its heart. The

ruby glow touches the dark face leaning closer, ever closer, fascinated, eager . . .

The egg hatches.

"**W**hat now?" whispers Sysselore, and the quiet in her voice
is almost that of awe. "Where will it go? They cannot call it holy
now, and . . . it won't stay hidden. Not long."

"We shall see."

"**W**hat's happening?" Will asked the darkness. "Even allow-
ing for circumstances, I've never known Fern so on edge."

"I dinna ken," said the darkness, predictably. "But there's
Trouble coming. I can smell him."

The smoke thins, swirls, re-forms, showing us great events and
small. The moor unrolls like a carpet beneath a sky tumbling with
clouds. The valley opens, the hillside plunges, the wind rushes
in from the sea. And there is the house, lifting blind windows to
the rain. Behind closed curtains there is firelight and lamplight, the
murmur of conversation, the smell of roasting meat uncoiling from
the oven. The sunless evening blurs gradually into night. When
dinner is long over, feet climb the stairs to bed. A glass tumbler
stands alone on a sideboard in the kitchen, containing a small measure of golden liquid. Not discarded or forgotten but placed there
deliberately. A gesture. Presently the house-goblin materializes,
sitting on the end of the table. He samples the leftover roast and
drains the tumbler, declaiming an incomprehensible toast, probably to the red-bearded laird who swatted his foes with a tree trunk.
Then he roams through the house, patrolling his domain.

In a bedroom on the second floor a girl is seated in front of an
antique dressing table, studying herself in the mirror. There is no
vanity in her contemplation: her expression is grave and unusually

detached. She stares at her reflection, you feel, simply because it is there. Yet she might be termed beautiful, if mere youth is beauty, clarity of skin and eye, elfin slenderness of body. I was beautiful once, I and Morgun, my twin, but beauty alters with time, as all else, and in a different age Helen wears a different face. So maybe she is beautiful, this pale, dispassionate girl, with her gravity and her small breasts. Fashion is a poor judge of such things. The adjacent lamp puts a gloss on her short hair that it may not merit and shades the molding of invisible bones. But as we look closer I see *something* in her face, or in its reflection, something beneath the unblemished exterior. Imperceptible. Almost familiar. A secret too well hidden, a scar too perfectly healed. It shows in a certain fragility, a certain strength, a trace element of pain. But the image begins to withdraw from her, and the flicker of not-quite-recognition is gone.

The goblin, too, is watching her, just inside the door, his crouched body only a shadow in the corner to the discerning eye. Even the mirror cannot see him. She is still staring at her reflection but now the direction of her gaze switches to a point beyond her shoulder. Her eyes widen; shock or fury expels the hint of color from her cheek. To us, the glass is empty, but *she* sees the intruder. *She sees him in the mirror.* "Get out!" She rounds on him, screaming like a virago. "Toad! Contemptible little sneak! Creeping in here, spying on me—how dare you! How *dare* you! Get out, do you hear? If I see even your *shadow* again, I'll—I'll squeeze you to pulp—I'll blast you into Limbo—I'll blow your atoms to the four winds! Don't you ever—*ever!*—come near me again!" The unleashing of power is sudden and terrifying: her hair crackles with it, the air thickens around her outstretched fingers. The goblin vanishes in a flash of startled horror. She is on her feet now but her rage ebbs as rapidly as it came, and she casts herself face-down on the bed, clutching the pillow, sobbing briefly and violently. When the storm is over she lifts her head; she is red eyed and tearless, as if tears were a rain that would not come. Her expression reverts to a wary stillness: her gaze roves round the room. "It's gone," she murmurs, "I know it's gone, but . . . there's someone . . . somewhere . . . watching me."

"She feels us," says Sysselore. "The *power*. Did you see the power in her . . . ?"

"Hush."

The picture revolves cautiously as I lean forward, close to the smoke; the fire draft burns my face. I am peering out of the mirror, into the room, absorbing every detail, filling my mind with the girl. This girl. The one I have waited for.

Slowly she turns, drawn back to the mirror, staring beyond the reflections. Our eyes meet. For the second time, the watcher becomes the watched. But this is no threat, only reconnaissance. A greeting. In the mirror, she sees me smile.

She snatches something—a hairbrush?—and hurls it at the glass, which shatters. The smoke turns all to silver splinters, spinning, falling, fading. In the gloom after the fire dies, Sysselore and I nurse our exultation.

She is the one. At last.

I will have her.

✦ IV ✦

F ern devoted the following morning to final preparations and thank-you letters, which she, being efficient, penned beforehand. Then there were long phone calls—to the caterers, to prospective guests, to Marcus Greig. Will, not so much unhelpful as uninvolved, removed Gaynor from the scene and took her for a walk.

"What do you make of it all?" he asked her.

"Make of what?" she said, her mind elsewhere. "You mean—that business of Alison Redmond? Or—"

"Actually," said Will, "I meant Marcus Greig. Who's been talking to you about Alison? Fern tries never to mention her."

"Gus Dinsdale," Gaynor explained. She continued hesitantly: "I don't want to be nosy, but I can't help wondering . . . *Was* her death really an accident? You're both rather—odd—about it."

"Oh no," said Will. "It wasn't an accident."

Gaynor stopped and stared at him, suddenly very white. "N-not *Fern*—?"

Will's prompt laughter brought the color flooding back to her cheeks. "You've been thinking in whodunits," he accused. "Poor Gaynor. A Ruth Rendell too many!"

"Well, what *did* happen?" demanded Gaynor, feeling foolish.

"The truth is less mundane," Will said. "It often is. Alison stole a key that didn't belong to her and opened a Door that shouldn't be opened. I wouldn't call that an accident."

"Gus said something about a *flood*?"

Will nodded. "She was swept away. So was Fern—she was lucky to survive."

Gaynor felt herself becoming increasingly bewildered, snatching at straws without ever coming near the haystack. "I gather Fern was ill," she said. "They thought—Gus and Maggie—that she would have told me, only she never has. Some sort of post-traumatic shock?"

"Shock leading to amnesia, that's what the doctors said. They had to say *something*. She was gone for five days."

"*Gone?* Gone where?"

"To shut the Door, of course. The Door Alison had opened. The flood had washed it away." He was studying her as he spoke, his words nonsense to her, his expression inscrutable. She could not detect either mockery or evasion; it was more as if they were speaking on different subjects, or in different languages.

"Can we start again?" she said. "With Alison. I was told— She was a girlfriend of your father's?"

"Maybe," said Will. "She slipped past Fern—for a while. But she wasn't really interested in Dad."

"What did she do?"

"She stole a key—"

"I mean, what did she do for a living?"

"She worked in an art gallery in London. At least, that was what you might call her cover."

"Her cover? She was a *crook*?"

"Of course not." He smiled half a smile. "Well, not in the sense you mean."

"In what sense, then?"

"She was a witch," said Will.

She looked for the rest of the smile, but it did not material-ize. The narrowing of his eyes and the slight crease between his brows was merely a reaction against the sun. His expression was unfathomable.

After a pause that lasted just a little too long, she said: "Herbal remedies—zodiac medallions—dancing naked round a hilltop on Midsummer's Eve? That sort of thing?"

"Good Lord no," Will responded mildly. "Alison was the real McCoy."

"Satanism?"

He shook his head. "Satan is simply a label of convenience. Mind you, if Jesus had come back a few hundred years later, and seen what had been done in his name—the Crusades, or the In-quisition, or even just a routine schism with heretics burning at the stake over a point of doctrine—he'd probably have given up on all religion then and there. The atheist formerly known as Christ. He might even have decided it would be best—or at least much easier—to corrupt and destroy the human race instead of wasting time trying to save it. You get the gods you deserve."

"You're wandering from the point," Gaynor said, determined the discussion was going to go somewhere, though she had no idea precisely where. It occurred to her that his outlook—she could not think of a better word—must have something to do with his paintings, or vice versa, but it didn't seem to clarify any-thing. "What kind of a—what kind of a witch was Alison?"

"She had the Gift," Will explained. (She could hear the capital letter.) "The ability to do things . . . beyond the range of ordinary human capacity." He did not appear to notice the doubt in Gaynor's questioning gaze. "When the universe was created, something—alien—got into the works, a lump of matter from outside. They called it the Lodestone. A friend of ours had the theory that it might have been a whole different cosmos, imploded into this ball

of concentrated matter, but . . . Well, anyhow, it distorted everything around it. Including people. Especially people. It affected
their genetic makeup, creating a freak gene that they passed on
even when the Stone itself was destroyed. A sort of gene for witchcraft." He gave her a sudden dazzling and eminently normal smile.
"Don't worry. You don't have to believe me. I just think you ought to
know. In case anything happens that shouldn't."

"Do you think something is going to happen?" asked Gaynor,
mesmerized.

"Maybe. I'd whistle up a demon if I could, just to stop this idiotic wedding."

"Idiotic?" She was bemused by his choice of adjective.

"Can you think of a better word? Fern's marrying a man she
doesn't love, probably as a gesture of rejection. That seems fairly
idiotic to me."

"What is she supposed to be rejecting?"

"The Gift," he said. "That's the whole problem. Don't you
understand? Fern's a witch, too."

Gaynor stopped abruptly for the second time, staring at him
in a sudden violent uncertainty. They had walked quite a way and
she was aware of the empty countryside all around them, the
wind ruffling the grasses, the piping voice of an isolated bird. The
wild loneliness of it filled her with an upsurge of panic that
nudged her into anger. "If this is your idea of a joke—"

And then normality intruded. The dog came out of nowhere,
bounding up to them on noiseless paws, halting just in front of
her. Its mouth was open in a grin full of teeth and its tongue lolled.
Will bent down to pat its muzzle but the yellow-opal eyes were
fixed on Gaynor. The man followed briskly on its heels. He, too,
gave the uncanny impression of appearing from nowhere. But this
was normality, or so Gaynor assured herself. A man and his dog,
walking on the moors. The dog was friendly, the man, dressed like
a tramp, at least unequivocally human. Will evidently knew them.

"This is Ragginbone," he told Gaynor. The man, not the dog. And: "This is Gaynor Mobberley. She's a close friend of Fern's." A firm handclasp, bright eyes scanning her face. He looked very old, she thought, or perhaps not so much old as aged, reminding her of an oak chest her mother had inherited recently from an antique relative. The wood was scored and blackened but tough, unyielding, halfway to carbonization. The man's face seemed to have been carved in a similar wood, a long time ago, scratched with a thousand lines that melted into mobility when he smiled at her. His scarecrow hair was faded to a brindled straw but his brows were still dark and strong, crooked above the bright eyes that shone with a light that was not quite laughter but something deeper and more solemn. She wondered about his name (a soubriquet? a nickname?) but was too polite to ask.

"And Lougarry." Will indicated the dog. A shaggy animal without a collar who looked part Alsatian and all wolf. But Gaynor had grown up with dogs and was not particularly deterred. She extended her hand and the dog sniffed briefly, apparently more out of courtesy than curiosity.

"And how is Fernanda?" asked the man called Ragginbone.

"Still resolved on matrimony," said Will. "It's making her very jumpy. She picked a fight with me last night, just to prove she was doing the right thing."

"She has to choose for herself," said the old man. "Neither you nor I have the right to coerce her, or even advise."

Gaynor found his air of authority somewhat incongruous, but before she had time to consider her surprise he had turned to talk to her, and was enquiring about her work and displaying an unexpected familiarity with the subject. The three of them walked along together for some distance, the dog padding at their heels. Will said little. They turned back toward Yarrowdale, following a different path that plunged down into the valley and brought them eventually to the river. Spring was unfolding among the trees but the leaves of many winters lay thickly on the ground.

"Was this where Alison drowned?" Gaynor said suddenly.

"Yes and no," said Will. "This is where they found her. In the Yarrow. Farther down from here."

Ragginbone made no comment, but she felt his gaze.

Where the path branched they separated, man and dog going their own way.

"You'll stay around, won't you?" Will said to him.

"There's nothing I can do."

"I know, but . . ."

"Something troubles you? Something more than your sister's obduracy?"

"There's too much tension in the air. I don't think it's all coming from her." He appealed to Gaynor. "You've felt it, too, haven't you?" She remembered her nightmare in front of the television and the owl dream, and for no reason at all there was a sick little jolt of fear in her stomach. "It isn't like the last time, hounds sniffing in the night: nothing like that. But I have a sense of someone or something watching . . . spying. An uncomfortable tingle on the nape of my neck. I might be imagining it."

"We'll be here," said Ragginbone.

He strode off at great speed, the dog always beside him, unbidden and silent. "I suppose he's a wizard?" Gaynor said with a wavering attempt at sarcasm.

"Oh no," said Will. "Not anymore."

Fern was sitting at the kitchen table, an untidy pile of cards, gifts, and wrappings on one side of her, a tidy pile of sealed and addressed envelopes on the other. There was a cup of coffee at her elbow, almost untouched. She glanced up as her friend came in, her expression preoccupied, a brief smile coming and going. Perhaps because she wore no makeup she looked visibly strained, the small bones showing sharply beneath her skin, faint shadow bruises under her eyes. But she did not look like a witch. Gaynor's concept of the twenty-first-century sorceress was drawn from books and films: she visualized something between the Narnian Jadis and Cher in one of her more glamorous roles, a statuesque creature with aquiline profile and waist-length elflocks. Fern looked compact, practical, wearily efficient. A PR executive frustrated by rural privations. A bride with premarital nerves. The antithesis of all that was magical and strange. "I've run out of stamps," she announced. "I wish I could do these things on the laptop: it would take half the time and at least they'd be legible. My handwriting's turning into Arabic."

"Why can't you?"

"The older generation would be offended. Etiquette hasn't caught up with technology yet."

"Shall I go and get the stamps for you?" Gaynor offered. "I can find the post office. I saw it yesterday."

"That would be wonderful," Fern said warmly, "but you've only just got in. Have some coffee first. The pot's on the stove. I made the real thing: I thought we might need it. Instant doesn't have the same kick."

Gaynor helped herself and replaced the contents of Fern's mug, which had begun to congeal.

"How are you getting on with my brother?" Fern enquired, scribbling her way automatically through another note.

"I like him," Gaynor responded tentatively, thinking of the row the previous night.

"So do I," said Fern. "Even if he is a pain in the bum."

"He lives in a world of his own, doesn't he?" Gaynor said rather too casually, seating herself on the opposite side of the table.

"Not exactly." Fern's head was still bent over her work. "He lives in someone else's world—a world where he doesn't belong. That's just the trouble."

*   *   *

Now we search the smoke for her, skimming other visions, bending our dual will to a single task. But the fire-magic is wayward and unpredictable: it may sometimes be guided but it cannot be forced. The images unravel before us in a jumble, distorted by our pressure, quick-changing, wavering, breaking up. Irrelevancies intrude, a cavalcade of monsters from the long-lost past, mermaid, unicorn, Sea Serpent, interspersed with glimpses that might, or might not, be more significant: the hatchling perching on a dark, long-fingered hand, a solitary flower opening suddenly in a withered garden like the unlidding of a watching eye. Time here has no meaning, but in the world beyond Time passes, years maybe, ere we see her again. And the vision, when it comes, takes us off guard, a broad vista unwinding slowly in an interlude of distraction, a road that meanders with the contours of the land, white puffball clouds trailing in the wake of a spring breeze. A horseless car is traveling along the road: the sunlight winks off its steel-green coachwork. The roof is folded back to leave the top open; music emanates from a mechanical device within, not the raucous drumbeat of the rabble but a music of deep notes and mellow harmonies, flowing like the hills. The girl is driving the car. She looks different, older, her small-boned face hollowed into shape, tapering, purity giving way to definition, a slight pixie look tempered by the familiar gravitas. More than ever, it is a face of secrets. Her hair is cut in a straight line across her brow and level with her jaw. As the car accelerates the wind fans the hair out from her temples and sweeps back her fringe, revealing that irregularity of growth at the parting that we call the Witch's Crook. Her mouth does not smile. Her companion—another girl—is of no importance. I resist the urge to look too closely, chary of alarming her, plucking Sysselore away from the smoke and letting the picture haze over.

When we need her, we will find her. I know that now.

We must be ready.

✦ V ✦

Long before, when she was five or six years old, Gaynor had stayed in a haunted house. She still retained a vivid memory of the woman who had bent over her bed, staring at her with eyes that saw someone else. A woman in a long dress, shadowy in the semidark. She had brought a chill into the room that made Gaynor shiver, even under the bedclothes, but she could remember no sense of evil. Only a presence, and the cold. "She's a sensitive," a friend had told her mother, and for some time she had worried about that, afraid of what she might sense, but no further incidents had occurred and the matter had faded from her mind, though her recollection of the phenomenon remained very clear. Now she found herself reviving that image, reaching out with her so-called sensitivity, half in hope, half in fear, though the house did not respond. It felt not so much haunted, she decided, as *inhabited*: she always had the impression there were more people around than was actually the case.

After she returned from the post office Fern had to drive into Whitby to sort out a problem with the caterers. "Do you want to come?" she asked, but Gaynor declined. Will was out painting somewhere and she welcomed the idea of some time to herself.

She stood in the room gazing in the mirror—Alison's mirror—willing it to show her something, part fanciful, part skeptical, seeing only herself. A long pale face, faintly medieval, or so she liked to think, since medieval was better than plain. Brown eyes set deep under serious eyebrows. A thin, sad mouth, though why it should be sad she did not know, only that this was what she had been told. And the hair that was her glory, very long and very dark, falling like a cloak about her shoulders. Alison Redmond had had such hair, Maggie had said, though for some reason Gaynor pictured it as fairer than her own, the color of dust and shadows.

"You stare much harder at t'glass you'll crack it," came a voice from the doorway. Gaynor had forgotten Mrs. Wicklow. She jumped and flushed, stammering something incoherent, but the housekeeper interrupted. "You want to be careful. Mirrors remember, or so my mother used to say. You never know what it might show you. That was the one used to hang in *her* room. I've cleaned it and polished it up many a time, but the reflection never looks right to me."

"What was she like?" asked Gaynor, seizing the opportunity. "Alison, I mean."

"Out for what she could get," Mrs. Wicklow stated. "This house is full of old things—antiques and stuff that the Captain brought back from his travels. Her eyes had a sort of glistening look when she saw them. Greedy. Wouldn't have surprised me if she were mixed up with real criminals. She didn't like anyone in t'bedroom when she was away. We didn't have no key then but she did something to the doorknob—something with electricity. Funny, that." She turned toward the stairs. "You come down now and have a bite of lunch. You young girls, you're all too thin. You worry too much about your figures."

Gaynor followed her obediently. "I gather Alison drowned," she continued cautiously. "In some kind of freak flood?"

"That's what they *say*," said Mrs. Wicklow. "Must have been an underground spring, though I never heard of one round here. Swept most of the barn away, it did; they pulled down t'rest. She'd had the builders in there, 'doing it up' she said. Happen they tapped into something."

"I didn't know there was a barn," said Gaynor.

"The Captain used to keep some of his stuff in there. Rubbish mostly, if you ask me. He'd got half a boat he'd picked up somewhere, part of a wreck he said, with a woman on the front baring her all. Fern insisted they give it to a museum. Will wanted to keep it, but it wasn't healthy for a young man. There's trouble enough him messing around with Art."

"Alison worked for an art gallery, didn't she?" Gaynor persisted, resisting diversion.

"Aye," said the housekeeper. "She and that man with the white hair. I didn't like *him* at all, for all his greasy manners. Oily as a tinned sardine, he was. They never found out what happened to him."

"What do you mean?" Gaynor had never heard of a man with white hair.

"Done a bunk, so they said. Left his car here, too: a flash white car to match the hair. Happen that's why he bought it: he was the type. A proper mystery, that was. He walked into t'drawing room and never walked out. Mind, that was the same time Fern got lost, so we thought she might have gone with him, though not willing, I was sure of that. They were bad days for all of us, and bad to remember, but she came back all right. They said she'd been sick, some fancy name they gave it, one of these newfangled things you hear about on t'telly. She was well enough after, but she wouldn't talk about it."

"I know," said Gaynor as they entered the kitchen. "But—the man . . . ?"

"I reckon he was a crook, like his Alison. They were in it together, whatever it was. Anyhow, that fancy car of his sat here and sat here till the police came and towed it away. He didn't come back at all." She concluded, with a certain grim satisfaction: "And good riddance to both of 'em."

Gaynor digested this with the sandwich lunch Mrs. Wicklow insisted on feeding her, though she wasn't really hungry. Afterward, Fern and Will still being absent, she returned to her room. A flick through the newspaper had reminded her there was a program she wanted to catch on the television, an afternoon repeat of a documentary that she thought might be of professional interest. She told herself it was stupid to be nervous about switching the set on. She had had a nightmare the previous day, that was all, probably suggested by an item on the news—one of those vivid, surreal spasms of dreaming that can invade a shallow sleep. (Nightmares and dreams, pervading the dark, spilling over into reality . . .) All the same, she was secretly relieved when she pressed the button on the remote and a normal picture appeared, flat and off-color. Her program was already under way, the camera following a conscientiously enthusiastic presenter around a succession of museums and private collections. Presently Gaynor forgot her qualms, becoming totally absorbed in her subject. The camera panned over early printing on cracked paper, incunabula and scrolls, wooden plaques and broken sections of stone tablets. "Here we are in the little-known Museum of Ancient Writings," announced the presenter, "hidden away in a back street in York . . ." Near enough, thought Gaynor. I ought to pay it a visit. The curator, a dingy young man of thirty-odd who appeared to have been prematurely aged by the manuscripts that surrounded him, talked in a lengthy drone that Gaynor tuned out, wishing instead that the image would focus longer and more closely on some of the documents. "A Historie of Dragonf," she read on the cover of a medieval book gloriously inlaid with serpentine monsters in gold leaf. Invisible hands turned the pages, but too swiftly for her to catch more than a line here and there. "A grate dragon, grater than anye other lyving beaste . . . and the Knyghte cast his speare at yt, but yt was not slaine . . . Its mouthe opened, and the shafte was consumed with fire, but yt swallowed the hedde, which was . . . stone yet not stone, a thyng of grate power and magicke . . ." The picture changed, returning to the presenter, now interviewing a much older man who was evidently on the board in some significant capacity. A subtitle indicated that this was Dr. Jerrold Laye, a university lecturer specializing in this field. "Not a name I know," Gaynor said aloud, and for a fraction of a second his hooked profile froze, almost as if he had overheard.

Gaynor felt suddenly very cold. The camera veered from profile to full face, closing in until Dr. Laye's physiognomy filled the whole screen. She was staring at him as if hypnotized, unable to avert her gaze without a degree of effort that seemed all but impossible. She saw a high, sloping brow from which the hair was receding in a double arch, the nose of a Roman emperor, the flinty jawline of a fanatic. Pronounced cheekbones pulled his skin into taut, sharp creases that had little to do with smiling. What hair he still possessed was gray; so was his complexion, gray as paste, though whether this was the result of poor color quality on the television or the aftereffect of disease she could not guess. His eyebrows formed another double arch, shaggy with drooping hairs, beneath which his eyes lurked, half hidden by membranous lids of a curiously scaly appearance, like the extra eyelid possessed by certain reptiles. As the camera angle altered so did the direction of his regard, until he seemed to be looking not at the interviewer but at the viewer, staring straight out of the screen at Gaynor herself. His eyes were pale blue, and cold as a cleft in an ice floe. He can't really see me, she told herself. He's just looking into the lens: that's all it is. *He can't see me.* The interview wound down; the voice of the presenter faded out. Dr. Laye extended his hand—a large, narrow hand, the fingers elongated beyond elegance, supple beyond nature. He was reaching toward her, and toward her . . . out of the picture, into the room. The image of his head and shoulders remained flat but the section of arm emerging from it was three-dimensional, and it seemed to be pulling the screen as if it were made of some elastic substance, distorting it. Gaynor did not move. Shock, horror, disbelief petrified every muscle. If it touches me, she thought, I'll faint . . .

But it did not touch her. The index finger curled like a scorpion's tail in a gesture of beckoning, at once sinister and horribly suggestive. She could see the nail in great detail, an old man's nail like a sliver of horn with a thin rind of yellow along the outer edge and a purplish darkening above the cuticle. The skin was definitely gray, the color of ash, though the tint of normal flesh showed in the creases and in a glimpse of the palm. On the screen, something that might have been intended for a smile stretched Dr. Laye's mouth.

"I look forward to meeting you," he said.

The hand withdrew, the bent fingertip wriggling slowly to emphasize its meaning. Then the flat image swallowed it, and it was back in its former place on Dr. Laye's lap, and he turned again to the presenter, who appeared to have noticed nothing out of the ordinary. Her voice gradually resumed its earlier flow, as if someone were gently turning up the volume. Gaynor switched off the television, feeling actually sick from the release of tension. When she was able she went over and touched the blank screen, but it felt solid and inflexible. She ran downstairs to find Mrs. Wicklow, not to tell her what had happened—how could she do that?—but for the reassurance of her company.

But she had to tell someone.

Will came home first.

"There was this amazing cloud effect," he said, pushing his studio door open with one shoulder, his arms full of camera, sketch pad, folding stool. "Like a great gray hand reaching out over the landscape . . . and the sun leaking between two of its fingers in visible shafts, making the dark somehow more ominous. I got the outline down and took some pictures before the light changed, but now—now I need to let the image develop, sort of grow in my imagination . . ."

"Until the cloud really *is* a hand?" suggested Gaynor with an involuntary shudder.

"Maybe." He was depositing pad, stool, camera on various surfaces but he did not miss her reaction. "What's the matter?"

She told him. About the program, and Dr. Laye, and the hand emerging from the television screen, and her waking nightmare the preceding evening, with the idol that came to life. She even told him about the dreams and the sound of bagpipes. He listened without interruption, although when she came to the last point he laughed suddenly.

"You needn't worry about that," he said. "It's just the house-goblin."

"House-goblin?" she echoed faintly.

"In the old days nearly every house had its own goblin. Or gremlin, bogey, whichever you prefer. Nowadays, they're much rarer. Too many houses, too much intrusive technology, too few goblins. This house had one when we first came here, but Alison . . . got rid of him. She was like that. Anyway, the place felt a bit empty without one, so I advertised for a replacement. In a manner of speaking. Bradachin came from a Scottish castle and I think his heart's in the Highlands still—at least in the wee small hours. He turned up with a set of pipes and a rusty spear that looks as old as war itself. Anyway, don't let him trouble you. This is his house now and we're his people: that means he's *for* us."

"Have you ever seen him?" asked Gaynor, skepticism waning after her own experiences.

"Of course. So will you, I expect—when he's ready."

"I don't particularly *want* to see a goblin," Gaynor protested, adding somberly: "I've seen enough. More than enough."

Will put his arms around her for the second time, and despite recent fear and present distress she was suddenly very conscious of his superior height and the coiled-wire strength of his young muscles. "We'll have to tell Ragginbone about all this," he said at last. "He'll know what's going on. At least, he might. I don't like the sound of that business with the idol. We've been there before." She glanced up, questioning. "There was a statue here when we came, some kind of ancient deity, only a couple of feet high but . . . Fortunately, it got smashed. It was being used as a receptor—like a transmitter—by a malignant spirit. Very old, very powerful, very dangerous."

"What spirit?" said Gaynor, abandoning disbelief altogether, at least for the present.

"He had a good many names," Will said. "He'd been worshiped as a god, reviled as a demon . . . The one I remember was Azmordis, but it's best not to use it too freely. Demons have a tendency to come when they're called. Ragginbone always referred to him simply as the Old Spirit. He is—or was—very strong, too strong for us to fight, but because of what Fern did he was weakened, and Ragginbone thought he might not return here. It seems he was wrong."

"I don't like any of this," said Gaynor. "I've never trusted the supernatural."

Will smiled ruefully. "Neither have I."

"I went to a séance once," she continued. His arms were still around her and she found a peculiar comfort in conversing with his chest. "It was all nonsense: this dreadful old woman who looked like a caricature of a tea lady, pretending to go into a trance and faking these silly voices. If I were dead, and I wanted to communicate with somebody, I'm sure I could do it without all that rigmarole. But there was something coming through, something . . . unhealthy. Maybe it was in the subconscious minds of the participants. Anyway, whatever it was, it felt *wrong*. I don't want to be mixed up in anything like that again."

"You could leave," said Will, releasing her. "For some reason, you're a target, but away from here you'd be safe. I'm sure of that."

She didn't like the word "target," but she retorted as hotly as she could: "Of course I won't leave! For one thing, I can't miss the wedding, even if I'm not mad keen on the idea. Fern would never forgive me."

"You know, I've been wondering . . ." Will paused, caught on a hesitation.

"Yes?"

"It's too much of a coincidence, everything blowing up again just *now*. There has to be a connection."

"With Fern's *wedding*?"

"It sounds ridiculous, but . . . I think so."

They discussed this possibility for some time without arriving at any satisfactory conclusions. None of this is true, Gaynor told herself. Witchcraft, and malignant spirits, and a goblin in the house who plays the bagpipes at six o'clock in the morning . . . Of course it isn't true. But although much of what had happened to her could be dismissed as dreams and fancy, her experience in front of the television with the reaching hand had been hideously real. And Will had not doubted her or laughed at her. As he had believed her, so she must believe him. Anyway, it was so much easier than agonizing about it. Yet even as the thought occurred, uncertainty crept in. "If you're inventing this to make fun of me," she said, suddenly shaky, "I'll—I'll probably kill you."

"I don't need to invent," he said, studying her with an air of gravity that reminded her of Fern. "You saw the hand. You dreamed the idol. You heard the pipes. The evidence is all yours. Now, let's go up to your room. At least I can get rid of that bloody TV set."

They went upstairs.

The television stood there, squat, blank of screen, inert. Yet to Gaynor it seemed to be imbued with a new and terrifying potentiality, an immanent persona far beyond that of normal household gadgetry. She wondered if it was her imagination that it appeared to be waiting.

She sat down on the bed, feeling stupidly weak at the knees, and there was the remote under her hand, though she was almost sure she had left it on the side table. The power button nudged at her finger.

"Please take it away," she said tightly, like a child for whom some ordinary, everyday object has been infected with the stuff of nightmares.

Will crouched down by the wall to release the plug—and started back abruptly with a four-letter oath. "It shocked me!" he said. "The bloody thing *shocked* me!"

"Did you switch it off?"

He reached out once more, this time for the switch—and again pulled his hand back sharply. Gaynor had glimpsed the blue spark that flashed out at his touch. "Maybe you have a strong electric aura," she offered hesitantly, coming over and bending down beside him. The instant her tentative finger brushed the socket she felt the stab of pain, violent as a burn. For a fraction of a second a current of agony shot up her arm, her fingertip was glued to the power source, the individual hairs on her skin crackled with static. Then somehow she was free, her finger red but otherwise unmarked.

"Leave it," said Will. "We need Fern. She could deal with this. She has the right kind of gloves."

They went down to the kitchen, where they found Mrs. Wicklow extracting a cake from the oven. With her firm conviction that young people nowadays were all too thin and in constant need of sustenance, she cooked frequently and to excess, although only Will could be said to justify her efforts. But after the horrors of the afternoon Gaynor munched happily on calories and carbohydrates, thankful for their comforting effect. Fern was late back, having gone from the caterers to the wine merchants, from the wine merchants to the church. "We're invited to the vicarage for dinner," she called out as she came in. "Is the bath free?"

Gaynor called back in the affirmative and was vaguely relieved to hear Will following his sister upstairs, sparing her the necessity of relating her story again. Despite all that Will had told her, she could not visualize her friend receiving it with anything but polite disbelief. She waited several minutes and then she, too, went up to the second floor.

Fern was standing in the bathroom doorway, with the chundering of the hot tap coming from behind her and translucent billows of steam overflowing into the corridor. She had obviously been in the preliminary stages of undress when Will interrupted her: her shoes lay where they had been kicked and her right hand was still clutching a crumpled ball of socks that she squeezed savagely from time to time, apparently unaware of what she was doing. There was an expression on her face that Gaynor had never seen before, a kind of brittleness that looked as if it might fragment at a touch and re-form into something far more dangerous. Gaynor could smell a major row, hovering in the ether like an inflammable gas, waiting for the wrong word to spark it off.

But all Fern said was: "I told you that TV was a mistake."

She led the way up to Gaynor's room and headed straight for the socket where the set was plugged in.

"You'll need the gloves," Will said. "Alison's gloves . . ."

Fern rounded on him, her eyes bright with pent-up rage and some other feeling, something that might have been a deep secret hurt. "That's what you want, isn't it? That's what you're *really* after. You want me to open her box—Pandora's box—play with her toys. You want to drag me down into her world. It's over, Will, long, long over. The witches and the goblins have gone back into the shadows where they belong. We're in the real world now—for good—and I'm getting married on Saturday, and you can't stop it even if you call up Azmordis himself."

"From the sound of things," Will said quietly, "he's coming anyway."

"If I didn't know you better," Fern said, ignoring him, switching the glare to her friend, "I might think you'd been primed."

Gaynor, absorbing the accusation with incredulity, opened her mouth to refute it, but Fern had turned away. She bent down to the socket, the sock ball still crumpled in one fist, and flicked the switch on and off with impunity. "Well, well. Seems perfectly normal to me. On, off. On, off. How unexpected. And the plug—plug out, plug in, plug out. What do you know. If you've finished with this farce I'm going to have my bath. I told Maggie we'd be there at seven; please be ready promptly. Let's not add bad manners to everything else."

And to Gaynor: "I thought better of you. I know you don't like Marcus—"

"I *do* like him," Gaynor said, speaking faster than she thought. "But I'd like him a lot more if you were in love with him."

"Love!" Fern cried scornfully—but for all the scorn her voice held an undertone of loss and suffering that checked Gaynor's rising anger. "That belongs with all those other fairy tales—in the dustbin."

She ran out and downstairs: they heard the bathroom door slam. Gaynor had moved to follow but Will held her back. "No point," he said. "If there's trouble coming she can't stop it, not even by marrying boring Marcus."

"But I still don't see what her marriage can have to do with—this?" Gaynor said in bewilderment, indicating the television set. "Why is everything getting mixed up?"

"I *think*," Will said, "it's all to do with motives. Her motives for getting married."

"She's in pain," said Gaynor. "I heard it in her voice."

"She's in denial," said Will.

It was not a scene that augured well for the forthcoming dinner party, but although the three of them walked down to the vicarage in comparative silence, once there the warmth of the Dinsdales' welcome, the aroma of roasting chicken, and copious quantities of cheap red wine all combined to bring down their hastily erected barriers. Will relaxed into his usual easygoing charm of manner, Fern, perhaps feeling that she might have over-reacted earlier on, made a conscious effort to unwind, appealing to her friend for corroboration of every anecdote, and Gaynor, too generous to nurse a sense of injury, responded in kind, suppressing the bevy of doubts and fears that gnawed at her heart. By the time they were ready to leave, their mutual tensions, though not forgotten, were set aside. They strolled homeward in harmony, steering the conversation clear of uncomfortable subjects, admiring the stars that had chosen to put in an appearance in the clearing sky, and pausing to listen for night birds, or to glimpse a furtive shadow that might have been a fox, slinking across the road toward the river. For Gaynor, a city girl like Fern, though more from career necessity than choice, the country held its own special magic. The belated child of a flagging marriage with three siblings already grown up, she had never really felt part of a family, and now, with Fern and her brother, she knew something of the closeness she had missed. The wine warmed her, the night bewitched her. She would have subordinated a whole catalogue of private doubts to preserve that feeling undamaged.

"Perhaps we'll see the owl," she said as they drew near the house.

"I thought that was a dream," said Will. "Riding on the back of a giant owl . . . or did you see a real one?"

"I'm not sure," Gaynor admitted. "Maybe it *was* just a dream."

"I've heard one round here at night," Fern said, and a quick shiver ran through her, as if at a sudden chill.

Indoors, they said good night with more affection than was customary, Fern even going so far as to embrace her friend, although she had never acquired the London habit of scattering kisses among all and sundry. Gaynor retired to her room, feeling insensibly relieved. As she undressed she found herself looking at the television set, disconnected now but still retaining its air of bland threat, as if at any moment the screen might flicker into unwholesome life. She thought: I don't want it in here; but when she tried to move it, overcoming a sudden reluctance to approach or handle it, the machine felt awkward, at once slippery and heavy, unnaturally heavy. She could not seem to get a grip on it. In the end she gave up, but the blank screen continued to trouble her, so she draped a towel over it, putting a china bowl on the top to prevent the makeshift covering sliding off. Will would probably be asleep now; she could not disturb him just to help her shift the television. She climbed into bed and after some time lying wakeful, nerves on the stretch, she, too, slept.

She was standing in front of the mirror, face-to-face with her reflection. But it looked different from earlier in the day: it had acquired a sort of intense, serious beauty, an antique glamor that had little to do with the real Gaynor. It isn't me, she thought, but I wish it was. Behind the reflection her room, too, had changed. There were books, pictures, a potted plant whose single flower resembled puckered red lips, a bedspread made of peacock feathers. A smoked glass shade softened the lightbulb to a dull glow. This isn't my room, she realized. This is Alison's room, the way it must have looked when she lived here. Mirrors remember. Her gaze returned to her own image with awakening dread: she knew what would happen with that dream-knowing that is both terrible and ineffectual, a vain striving to alter the unalterable. Dream turned to nightmare: the face before her shrank into a tapering oval, hollow cheeked, broad browed; the deep eyes were elongated into slits, not dark but bright, shining with the multifaceted glitter of cut crystal. A dull pallor rippled through her hair, transforming it into the dim tresses of a phantom. Gaynor was paralyzed, unable to twitch a muscle, but in the mirror her mouth widened into a thin crimson smile, curling up toward her cheekbones, image surveying reality with cold mockery. The surface of the glass was no longer hard and solid: it had become little more than a skin, the thickness of a molecule, dividing her from the other room, the other person. And then the reflection reached out, and the skin broke, and the stranger stepped out of the mirror into Gaynor's bedroom.

"Alison," said Gaynor.

"Alimond," said the stranger. "Alison was just a name. Alimond is my true Self."

"Why have you come back?"

The smile became laughter, a tinkling silvery laughter like the sound of breaking glass. "Why do you think?" she said. "To watch television, of course. I'll tell you a secret: there is no television beyond the Gate of Death. Neither in heaven nor in hell. All we are allowed to see is our own lives and the lives of those we touched; an endless replaying of all our yesterdays, all our failures, all our mistakes. Think of that, ere your time comes. Live yourself a life worth watching, before it's too late."

She took Gaynor's hand as she spoke: her grip felt insubstantial, light as a zephyr, but cold, so cold. The icy chill stabbed Gaynor to the bone.

Alimond said: "Plug the television in, and switch it on."

Gaynor tried to pull free of the cold ethereal grasp but her nerve withered and her strength turned to water. "You are too sensitive," murmured Alimond. "Too delicate to resist, too feeble to fight. You have neither the backbone nor the Gift to stand against me. Fernanda chooses her friends unwisely. Push the plug in . . ."

She's right, Gaynor's thought responded, taking control of mind and body. You're betraying Fern, betraying yourself. You cannot help it . . .

She was on her knees by the wall; she heard the click of reconnection as the plug slid home. Alimond guided her hand toward the switch. Then the dream faded into sleep, and darkness enveloped her.

When she woke again, the room was shaking. The bed juddered, the floor vibrated; above her she could make out the old-fashioned fringed lampshade twitching like a restless animal. She struggled to sit up and saw the television rattling and shuddering as if seized with an ague. Its fever seemed to have communicated itself to the rest of the furniture: even the heavy wardrobe creaked in response. As she watched, the china bowl on top of the set danced sideways, trembled on the edge, and fell to the ground, rolling unbroken on the carpet. The towel followed suit, sidling inch by inch across the screen and then collapsing floorward in a heap. In a sudden access of terror Gaynor reached for the remote and flung it with all her strength against the wall, but the impact must have jolted the power button, for even as it hit the television screen exploded into color. The furniture was still again; the picture glowed in the darkness like an extraterrestrial visitation. Gaynor sat bolt upright, clutching the bedclothes. It felt like a dream, dreadful and inexorable, but she knew she wasn't dreaming now. The image was flat, two-dimensional, not the hole in the very fabric of existence through which she had seen the idol in the temple. But it had been from an apparently normal image that Dr. Laye had turned and looked at her, and stretched out his hand . . .

She was watching a vintage horror film. Pseudo-Victorian costumes, men with sixties sideburns, a heroine with false eyelashes and heaving bosom. It was low camp, reassuringly familiar, unalarming. Improbable plastic bats circled a Gothic mansion that had loomed its way through a hundred such scenes.

Presently one of the bats came too close to the screen, thrusting its wing tip into the room . . .

Fern and Will woke to the sound of screaming.

The room was full of bats. They blundered into the passage when Will opened the door, ricocheted to and fro as he switched on the light. Gaynor was covered in them, her pajamas hooked and tugged and clawed, her hair tangled with wildly threshing wings. She beat at them in a frenzy, irrational with terror, but her fear only served to madden them, and they swarmed around her like flies on a corpse. Their squashed-up snouts resembled wrinkled leaves, their blind eyes were puckered, their teeth needle pointed. More flew out of the television at every moment, tearing themselves free of the screen with a sound like lips smacking. Miniature lightnings ran up and down the power cord.

"Help her," Fern said to her brother, and raced back to her room, extricating the box from under her bed—the box she never looked at, never touched—catching the scent of the long-lost forest, fumbling inside for the gloves she had always refused to wear. Upstairs, Will was trying to reach the figure on the bed, arms flailing in a vain attempt to disperse the bat cloud.

When Fern reentered, the gloves were already on her hands. The scales grew onto her flesh, chameleon patterns mottled her fingers. She reached for the socket with lizard's paws; the plug spat fire as she wrenched it out. There was no explosion, no noise, just the suddenness of silence. The screen reverted to blank; the bats vanished. Gaynor drew a long sobbing breath and then clung to Will, shaking spasmodically. Fern gazed down for a minute at the hands that were no longer hers, then very carefully, like a snake divesting itself of its skin, she peeled off the gloves.

They deposited the television outside by the dustbins after Will, at Fern's insistence, had attacked it with a hammer. "What about the mirror?" he said. "We can't leave it there."

"Swap it with the one in the end room," Fern suggested. "It's even dirtier, I'm afraid," she apologized to Gaynor, "but at least you know the nastiest thing you'll ever see in it is Will, peering over your shoulder."

Gaynor managed an unsteady laugh. They were sitting in the kitchen over mugs of strong, sweet cocoa, laced and chased with whiskey. Mindful of the shuddering cold that so often follows shock, Fern had pressed a hot-water bottle on her friend and wrapped her in a spare blanket. "If you want to leave," Fern said, "I'll understand. Something, or someone, is trying to use you, victimize you . . . perhaps to get to me. I don't know why. I wish I did."

"Ragginbone might know," Will offered.

"Then again he might not." Fern opened a drawer and fished out a crumpled packet of cigarettes, left behind by a visitor months or even years ago. They were French, their acidic pungency only enhanced by the passage of time. She extracted one, remolded its squashed contours into a vaguely tubular shape, and lit it experimentally.

"Why on earth are you doing that?" Will demanded. "You never smoke."

"I feel like making a gesture." She drew on the cigarette cautiously, expelling the smoke without inhaling. "This is disgusting. It's just what I need."

"It has to be Azmordis behind this business, doesn't it?" Will said after a pause.

"Don't name him," his sister admonished. "Not if he's around.

Ragginbone said he would be seriously weakened after Ixavo's death, maybe for a long time—but how long is that? Twelve years? And what *kind* of time—real time or weretime, time here or elsewhere?"

"Do you think what Gaynor saw was really Alison?" Will pursued. "Alison returned from the dead?"

"N-no. The dead don't return. Ghosts are those who've never left, but Alison had nothing to stay for. I suppose *he* might use a phantom in her image, possibly to confuse us."

"I'm confused," Gaynor confirmed.

"Will you be okay for the rest of the night?" Fern asked. "We could change rooms if you like. I'll drive you into York in the morning: there are trains for London every hour."

"I'm not leaving." Behind the dark curtains of her hair Gaynor achieved a twisty smile. "I'm frightened—of course I am. I don't think I've ever been so frightened in my life. But you're my friend—my *friends*—and, well, you're supposed to stand by friends in trouble . . ."

"Sentimentality," Fern interjected.

"Hogwash," said Will.

"Whatever. Anyway, I'm staying. You invited me; you can't disinvite me. I know I wasn't very brave just now but I can't help it: I hate bats. I hate the way they flutter and their horrible ratty little faces. That's what they are: rats with wings. I'll be much braver as long as there are no more bats."

"We can't absolutely guarantee it," Fern said.

"Besides," Gaynor continued, ignoring her, "you're getting married on Saturday. I'm not going to miss that."

For an instant, Fern looked totally blank. "I'd forgotten," she said.

They went back to bed about half an hour later, warm with the twin comforts of chocolate and alcohol. Will bunked down in the room next to Gaynor's, wrapped in the ubiquitous spare blanket. Worn out by events, reassured by his proximity, she fell asleep almost at once; but he lay with his eyes open, staring into the dark. Presently he made out a hump of shadow at the foot of his bed that had not been there before.

He said softly: "Bradachin?"

"Aye."

"Did you see what happened?"

"Aye."

There was an impatient silence. "Well?" Will persisted. "Did you see a woman come out of the mirror?"

"I didna see ony woman. There was a flaysome creature came slinking through the glass, all mimsy it was, like a wisp o' moonlicht, and the banes shining through its hand, and cobwebs drifting round its heid. Some kind o' *tannasgeal* maybe. It was clinging round the maidy like mist round a craig. She seemed all moithered by it, like she didna ken what she was doing."

"Where did it go?" Will asked.

"Back through the glass. I'm nae sure where it gaed after, but it isna here nae mair."

"But how could it get in?" Will mused. "No one here summoned it, did they?"

"Nae. But a *tannasgeal* gangs where the maister sends it—and ye asked *him* in long ago, or sae ye seid."

"You mean Az—the Old Spirit sent it?"

"Most likely."

"Yes, of course . . . Bradachin, would you mind spending the night in Gaynor's room? Don't let her see you, just call me if—if anything happens."

"I'm no a servant for ye tae orrder aboot."

"Please?" Will coaxed.

"Aye, weel . . . I was just wanting ye tae keep it in mind. I'm nae servant . . ."

The hunched shadow dimmed, dissolving into the surrounding dark. After a few minutes Will closed his eyes and relapsed into sleep.

In the room on the floor below, Fern was still wakeful. She was trying to concentrate on her marriage, rerunning a mental reel of her possible future with Marcus Greig. Cocktail parties in Knightsbridge, dinner parties in Hampstead, all-night parties in Notting Hill Gate. Lunches at the Ivy, launches at the Groucho. First nights and last nights, previews and private views, designer clothes, designer furniture. The same kind of skiing trips and Tuscan villas that she had experienced as a child, only rather more expensive. In due course, perhaps, there would be a second home in Provence. Her heart shrank at the prospect. And then there was Marcus himself, with his agile intelligence, his New Labor ethics, his easy repartee. She liked him, she was even impressed by him—though it is not difficult for a successful forty-six to impress a rising twenty-eight. She knew he had worked his way up from lower-middle-class origins that he preferred to call proletarian, that his first wife had been a country type who left him for a farmer and a horse. Fern had contemplated marrying him on their third date. He fulfilled the standards she had set for her partner, and if his hair was thinning and his waistline thickening, he was still generally considered an attractive man. She was nearly thirty, too old for fairy tales, uninspired by casual love. The more she thought about it, the more she had wanted this marriage—and she still wanted it, she knew she did, if only she could keep hold of her reasoning, if she could just remind herself what made those scenes from her life-to-be so desirable. She should never have left London. Away from the polluted air and the intrusive voices of traffic, telephones, and technology, her head was so clear it felt empty, with too much room for old memories and new ideas. She had done her best to fence them out, to fill up the space with the fuss and flurry of wedding preparations, but tonight she sensed it had all been in vain. The future she had pursued so determinedly was slipping away. She had worn the witch's gloves, opened her heart to power. Trouble and uncertainty lay ahead, and the germ of treachery in her soul was drawing her toward them.

She languished in the borderland of sleep, too tired now to succumb. Her mind planed: recollections long buried resurfaced to ensnare her, jumbled together in a broken jigsaw. Alimond the witch combing her hair with a comb of bone like a Lorelei in a song, her lips moving in what Fern thought was an incantation, until she heard the words of an antique ballad: *Where once I kissed your cheek the fishes feed* . . . And then the siren dived into deep water, and there was the skeleton lying in the coral, and she set the comb down on its cavernous breast, and Fern saw it slot into its place among the ribs. And the head looked no longer like a skull: its eyes were closed with shells, and its locks moved like weed in the current. *Sleep well forever there, my bonny dear.* A ship's foghorn drew her out of the depths—no, not a foghorn, an albatross, crying to her with a half-human voice. They said in Atlantis that albatrosses were the messengers of the Unknown God. It was very near now, almost in her room. How ridiculous, thought Fern. There are no albatrosses in Yorkshire. It must be the owl again, the owl Gaynor talked about . . .

She was not aware of getting up but suddenly she was by the open window, leaning out into the night. She heard the sough of the wind in the trees although there were no trees anywhere near the house. The owl's cry was somewhere in her dream, in her head. And then it came, hurtling out of the dark, a vast pale blur too swift and too sudden to see clearly. There was a rushing tumult of wings, the close-up of a face—a mournful heart-shaped face with nasal beak and no mouth, black button eyes set in huge discs, like a ghost peeping through the holes in a sheet. She thrust out her hands to ward it off, horrified by the impression of giant size, the predatory speed of its lunge. The power came instinctively, surging down her arms with a force dream-enspelled, unsought and out of control . . . The owl reeled and veered away, gone so fast she had no time to check if its size had been real or merely an illusion of terror. But its last shriek lingered in her mind, haunting and savage. She stumbled away from the window, her body shaking with the aftermath of that power surge. When she touched the bed she collapsed into it, too exhausted to disentangle herself from the blankets, helpless as with a fever. Dream or reality faded, and in the morning when she finally awoke, late and heavy eyed, she was not sure if it had happened at all.

◆ VI ◆

(W)eddings have their own momentum. Once the machinery has been set in motion—once invitations have been issued and accepted, present lists placed with suitable department stores, caterers conjured, live music laid on, flowers, bridesmaids, and multistory cakes all concocted—once male relatives have hired or resurrected morning suits and female ones have bought outfits in the sort of pastel colors that should be worn only by newborn infants—the whole circus rolls on like a juggernaut with no brakes, crushing anything and anyone who may get in its way. The groom is sidelined, the bride traumatized. Couples who are madly in love lose track of their passion, floundering in a welter of trivial details, trapped by the hopes and expectations of their devoted kith and kin. Those less in love find in these chaotic preliminaries the wherewithal to blot out their doubts, giving themselves no leisure to think, no leeway to withdraw. So it had been with Fern. She had made her decision and intended to stand by it, obliterating any last-minute reservations; and now, when she felt a sudden need to stop, to reconsider, to take her time, there was no time left to take. It was Friday already, and although she had overslept she did not feel rested, and the morning was half-gone, and the phone was starting to ring down-stairs. Someone answered it, and Fern stretched and lay still, temporarily reprieved, and for the first time in more than a de-cade she opened her waking mind to memories of Atlantis. A villa on a mountainside, a room golden with lamplight and candlelight, the blue evening deepening outside. The echo of a thought, bitter-sweet with pain: *This is how I shall remember it, when it is long gone* . . . She got up in a sudden rush and began rummaging furi-ously in her dressing-table drawer, and there it was, tucked away at the back where she had hidden it all those years ago. A skein of material, cobweb thin and sinuous as silk, so transparent that it appeared to have neither hue nor pattern, until a closer look re-vealed the elusive traces of a design, and faint gleams of color like splintered light. As Fern let it unfold, the creases of long storage melted away, and it lay over her arms like a drift of pale mist. She was still holding it when she went down to the kitchen in search of coffee. Will frowned: he thought he had seen it before.

"It's beautiful," said Gaynor, touching it admiringly. "It's the most beautiful thing I've ever seen. What is it—a scarf?"

"Something old," said Fern. "Like it says in the rhyme. Some-thing old, something new, something borrowed, something blue. This is very old."

"What will you do for t'rest of them?" asked Mrs. Wicklow.

"A new dress, a borrowed smile, the three-carat sapphire in my engagement ring. That should cover it."

Gaynor started at her flippancy; Mrs. Wicklow found excuses for it. "Poor lass. Happen it's all been too much for you. It's al-ways hard on t'bride just before t'big day, specially if she hasn't a mother to help her. You don't want to go drinking so much coffee: it'll wind up your nerves even tighter."

Fern smiled rather wanly, pushing the empty cup away. "I'll switch to tea," she said.

After a breakfast that only Will ate, Mrs. Wicklow departed to make up beds and bully Trisha, and Will and Gaynor went out in search of Ragginbone.

"You won't find him," said Fern. "He's never there when you want him. It's a habit of his."

She went to the upstairs room where the dress waited in solitary splendor. It was made of that coarse-textured Thai silk that rustles like tissue paper with every movement, the color too warm for white but not quite cream. The high neck was open down the front, the corners folded back like wings to show a glimpse of hidden embroidery, similar to the neckline worn by Mary Tudor in so many somber portraits. The sleeves were tight and long enough to cover the wrist; the waist tapered; the skirt flared. Further decoration was minimal. It had beauty, simplicity, style: everything Fern approved of. If I was in love, she thought irrationally, I'd want frills and flounces and lace. I'd want to look like a cloud full of pearls, like a blizzard in chiffon. No woman in love wants understatement. But there was no such thing as love, only marriage. On an impulse she took the dress off the dummy and put it on, wrestling with the inaccessible section of the zipper. There was a hair ornament of silver wire, fitting like an Alice band, in order to secure the veil. She arranged it rather awkwardly and surveyed herself in the mirror—Alison's mirror, which Will had moved from Gaynor's room. In the spotted glass the sheen of the silk was dulled, making her look pale and severe. Her face appeared shadowed and hard about the mouth. I look like a nun, she decided. The wrong kind of nun. Not a blossoming girl abandoning her novitiate for the lure of romance, but a woman opting out of the world, for whom nunhood was a necessary martyrdom. A passing ray of sunlight came through the window behind her, touching that other veil, the gift of Atlantis, which she had left on the bed, so that for an instant it glowed in the dingy mirror like a rainbow.

Fern turned quickly, but the sun vanished, and the colors, and her dress felt stiff and cumbersome, weighing her down; she struggled out of it with difficulty. I must have time to think, she told herself. Maybe if I talk to Gus . . .

She could hear Mrs. Wicklow coming up the stairs and she hurried out, feeling illogically guilty, as if in trying on the dress before the appointed hour, she had been indulging in a culpable act. Mrs. Wicklow's manner was even more dour than usual: Robin, Abby, and Robin's only surviving aunt were due later that day, and it transpired that although Dale House was lavishly endowed with bedrooms, there was a shortage of available linen. An ancient cache of sheets had proved to be moth eaten beyond repair. "It's too late to buy new ones," Fern said, seizing opportunity. "I'll go down to the vicarage and see if I can borrow some."

She felt better out of doors, though the sky to the east looked leaden and a hearty little wind had just breezed in off the North Sea. At the vicarage, she explained to Maggie about the bedding and then enquired for Gus.

"He had to go out," Maggie said. "Big meeting with the archdeacon about church finances. It's a funny thing: the smaller the finances, the bigger the meeting. Did you want him for anything special?"

Maybe she would be better off talking to Maggie, woman to woman, Fern thought, tempted by the hazy concept of universal sisterhood. Haltingly she began to stammer out her doubts about the forthcoming marriage. She felt like a novice curate admitting to the lure of religious schism. Maggie's face melted into instant sympathy. Her normal Weltanschauung combined genuine kindness and conscientious tolerance with the leftovers of sixties ideology at its woolliest. In her teens she had embraced Nature, pacifism, and all things bright and beautiful, Freudian and Spockian, liberal and liberationist. She had worn long droopy skirts and long droopy hair, smoked marijuana, played the guitar (rather badly), and even tried free love, though only once or twice before she met Gus. At heart, however, she remained a post-Victorian romantic for whom a wedding day was a high point in every woman's life. Relegating the loan of sheets to lower on the agenda, she pressed Fern into an armchair and offered coffee.

"No, thanks, I . . ."

"It's not too much trouble, honestly. The percolator's already on. What you need is to stop rushing around and sit down and relax for a bit. All brides go through this just before a wedding, believe me. I know I did. It's all right for the men—they never do any of the work—but the poor bride is inundated with arrangements that keep changing and temperamental caterers and awkward relatives, and there always comes a moment when she stops and asks herself what it's All For. It's a big thing, getting married, one of the biggest things you'll ever do—it's going to alter your whole life—so it's only natural you should be nervous. You'll be fine tomorrow. When you're standing there in the church, and he's beside you, and you say 'I do'—it all falls into place. I promise you." She took Fern's hand and pressed it, her face shining with the fuzzy inner confidence of those fortunate few for whom marriage really is the key to domestic bliss.

"But I'm not sure that I—"

"Hold on: I'll get the coffee. Keep talking. I can hear you from the kitchen."

"I had this picture of my future with Marcus," Fern said, addressing the empty chair opposite. "I'd got it all planned—I've always planned things—and I knew exactly how it would be. I thought that was what I wanted, only now I—I'm not sure anymore. Something happened last night—it doesn't matter what—that changed my perspective. I've always assumed I liked my life in London, but now I wonder if that was because I wouldn't let myself think about it. I was afraid to widen my view. It isn't that I *dis*like it: I just want more. And I don't believe marrying Marcus will offer me more—just more of the same."

"Sorry," said Maggie, emerging with two mugs in which the liquid slopped dangerously. "I didn't catch all that. The percolator was making too much noise. You were saying you weren't sure—?"

"I'm not sure I want to get married," Fern reiterated with growing desperation.

"*Of course* you're not." Maggie set down the mugs and glowed at her again. "No one is ever one hundred percent sure about anything. Gus says that's one of the miraculous things about human nature, that we're able to leave room for doubt. People who are too sure, he says, tend to bigotry. He told me once, he even doubts God sometimes. He says that if we can deal with doubt, ultimately it strengthens our faith. It'll be like that with your marriage: you'll see. When you get to the church—"

"Maggie," Fern interrupted ruthlessly, *"I'm not in love with Marcus."*

The flow of words stopped; some of the eager glow ebbed from Mrs. Dinsdale's face. "You don't mean that?"

"I've never been in love with him. I like him, I like him a lot, but it's not love. I thought it didn't matter. Only now—" Seeing Maggie's altered expression, she got to her feet. "I'm sorry. I shouldn't have saddled you with all this. I've got to sort it out for myself."

"But Fern—my dear—"

"Could I have the sheets?"

Equipped with a sufficiency of linen, Fern and Trisha made up the beds together while Mrs. Wicklow prepared a salad lunch for anyone who might arrive in time to eat it. Marcus and his family were to stay in a pub in a neighboring village, maintaining

a traditional distance until D-Day—something for which Fern
was deeply grateful. Having to cope with her own relations was
more than enough, when all she wanted, like Garbo, was to be
left alone. Shortly after one the sound of a car on the driveway an-
nouced the advent of Robin, Abby, and Aunt Edie, the latter an
octogenarian with a deceptive air of fragility and an almost infi-
nite capacity for sweet sherry. Robin, at fifty-nine, still retained
most of his hair and an incongruous boyishness of manner,
though where his children were concerned he radiated an aura of
generalized anxiety that neither their maturity nor his had been
able to alleviate. Abby, in her forties, was getting plump around
the hips but remained charmingly scatty, easily lovable, impracti-
cal in small matters but down-to-earth in her approach to major
issues. They had lapsed into the habits of matrimony without ever
having formalized the arrangement and Fern, suspecting her father of a secret mental block, had never pushed the subject. Abby
had received her seal of approval long before and Fern was content not to disrupt the status quo. However, even the nicest people have their defects. Abby had a passion for pets, usually of the
small furry variety and invariably highly strung to the point of psy-
chosis. There had been a vicious Pomeranian, a sickly Pekinese, a
succession of neurotic hamsters, gerbils, and guinea pigs. Unfortunately, she had brought her latest acquisition with her, a Chi-
huahua salvaged from a dogs' home whom she had rechristened
Yoda. Fern tried not to fantasize about what might happen if the
canine miniature came face-to-face with Lougarry. There was
much cheek-to-cheek kissing, hefting of luggage, and presenta-
tion of presents. Fern felt she was functioning increasingly on automatic pilot: her mouth made the right noises while inside her
there was a yawning emptiness where her uncertainties rattled to
and fro like echoes in a gorge. At Abby's insistence she showed
her the dress, thrown in haste back over the dummy, and while

Abby touched and admired it, a sudden cold fatalism told Fern that all this was meaningless, because she would never wear it now. She would never wear it at all.

"What's this?" Abby enquired, picking up the drift of gossamer on the bed.

"It's mine," Fern said quickly, almost snatching it from her. "It was given to me—ages ago. Ages ago." And then, seeing Abby's expression of hurt: "I'm sorry if I . . . It's very fragile. I must put it away. I shouldn't have left it lying about."

The intrusion of Yoda put paid to further embarrassment. Abby scooped him up in her arms to prevent him soiling the dress and marveled aloud how he could have managed to climb so many flights of stairs when the treads were nearly his own height. Fern could not resist a sneaking hope that he might slip on the descent and roll all the way to the bottom.

Will and Gaynor walked up the hill toward the moors. The same gleam of sunlight that spun a rainbow from the Atlantean veil as Fern gazed into the mirror danced across the landscape ahead of them, pursued by a gray barrage of cloud. The sun's ray seemed to finger the farthest slopes, brushing the earth with a fleeting brilliance of April color: the green and straw-gold of the grasses, the brown and bronze and blood-purple of thrusting stems, vibrant with spring sap, and in an isolate clump of trees the lemon-pale mist of new leaves.

"Spring comes later here than in the south," Gaynor said.

"Like a beautiful woman arriving long after the start of the party," Will responded. "She knows we'll appreciate her that much more if she keeps us waiting."

He seemed to know where he was going, changing from track to track as if by instinct, evidently treading an accustomed route. In due course Lougarry appeared, though Gaynor did not see from where, falling into step beside them. Her coat was scuffed and ruffled as if she had slept out, the fur tipped here and there with dried mud, burrs and grass seeds adhering to her flank. Gaynor tried to imagine her and her owner living in an ordinary house, sharing a sofa, watching *Eastenders*; but it was impossible. They were, not quite wild, but outsiders: outside walls, outside society, outside the normal boundaries in which we confine ourselves. She sensed that Ragginbone's knowledge, his air of culture, had been acquired by watching and learning rather than taking part—endless years of watching and learning, maybe even centuries. She could picture him standing sentinel, patient as a heron, while the tumult of history went rushing and seething past. The wind would be his cloak and the sky his shelter, and Lougarry would sit at his heels, faithful as his shadow, silent as the wolf she resembled.

"If Ragginbone is a retired wizard," she asked Will, "where does that leave Lougarry? Is she a retired werewolf?"

"Reformed," said Will.

Gaynor had spoken lightly, her manner mock-satirical; but Will, as ever, sounded purely matter-of-fact.

They found Ragginbone on the crest of a hill where the bare rock broke through the soil. Gaynor did not know how far they had come but she was tired and thirsty, grateful for a long drink from the flask he carried. It was cased in leather like a hip flask, though considerably bigger, but the contents tasted like water— the way water ought to taste but so rarely does, cool and clear and straight off the mountain, without that tang of tin and the trace chemicals that so often contaminate it. But afterward she thought perhaps its purity was mere fancy: thirst can transform any drink into an elixir. Will related most of her story, Gaynor speaking only in response to direct questions from Ragginbone. He made her repeat the description of Dr. Laye several times.

"Could he be an ambulant?" Will suggested.

"Maybe. However . . . You are sure his skin was actually *gray*? It was not an effect of the television?"

"I'm sure," said Gaynor. "When his hand reached out I could see it quite clearly. I can't describe how horrible it was. Not just shocking but somehow . . . obscene. The grayness made it look dead, but it was moving, beckoning, and the fingers were very long and supple, as if they had no bones, or too many . . ." She broke off, shuddering at the recollection.

"Yet the picture remained flat—it wasn't like your three-dimensional vision of Azmodel?"

"The screen went sort of rubbery, and the arm was pushing at it, stretching it out like plasticine, but—yes, the image behind stayed flat."

"And this was a program you expected to see?" Ragginbone persisted. "It was listed in the newspaper?"

"Yes."

To her frustration, Ragginbone made no further comment, his bright eyes narrowing in an intensity of thought. Will, better acquainted with him, waited a while before resuming the subject. "You know him, don't you?"

"Let us say, I know who he might be. If the skin tint is natural, and not the result of disease, that tone—or something like it—was a characteristic of a certain family, though it has been diluted over the ages. There is the name, too . . . Clearly, since this was a real program, and he was invited to appear on it, he is a person of some standing in his field. Possibly Gaynor could use her contacts to learn more about him?"

"I never thought of that," Gaynor admitted. "Of course, it's obvious. How stupid of me."

"Not at all." Unexpectedly, Ragginbone smiled at her, a maze of lines crinkling and wrinkling at eye and cheek. "You had a disconcerting experience, but you seem to have kept your head very well. It was a pity you were so upset by the bats."

"I *hate* bats," said Gaynor.

"What about the Old Spirit?" asked Will. "He has to be behind all this."

"I fear so. He was weakened by his failure in Atlantis, but alas, not for long. And no other has ever laired in Azmodel."

"But why is he targeting *Gaynor*?"

"Possibly because you put Alison's television set in her room," Ragginbone retorted with a flourish of his eyebrows. "Technology lends itself to supernatural control, and after all, what is a television but the mechanical equivalent of a crystal ball? Gaynor was not targeted, she was merely on the spot. It is Fern, I suspect, who is the target."

"Revenge?" Will asked after a moment's reflection.

"Possibly. *He* has always been peculiarly subject to rancor, especially where the witchkind are concerned. The first Spirits hated the rumor of Men aeons before they arrived, fearing them as potential rivals for the dominion of the planet, knowing nothing of who they were or from whence they would come. When they realized that their anticipated enemies were no fiery angels descending from the stars but only hairless apes who had clambered down from the trees, their hatred turned to derision." Ragginbone paused, smiling a wry smile as if at some secret joke. "Time passed. For the immortals, time can move both very fast and very slow: a week can stretch out indefinitely, or a million years can slip by almost unnoticed. Man grew up while their eyes were elsewhere, the Gift was given, and Prospero's Children learned to vie with the older powers. And of all the Spirits, *his* self-blame for such willful myopia— the contempt and enmity that he has nourished for mortals ever after—was the greatest. Yet he yearned for Men—to rule, to manipulate, to control. And down the ages he has grown close to them, learning too well their follies and weaknesses, becoming their god and their devil, their genius and nemesis. Learned but never wise, he has remade himself in their image: the dark side of Man. Revenge gnaws him, but power motivates him. And Fern . . . Fern has power. How much, I do not know. In Atlantis, he must have seen more than we. In the years when the loss he had suffered there drained him like a slow-healing wound, he may still have dreamed of using her, turning her Gift into his weapon. The Old Spirits have sought before now to corrupt witchkind and force them into their service, though such bargains have usually achieved little for either partner in the end. Remember Alimond. Still, it is said that the Fellangels, his most potent servants, were numbered among Prospero's Children, until both their souls and their Gift were warped into the form of his purpose. Fern would not listen to the whispers of the Old Spirit—at the moment, she listens to no one—but . . . she might be subjugated through those she loves. Or so *he* may calculate. I think . . ."

"You mean us?" Will interrupted.

"You, and others. You two seem to be the most readily available. You will have to be careful."

"You aren't very reassuring," said Gaynor. "I thought I was scared before, but now . . . I suppose I could decide not to believe in any of this: it might be more comfortable."

"Is it comfortable," Ragginbone enquired, "to be afraid of something you don't believe in?"

Gaynor did not attempt to respond, relapsing into a nervous habit of childhood, restless fingers plaiting and unplaiting a few strands of her hair. Presently she broke into Will's murmur of speculation, addressing the old man: "Why did you say 'them' all the time?" Ragginbone frowned, baffled. "When you talked about mankind, you said 'them,' not 'us.' I was wondering why."

"I wasn't aware of it," Ragginbone admitted. "You are very acute. Little things betray us . . . I was born into the dregs of humanity, my Gift raised me higher than the highest—or so I thought at the time—and when I lost it I felt I was neither wizard nor man. The human kernel was gone: all that remained was the husk of experience. I became a Watcher on the periphery of the game, standing at the elbow of this player or that, giving advice, keeping the score. The advice usually goes unheeded and the score, at least on this last hand, was evidently wrong."

Will grinned. "That's how it goes."

"You're an outsider," said Gaynor. "I thought so on the way here. Outside life, outside humanity, perhaps even outside time. Are there—are there others like you?"

"Some that I know of. Probably some that I do not. We are the invigilators: events unfold before us, and occasionally we may try to give them a nudge in the right direction, or what we hope is the right direction. Our task is neither to lead nor to follow, only to be there. I have been an onlooker for so long it is hard to remember I was once part of the action. The human race . . . that is a club from which I was blackballed centuries ago."

"But—" Gaynor broke off, gathering her courage for the question she was suddenly afraid to ask.

"But?" Ragginbone repeated gently.

"Who appointed you?" asked Gaynor. "There must be someone—someone you work for, someone who gives you orders . . ."

"There are no orders," said Ragginbone. "No one tells us if we have succeeded or failed, if we have done right or wrong. We work for everyone. All we can do is all anyone can do: listen to the voice of the heart, and hope. I should like to think that we, too, are watched, and by friendly eyes."

"You will never get a straight answer from him," Will said. "Only twisted ones. He could find curves in a plumb line. Ragginbone, Bradachin said the thing that came out of the mirror was not Alison but a *tannasgeal*. What did he mean?"

"They are the spirits of those who died but feared to pass the Gate. They have long forgotten who they were or why they stayed; only the shreds of their earthly emotions linger, like a wasting disease. Hatred, greed, bitterness: these are the passions that bind them here. They loathe the living, and lust after them, but alone they have little power. However, the Oldest has often used such tools."

"How could it look like Alison?" Will demanded.

"People—and events—leave an impression on the atmosphere. Such creatures are parasites: they batten on the memories of others, taking their shape. No doubt the *tannasgeal* saw her in the mirror."

"Mirrors remember," said Gaynor.

"Exactly."

They were silent for a while, leaning against the rock where once, long before, Ragginbone had shown Will and Fern the Gate of Death. Every so often there was the rumor of a passing car on the distant road, but nearer and clearer were the tiny sounds of insects, the call of an ascending skylark. The colors of the landscape were dulled beneath the cloud cover; the wind was chill.

"What can we do to protect Fern?" Gaynor said eventually, shivering now from cold rather than the recollection of horror.

"I don't know," said Ragginbone.

"I thought you were supposed to advise us?" Gaynor protested indignantly.

Will laughed.

"Advice is a dangerous thing," the Watcher responded. "It should be given only rarely and cautiously, and taken in small doses with skepticism. What can I say? Keep your nerve. Use your wits. Premonition is an unchancy guide to action, but there is a shadow lying ahead of you through which I cannot see. Remember: the Old Spirit is not the only evil in the world. There are others, less ancient maybe, less strong—as the tempest is milder than the earthquake, the tsunami cooler than the volcano—but not less deadly. And mortality gives the Gifted an edge that the undying cannot match. Your dream about the owl puzzles me,

Gaynor. Of all the things you have told me, that is the one that does not fit. There is something about it that I ought to recognize, a fragment that eludes me. Tread carefully. The shadow ahead of you is black."

"We're supposed to be having a wedding tomorrow, not a funeral," said Will somberly.

"Maybe," said Ragginbone.

When Will and Gaynor left him they found a lonely pub that served a ploughman's lunch and stopped for a snack. A little to their surprise, Lougarry accompanied them. They fed her the rind of the cheddar and some crusts under the table. "What will Fern say if she comes home with us?" asked Gaynor. "Or Mrs. Wicklow?"

"Oh, they're accustomed to her," said Will. "She comes and goes very much as she pleases. All the same, she's usually rather more unobtrusive about it. She obviously thinks we need looking after."

"She can sleep in my room," said Gaynor, "if she likes."

Back at Dale House, Abby was less enthusiastic. "Couldn't you have told your friend it wasn't convenient?" she said. Will had explained that he was minding Lougarry for an absent owner. "I know you enjoy having her around, and she's always been well-behaved, but—she's so *big*. She may frighten Yoda. He's very highly strung. I'm sure she wouldn't hurt him *really*, it's just—"

"She's an excellent guard dog," Will interposed. "We think there's been someone sneaking around at night. Yoda wouldn't be much good at dealing with a burglar."

"No—no, he *wouldn't*," Abby agreed warmly. "He attacked a spider the other day, a big one with knobbly legs, but . . . Anyway, you will keep her away from him, won't you?"

"I'll try," said Will.

Meanwhile, the juggernaut rolled on. A tent sprang up on the

site of the old barn and ranks of tables and chairs were frog-
marched inside. People rushed to and fro carrying boxes of glass-
ware and cutlery, tablecloths, napkins, potted palms. Everything
was carefully arranged and then had to be completely rearranged
in order to leave room for the band. As so often on these occasions, there was a great deal of pale pink in evidence: the table
linen, the roses and carnations in vase and garland, the lipstick of
the female supervisor who gave the orders and subsequently pre-
sented Fern with the appropriate forms to sign. And Fern duly
signed, smiled, said "thank you," made and answered last-ditch
phone calls, spoke for half an hour to the caterers, for five minutes
to Marcus Greig. Gaynor thought she looked exhausted, not so
much from shortage of sleep but from that weariness of the will
that shows itself in a certain glassy-eyed fragility, an abstracted
manner, a slowness of response. For all her polite competence, her
mind was elsewhere. Minor frictions enlivened the afternoon.
Abby upset Mrs. Wicklow with constant offers of tea to all and
sundry, something the latter felt was within her sole jurisdiction.
Trisha surveyed the preparations and suddenly burst into tears,
revealing upon sympathetic enquiry that her fiancé had just termi-
nated their engagement. The mother of the bridesmaids, seven-
year-old twins with coordinated faces, curls, and clothes, rang to
announce that a drop of cola had been spilled on the front of one
of the dresses ("She can hold the bouquet over it," said Fern).
Someone bearing a box of champagne glasses tripped over Yoda,
with consequent oaths and breakages. However, by seven o'clock
the final place card had been laid, the excess helpers were gone.
Food and wine were due to arrive in the morning. Fern and Gaynor went out to survey the results. The tent looked like a huge
wedding cake. The wedding cake looked like a small tent. In the
kitchen, Abby and Mrs. Wicklow were talking to Trisha, Abby
vaguely soothing, Mrs. Wicklow astringent, while Will dosed her

periodically with medicinal sherry. In the background, Aunt Edie assisted with the dosage, presumably in the role of taster.

"Well," said Fern, "that's that."

"I'm afraid I haven't done very much," Gaynor said guiltily, conscious of a day's truancy with Will.

"You stayed," said Fern. Unexpectedly she took her friend's hand. "That means a lot. Anyway, I'm used to organizing things: it's my job. All this—it's just another product launch. Fern's wedding: the latest thing in rural chic. Don't drive your Range Rover without one. I only hope it doesn't rain."

Outside the tent, the gray afternoon was darkening into a murky evening. Clouds mobbed the horizon. If the light sought a chink, in order to provide the obligatory flash of sunset, it did not find one. Gaynor was suddenly aware of an overwhelming sense of oppression. The farrago of matrimonial preparations, which had seemed frivolous and almost grotesque after the events of the previous night, an element of farce in a potential tragedy, now felt ill-fated, part of a deadly momentum, building toward an unimaginable climax. Her brain told her that tomorrow everything would go according to plan, Fern would be married, and the surreal world of which she had had a brief, horrifying glimpse would vanish. But her heart quailed at the receding daylight, and the dark hours stretched endlessly ahead of her. She knew she must find time to tell Fern what Ragginbone had said, to warn her, but Robin appeared, laying a hand on his daughter's shoulder that made her jump, and the opportunity was lost.

"Nervous?" he said.

"A little." Her expression of pale composure defeated any scrutiny.

"You'll be all right. Marcus is a pretty good chap. Bit old for you, but—" He broke off, doubtless remembering the list of subjects that Abby had primed him not to mention.

Fern's gravity lightened with a glimmer of mischief. "I like older," she said. "It's my Oedipus complex."

Robin grinned, inexplicably relieved, and they went back indoors.

Fern had rejected the concept of a hen night on the grounds that she didn't wish to lay an egg and Abby had suggested dinner out at a local pub, but in the rush of the afternoon no one had made any reservations. "If you don't mind," Fern said diffidently, accepting a restorative gin and tonic, "what I'd really like is to go out with Gaynor somewhere and talk. Not exactly a hen party—no clucking—just a quiet supper for the two of us. If that's okay with you?" She turned to appeal to her friend.

"I'd love it," Gaynor said.

On Will's recommendation they booked a table at the Green Man, a pub in a village about half an hour's drive from Yarrowdale. Gaynor took the car keys so Fern would be free to drink and scribbled down directions from Will. Lougarry, who had spent much of the afternoon loftily ignoring Yoda, padded after them out to the car, apparently intent on coming, too, but Fern dismissed her. "Take her inside," she told her brother. "Most restaurants don't allow dogs. We'll be fine."

"The weather looks ugly," said Will. "We could be in for a storm."

"Good," said Fern. "I need a storm. It would suit my mood."

"Ragginbone said—"

"He talks too much."

She felt curiously light-headed—a light-headedness born not of elation but of emptiness, the aftermath of that yawning sensation when the last bridges are burned, the one remaining lifeboat is sunk, and the future looms ahead with no loopholes and no way out. As Gaynor drove up out of the Yarrow valley the wind hit them, buffeting the car like a punching bag. Breaks in the cloud showed more cloud, piled up into enormous towers: one great shape resembled a sumo wrestler, leaning threateningly over the landscape, its sagging belly black with forthcoming rain. "It looks awful," said Gaynor. "Maybe we should have stayed in."

"It looks wonderful," said Fern, and Gaynor, glancing sideways, saw the gleam of an elusive wildness in her face.

"So what *did* Ragginbone say?" she enquired after a while.

Gaynor told her, trying to remember everything, but Fern's reaction was not what she expected. "Beware the Ides of March," she concluded flippantly. "Or April, in this case—if April has any ides. Doom is at hand. Ragginbone was always telling us that: it was his favorite line. Doom, doom. Perhaps Azmordis will come to my wedding, and bore everyone with ranting. *He holds him with his glittering eye—The Wedding Guest stands still, And listens like a three-years' child*: Azmordis *hath his will.*"

"I thought it was dangerous to name him?"

"So they say. Azmordis. Azmordis! Let him come."

"Stop it," said Gaynor. "There isn't room in the car."

"Sorry," said Fern. "No lunch, and too much gin in too little tonic. I'll be better when I've eaten."

She's not drunk, thought Gaynor, struggling to suppress her fear. She's fey . . .

The first squall struck just before they reached their destination. Fortunately Will's directions were straightforward and Gaynor found the pub without difficulty, though it was identifiable only as a splash of colored lights through a blowing curtain of rain. She pulled into the parking lot and they got out, making a dash for the entrance. It was not until they were inside and the manageress had shown them into the restaurant that Fern, looking around, said: "I've been here before." For an instant, her expression had frozen; she halted as if unwilling to proceed—but at a nudge from Gaynor she moved on. They sat down at a corner table, ordered drinks. Fern, not normally a heavy drinker, asked for a double gin, Gaynor a St. Clement's. A waiter came to light the candle in the center of the table. Fern watched with peculiar intentness as the flame flickered and caught, settling into a tiny cone of brilliance. When the waiter had gone she moved it carefully to one side. "I can't see you," she told Gaynor, "behind the light." Her friend had a feeling the phrase meant more than it said.

"Are you sure you want to stay here?" she asked in a low voice. "You looked as if . . . as if this place has some unpleasant association."

"It's not important," said Fern. "It was a long time ago. Funny: I never noticed the name of the pub then, or even the village." She paused a moment to reflect. "Anyway, I can't remember much about the food myself but Will says it's the best in the district. I don't know the area at all well; we could drive round for hours looking for somewhere else."

"What happened here? If you don't mind talking about it . . ."

Fern shook her head. "I don't mind *now*."

Their drinks arrived; Fern tipped the tonic slowly into her glass, watching the brief rush of bubbles up the sides. "It's as if I spent the last twelve years—nearly twelve—looking at life through the wrong end of a telescope, so everything seemed small and cold and far away. And then last night the telescope flipped over, and now the world looks huge and close, and very bright. It ought to be frightening, but I'm not frightened. Maybe I'm just a bit numb."

"What about the wedding?" Gaynor asked before she could stop herself.

But Fern was no longer on the defensive. "The strange thing is, I can't really believe it's going to happen. When we stood in the tent this evening, and I saw the tables all laid out—what a choice of verb, *laid out*, like a body dolled up for a funeral—when I saw them all there, with their rose-pink tablecloths and rose-pink napkins and rose-pink roses in every vase, my brain told me this was the end but my—my *instinct* denied it. My brain said: She got

married and lived happily ever after. Instinct said: In a pig's eye. I
can't imagine it, you see. I can't imagine wearing the dress, walking up the aisle on Daddy's arm, saying 'I do.' I can't imagine—any
future." A sudden shiver seemed to run down her spine. "Anyway,
if you can't imagine something, it can't happen."

"It *will* happen," said Gaynor, "if you don't call it off."

"Poor Marcus: how could I? He'd be so humiliated. Not heart-
broken, just humiliated. You know, when I spoke to him today he
sounded so . . . distant. Not his manner, I don't mean that, nor the
telephone line. It was the way I heard him, as if his voice was
reaching me from somewhere years and years in the past . . ." She
laughed, shrugged, the two gestures becoming confused, uniting
in a single motion of uncertain meaning. "Maybe a whirlwind will
sweep away the tent with all the wedding guests and spin them
over the rainbow. Maybe moles will undermine the church foundations and the whole building will collapse. Maybe Marcus will
lose his way on the moors and be kidnapped by boggarts."

"What are boggarts?" Gaynor enquired.

"I've often wondered," Fern admitted. "Some special kind of
Yorkshire pixie, I think." And then they both laughed, and the
constraint and tension of the previous day melted away, and
Gaynor saw her dearest friend again, with no shadows coming between them. They had scrutinized the menu and given their order
before Gaynor reverted to her earlier question. "You were going to
tell me what happened, the last time you came here. Who were
you with?"

"A man named Javier Holt. He was an art dealer of sorts: he
ran the gallery in London where Alison worked. I never knew if
she realized the truth about him."

"The truth—?"

"He was an ambulant," Fern said, adding, in response to
Gaynor's bewildered expression: "A human being possessed—
expelled—by an alien spirit. In this case, the Oldest of all Spirits.

What became of the real Javier, the original person, I don't know. Lost perhaps, or in Limbo, or thrust through the Gate before his time. The Javier that I knew was—a vehicle. A puppet with the eyes of the puppeteer. A dead thing that spoke and breathed only because someone pressed the requisite buttons. We sat here and discussed literature and drama and witchcraft, and suddenly the walls of the restaurant disappeared, and we were on a bare heath, and there were trees floating above the mist, and stars above the trees. Javier had the power of his occupant: he could conjure the past, or an illusion of the past, and use it against you. That wasn't the only time he did it. I remember how the candle flame between us burned thin and tall, a needle of light, and how I looked at him and thought: I'm dining with a demon."

Gaynor's face showed her horror and sympathy. "You must have been terrified," she said.

"No," said Fern. "Not *then*. That was the dangerous part. I was—exhilarated."

There was no background music in the restaurant and general conversation broke off at a sudden crack of noise outside, which melted into a rolling growl as if some vast ill-tempered animal were stravaiging around the building. The lights flickered.

"Lovely weather for a wedding," said Gaynor with a dash of bravado. She disliked storms.

For a moment the sound of the rain penetrated, streaming down the night-darkened windows. "Never mind," said Fern. "With luck, by the time we want to leave it should have blown over."

She had graduated from gin and tonic to red wine, a half bottle since Gaynor would take only a single glass, and she now tipped the dregs into hers. Despite a career spent at PR parties she was not normally a heavy drinker, and Gaynor wondered if she should be concerned. But Fern, having at last opened up the secret closet of her memories, seemed determined to spill all the contents, and Gaynor forgot her niggling anxiety as she listened and listened, needing no more questions to prompt. She knew she would have been incredulous and even downright cynical if it had not been for her own recent experiences and her knowledge of her friend. This was Fern talking, cool, pragmatic Fern, relating her incursions into the darker side of Being, dreams and spirit journeys beyond the boundaries of the normal world, the search for a key that would open a Door in space and time. Finally, she came to the last part of her tale, a hopeless, fearless venture into the Forbidden Past, to the downfall of Atlantis more than ten thousand years ago. Dessert had come and gone, largely untouched, and she was cupping a brandy bubble in her hands, gazing at the tilting liquid as it curved its leisurely way around the glass. "The trouble with the past," she said, "is that it takes over. History protects itself. Wherever you are, you think that's where you belong. I had a whole background, a life story, a stockpile of memories. I knew what I had to do, but I didn't properly understand why. I didn't know what had happened before or what was to come. I arrived in a city on the edge of doom, and all I could see was the wonder of it. There were people there who became my friends and allies, people I cared for. And I fell in love. We met in a dungeon and fled the city together and hid out in a cave on the beach. We had two . . . three days. I can't really recall how it felt, or even how he looked: just occasional glimpses of memory, stabs of feeling, twisting inside . . . Funny: I used to try and blot it out, afraid to remember, and now—now I *want* to remember, I can't. But I'll never forget the sound of the sea there. I hear it sometimes, in the hollow of a shell, or walking along the shoreline here, listening to the falling waves, like an echo of those waves long ago. And sometimes I get it mixed up, and the golden beaches of Atlantis turn to silver, and the sea sound is the wash of starmelt on that other beach, the endless beach where I rode the unicorn along the Margin of the World."

Gaynor stared at her, uncomprehending; but Fern seemed

hardly aware of her anymore. "I sent my lover to his death," she said. "I didn't know it—I was trying to save him—but I sent him to his death. Atlantis was broken by the earthquake, and swallowed by the storm. Everyone in it perished. And the unicorn will never come again. I have lost the qualification to tame him." She was silent for a minute, still toying with the brandy. Outside the thunder, which had been rumbling on and off for the last half hour, pulled itself together for a final drumroll. "Sixteen is very young to lose so much. It's very young to gain so much—to live so much—to die so much. Azmordis wants revenge, you said? He has no need. I made my own punishment. I've been running away ever since: from the pain, the responsibility, the—the Gift." It appeared to cost her an effort to say it. She uncurled her right hand from the glass and gazed into the palm as if she expected to see her doom written there. But the lines of fate were few, and inscrutable. "Enough is enough," she concluded. "It's time to stop hiding my eyes." She smiled an unlikely smile, wan in the candlelight. "I suppose . . . this is a hell of a moment to choose."

Gaynor's response was drowned out as a crack of thunder sounded directly overhead, so loud that it shook the room. She clasped her hands to her skull, covering her ears; for a second she seemed to see the other diners, the tables and chairs rattling like dice in a box. The lingering rumble that followed made the floor continue to vibrate as if to the padding of giant paws. A bolt of lightning, so near it must almost have struck the building, turned the windows white, bleaching the checked curtains into transparency.

And then the lights went out.

Fern's face remained suspended in front of her, isolated against the darkness: a golden ovoid, conjured by the candle flame that hovered a little to one side of it. In that instant Gaynor could see nothing else. The buzz of dinner-table conversation had been wiped out; the silence was absolute. Slowly, almost reluctantly, Gaynor let her gaze travel around them. There were no other candles, no other faces. They were in the center of a pool of absolute blackness. But gradually, as she stared, she began to make out something beyond: the pale glimmer of snow, the spectral branches of a few lean winter trees. And far above there were stars, small and hard as grains of frost. She was bitterly cold.

The whisper came so close to her ear she found herself imagining writhing lips, all but touching her. *You called me, Fernanda,* it said, and somehow she knew it was equally close to Fern. *You called me, and I have come. What do you want?*

For a minute Fern made no answer. When she spoke at last, it was in a language Gaynor did not know, in a voice she hardly recognized. The words crackled with power like damp wood thrown on a fire. *"Envarré! Varré inuur ai néan-charne!"*

The ghostly snow scene faded. There were walls around them again, dim in the glow of scattered candles; tables; people. People turning to gape at them as Fern's voice died away. A waitress sidled up to their table. "The lights will be on again very shortly," she said. "Is there anything I can get you?"

Fern lifted her brandy, finishing it in a single swallow. "Another," she said.

It took time and coffee before Gaynor felt able to drive.

"It's my fault," said Fern, a little muzzily. "I called him. In a twisted sort of way, I hoped he would come."

"What *did* you want?" asked Gaynor, echoing Azmordis's question.

"To make an end," said Fern. But that final brandy had been a drink too far, and she would not or could not elaborate, merely sitting gazing in a zombielike fashion at her empty glass. Gaynor had seen other drunks in this condition, but never Fern, and coming on top of everything else she found it deeply disturbing.

"She's in a bit of a state, isn't she?" said the waitress.

"She's supposed to be getting married," Gaynor said.

"That explains it."

The electricity had been restored and Gaynor enquired after a telephone; she had no cell phone and Fern's had been left in London. She knew Will would come on demand, and she felt the need of reinforcements. But the lines were down because of the storm.

"Thunder's stopped," said the waitress encouragingly, wanting her bed. "It's just raining."

The staff offered to help her shepherd her friend out to the car, but Fern stood up without assistance and Gaynor availed herself only of an umbrella that she returned once Fern was in the passenger seat. She got wet sprinting back to the car and she shut the door in haste, switching on engine and heating. Windshield wipers swept ineffectually at the unrelenting rain. She hoped she would not miss the road back to Yarrowdale. She still had Will's instructions, but pouring curtains of water obliterated the landscape and she could see nothing beyond the short range of the headlights. "Are you all right?" she asked Fern, and was thankful to get a response, although Fern's conversation had shrunk to the purely monosyllabic.

The side road where the pub was situated had no markings for Gaynor to follow, but when she turned onto the main road there were reflectors winking at her like cats' eyes through the dark. She clung to them as if to a guiding thread in a labyrinth, craning forward over the wheel. Wind gusts shook the chassis until every joint rattled; the battery of the rain eased for a short while only to return in force, hitting the car with all the violence of a monsoon. Gaynor told herself there was nothing supernatural about rain, but after the horror in the restaurant even the elements seemed untrustworthy, and it seemed as if she was having to contest every yard of her progress with some invisible power. For all her resolution, she felt weak willed and helpless. A quick sideways glance showed her Fern's head drooping against the back of the seat, her eyes closed. Gaynor was half-relieved to see her sleeping, half-afraid because now, with Fern unconscious, she was completely alone. She drove more slowly, checking the verge constantly for road signs. Sooner or later, she knew, she must reach the turning for Yarrowdale. A spiky belt of conifers loomed up to her left; she tried to fit them into her recollections of the drive out but could not. There was no other traffic. She had almost convinced herself she was on the wrong road when the sign appeared ahead of her. And *there* was the turning, veering sharply to the right, undefined by any white lines. She swung the car around, leaving the friendly cats' eyes behind, the headlights picking out only the black gleam of tarmac, the long streaks of rain.

The drive had taken on the qualities of nightmare: it had become a timeless striving for an unattainable goal. The momentary hope that had flickered in her heart when she found the turning shriveled as the car crawled on into the darkness, following the twin beams that peered myopically ahead. Gaynor's mind was in suspension: all her senses were concentrated on the car. She was never sure exactly how it happened—*something* hurtling into the radius of the headlights, the judder of impact, the crack of breaking glass. The right-hand beam was abruptly extinguished. She stopped the car, her pulse thumping. When she summoned the courage to get out she barely noticed the rain that transformed her long hair into rats' tails and made her skirt cling heavily to her legs. A broken branch lay in the road, though there were no trees around. The thick glass that had shielded the light was gone. She kicked the branch aside; there was nothing else to be done. Then she got back into the driver's seat.

The other headlight went minutes later. There was no flying branch this time, just a sudden explosion—a flash of brilliance that faded swiftly, leaving her in utter dark. She pulled up again but did not get out, clutching the wheel, her breath coming in gasps. Gradually her eyesight adjusted to the blackness. She became aware of a faint pallor all around her, a change in the nature of the rainfall. Instead of somber curtains, white flecks showed against the brooding shadow of the sky. And in a landscape that had been treeless she saw horned branches uplifted like the antlers of a watching stag. She had switched off the engine, and the snow-silence wrapped her like a pale blanket. She shook Fern, gently at first, then harder, but without result. She called her name: "Fern! *Fern!*" but her own voice sounded alarmingly close to panic and the sleeper still did not respond. Her fear for herself was replaced by another, far more deadly: the fear for her friend. She had seen plenty of drunks who passed out but none who could not be roused, if only to a grunt of acknowledgment. She restarted the engine, knowing she had little alternative. She might get out of the car and seek help on foot, but where? And outside the car was the snow, falling steadily, snow in April—if it was April, if it was snow. Azmordis could summon an illusion of the past, Fern had said. In front Gaynor saw a cart track where the road had been, the defining ruts partially smothered under a white mantle. "It's a road," she said out loud. "It's tarmac; it's wide and smooth and safe. There's no snow, no trees. It's just bare road and bare moor." She released the brake, let out the clutch. Nervously, as if imbued with her terrors, the car inched forward.

The ground felt level beneath her wheels, like a modern road. Gaining confidence, she accelerated a little. The wipers had cleared the windshield after her halt but now the snow was falling faster, piling up around them, slowing them down. She had to resist a desperate urge to press hard on the pedal and speed away from the thickening snowfall, the illusion, the fear. She found she was saying to herself, over and over: Don't panic. Don't panic. It might have been funny if it hadn't been real. Idiot, Gaynor. Cowardly idiot. It's just *snow*. How can you be afraid of snow?

The owl came at her so fast she had barely time to swerve. She saw the wide tilt of its wings rushing toward her, the ghost face with its staring eyes. It appeared bigger than the windshield, almost as big as the car. Reflexes betrayed her: she jerked the wheel into a spin, swinging the vehicle around, off the track, out of control. Uneven terrain bounced the chassis—a stag was charging straight at her, its vast antlers filling the sky. *It's an illusion—just an illusion—* Her foot was on the brake and they skidded to a halt; hood met tree trunk in a terminal crunch. Gaynor tried to reverse but the tires would not grip, sliding on slush or mud. The owl had vanished. She shut off the ignition, leaned her forehead against the wheel. Beside her, Fern still slept, secured by the seat belt, soundless and undisturbed. Gaynor's hammering pulse gradually subsided: she sat back in her seat, gazing around her with night eyes. There was only the one solitary tree; the white snow mantle made the world formless and unfamiliar. I'm near Yarrowdale, she thought. A mile or two. I could go for help. Fern might die of hypothermia. Gaynor didn't want to start the engine again in case there was fuel leaking somewhere: she almost imagined she could smell it. But above all, she didn't want to get out of the car. A glance at her watch told her it was well past midnight. Someone will come looking for us, she thought. I have only to wait.

Time passed, and she grew colder. When she touched Fern's hand it was icy. She couldn't flick the wipers on to sweep the windshield but she wound down her side window to clear it. Then she reached across Fern to do the same with hers. But when she went to close the window again, it jammed halfway. Bitter air sliced through the gap. She was seized with a fresh dread, a frenzy beyond all reason, unlike anything she had felt before. She yanked in vain at the handle, got out and floundered around to Fern's side of the car. But the door, too, was stuck fast. She beat on the roof, crying out for help. But the snow deadened her voice, and no one came. A mist was rising, mingling with the snowflakes, and in the mist was something like a shape, changing, billowing, elusive as smoke. Boneless arms uncoiled like tentacles; where the face might have been, skull features wavered like a pattern on water, yawning eye sockets and nose hole, a jaw that narrowed into nothingness. She remembered Will's description of the thing Bradachin had witnessed emerging from the mirror, the thing she had seen as Alison. In front of her the skull melted briefly into the semblance of a woman, mist strands fanning out behind it like hair. But the features drifted, unfixed, and teeth showed through the shadowy lips. Gaynor was backed up against the car, trying to cover the window gap, inadequate fingers spanning the remaining space, but the smoke shape poured through every chink, and its touchless contact made her too cold to resist, weak and faint. She saw it wind itself around Fern, pulling her upward, drawing the spirit from her body. Now there were two phantoms, twining mist with mist, though one seemed inert, its head hanging as if still in slumber. Gaynor beat at them to break their bond, but her hands numbed, and they floated away from her. She strained to recall the word Fern had used in the restaurant, dismissing Azmordis. *Envarré . . . ?* *"Envarré!"* But she had not Fern's Gift, and the command sounded brittle and ineffectual: the *tannasgeal* barely faltered. She tried to follow them, slipping in the snow, crashing to her knees . . .

She never saw from where the owl came. Huge pinions pounded the air, beak and talons slashed the mist into shreds. Snow whirled in a blizzard around it. The incubus disappeared with a thin wailing sound like the wind in a hollow tree. As the owl wheeled, Gaynor thought she glimpsed the phantom Fern, wide-eyed and blank-faced, just behind its shoulder. Then the wings dipped and rose, feather tips brushing the ground, and it was gone in a cloud of frosty spray, dwindling like a snowflake into the night.

Gaynor ran after it, screaming until her breath failed. She for-

got the damaged car, and Fern's body lying inside, and the perils
of this world into which she had strayed. On she ran, up toward
the road, or where the road ought to be. The wolf loomed up suddenly ahead of her. It occurred to Gaynor, somewhere at the back
of her mind, that there must have been wolves in Yorkshire long
ago, in the dim past that enmeshed her. There was no snow on its
ragged fur, and its fire-opal eyes shone with a glow of their own.
Gaynor stood rigid as it trotted over to her, lifting its muzzle to fix
her with a steady gaze. And then the truth dawned, and she slid to
her knees, burying her face in the wet ruff, repeating: "Lougarry,
Lougarry," while tears of thankfulness spilled down her cheek.
She was kneeling in mud, and the snow was gone, her clothing
was drenched and her hair matted, and the rain poured down on
them both.

· VII ·

ill saw her first. She pushed open the back door into the kitchen where he was sitting at the table with Robin, a tumbler of whiskey at his elbow. His expression went blank with shock. She stepped inside, and the water ran off her into puddles on the floor. There was mud on her shoes, on her skirt, on her hands where she had tried to stop herself from falling, on her face where she had reached up to sweep the sodden hair from her eyes. She looked dazed beyond speech, exhausted beyond fear. Will sat her down on a chair and pressed the tumbler to her lips. "Drink it," he ordered. "All of it. Now." She gulped obediently, coughing as the raw spirit seared her throat, the blood flooding to her cheeks. Robin kept saying: "Where's Fern?" but Gaynor did not answer. Will said to him: "Get Abby," and began to towel her hair vigorously with the nearest dishcloth.

"But Fern . . ." Robin persisted. "Has there been an accident?"

"Not bad," Gaynor managed. "Came off the road—hit a tree. Fern—wasn't hurt."

"Should have got a cab," said Robin. "Big mistake, drink and drive, even on these quiet roads. Where is she?"

"I wasn't drunk," Gaynor said. "Fern was drunk. She's asleep . . . in the car. I think."

"You *think*?" said Will.

"I couldn't wake her. She . . ."

"Finish the whiskey. Dad, for God's sake do something useful. Go and get Abby. We want a couple of large towels, a bathrobe— there's one in my room—and a hot-water bottle. Fern will be all right for the minute. If she's in the car she's dry." When he had thrust Robin from the room Will turned back to Gaynor. "Did you see Lougarry? She's been restless all evening; I assumed she'd gone to look for you."

"She found me," said Gaynor through a falling wave of hair. Having saturated the first dishcloth, Will had set to with a second. "When I was sure I knew the way I sent her back to the car. I thought—she would watch over Fern. Thanks," she added, re-ferring to Will's drying efforts. "That's enough, honestly. As long as it's not dripping . . . I must get these clothes off."

Once Abby had appeared to minister to her, Will and Robin set out to find Fern. Gaynor's directions were vague—she had no idea how far she had walked—but she maintained that if they fol-lowed the road and stopped at intervals to call Lougarry, the she-wolf would come to guide them. Robin was dubious, finding it difficult to believe that a half-feral mongrel, the property of an ec-centric tramp, could be, as he put it, sufficiently well-trained. But Will waived his reservations aside and, clad in weatherproof clothing snatched from the hall closet, they went out to Robin's car. In the kitchen, Gaynor was mopped clean of excess mud, stripped, dried, enveloped in Will's bathrobe, and padded with hot-water bottles. She wanted to have a bath, but Abby dissuaded her. She was shivering in spasms now, her teeth chattering from the aftermath of cold and shock. "The main thing is to get you really warm," Abby said. "Will's very sensible. It always surprises me—although I don't know why it should, because, of course,

Fern is sensible, too." She scooped up Yoda, who had followed her downstairs. "Perhaps you'd like to stroke him? It's supposed to be awfully therapeutic. Oh, well . . . have some more whiskey. There's always lots in this house, though no one drinks it much. I'm never sure whom it's for."

Bradachin, thought Gaynor, but she only stammered, through her shivers: "M-medicinal."

"I'll make you some coffee," said Abby, depositing Yoda on a spare chair. He promptly jumped down and wandered around the kitchen, looking for scraps that he could chew and spit out again in disgust. It was the bad habit that had earned him his name, after Yoda's first screen appearance where his rooting about irritates Luke's fragile patience. "Are you . . . are you quite sure Fern wasn't injured? It's so unlike her to drink too much, and I've never known her to pass out before."

"N-nor me," said Gaynor. She saw no need to elaborate.

"I do hope she'll be all right for tomorrow," Abby said.

To that, Gaynor made no answer at all.

It was nearly three when they brought Fern home. By that time, Gaynor was dry and the men were wet. Lougarry endeared herself to no one by shaking her coat heartily in the middle of the kitchen, soaking Yoda who had appropriated her place by the stove. The small dog fled into the hall, for once ignored by Abby, who had other things on her mind. They carried Fern to her room and put her to bed. Her condition appeared normal: her pulse was steady if slow, her breathing ditto. She was cold from her long sojourn in the damaged car, but assisted by Gaynor's discarded hot-water bottles she warmed up fairly quickly. Yet she made no sound—not the wisp of a snore, not a grunt, not a sigh—and her body stayed where it had been placed, unmoving, inanimate as a broken dummy. Robin wanted to call a doctor but the others overruled him. "What would you tell him?" Will demanded. "That she had too much to drink and slept through a minor car crash in which she wasn't hurt? There isn't a mark on her."

"Perhaps we should tell Marcus . . ."

"Good God, no," Gaynor murmured faintly.

"I'm sure she'll be fine in the morning," Abby said. "She's just—sleeping it off. Anyway, there's nothing more we can do now. We ought to go to bed before all this bother wakes Aunt Edie."

"I'll stay with her for a bit," said Gaynor.

Abby herded Robin down the corridor to their own room and Will and Gaynor were left alone with Fern. Gaynor took the chair, Will the low stool from in front of the dressing table. "What haven't you told me?" he asked.

Carefully, pausing often to ask or answer extra questions, Gaynor went through her story. At some point Lougarry came in and began to lick Fern's hand, a typical doglike gesture that was rare for her. When Gaynor had finished Will stood up and went to the window, pulling back the curtain. But whatever he was looking for, it wasn't there. "We need Ragginbone," he said, moving irresolutely to the bedside. "He probably won't know what to do, but he might be able to explain this. Well . . . if she doesn't wake up at least the marriage is off. Funny: that seemed such a good idea earlier on, and it seems such a bad one now."

"She won't wake up," said Gaynor. "She isn't there."

Fern's still face appeared no longer tired, or strained, or tense. It was just a face, arranged into features, unmarked by thought or dream, with less expression than a statue. Gaynor had once done some voluntary work in a hospice and she knew that peaceful look that comes after the passage of death, when the vacant body subsides into a semblance of tranquility. But here was no peace, no death; only vacancy. The full realization was so horrifying, there in that quiet, safe room far away from the perils of an illusory past, that panic rose in her, and she had to fight herself not to start screaming. Instead she demanded, in the age-old cliché of helplessness and desperation: "What can we *do*?"

Will put his arms around her, and said nothing.

The following morning was one that all of them would later prefer to forget. No one had slept well, except Aunt Edie. Abby was the first to try to rouse Fern; Will and Gaynor knew it would be fruitless. Subsequent events unwound with a combination of chaos and inevitability, disaster broken with moments of pseudo-comic relief. Afterward, Gaynor remembered everything as a blur, shot here and there with highlights of detail, where her mind would focus briefly on some trivial point before losing its grip again. She found herself thinking, idiotically: If only Fern were here. She would be able to manage. The half-world on the shady side of existence, a world of dark magic and ethereal horror, had become a hideous reality.

They telephoned the doctor, they telephoned the vicar, they telephoned Marcus Greig. They telephoned a garage to tow away the smashed car. An ambulance came and went, taking Fern, accompanied by Robin, to a hospital for tests, and thence to a private nursing home specializing in coma patients. Marcus followed in his Saab. Meager information percolated back: *She's doing well. There's nothing wrong with her. The doctors are baffled.* Abby, supported by Gus and Maggie Dinsdale, struggled to unarrange all the arrangements, delaying, canceling, collapsing into confusion when asked for definite directives. Stray guests arrived at the house and were rounded up by Will, who dispatched them, in default of other entertainment, to enjoy the Yorkshire countryside. Yoda located the wedding cake and ate a portion of the bottom tier, since that was all he could reach. Lougarry went to fetch Ragginbone and Gaynor took him into Will's studio to relate the saga of the previous night. Mrs. Wicklow astonished everyone by bursting into tears. Endless cups of tea circulated, but nobody appeared to drink them, lunch sank without trace, morning staggered into afternoon, afternoon trickled into evening. The tent removers refused to remove the tent. Aunt Edie drank an entire bottle of sherry and claimed to have had a conversation with a hirsute Scottish gnome, thus convincing Abby that she was even farther down the road to alcoholic senility than they had realized. Yoda was sick.

Around seven the house lapsed into a species of dumb lassitude. Mrs. Wicklow and the Dinsdales went home; Ragginbone had already gone, promising to return later. Abby was in the sitting room with Aunt Edie, who had the constitution of a navvy and was proving obdurate about having an early night. The phone still rang intermittently: they didn't dare take it off the hook in case it was Robin or Marcus with news of Fern. Will went to look for Gaynor, locating her eventually in the tent. The tables were still immaculately laid, the flowers only just beginning to wilt. Everything was spotlessly pink. The wedding cake alone appeared somewhat the worse for wear: Yoda's inroads on the foundations had caused the upper stories to collapse, and now it resembled a block of jerry-built flats in an earthquake zone. Gaynor was standing in the middle of the tent, surveying the wedding that wasn't. Even the reflection from so much pink could not hide the whiteness of her face. "What are you doing *here*?" said Will.

"Thinking." Gaynor did not look at him. Her regard was fixed on the empty top table. "This was the only place I could be on my own. I keep wondering . . . if things could have been different. I mean, if I'd acted differently, or been more supportive, or—"

"No," Will said shortly. "For God's sake, don't start feeling guilty. People who blame themselves for every single thing that happens really get on my tit."

"I don't care who—or what—gets on your *tit*!" Gaynor flashed.

"Good. You know what's wrong with you? You've had a bad shock, very little sleep, and no food. No wonder you look as if you're about to faint. Maggie's left a stack of sandwiches in the kitchen for us, and there's stuff in the cupboard that's been there for years. This is the kind of house where tins of soup accumulate on upper shelves, fermenting quietly. Some of them should be quite mature by now."

Gaynor laughed weakly, but declined to eat. "I'm really not hungry."

"That's just in your mind," said Will. "Your body's famished."

He took her back into the house, heated soup, teased her into eating a sandwich. After the first bite, she was a little shocked to discover she was hungry after all. "Don't be silly," Will adjured her. "Fern wouldn't thank you for starving yourself. How could that help?"

He carried more soup and sandwiches into the sitting room for Abby and Aunt Edie, although Gaynor had to forcibly discourage him from adding pounded-up sleeping pills to the mug prepared for the latter. ("I didn't know you had these Borgia tendencies.") After the chaos of the day, the evening dragged. Robin rang to say he was staying at the nursing home and Marcus had booked himself into the nearest hotel. No, there was no change in Fern's condition. Aunt Edie was finally coaxed up to bed; a worn-out Abby followed shortly after.

Ragginbone returned at ten-thirty, when Will and Gaynor were alone. Lougarry was with him.

"What do you make of it?" said Will without preamble.

The old man sighed. He had pushed back his hood and disheveled wisps of hair stood out from his head, making him look more like a scarecrow than ever. His coat steamed gently from the rain that had punctuated the afternoon. He smelled of wet cloth and leaf mold, and his face was sere and withered, like the residue of autumn. Somewhere among the lines and folds his eyes lurked under lowered lids, flickering into brightness in his rare upward glances. Only those eyes still seemed to hold some secret strength. For the rest, he looked ancient and frail, no longer a knotted oak but a twig that would snap at a touch, a leaf that would fall in the wind. "I don't know," he said at last. "We've been going over the area, Lougarry and I. There was little to find. I picked up this—" He laid a long feather on the table, its pallor barred with dun ghost markings. "It might have come from the wing or tail of an owl. A very large owl. I think . . . I'm not sure what I think." There was a further pause. Gaynor was too weary to ask questions; Will knew better. "It's clear the Old Spirit was involved," Ragginbone resumed. "Fern called him. Folly—rashness—bravado—who knows? He was here anyway. The specter that came for her must have been under his control. But the owl—the owl still puzzles me. That dream of yours—" he nodded to Gaynor "—tell me about it again."

She complied, trying to recollect details submerged in later events. "I was flying, like you do in dreams, only sitting on its back . . . I saw fields, and houses . . . That part was magical. And then everything became very rapid and muddled. It felt as if a lot of time went past. I was—somewhere dark, and there was a face floating in front of me . . ."

"Describe it."

"Sort of pale and flabby . . . like a slug. The way a slug might look if it were human size and had human features and the personality of a psycho. The eyes were horrible: black and malevolent. It said—I can't remember. *Not the one* . . . something like that. Then it went away, or I went away, I'm not sure. There was a nasty smell, too. Decayed vegetation. Dryness. Dampness."

"Which?" asked Will.

"All of them."

"*Not the one,*" Ragginbone mused. "So perhaps . . . Fern was the one. But who—"

"Do you think it was more than just a dream?" Gaynor said.

"What is a dream? The mind can move in other worlds; so can the spirit. Who knows where we go, when the body sleeps? Or when the body dies?"

"Fern won't die, will she?" said Will brusquely, betraying a child's need for reassurance. It was the first time Gaynor had been conscious that she was older.

"We all die," said Ragginbone, "eventually. Still, she's young and strong. I must see her. It is plain that she has gone, but until we know where it will be impossible to find her. I fear—" He stopped.

"What do you fear?" Will demanded.

"Many things. I have lived my life in fear; I am accustomed to it. Courage is a delusion of the young. Hold on to yours."

After that, he refused to venture more than cryptic utterances, and they said good night, watching him stride off into the gloom. "Where does he sleep?" asked Gaynor.

"Out," said Will. "Under the trees, under the stars, under the rain. Maybe he doesn't sleep at all. I've known him to spend days— weeks—sitting like a boulder on a hillside. And I don't mean that as a metaphor. Bugger him. Let's have a drink."

It was Monday before they got to see Fern. Gaynor rang the museum where she worked and extended her holiday; Will seemed to be permanently on vacation. "That's the point of a thesis," he said. "You do nothing for a couple of years or so and then slog like hell for the last three months. I drop in on the college once in a while, read a book, paint. I've never really absorbed the work ethic."

"I'd noticed," said Gaynor.

Abby had driven Aunt Edie back to London; Robin stayed on. Marcus declined to move to Dale House—"There's no fax"— conducting his life from hotel and nursing home by mobile and modem. On Sunday night he drove over to have supper with them, showing himself properly appreciative of Mrs. Wicklow's cooking. He was a stocky, well-built man, his thickening waistline counterbalanced by breadth of shoulder, his dress of the sort usually labeled expensively casual (no tie and a vicuna coat). He had an aura of intense masculinity, the eyes of an intellectual, the mouth of a sensualist. He wore both his costly coat and his bald patch with a negligent air. Even Will admitted afterward that he was good company. But he shouldn't be, thought Gaynor. *The girl he was due to marry is lying in a coma from which she can't be roused and he still sounds clever, well-informed, wryly amusing.* It occurred to her that at no time during the dinner-table conversation had he revealed his deeper feelings, using witticism or generalization to fend off personal comment. After all, he was forty-six years old, a worldly-wise sophisticate who would never wear his broken heart on his sleeve. "But Fern's twenty-eight," she said to Ragginbone, driving to the nursing home on Monday afternoon. "She deserves to be loved madly, even on the surface. He should be weeping and wringing his hands—pacing the floor—abandoning himself to despair. He shouldn't be cool and calm and collected and entertaining at dinner."

"Only the very young and the very old love madly," sighed Ragginbone. "Enjoy it while you can. In old age love becomes embarrassing, often pathetic. The doter in his dotage. Don't be too hard on Marcus Greig. He's reached the years of caution: he loves carefully, grieves privately, and refuses to put either emotion on show. You shouldn't condemn him for reticence."

"Anyway, I thought you liked him," Will interpolated from the backseat.

"I did," said Gaynor. "I do. I just feel he's picked the wrong time to make himself likeable."

They had arranged to visit Fern at an hour when she would be alone: Robin was at home catching up on sleep, Marcus was working in his hotel. She lay on her back in the high white bed, her head raised up on the pillows, her arms at her sides. The fold of the sheet across her breast was immaculate, the plumpness of the pillows undented save for the slight pressure of her skull. Electrodes attached to her chest monitored her heart rate: they could see the thin green line on screen, broken here and there into the hiccup of a pulse beat. "It's very slow," said Ragginbone. Transparent plastic tubes pumped essential nutrients into her at one end and removed waste products from the other. A video camera kept a mechanical eye on her. She looked shrunken, scarcely bigger than a child, and very fragile, a doll-like thing animated only by the machines to which she was wired. Life was fed through her automatically, its passage recorded, alarms poised to go off at any significant change. But there would be no change. They could see that. Her face was white, and very still. Ragginbone lifted an eyelid: her eyes were turned up so hardly any iris showed. The three of them found chairs and seated themselves on either side of the bed. Herself horribly distressed, Gaynor saw Will had shed his customary laid-back attitude: he was shaking and seemed close to tears. Tentatively she took his hand.

"Is it my fault?" she said after a while, guilt returning. "Was there . . . something more . . . I should have done?"

"No." Ragginbone emerged briskly from some faraway place to which his thoughts had strayed. "When the Oldest One comes, there is nothing to be done. You showed great courage under difficult circumstances; somewhere, Someone takes note. Or so I have come to believe. As it is, we have no time for the indulgence of what-ifs and maybes. What matters is how we act now."

"Where is she?" asked Will, his voice sharpened with bitterness or pain. "She isn't here." He did not appear to notice how tightly his fingers gripped Gaynor's.

"Where indeed?" said Ragginbone. "*That* is the question. The *tannasgeal* drew her from her body, but it seems clear—if Gaynor's recollection of events is accurate—that the owl intervened. But who would send the owl? There are many evil creatures in the world, some less than human, some . . . more. Fern is the first in a long while to manifest the Gift so strongly. That might attract the attention of other Old Spirits: the Hag, the Hunter, the Child. Even She Who Sleeps. And there are too many among the Gifted who have turned to the cult of Self, to strange obsessions, ancient lusts: they, too, would be interested, though few remain who have not passed the Gate. I have been trying to remember . . ."

"Fern was always afraid it would send her mad," Will said. "Like Alison. Or Zohrâne."

"They made their own madness," Ragginbone responded. "The Gift only gave them the power to exercise it."

"She's never used it," said Will. "Not since Atlantis."

"It would not take much to be noticed," said Ragginbone. "If someone was watching."

Will frowned suddenly. "I know she lost her temper with Bradachin, when he first came to us. He said you could *see* the power, like lightning stabbing from her hand. But he wouldn't—"

"You cannot trust a malmorth. Remember Pegwillen."

"He's different." Will was decisive. "Stronger. He's talked to me more than once about the honor of the old lairds—the Mc-Crackens of Glen Cracken. He says they can trace their kinship to Cuchulain of Ulster. He sees their honor as his. I know he would never betray us."

"Maybe." Ragginbone looked unconvinced. "I . . . advertised . . . for him; when he arrived, I checked his references. It is unusual for a house-goblin to change his residence, all but unthinkable for one to travel so far. The goblinkind are not like people: their behavior patterns do not alter. None of the werefolk are subject to evolution."

"He's spent a lot of time in human company," said Will. "He might have picked up a few bad habits."

"I believed him capable of loyalty," Ragginbone conceded, "up to a point. But such elemental spirits have no moral fiber; their substance is too slight for it. Treachery comes easily to them: a little bribe, a little threat, and the thing is done. They care for humans as we care for pets. One dead goldfish can always be replaced by another."

"You're wrong," said Will doggedly. "You're often wrong."

Ragginbone darted him a swift, sharp glance before returning to his contemplation of Fern. "It's possible. It may have been . . . bad luck. The spellfire shows many things, if you know how to look. I have always guessed that was how Alimond first traced the key to Dale House, all those years ago. But the fire is wayward, like all magics; what you see is not always yours to choose. Still, the searching eye will always find what it seeks, in the end."

"If someone other than the Oldest Spirit found out about Fern and wants to use her," Will said rather desperately, "you *must* have an idea who it is."

There was a silence while Ragginbone's face seemed to fold in on itself, the furrows drawing together, closing over his features, until eyes and mouth were mere slits of concentration in a nest of woven lines. Gaynor imagined him reaching far and deep into the wells of memory, sorting through the jumbled experience of centuries, through moments of hope and joy and pain and sorrow, looking for the lost connection, the forgotten image. She wondered how it must feel to live through so many lifetimes, to store so much, to *know* so much, until the great weight of that knowledge sank without trace into the depths of the soul. When Ragginbone's eyes reopened their expression was bleak. "As you remarked," he said, "I am often wrong." He would not venture any more on the subject, though Will pressed him. "At least her body is safe," he pointed out. "I feared, at first, that *he* might have entered her, taken possession of her. She had called him, on territory with which he was familiar; the alcohol had numbed her brain; she had laid herself wide open to him. He would have made her an ambulant, his instrument, her spirit lost or trapped in some corner of her mind, aware but powerless. That would have given him both vengeance and control. Fortunately, her Gift—or some other factor—protected her. Even her emptiness is barred to him."

"Fern would never let herself be possessed," said Will. "With or without the Gift, she's as strong as steel."

The sudden movement caught them all off guard. Discussion and argument were both forgotten; all their attention was focused on the patient. The motion had been very slight, a barely perceptible twitch of the right arm, perhaps nothing more than a muscular reflex. But in Fern's inert condition even so tiny an indication of life was somehow shocking, as unnerving as a gesture from a corpse. "Look!" Will cried. "Her heart rate's up." On the monitor, the blips became more frequent. Will bent over her, calling her name, but her face remained blank and empty. It was Ragginbone, on her right, who first saw the cut. Her arm stiffened, shuddering, though the rest of her body stayed utterly limp. A thin line of red appeared on the underside, between elbow and wrist, fine and shallow as a paper cut. It was as if someone was drawing an invisible knife across her flesh. Ragginbone pinched the wound shut, demanding gauze, bandages, Elastoplast. "She mustn't bleed!" he said, his tone so fierce that neither Will nor Gaynor questioned him. "Call a nurse!"

The next half hour was an ordeal. Staff agreed that the injury was trivial; it was its origin that puzzled them. Initially Ragginbone was regarded with deep suspicion, an officious ward nurse muttering: "Munchausen syndrome by proxy," but the videotape bore out the story related by all three witnesses. Robin arrived opportunely, and was taken aside by a senior doctor and asked if Fern had any history of what he described as "unusual psychosomatic phenomena." Robin admitted reluctantly that some twelve years earlier there had been an incident that had been labeled at the time "post-traumatic amnesia," but although he detailed everything he knew about it, and the doctor agreed there must be some connection, they were no further on. "The video camera is a very inadequate guardian," Ragginbone said to Will. "One of us should be with her at all times. I fear she is in great danger. Persuade your father." But Robin needed little persuasion. The weekend had turned from romance into tragedy and overnight his habitual expression of slight anxiety had evolved into one of chronic stress. No amount of care was excessive for his little Fernanda. The fact that Fern, although built on the small side, had never been petted and protected as her father implied, somehow made her present plight yet more pathetic and difficult to endure. She had bossed, bullied, and manipulated Robin from the time of her mother's death, delegating only a few such duties to Abby over the years, and he could hardly bear to see her lying there, so deathly still, neither dead nor alive. Her motionless figure appeared somehow broken, defenseless, drained of all that was Fern.

"You must let us take turns on watch," Will said to him. "This could go on for some time, and you're worn out already. As long as there's *one* of us here . . . It would be awful if she were to wake and find only the nurses and a rack of machines."

"Awful," Robin echoed automatically. The fact that she might never wake eclipsed such minor horrors.

Convincing him to accept Ragginbone was harder. However, by dint of dramatizing the latter's prompt action when the cut appeared, and hinting at a superior knowledge of medical arcana (Robin had always suspected the old man, whom he knew as Mr. Watchman, of being a scientist or professor fallen on hard times), Will won his point. Before Robin quite understood how, it had been agreed that Ragginbone would relieve him at eleven o'clock. They left him as another doctor arrived, joining what was rapidly becoming a symposium around Fern's bed. "They think she's an 'interesting case,'" Will muttered angrily. "Not just an ordinary coma. 'Many unusual features'—I heard one of them say it. As if he was an estate agent selling an awkward house."

"Stop it," said Gaynor. "They'll look after her. That's what matters."

"Precisely," Ragginbone affirmed. "Her body, at least, is in good hands. As for her spirit: that's for us to locate. If we can."

"Where do we start?" asked Will.

"Nowhere," said Ragginbone. "You can only look for a spirit in a spiritual dimension. Feel for her with your intuition, seek her in your dreams. Nowhere is the only place to begin. Remember, there is a little of the Gift in most of us. Gaynor has already shown herself sensitive to both influence and atmosphere. As for you, Will, you are Fern's brother in blood: you share the same heritage, kindred genes. Your spirit can call to hers wherever she is."

"What about you?" said Will. "What will you do?"

"Think," said Ragginbone.

The Watcher shared their supper and then left to return to the clinic, declining a lift. "I can get about," he said, "as fast as I need to." Lougarry went with him, though she knew the clinic permitted no animals on the premises.

"He may hitch a ride," said Will. "Or he might walk it. He can walk very quickly when he wants to. Much quicker than me." He and Gaynor ran through the events of the past few days for the fourth or fifth time, winding up with a recap of the incident that afternoon, coming to no new conclusions, seeing nothing at the end of the tunnel but more tunnel. Will had opened a bottle of wine and they finished it slowly, unwilling to go to bed, though they were both tired and there was little to be gained by staying up and recycling their problems. Eventually Will poured a dram of whiskey for Bradachin and the two of them went upstairs.

"Maybe we will dream of Fern," said Gaynor, "if we concentrate."

"You might," said Will. "I never dream of anything. I'm always too busy being asleep." He did not want her to see how frightened

he was by his sister's condition, or how much his own helplessness galled him. When he and Fern had first met Ragginbone and
become involved in the search for the key, he had been twelve
years old, too much a child still to prevent his sister taking the
lead and assuming responsibility. Now that he was an adult he
felt he should be sharing her danger, not watching it; acting, not
dreaming. He knew it was she who had the Gift—he knew at
least a part of his attitude might be frustrated machismo—but he
was not one to probe his motives or prove his New Manhood by
waiting on the sidelines. He had sensed the proximity of the
shadow world and its denizens for too long now to regard it with a
child's formless dread; his fear, too, was an adult thing, intelligent,
knowing. Knowing too much for comfort, too little for action. In
bed he lay sleepless, listening for the owl's hoot, hearing only
wind murmurs, and the soft creakings of an old house twitching
in its slumber. A bird called, but it was not an owl. Oblivion crept
up on him unawares.

He dreamed. It was a nightmare from infancy, when he had
first heard about dinosaurs, and their hugeness, their monstrous
teeth, their tiny glittering eyes had dominated his terrors. The
slightest bump in the night would be translated, in his dreams,
into the distant tread of thunderous feet. When he saw the skeletons in the Natural History Museum, taking them out of the domain of imagination and into reality and science, they became
just big lizards, manageable and not so awesome, and his nightmares had ceased. But now the horror returned.

The gigantic head was resting on the ground beside him, so
close he could have reached out and touched it. He saw it in extraordinary detail: the elongated jaw with reptilian fangs extruding
beyond the lip, the gaping trumpet of the nostril, the eye, not tiny
now but a huge bulbous sphere, lidded with horn, lashed with
spines; its murky colors, all red, swirling like gasoline on water, its
slitted pupil a crevasse opening onto the abyss. The body was lay-

ered thickly with scales that shone with a dull metallic luster; the armored brow was jagged and spiked and notched; a ridge of triangular bone plates extended down the spine, vanishing into the darkness. Nearby he could see the outline of a foreleg, the crooked elbow higher than the creature's back, and an outstretched claw the length of an elephant's tusk, gleaming in the half-light. It couldn't be a tyrannosaur, he thought, with the small part of his brain not paralyzed with terror. The teeth were wrong, the foreclaw too big. It must be some species of crocodile, an antique behemoth from the vast swamps of prehistory. He could see little in the gloaming, but they seemed to be hemmed in between low cliffs, perhaps leading to a cave mouth. The sky above was evening-blue, still sparsely starred; the bloodstained traces of sunset lingered somewhere on the edge of his vision. When he dared to turn his head, he saw the cliffs opening out before them to show a broad valley, dimly patterned with fields, and very far away what looked like city walls and a tall spire like a black needle against the dying glow in the west. It took a dreadful effort to turn back. He knew now the monster beside him wasn't a dinosaur. He saw the smoke trail rising from its nostril, thin and somehow oily, like the fume from some slow-burning pollutant. The nostril itself was as blackened as an ancient chimney, but somewhere deep in its cavern he glimpsed a tiny red smolder, an ember that would not go out. He had realized by then that it could not see him—he was trapped in a fantasy of his sleeping mind or someone else's memory of the distant past—yet he felt horribly visible, flattened against the cliff face, cowering from the basilisk gaze of that enormous eye.

The clatter of iron-shod hooves on stone, the shout of challenge, the irregular tramp of following feet—these sounds came to him as if from a long way away, though in reality they were close at hand. He saw the warrior in his strange armor, made of some dark, unreflecting metal, triple-plated like rhinoceros hide, scratched and pitted from a hundred fights. The visor was lifted and what little Will could distinguish of the face between the cheek guards was similarly battered, no youthful hero but a man callused with years, pockmarked with battles. His eyes were mere chinks of brilliance between leathern folds of skin. He wore a broadsword and carried a heavy shield, so scarred the original bla-zon could no longer be guessed, and a lightweight throwing spear. The men behind him were a motley collection, mounted and on foot, armed with assorted weapons. Yeomen and bowmen, villeins and villains, they stood in a half circle at a range chosen by some intuitive accord, close enough to threaten, far enough for flight. For all the diversity of faces every expression was the same: part fearful, part brave, desperately stubborn, yet with an underlying element that Will could not immediately identify. The monster will fry them, he thought, forgetting his own dread, and only their arrows will reach it—if they can shoot fast enough. They must hope it will concentrate on the warrior. And then he understood the significance of that careful space. This was no safety margin: it was the arena of battle, the killing ground. The men, despite their courage and their doggedness, were not an army but an au-dience, and the undercurrent that united their expressions, draw-ing them to that place, holding them within the periphery of danger, was curiosity.

Dream or visitation, Will would remember what followed all his life. The scraping noise of great wings unfolding, catching the breeze like spinnakers—the rattlesnake speed of the uncoiling neck—the hiss of indrawn air as the jaws opened. The warrior dropped to a crouch in the lee of his shield and cast his spear. At the same instant, the dragon flamed. There were screams, terrible but brief. The cliffs glowed red. Will knew he was burning, he sensed the heat searing through him, yet he felt no pain. When the blast struck he saw rock melt and bubble; plant life within a ten-yard radius was incinerated, blown away in a cloud of ash flakes. He did not know what became of the warrior, though he thought he caught a glimpse of him, through a veil of fire, still down on one knee, protected by some power in his shield. But what he saw most clearly was the spear. It must have been thrown with incredible force, or perhaps it had an impetus of its own, for it sped on against the jet-powered blast of the dragon's breath. The shaft kindled and became a streak of white flame, but the sharpened head appeared untouched, even unwarmed. Will saw it with perfect definition, a black splinter against the streaming fires. He sensed that it was neither rock nor metal, but made of some other, more potent substance. The air was split in its path, the flames parted. Straight down the dragon's throat it flew; the monster hiccuped as if swallowing a pill, and it was gone.

For perhaps a minute nothing happened. Then the dragon in-haled, sucking both heat and flame from the atmosphere so swiftly that Will shivered in the sudden cold. And now the fire was inside its body, coursing through its veins like liquid light-ning. Every scale glowed red-hot, every horn, spike, spine was limned with a flickering radiance. The dragon was translucent with fire: its back-flung head arched and strained at its neck; its wings lashed; its eyes were globes of blood. Through the curve of its breast Will saw the burning coal of its heart, dark as a ruby, pulsing like an enormous drum. Then a column of flame shot from the gaping vent of its jaws, blazing starward. Endlessly high it soared, until the last of the fires were expelled, and the dragon sank back into darkness. The pillar hung in the sky for a while like a contrail, then gradually it wavered, breaking into separate tongues of flame that floated away, coiling and dancing like snakes, fading to a glimmer that was swallowed up at last in an in-finity of blue.

The dream, too, was fading, its intensive reality blurring into a mere nocturnal fantasy. The dragon's dead, Will told himself, snatching at the thought even as it slipped away from him, and his relief was mingled with regret, because in its rage and destruction there had been a terrible splendor that might never come again. But as the dream receded he seemed to see the mythical reptile arise once more, dark against the myriad stars, its fires spent or hidden, and it appeared to grow, and grow, until its head was silhouetted against the moon, and the span of its wings eclipsed whole galaxies. But the image was no longer clear and immediate, only an ethereal impression, which dimmed into the shadows of sleep. In the morning the dream remained with him, vivid as experience, but that last fleeting chimera endured only as an afterthought, a cobweb clinging to the borders of memory.

"Did you dream?" Will asked Gaynor at breakfast.

"I think so," she said. "But it's all mixed up. I can't remember anything properly. What about you?"

"Yes," he said, after a pause, but he didn't elucidate.

Mrs. Wicklow, busying herself about the kitchen, added her bit. "It's no wonder you're dreaming," she said, "the way things have been here. Happen troubles always upset your sleeping, one way or t'other. I had a strange dream myself, only last night."

"What was it?" Will enquired.

"Fern was getting married, wearing the dress upstairs. Lovely, she looked, quite lovely. But when I saw the groom, it wasn't Marcus Greig. It was that man from the gallery, the one who disappeared all them years ago. Javier Holt, that was the name. What do you make of that?"

"I don't like it," Will said frankly. "I don't like it at all."

Trisha was still on compassionate leave and Mrs. Wicklow appeared to find a panacea in housework, attacking the most furtive corners with the vacuum cleaner, poking a long-handled feather duster into crevices hitherto unexplored. Will and Gaynor retreated to his studio—off limits to the housekeeper except for supervised hoovering—to discuss his dream. He began to sketch the dragon—not a fairy-tale depiction of an elegant reptilian form but a close-up of the head: the crocodile grin studded with uneven teeth, the rough-hewn scales laminated like oyster shells, the humps and jags of bone that crested its brow. But when it came to the eye, he could manage only the outline. "It must have been terrifying," said Gaynor, peering over his shoulder.

"Yes." Will grimaced at the memory. "Magnificent—and terrifying. Afterward, you tend to forget the fear. Of course, if I'd really been there I'd have been fried to a crisp. But I don't see what it has to do with Fern. Unless . . ."

"Maybe Ragginbone will know," Gaynor said, missing that last uncertain word.

"Ragginbone knows some of the answers some of the time," said Will. "Don't let his air of venerable wisdom fool you. He'd be the first to admit that what he expounds are theories, not facts. We have the clue: it's for us to work out what it means."

"It reminds me of something," Gaynor said abruptly. "Something I've seen recently . . . only I can't remember where." She clutched her head in sudden frustration, tugging at her hair. "I think . . . it was an incunabulum. I can see Gothic lettering . . . illuminated capitals. It must have been at work—no, that's not right . . ."

"Don't force it," said Will. "It'll come."

He retreated into his own thoughts and Gaynor tried not to strain after that elusive recollection still nagging at the fringes of her mind. It will come, she told herself, echoing his words. Stop thinking about it, and it will come.

They had arranged to be at the clinic at three o'clock, taking over from Marcus, but the first person they saw when they got there was Ragginbone, waiting on a wooden bench in the garden with Lougarry at his feet. There was a lawn to the left of the driveway overlooked by a terrace where patients on the way to recovery could sit in sun or shade. The bench was in the midst of the lawn, under a tree with hanging branches; not a willow, Gaynor thought, maybe a weeping ash. The leaves were just beginning to open: their color was that fresh light green that is the essence of spring. They sat there in a leaf-curtained grotto, talking about Will's dream.

"That cut on Fern's arm," Will said, "that was something done to her spiritual body—her absent self—that affected her physical body. Is that right?"

Ragginbone nodded. Gaynor said: "What does that have to do with—" but the Watcher silenced her with a peremptory gesture.

"So," Will pursued slowly, "it ought to work the other way. If we could somehow strengthen her physical body, it should increase the power of her spirit—wherever that is."

"How do you propose to *strengthen* her?" Gaynor said crossly, annoyed because she did not understand, and angry at her own petty annoyance. "Vitamins?"

Will ignored her. "The spearhead," he said. "I'm sure—I *think*—that it was a fragment of the Lodestone. You told us—" he was addressing Ragginbone "—that when it was broken the Ruling Families of Atlantis kept the pieces. If that warrior was a descendant of the exiles, he might have owned one. And against the dragon, it could have represented his only chance. I know this is all ifs and maybes, but . . . Fern's Gift was reinforced by contact with the matrix. If we could find that spearhead, lay it in her hand, perhaps it would give her the power to return to herself."

"It's an idea," said Ragginbone. "The first we've had. As to whether it would work—I do not know. But any plan is better than no plan. I will tell you this much. There is a story of Pharaïzon, one of the greatest of dragons, that says that at one time he was wounded by an arrow or spear whose head was made from a holy relic. It may be true; it may simply be that the Christians got hold of a good legend and adapted it. Anyway, the holy object en-

tered into his body and endowed him with a strength immeasurable, so that he was called the Curse of God, and if he had been
evil before, now he was mad with a sacred madness, and no one
would challenge him. In the end, according to some sources, he
perished in his own fires; but the holy thing, whatever it was, was
never recovered. Some said it was a jewel, some said a fingerbone
of Christ or one of the saints: those early Christian martyrs scattered their bones widely. It hadn't occurred to me to connect the
legend with the Lodestone, but it might fit. Three of the splinters
were rumored to have been saved from the downfall of Atlantis.
However, little is known of what became of them, only myths,
and stories without endings. How will you begin your search?"

"I don't know," Will admitted. "Gaynor thinks she remembers
reading something about this in an old book, but she can't recall
where."

"I wish you luck," said Ragginbone, "if there is any. Do nothing rash. Watch over Fern. I must go south for a while—"

"I thought you were going to help?" Will interjected.

"That's why I'm leaving," Ragginbone replied. "Like Gaynor, I
am chasing something on the verge of memory, something from
very long ago. That chase takes me elsewhere. I will keep your
ideas in mind, and find out what I can, and return when I can."

"But what about Fern?" said Will.

"This *is* about Fern. I repeat, take care of her. Be cautious.
Lougarry will stay with you."

Will bombarded him with further questions and pleas to remain, or at least explain, but he would not be persuaded. He
strode off toward the main road and they entered the clinic via
the front door, while Lougarry sat patiently outside.

In Fern's room, Marcus Greig got to his feet. Will's mind was
elsewhere and it took several moments before he realized that
Marcus had launched into what was clearly a prepared speech.

He sounded embarrassed, upset, uncomfortably determined. "I can't stand it," he was saying, "just sitting here, staring at her, day after day, unable to *do* anything."

"It's been only four days," Will murmured; but Marcus continued regardless.

"The inaction is driving me insane," he said. "One minute we're getting married, and then—this. I can't cope. I know I don't show it, but deep down I'm a sensitive person, and it's starting to get to me. I'm going back to London. I need distraction—I need *work*—I need something to pass the time. Otherwise I'm just going to sink into the most awful condition of apathy and gloom, and I won't be the slightest use to anyone, least of all Fern. I'll phone every day. I want to know if she so much as twitches an eyelash—"

"If?" said Will.

"When. Dear God, I mean *when*." He doesn't even blush, thought Gaynor. "Look, if there's anything I *can* do, just say the word. Call, and I'll come whizzing up the motorway. But there's no point in my hanging around here ad infinitum, like some poor mug waiting for a bus that's been canceled."

"No," Will said very coolly. "No point."

"I knew you'd understand. Tell your father, won't you? It was a bloody difficult decision, but it had to be made. Life must go on, cliché though it may be. You can't hold the pause button down indefinitely." He shook hands with Will, kissed Gaynor, took one last, long look at Fern. Then he was gone. A sense of bustle went with him, leaving the room as still and quiet as a sepulchre.

"It's just us now," said Will, temporarily discounting his father's contribution.

They felt very alone.

· VIII ·

J n a side street somewhere in the heart of London stood a shop that was never open. So narrow was the street that it would have been more accurately classified as an alley: there was no passage for a car, and the upper stories overhung the lower, constricting the available air space until only a blue vein of sky could be seen zigzagging between the rooftops. It was called the Place, Selena Place; the buildings there, though shabby, bore traces of architectural pedigree; one or two had been partially renovated. Inside, the houses were honeycombed with precipitous staircases and haphazard rooms. There was a club on some of the higher floors where people drank and talked about literature and a club in a basement that required references and a password to gain admittance. A video store specialized in pornography from the silent era, a secondhand bookseller in vintage *Boys' Own* annuals, a kosher snack bar in salt beef sandwiches. The shop that never opened was tucked away between the bookseller and a dilapidated building formerly a squat, now too dangerous for human habitation, that served no purpose at all. There was a narrow window dingy with dirt that was not so much ingrained as artfully blended with the glass, permitting minimal visibility. It was framed by a species of canopy that resembled a Victorian bonnet, the kind that hid the wearer's face from view. Beyond the window, the perceptive might distinguish an occasional table, a couple of items of bric-a-brac, and in the background a curtain of dull brocade, discolored with mildew that seemed to mingle with the pattern and become part of it. There was also a case of stuffed birds in various stages of molt that appeared and disappeared on a weekly basis, though it was never removed. No one knew what the shop actually sold. The door was inset with more bleared glass, showing only a glimpse of the barred grille within. If a notice materialized declaring the establishment open, invisible hands would turn it over on the approach of a customer, and no amount of knocking and calling would elicit any response. Nobody ever went in, nobody ever came out, though there was a cat in the area, a moth-eaten ginger tom with half an ear missing and an array of balding battle scars, whose ownership was attributed to the unseen occupant. But in the vast, seething hotpot of London, a stew that contains every ingredient in the world and is flavored with every spice, the odd morsel of gristle can go unremarked. The neighbors in Selena Place were mildly intrigued but never inquisitive: none of them could remember a time when the shop had not been there, and its furtive attitude to opening hours was part of the local scenery, something to be both respected and ignored. In Soho, a king in exile and a beggar on the make can live side by side, and no one will ask awkward questions.

It was early on a Thursday afternoon when a man came to the shop and tapped lightly on the door. What made this knock different from all other knocks it would have been impossible to say, but after a pause lasting several minutes the door opened a chink—just a chink—as far as might be allowed if there were a safety chain inside. Neither face nor voice featured in the gap, though the visitor certainly spoke, perhaps in response to a question. There were plenty of people about at that hour—a bearded young man in the bookstore, a skinhead with an earring in the video shop, a queue for the salt beef sandwiches—yet they paid no attention. The door closed again; a chain rattled. When it reopened, a hand emerged from the inner darkness, snatching the newcomer and pulling him through the gap. This time, when the door shut, it was with the finality of a last curtain call, though nobody had been watching the show. The ginger cat, alerted by these unusual proceedings, plunged into the derelict building next door, no doubt seeking his own means of ingress. The shop front resumed its customary air of shabby inscrutability. Something all but revolutionary had occurred, a major upheaval in a long history of inertia, yet the incident passed strangely unremarked, potential witnesses were looking the other way, the bustle of the ancient metropolis absorbed it without even a ripple. Selena Place went about its business undisturbed.

Inside, the visitor was led through a dim room hazardous with looming furniture, along an unlit corridor, down a twisting stair. At the bottom, another door swung back with an eloquent creak that sounded disturbingly like a voice, and the guest followed his hitherto unseen host into a basement room. The only daylight was admitted through a slit window set high in the wall at the far end; the remaining illumination came from sallow electric bulbs under shabby fringed lampshades, but the fringes seemed to have grown, like lianas, some of them trailing on the chair back or table beneath. Old candles crouched on available promontories, shapeless humps of wax in chipped saucers, half-melted and apparently forgotten. The walls were lined with books that looked more dated than antique, thrillers long out of vogue, melodramas and morality tales by unmemorable Victorian scribes. In the few spaces in between there were random glimpses of brick and plaster and a collection of yellowing prints at once lewd and faintly horrible: a crinolined woman coyly lifting her skirt to show a cloven hoof, another exposing a breast where a clawed imp sucked greedily, a rearview nude admiring in a hand mirror the countenance of a malignant ape. A huddle of chairs filled one end of the room; at the other stood a large table littered with equipment of an alchemical appearance, including a Bunsen burner and several retorts of assorted shapes and sizes, all cloudy with the dust of neglect. Furtive cupboards lurked in corners; the visitor almost tripped over a cakestand stacked with ornaments. He saw a blue china rabbit, an art deco nymph, a green glass ball twined with a wisp of fishing net, a toad carved in jade with a gold leaf crown and eyes set with crystal.

"I'm afraid," said his host, "the place has grown a bit—cluttered. Over the years." He had a curious habit of punctuating his phrases with odd pauses, audible full stops, as if he were out of practice with conversation and had lost the knack of making his sentences flow. "I keep things, you know. Things that interest me, or amuse me, or . . . remind me. That blue rabbit, now. I used to see blue rabbits, at one time. I believe it was the absinthe. Or the laudanum. I don't indulge now, of course."

He sat down in one of the chairs after first checking it was unoccupied, perhaps by more blue rabbits; his guest followed suit. The ginger cat negotiated the narrow window, which was slightly open, pouring itself through the gap like oil, depositing its scabious orange form in its owner's lap. Choppy fingers began stroking automatically.

The resident of Selena Place bore an extraordinary resemblance to a spider, one of the spindle-legged kind with a small fat body and a shambling, wavering gait. His head was sunken into rounded shoulders; his concave chest swelled out below the rib cage into the sudden mound of his paunch. Carpet-fluff hair clung erratically to his scalp or fanned out as if animated by invisible static. He had the bleached complexion of someone who rarely sees the sun and eyes like sloes, matte black, both iris and pupil, and as expressive as plastic buttons. His clothes appeared so much a part of him it was impossible not to suspect he never took them off. A buff-colored waistcoat wrinkled over his stomach; above it he wore several layers of cardigan trailing frayed woollen threads, all evidently in varying stages of gentle disintegration. Presumably he put a fresh garment on top even as the nethermost one rotted away. His trousers were both too loose and too tight, baggy around the seat yet clinging awkwardly to knob knee and shrunken calf. They stopped well short of his ankles, revealing socks that sagged in laminated folds above slippers corroded with constant shuffling. He appeared quintessentially an *indoor* person: a house spider spinning web after web in the same inglenook, a cave dweller who would live and die out of range of the daylight. The other man, in contrast, wore the countryside like a patina, his face rugged as bark, his hooded coat, after a recent shower, having both the color and texture of rain-soaked earth. In that musty atmosphere he steamed faintly, exuding a distillation of pastoral odors.

"It has been a long, long time, Moonspittle," he remarked, "but you haven't changed. Literally, I fear. Do you still trade in—"

"Not *trade*." The man called Moonspittle responded before the question had been completed. His real name, or one of them, was Mondspitzl, but it had lost something in translation. "I helped people. For a fee. An acknowledgment of my skill. Not ordinary people, of course. Princes, statesmen, lovers. They came by night; they knew how to knock. They wanted potions and philters, dreams and visions. They don't come now. Maybe there are other dream sellers out there. Less careful, less . . . particular. I haven't changed, but the world changes. You would know. You were always . . . striding to keep up." He added, inconsequentially: "I'm glad you didn't bring the . . . er . . . dog. Mogwit never took to her."

Ragginbone eyed the tattered sack of feline temperament unenthusiastically. "I believe it's mutual."

"Time doesn't really matter *here*," Moonspittle continued, backtracking. "I blend in, you see. Anyone and everyone blends in. That's what I like about the city. It's like a giant forest—life is evolving even now, in the leaf mold, in the underbrush—growing, spreading, dying out. And I just stay here, deep in my hollow tree, ticking over. Like a beetle. The branches above could be full of owls, but I don't notice. I stay in the dark. In the warm."

"Owls?" Ragginbone queried with a frown. "What made you think of owls?"

"Owls and trees. Trees and owls. They go together."

"I've always associated owls with barns. Or belfries."

"You've learned too much," said Moonspittle. "In the old stories, before there were barns or belfries, owls lived in trees."

Ragginbone's frown persisted, as though he had plunged into a sudden quagmire of thought.

"Was there something you wanted?" Moonspittle enquired eventually. "This is not—surely—a social call. No one ever calls on me. Socially."

"I want your help." Ragginbone returned to the present, subjecting the other to a swift scrutiny. "I need to draw the circle. You have the Gift, after a fashion. Mine is gone. Together—"

"You want to *use* me." Moonspittle's thin, rather high voice dropped to a murky whisper. "My power—your will—is that the idea?"

"Put it how you like," said Ragginbone. "I wouldn't ask if it wasn't important."

"Ah, but how important? What will you give me, Caracandal,

for my Gift? A black diamond—a blue rose—a lock of angel's hair?"

"I brought you this," said Ragginbone. From an inner pocket he extracted a transparent plastic globe containing a tiny model of St. Paul's in winter. He shook it, and it filled with snow, a blizzard in miniature.

Moonspittle's face shone with a childlike greed. "My city!" he said. "My city in a bubble—a snowstorm city to hold in my hand. *That* is enchantment. Even in the crystal ball it is not so clear. This is a precious thing. Give it me!"

"After," said Ragginbone, putting it away in the folds of his coat. "First, we will draw the circle."

They cleared a space in the center of the room, pushing furniture aside, rolling back a ragged strip of carpet. The outline was already there, a shadow-marking on the floorboards. Moonspittle took a jar from one of the cupboards and dribbled a grayish-white powder around the perimeter, muttering to himself in a sotto voce mumble that might have been incantation or merely complaint. There was no solemnity, no stately ritual. Ragginbone covered the window, lit the candles, switched off the lights. Mogwit jumped on a chair to watch: in the artificial dark he became a furry shadow whose eyes glowed balefully. And gradually the gloom intensified and the room seemed to alter, expanding, mutating. There was no visible movement, yet chairs and tables appeared to lean away from the circle, crowding toward the wall. Some shapes swelled, others shrank. The ceiling arched far above, the bookshelves became a ladder into infinity. Moonspittle spoke the word, and the circle burned with an unsteady glimmer, hissing like green wood on a fire. Then Ragginbone laid a hand on the back of Moonspittle's neck and he dropped to his knees in sudden weakness, folding up as though stricken, the spider swatted. "Elivayzar," Ragginbone said softly. "Elivayzar."

"You take—too much," gasped Moonspittle. "You would steal my very soul . . ."

"Not steal, borrow. And only your power. Is it agreed?"

Elivayzar struggled to rise, subsiding into a chair that Ragginbone thrust beneath him. Then the hand closed on his nape again. If he acquiesced, it went unheard. He began to speak in a strange language, full of knife-edged consonants, pulsing vowels, crackling Rs and sibilant Ss. A language of deep notes and clarion commands that made the stale air vibrate with a tuneless music. The language of the lost, the forgotten, the forbidden. Atlantean. But there was more fear than authority in his voice; his accent wavered; the words ran together, losing their native clarity. Within the circle a vaporous substance formed that thickened and thinned according to the rhythm of the incantation, condensing into half shapes, spectral impressions of torso and limb that dissolved even as they began to solidify. The glimmer of a face dwindled into the parallel bars of cheekbone and browbone, with yellow eyes fading in between, and then the smoke strands blurred and divided, becoming the flickering haunches of some goatish intermediary, before lengthening into hair, spreading into hands, sharpening into claws. "Concentrate!" exhorted Ragginbone, while his grip tightened on the helpless Moonspittle, gnarled fingers probing the bowed shoulders like burrowing roots. Ragginbone's lips moved on the words even as Elivayzar spoke them aloud, and the uncertain voice seemed to be charged with a conviction and a force from elsewhere. At the heart of the circle a humanoid form grew and condensed, becoming fixed in being. It was an old, old woman, so ancient she might have been all but fossilized, withered into stone. She was as ugly as a gargoyle, as shrunken as a thornbush in a drought. Bristles of coarse hair stood out on one side of her scalp; on the other the scabby craters of vanished sores encroached on her face. A single fang jutted from her arid mouth, stabbing the brown verge of her lower lip. Her eyeballs were encased in wrinkled pouches of skin that permitted only a sliver of vision between twitching lids. The sound that came from her vocal cords was a croak whose softer cadences had long gone.

"What do you want of me?" she said.

"Hexaté," Moonspittle began, but the crone mumbled on.

"I was sleeping—I sleep a lot now. Why did you disturb me? I am no longer young; I need my sleep. I will wake at the full of the moon."

"Ask her," said Ragginbone, "if she has the girl."

"What girl?"

"Ask her."

But Hexaté only licked her lips with a tongue like cracked leather. "A girl? What kind of a girl? Give me a girl, let her be plump and toothsome. I will roast her over a slow fire and suck the youth from her sweet flesh—"

Ragginbone made an impatient gesture, and the hag was gone, diminishing into her own ramblings like a leaf whirled away on a muttering wind. Others followed her into the circle: an antlered man dressed only in a doeskin; a child with the face of a celestial choirboy and the eyes of a satyr; a blind woman, veiled in red, holding a small bright sphere little bigger than a marble, marked with staring circles like the patterns on a sardonyx.

"We are seeking a girl," said Moonspittle. "One of Prospero's Children. New to her Gift. Her spirit wanders. Can you see her?"

The seeress lifted her veil. Beneath, the bones of her skull shone white through diaphanous skin. Her eye sockets were empty. She lifted the sphere and inserted it into the right-hand cavity where it glowed into life, roving to and fro, the lone ray of its gaze reaching out into a great distance, though it did not appear to pass the boundary of the circle.

"What do you see, Bethesne?" Moonspittle said.

"I see the Present." Her voice sounded hollow and full of echoes. "She is not there. She has gone beyond my Sight."

"Is she in the Past?" Ragginbone prompted. Elivayzar repeated the question.

"The Past is a busy place," said the sibyl. "We have all been there, including the one you seek. But she is not there now."

"Dragons," said Ragginbone, thinking of Will's dream, groping for further questions, for a hint, a clue, a spoor to follow. "Can she see *dragons*?"

The seeress was silent a while; the questing ray focused on some far-off vision. "The last dragon hatches. One is there to charm him, a man with a burnt face that is the stigma of his kindred. A burnt face that will not burn, legacy of that ancestor who was tempered in dragonfire. The burnt man lifts his hand. The descendant of Fafnir, the spawn of Pharaïzon dances at his word."

"The line of the dragon charmers is extinct," said Ragginbone. "Ruvindra Laï died long ago. Ask her—"

But the seeress continued. "One made a bargain with he who is not named. Ruvindra Laï slept the sleep of deep winter, until the fetus stirred in its egg. He sold his soul to tame the lastborn of dragonkind."

"Why would the Unnamed have struck such a bargain?" said Moonspittle.

"For the dragon. In selling himself, Laï has sold his Gift and his creature. He has bound the firedrake to the service of the Oldest Spirit. It is a weapon long sought."

"A clumsy weapon for the times," said Moonspittle. "Unpredictable—overheated—excessive. What use is a dragon nowadays? This is—" he hazarded a guess "—the eighteenth century."

"The twentieth," sighed Ragginbone. "The wheel has turned full circle. Dragon or firebomb: who will know the difference? Besides, the Oldest is not only of our time but of all Time, and in the domination of a dragon there is a prestige and glory unique to history. *He* would never resist flaunting such a symbol of his

might in the face of the otherworld. However, there might be another reason . . ."

"For what purpose does the Old Spirit covet the last of dragons, Bethesne?" Elivayzar asked.

"This was the sole remaining egg from the clutch of Senecxys
after her mating with Pharaïzon. Within the body of the dragonet
is the spearhead that entered his father long before. When he was
dying, Pharaïzon instructed his mate to devour his heart, that the
splinter of the Lodestone that had made him lord of fire and air
might be passed on to one of his offspring. Afterward, Senecxys
fled to the dragon's graveyard, laying her eggs there in a chasm of
flame ere she expired. But Ruvindra Laiï found them, even there
where no man had ever been, and he took the most precious and
destroyed the rest, breaking the shells with a hammer, crushing
the skulls of the unborn young."

"He loved dragons," objected Moonspittle. "That was the obsession of his house."

The seeress's tone did not alter. "Laiï had given himself to him
who is without pity," she said. "Though he may have wept, he
could not disobey. That was the price he paid."

"And now?" said Ragginbone. "Does the dragon charmer still
live? Ask her."

"One lives," said the sibyl. "Ruvindra Laiï is slain, but another
of his line has taken his place. Yet he is of corrupted race, and
both his blood and his Gift are diluted. He needs the Old Spirit
to increment his powers; thus the Unnamed has gained a
foothold in his soul."

"And the dragon?" said Ragginbone. "What of the dragon? It
would be difficult to hide such a creature in *this* world."

"Where has he hidden the dragon?" asked Moonspittle. "Is he
in the Here and Now, or Beyond?"

"I—cannot tell." For the first time, the sibyl faltered. Her single eye wandered; the attenuated beam flinched and receded,

withdrawing as if from a great depth of darkness. "It is . . . too well concealed. There is a mist over both dragon and demon."

"Will it manifest itself soon?"

"I do not know. I can see what was, and what is, but not what will be. There was only one of our sisterhood whose gaze could penetrate the future, and the dread of her visions weighed heavy on her heart. She foresaw too many horrors that could not be averted, and so she lost faith in the idle hand of Providence—she lost faith in Time itself—and now she sleeps too deeply ever to reawaken. Her spirit is gone, and her body molders. Even a necromancer could not summon Skætha again." She paused, and when she resumed the echoes were fading from her voice, leaving it cold and thin as an arctic breeze. "I grow tired now; I can see no more. Release me."

"Not yet." Ragginbone loomed behind Moonspittle like a venerable Mephistopheles: an insistent murmur in his ear, an iron pressure on his neck. "Ask her about the owl."

"The *owl*?"

"An owl bigger than an eagle, swifter than the beat of time. An emissary perhaps . . . a thief of spirits . . ."

When Moonspittle repeated the question, the seeress turned her solitary eye on him: a lidless orb pink veined and sheened with blue, where the double circles of iris and pupil stood out against the white like the center of a target. A target that might shoot back. The searching ray had dwindled to a nimbus around it; the transparent features were barely visible against the ivory perfection of the bones. "I am tired," she reiterated. "I have no strength for *bird-watching*." A faint contempt tinted her colorless monotone.

"Try." Ragginbone's voice spoke through Moonspittle's lips, hand followed hand in duplicate motion, tightening the perimeter, sealing the boundary against any departure. The muted fire glimmer crackled and grew.

The eye of the pythoness moved again, sending its piercing glance into some other dimension, a realm of distant night or twilit day. "The owl roosts," she said, and there was effort in the words. "It is far away . . . on the edge . . . the very edge of things . . . The Tree stands there forever, in a forest of its own shadows. Its topmost branches are above the stars . . ."

"How may I reach it?" Moonspittle's question was still in the harsher accents of Caracandal.

"There is no way there, no way back. Only the birds may come and go. The eagle and the owl fly where they will . . ."

"Look closer. There are other things than birds in the Eternal Tree."

"The heads of the dead ripen there in season, like hanging fruit . . . I can see no more. Release me!"

"Look closer!"

"I can . . . no more. *Release me!*" The shadowy mouth strained into a rictus over pearl-pure teeth; the skull glowed with an opalescent luster. But on the eyeball the blood vessels had darkened, standing out in ridges; the pupil was a black hole; the bluish nimbus had turned red. The lone ray was clouded, a murky fume reaching from another place to choke its radiance, forcing it back onto its source. The orb grew hot, throbbing visibly. Smoke rose from the socket. The seeress screamed, plucking at her head with skeleton fingers. And then the eye burst from its anchorage, arcing through the air on a trail of sparks, bouncing once before sailing over the outline of the circle—

Like a glittering marble it rolled across the floor. The cat Mogwit pounced upon it, entranced by this new plaything, patting it from paw to paw, evidently oblivious to the heat of its touch. In the circle the seeress howled with rage and agony, her empty socket weeping tears of blood. And around the periphery Moonspittle crawled on hands and knees, coaxing, threatening, wheedling, while the cat ignored his blandishments and slipped through his grasp, nudging the trophy so it was always just out of his master's reach. In the end it was Ragginbone who caught Mogwit by the scruff of the neck, plucking him into the air while Moonspittle retrieved the eye and passed it to its custodian. Her hand closed upon it; she pulled the veil over her face. Cursing him in a voice like the hiss of cold fire, she faded from their sight.

"The circle is broken," said Ragginbone, tossing his burden floorward. "We must start again."

"He might have *eaten* it," said Moonspittle, stroking his pet with unsteady fingers. Mogwit was still peering from side to side, clearly wondering where the fascinating bauble had gone. "He does, you know. Eat things. Rats, mice, cockroaches. Once it was a butterfly. I don't know where he found a butterfly in Soho. And things out of dustbins. His constitution is very strong—like a goat, or do I mean an ostrich?—but . . . Dear knows what *that* would have done to him."

"We must start again," said Ragginbone.

Outside, afternoon had flowed into evening, the uniform daylight giving way to the jumbled illuminations of the city dusk. Streetlamp and headlamp, arc light and neon, all competed for airspace, jostling the shadows out of existence, splashing reflections on paintwork and windowpane. The screams of the seeress must have been lost in the beat of music from the basement club, the cacophony of small talk spilling out of a neighboring bar. In the cellar room the flames hovered over the candle stumps, each sustaining its own diminutive zone of light, while in between the darkness thickened into that unrelieved midnight peculiar to caves and dungeons, places where neither moon nor star ever penetrate. The circle sprang into fire again, its wan glimmer very bright now against the increased gloom. This time, on Ragginbone's instructions, Moonspittle had traced runes of protection around the circumference. But when his confederate told him whom to summon he seemed startled, faintly disdainful.

"Why waste the power? Her little brain is full of trivia. She talks of nothing and knows less. She will be no use to you."

"That depends on what I wish to learn."

The words of summoning were spoken: at the center of the circle a cone of vapor, less than three feet high, swirled, shuddered, condensed into solidity. And there was a tiny creature—pixie or pygmy, leprechaun or homunculus—perched on a toadstool. Not an attractive picture-book toadstool, red capped and white spotted, but one of the noxious variety, a parasitic growth sprouting from an unseen tree trunk, its lip frilled into an alligator grin, its underparts emanating a sickly phosphorescence. It was leaking spores that drifted across the circle, and a smell came from it so unwholesome that Moonspittle almost gagged and Mogwit backed away, his fur on end. But the figure seated on the top, attenuated limbs curled beneath her, seemed untroubled by the stench. Standing, she might have reached the height of a four-year-old child, though she was far thinner, her jutting bones like flower twigs, her cunning hands and splayed feet adorned with more than the usual complement of digits. Many of them were twined with knotted tendrils and old-man's-beard like rustic jewelry, outward stigmata of a primitive vanity. She wore a misshapen garment that passed for a dress, woven of cobwebs and grasses, stuck with torn petals and iridescent fragments of insect wings that glinted in the furtive light. Other wings sprouted from her shoulder blades, bird's wings with many-shaded feathers, ripped from their original owner and rooted in place with goblin magic. Too inadequate to carry her in flight, they merely fluttered uselessly behind her, as though trying to break free of their moorings. Her small broad head was set on a neck so supple that she could twist a hundred and eighty degrees in either direction. Her skin was smooth, nut brown, and almost completely hairless, save for a short growth like mouse fur on her scalp; her ears were mobile and pointed; her slanting eyes utterly black from edge to edge, lustrous as polished coals. Across her brow she wore a chain of berries and daisy heads, like a woodland crown; but the berries were shriveled, last autumn's crop, the daisies molting. Nonetheless she seemed pleased with her appearance, as a child is pleased with fancy dress, admiring herself at intervals in a mirror chip held in one hand, virtually oblivious of her audience.

"I have some questions for you, Mabb," said Moonspittle.

She noticed him then; her chin lifted with exaggerated hauteur. "I am the goblin queen. You will address me correctly, or not at all." Her voice was half child, half woman, playing on every note from the shrillness of petulance to a husky effect intended for seduction. "Why have you summoned me? I am no antiquated spirit, to be at the beck and call of wizards. I have my own dominion. You have no right—"

"Right or wrong, you are here, the circle holds you, you may not depart until I give you leave," snapped Moonspittle, adding, belatedly: "Your Majesty."

"Highness," said the queen. "I am a Highness now. I have decided. What do you want?"

"Information," said Elivayzar, nudged on by his alter ego, "on one of your subjects."

"My subjects are legion, scattered throughout the north," said Mabb, preening herself in the glass. "How should I know one individual among so many?"

"Are you not the queen?" countered Moonspittle, echoing Ragginbone's whispered dictates. "Are you not omniscient and wise, both the emblem and the confidante of your people?"

"That is true." She lowered the mirror, diverted by his flattery. "Who—?"

"One Bradachin, a house-goblin, formerly a resident of Glen Cracken. Do you know him?"

"I know them all," said the queen, forgetting her lofty pose of moments before. "Bradachin . . . that is a human name. We gave him another, but I have forgotten it. No matter. Like all house-goblins, he spent too much time with Men. He wanted to play their games, squabble their squabbles, fight their silly wars. I fear he picked up bad habits: rashness, and folly, and the stupidity they call honor. Mortal stuff. I have not seen him in a long while. What comes to him?"

"He left the castle," said Moonspittle, "and crossed the border to a house on the moors."

"Why?"

"The castle was modernized. Central heating, bathrooms, too many visitors."

Mabb shuddered. "I hate bathrooms," she said, rather unnecessarily. "There is so little suitable accommodation for a housegoblin nowadays. Everywhere there are machines that whirr, and gibber, and bleep. No more quiet corners, no more cracks and crannies. We are being driven back to the woods—if they leave us those. Yes, I remember Bradachin. I remember him too well. He was obstinate—unreliable—a traitor to his own folk. I banished him once, but that was long ago. It had slipped my mind."

"Where did you banish him?" asked Moonspittle, and then, at a word from Ragginbone: "Why?"

"Elsewhere. Why? He had something—something I wanted—and he would not give it to me. I am his queen, but he denied me. *Me!* There was a witch who offered to pay me in phoenix wings—wings that would carry me up to the clouds—and all for a trinket, a piece of rusted metal, a giant's bodkin. But he would not give it to me, and I banned him from my sight. He said it was a sacred charge. I told him, *I* am all you should hold sacred. But he hid it from me, and I did not get my beautiful wings. I had forgotten. I will never forgive him."

"What was this sacred thing?"

"I told you. A bodkin. I don't want to talk of it anymore."

Moonspittle raised his hand, murmuring dismissal, and the pharisee was gone. The smell followed her more slowly.

"She is grotesque," he said to Ragginbone afterward. "An ugly little pixie as vain as a courtesan and as wanton as an alley cat." Mogwit groomed his belly fur complacently, unruffled by the chaos he had caused earlier.

"Malmorths are not noted for their moral fiber," said Ragginbone. "However, she was useful. I needed to be sure about Bradachin."

"What do you think it was—the artifact he refused to give her?"

"I believe it might be a spear. I recall Will telling me that Bradachin was carrying one when he arrived."

Moonspittle began to complain that Ragginbone abused his power and his hospitality while telling him nothing, but made little progress.

"Your power and your *what*?" said Ragginbone.

"Hospitality," said Moonspittle, defiantly. "I let you in. Didn't I?"

"You had no choice." Deep eyes glinted at him. "Come. We are not finished yet, and you are wasting time."

"Time is there to be wasted," grumbled Moonspittle. "What else would you do with it? You live your life like a rat on a treadmill. Running, running, running. Going nowhere."

"Probably," said Ragginbone. "Restore the circle. I need to call someone—anyone—from the vicinity of the Tree."

"You can't! You saw what came to Bethesne. She—"

"It must be tried," Caracandal insisted. "Concentrate."

But Moonspittle was nervous; his power of concentration, like his other powers, was limited. In the circle, leaf patterns formed and faded, livid gleams of werelight hovered like will-o'-the-wisps, wing shapes beat the air and vanished. The night noises of the city came to them for the first time, undimmed by the spell, faint as a distant music: the sound of traffic rumbling and generators humming, of people chatting, drinking, quarreling, making deals, mak-

ing love, of lives being lived, of a million different stories briefly in-
terlocking, of time passed not wasted, of minutes and seconds being seized and savored and devoured. A wonderful sound, thought
Ragginbone. The symphony of life . . .

"It's no use," whispered Moonspittle, though there was no
need to whisper. "I cannot reach . . . anything. There must be an
obstacle—a restriction of some kind. Or else there is no one there
to reach." There was a thin rime of sweat on his pallid brow, as
unlikely as dew on flowers long dried. He looked both frightened
and relieved.

The figure appeared without warning at the heart of the circle. There was no buildup of magic, no slow materialization: he
was simply *there*. A figure far more solid than his predecessors,
with an intense, virile reality that made the perimeter seem inadequate to contain him, a flimsy barrier against the impact of such
a presence. He looked part man, part monster, not tall but dispro-
portionately broad and heavy in the shoulder, his bare arms and
torso showing great knots and twists of muscle, ribbed with veins.
He was in deep shadow, but either he wore breeches made of animal fur or his legs were unnaturally hairy, matching the ragged
dark mane on his head. His outthrust brow branched into curling
horns, ridged like those of a ram; something behind him might
have been the sweep of a tail. His bulging, uneven bone structure
achieved an effect of ugliness that was close to beauty: a crude,
brutish beauty rendered more sinister by the lance of intelligence.
For there was a mind behind that face, agile and amoral, though
what it was thinking would have been impossible to guess. The
other beings summoned to the circle had all appeared in a strong
light, but he was in darkness, a red, sultry darkness that clung to
him like an odor. In twin clefts beneath his forehead the Watchers saw the ruby glitter of eyes at once feral and calculating.

"Well, well," he said, "if it isn't the spider. A leggy, whey-faced

spider babbling charms to summon flies into his web. You should
be careful, spider. I am big for a fly and I might snap the threads
that hold me—if hold me they can."

"What are *you* doing here?" demanded Moonspittle, unnerved. "You were not called."

"I came without a call, O gormless one—for the pleasure of
your company. The door was open, the way clear. Ask of me what
you will." The words were a taunt, the note of mockery vicious.

"Begone, half-breed," snapped Moonspittle, still shaken. "Back
to whatever midden you came from. *Vardé*—"

"You cannot dismiss me, half-wit. I am too strong for you.
Who is that sly shadow whispering orders into your ear?"

Ragginbone, who had determined to seize control of the encounter, was startled. Spirits who come to the circle can normally
see little beyond the rim and should hear only the voice of their
interlocutor. "Did you come merely to bandy words with an old
man?" He spoke directly to the unwelcome visitant. "That was
kind of you: we have so little to entertain us. How is your
mother?"

The ugly face grew a shade uglier. "As ever."

"Really? I had heard she was dead, but obviously rumor lied.
They said she had eaten herself in her insatiable voracity, poisoned
herself with her own bile. One should never believe all one hears.
Is she still pleased to see you, best-beloved of her children?"

"As ever." This time, it was little more than a snarl.

"Ah, well, blood is thicker than water, is it not? Even when diluted with the unholy ichor of the immortals. You have your
mother's beauty, your brother's charm. What did your father be-
queath to you?"

The figure in the circle, needled beyond detachment, gave
way to rancor. "I do not have to listen to this!"

"Then go."

Immediately the circle was empty. Moonspittle sank back into his chair; his wan face looked ghostly with fatigue. "It is enough," he insisted. "More than enough. You spoke rashly there—you often do. That one can be dangerous. He has no . . . proper . . . limitations."

"He was badly brought up." Caracandal allowed himself an unpleasant smile.

"I don't understand how he came here."

"I have an idea about that. Clearly his mother lives. I assumed the world's weariness had drained even her, and she had passed the Gate at last; but I was overoptimistic. Somewhere—_somewhere_ she must be hiding—waiting—chewing on her old plots like a jackal with a carcass of bones. I knew she had tutored Alimond, doubtless for her own ends—but that was long ago. I wonder . . ."

"Let me close the spell," begged Moonspittle, uninterested in such speculation.

"Not yet. There is one more question to be asked."

"Of whom?" Moonspittle's tone was dark with foreboding.

"Place the crowned toad in the circle."

"_No!_" The little remaining color quitted his face, leaving the small features looking uncomfortably isolated in a waxen façade. "You cannot—the risk is too great. I will not do it!"

"Fear clouds your judgement. The toad is a little god, a thing of few powers and forgotten myth. Only a handful ever worshiped it. _He_ must be bound by that."

"I will not—I _cannot_—"

"Why keep the thing," said Ragginbone, "if you do not mean to use it?"

"A curiosity. I am a collector . . ."

"So I see," Ragginbone said dryly. The gloom hid the lewd prints, the ill-assorted books, the jetsam littering and lining the room. "There are people who might be interested, if they knew of this place. Perhaps you should open the shop . . ."

"No—no—" Moonspittle's voice shriveled to a whisper; he huddled into himself, deep in the chair, a shivering bundle of terror. "Not people—not *customers*—" The word was pronounced with an inexpressible loathing. "I never open . . . *I never open* . . ."

Ragginbone did not smile. The Gifted have their own bogeymen, feeding on the imagination that is the source of all magic. In a lifetime lasting centuries, on the borderline of reality, such fancied demons may outgrow their more tangible rivals, dominating every nightmare.

"I opened once . . . I forget the date. I always forget dates. It was the last time . . . The city was burning. My city. A man came in without his wig. I knew him even so: he was a duke—a lord—a wealthy merchant—whichever. He carried a child in his arms with its face burnt off. 'Give me a potion,' he said, 'to heal my son,' but I sent him away. The dead are beyond healing. I shut the door, and locked it, and bolted the bolts, and chained the chains, and came down here until the fire was gone. Maybe it passed over me: I do not know. When I next went upstairs—it must have been a century or more later—the city had grown again as if it had never been lost. I could feel the busyness of it, the life. Heaving and bustling like an anthill. But I don't go out. Not now. And I never open."

The ensuing pause signified Ragginbone's understanding. Now he was calmer, Moonspittle seemed to have acquiesced, resigned to his visitor's recklessness. He placed the jade image at the heart of the circle.

"What of its name? Do you know it?"

"I hope so," said Ragginbone.

"I fear so," sighed Moonspittle.

He was back in his chair; Ragginbone's hand was on his shoulder; the wizard's voice spoke with his mouth. At the ominous words the darkness seemed to grow denser; the cat shrank into stillness. One by one the candle flames dwindled and went out, as if snuffed by damp fingers. There was no smoke. In the circle, the squat figurine began to glow with a green nimbus, like marsh light. Awareness grew in its crystal eyes, filling them with a baleful glare, sending spiked rays darting round the room. "Agamo—" Elivayzar's lips moved helplessly "—swamp god, mud god. Eater of the moon. In this name I conjure you, in this form I bind you. Come to me!"

The toad's throat flexed: the sound that issued from its mouth squeaked and crackled like a badly tuned radio. "I hear you. Who has—the insolence—to call me thus? Agamo—is long forgotten. I am no more—in this guise."

"It will suffice for my purpose."

"Your pur—pose!" Rage distorted the voice still further; the word cracked, ending on a shriek. "I serve—no man's *purpose*. Who are you? I will remember—your impudence."

"Caracandal."

"You lie. The Brokenwand—has sunk—to the level of a vagrant—a starveling beggar—homeless—powerless—dispossessed. He could not summon—the ghost—of a flea."

"I take my power on loan. I too have my instruments. Enough of this ranting. There are things I must ask you."

"I will not—be questioned by you!" Fury stretched the toad's mouth too wide: resistant to the pressures of spell and Spirit, the corners began to split.

"You are Agamo," his challenger intoned. "A lesser god of mangrove and marshland. There is no belief left to uphold you, no lingering myth to keep your memory green. Only the image in which you are bound. You *must* answer me."

"No—NO—"

"You sent the *tannasgeal* to take the girl, but her phantom eluded you. Where is she?"

"NOOO—"

The statuette shuddered as if in an earth tremor; the room

rocked; books fell from the shelves. The Watchers saw the cracks widening, dividing, spreading; snakes of lightning flickered from the crystal eyes. Then the mouth gaped to an impossible extent, wrenching the head in two, and with a report like a small bomb the image exploded. Jade fragments flew like shrapnel. Ragginbone ducked; Moonspittle scrunched himself into a ball, crossed arms screening his face. Silence came with the patter of the last few flakes of stone, the slither of a dislodged print descending the wall. On the narrow window the blind had been torn away, and remote streetlighting filtered through the shattered pane. They saw the circle quenched and scattered, pictures crooked, books tumbled. On the table at the far end of the room, several of the retorts were broken. A husk of ragged glass rocked on the carpet.

"Someone will have heard," Ragginbone remarked.

"Oh, no," said Moonspittle, plucking a splinter from his outermost cardigan. "They never do." For a moment, his button eyes shone dimly with the afterglow of power. *"They never do."*

Ragginbone stayed long enough to help Moonspittle clear up, offering to replace the shattered windowpane. Moonspittle was vaguely philosophical about the breakages, making temporary repairs to the window with tape and carefully collecting the segments of the smashed retorts in order to reconstruct them later with an ancient and evil-smelling pot of glue. "Don't worry about me," he said. "People bring me things. Deliveries. There's a little shop round the corner . . ."

"How do you know? I thought you didn't go out."

"It was there when I did. Maybe a hundred, a hundred and fifty years ago. I suppose it might have different owners now. I saw the boy once, when he came round. Through the grille, of course: he didn't see me. He looked very *dark*. Hobbs, the name was. He didn't look like a Hobbs. I've wondered if the new people might be *Welsh*." He made it sound impossibly exotic. "They're always dark, the Welsh. Little and dark. I never heard him sing, though."

Ragginbone considered explaining about the twentieth century, and abandoned the idea on the grounds that it would take most of the twenty-first.

"I send Mogwit round there," Moonspittle went on, "with a note on his collar. He's very intelligent, Mogwit."

"He must be," said Ragginbone. "He hasn't got a collar."

"Of course he has a collar!" Moonspittle was startled into indignation. "I'll put my hand on it in a minute . . ."

Eventually the collar was found, dangling from the corner of a bookshelf.

"See?" said Moonspittle proudly. "Now, you thought I'd forget . . . Didn't you? My payment—my city in a snowstorm. You thought you were going to keep it, but you shan't. Give it to me. You promised."

Ragginbone gave him the trinket and left him gazing raptly into its depths. No one saw him go. There was activity in Selena Place, very different from its daytime business: but the night people paid no attention to a stranger. The vast metropolis, with its motley inhabitants, its eccentric fashions, its myriad lives and lifestyles, seemed to absorb all comers into its shifting patterns: it had stood too long and seen too much ever to be surprised by anything. Wizards and warlocks, demons and dervishes might have passed unremarked in the crowd. Ragginbone strode off down the street and merged into the wilderness of the city.

aynor was in Fern's room at Dale House looking for her night cream when she found the Atlantean veil. At the hospital, she would rub moisturizer into her friend's face herself, as if in this act of touching, caring, performing Fern's own daily ritual, Gaynor would draw closer to Fern, hoping against hope that the gentle pressure of her fingertips might somehow reach into lost consciousness, lost mind. The body of an absentee remains a point of contact, a dear familiar thing, even when the spirit has strayed too far ever to return. When Gaynor came across the veil she held it up to the light, trying to catch the pattern, seeing only faint spectral shapes that seemed to melt and change even as she gazed at them. On an impulse, she thrust it in her bag to take with her.

That afternoon at Fern's bedside she pulled it out and folded it as best she could, though the gossamer was too soft to crease, too tissue-thin for her to make out where the creases should be. Then she draped it carefully around the sleeper's neck, tying the ends in a loose knot, feeling suddenly certain that in this futile gesture she had done something inexplicably significant, as if this silken bond might somehow protect its wearer from further harm and bind the distant spirit to its long-lost home. The nurse on duty said: "What a beautiful thing."

"Isn't it?" Gaynor glanced up, snatched from her reverie. "I don't suppose she knows it's there, but . . ."

"We can't tell what she knows," said the nurse. "Coma patients tell strange stories when they return to consciousness. Touch her, talk to her, go on hoping. She may hear you."

Gaynor sat clasping the limp hand as the long hours dragged past. She had brought a book but it could not hold her attention: her gaze and her thought kept returning to Fern's face. Sounds of activity reached her now and then from the corridor: the rattle of a trolley, a fragment of conversation, rarely medical in content. ("Where did you get that? It can't be true—" "Of course it's true: it was on the telly.") Birdsong came from the garden outside. A bee drifted through the window and began to investigate the vase of freesias on the table. Yet these small noises merely punctured the silence within the room, dimpling its surface, unable to penetrate the nucleus of quiet where Gaynor sat with Fern. Gaynor's mind planed, soaking up irrelevant details. *On the telly . . . it was on the telly . . .* And suddenly the elusive recollection clicked into place. The story about the dragon—the story she knew she had seen somewhere—had been in one of the manuscripts that came under the scrutiny of the camera on that television program. The program about the museum in York, the one with Dr. Jerrold Laye . . . She had tried very hard not to dwell on the incident—the elastic distortion of the screen, the horror of that beckoning finger— which was perhaps why she had mislaid the connection. But now the knowledge was there, in the forefront of her brain, and it could not be ignored. The core of quiet was broken, without the impact of sound. Her thoughts seemed to clatter in her head; her stomach quailed in advance of terror. They would have to follow up the clue—they would have to visit the museum. (*I look forward to meeting you,* he had said.) She found she was shaking and her grip had tightened on Fern's hand; hastily, she forced herself to relax. "It was a nightmare," she said aloud. "A nightmare in three-D." But she had moved into the borderland of a world where nightmares walked, and she could find no easy comforters. Instead she gazed at her friend's face, remote and aloof in its stillness, and at the drips that fed her and the catheter that purged her and the steady green line of her heartbeat, slow as a hibernating animal, and Gaynor knew that whatever her fears, she must do what she could.

It seemed an interminable length of time until Will arrived. She wanted to telephone him, but Ragginbone's instructions had been clear and she was loath to leave Fern. She told Will all she could remember of the few lines she had glimpsed so briefly: "It was the story of your dream, I know it was. The spearhead was mentioned specifically: *a thyng of grate power and magicke.* I can picture the words now . . ."

"Hmm." Will was frowning. "Odd, isn't it? One moment forgotten, then vividly clear. The clue materializes, just when we need it."

"I don't understand."

"It's too neat," he said. "Too pat. We're desperate—snatching at straws—and suddenly there's an obvious trail to follow. Even if it leads into a dragon's den—literally, perhaps—we can't afford to neglect it. I don't like it at all."

"You think it's some kind of a—what do you call it?—a plant?"

"I think . . . it's very convenient. Like the cigarette butt at the scene of the crime. The Old Spirit can send dreams, manipulate your thoughts . . . Did you get around to checking up on this Dr. Laye?"

Gaynor shook her head. "I meant to," she said, "but with everything that's been happening, I suppose it slipped my mind."

"Make a start when you get home," said Will, "if it's not too late to call people. Any background information would be useful.

Here—I came in Dad's car, you take it." He handed her the keys. "I'll get a taxi back."

Gaynor drove home to Dale House—it was curious how she had begun to think of it as "home"—feeling increasingly ill at ease. Overhead, a heavy sky seemed to reflect her sense of foreboding: clouds dark as indigo were rolling in from the sea, advancing rain obliterated the horizon. Trees lashed out in erratic gusts of wind and then were suddenly still, their new leaves shivering as if with cold. When she came to the barren moor the gale tugged and pummeled the car as if trying to push her off the road. It reminded her too much of the eve of Fern's wedding, and she was thankful to see the drive to Dale House approaching on her left. Indoors, there was a welcome smell of cooking emanating from the kitchen; Robin descended briefly from the study, his expression of forlorn hope dying as Gaynor shook her head. When she was able, she appropriated the telephone and sat down to make her calls.

"I didn't have much luck," she told Will the next day. "Several people had heard of the museum but no one seems to have visited it. Ditto Dr. Laye. He's supposed to be a private collector with academic pretensions—a doctorate from somewhere or other, an obscure publication or two. No known source of income but they say he has money, a bit too much money to be perfectly respectable. This morning I managed to get hold of the producer of that TV program. She can't have known what happened—his talking to *me*, I mean—but she said he was very manipulative about which manuscripts they showed, what questions they asked, that sort of thing. She obviously didn't like him. I said was his skin that awful gray color in real life and she said yes, if anything worse, they'd tried to do something with makeup but it didn't help much. Apparently they'd been warned by the curator not to mention it to him: it's a sensitive subject." She added after a moment's hesitation: "I feel it's important—this business of his skin color—but I don't know why."

"Hmm." Lost in reflection, Will made no comment. "We should talk to Ragginbone," he concluded eventually, "but God knows when he'll get back. As it is, we can't afford to wait. Fern's in danger—wherever she is—and we have to help her. We can't ignore a clue when it's the only one we've got—even if it means walking into a trap. I'd better go to York and take a look at this museum."

"Walking into a trap?" Gaynor echoed faintly. "That doesn't sound like an awfully good idea."

"So we walk warily. Anyway, you're staying with Fern. She can't be left alone."

"N-no," Gaynor demurred. "You need me. I'm the expert on ancient manuscripts."

After some argument, he conceded her point. "Someone has to stay with Fern, though. Dad can't be there all the time. I could ask Gus, I suppose . . ."

"Won't he think it odd," said Gaynor, "the two of us going off on a wild-goose chase in the middle of a crisis?"

"Not necessarily. I'll tell him the truth, or some of it. He's a vicar: belief in unearthly powers goes with his job. Demonic possession—or dispossession, in this case—should be something he can take in his stride. It won't be the first time he's known us to get mixed up in matters . . . outside normal experience."

"What about Lougarry?" asked Gaynor. "Should we take her with us?"

"That's up to her."

While he enlisted the support of the Dinsdales, Gaynor, with an abrupt access of practicality that kept her fears at a safe distance, checked the museum's opening hours and tried in vain to locate it on a rather basic street map of York. Mrs. Wicklow had produced the map—one of an armful—from Robin's study after tentative enquiries about the area. Gaynor rifled through Provence and Tuscany, the Peak District and the Brecon Beacons, before finding what she wanted. "We're going to see a . . . a doctor," she said feebly, tiptoeing round the facts. "He's a specialist in coma conditions."

"Ahh." Mrs. Wicklow gave the single syllable a wealth of hidden meaning that Garbo could not have equaled. "And Will's gone to see the vicar. Happen *he's* on the right track."

"What do you mean?"

"There's something bad in the house, something that came here near on twelve years ago. She may be dead, but if you ask me she's still around, that Ms. Redmond. My husband always says you shouldn't have no truck with the supernatural, but when the supernatural comes a-pestering you, there's little you can do about it. I saw her in the mirror t'other day when I went in to dust. Gave me quite a turn. Only for a minute, so I thought I'd been dreaming; but she wasn't no dream. I never liked her, never."

"I'm moving that mirror outside," Gaynor muttered.

"First the television, now the mirror," Mrs. Wicklow remarked sapiently. "Happen you've been seeing things, too."

"Happen," Gaynor said.

That night, Will sat with Fern until two o'clock. When his father arrived to take over, Will offered Gaynor's explanation for their forthcoming absence, this time with all the conviction of a gifted liar.

"A specialist?" said Robin, baffled. "But we've got a specialist coming next week. From Edinburgh," he added, as if it were a clincher.

"This chap favors the holistic approach," Will said, trying to recall the precise meaning of "holistic." "New Age stuff. We thought anything was worth a shot."

"Oh, yes," said Robin, with a sad, twisted look that made him appear very much older. "Anything."

*　　　*　　　*

In the kitchen at Dale House, Will poured whiskey into two tumblers with slow deliberation. A soft noise made him glance up: Gaynor was standing in the doorway wearing the type of candlewick dressing gown that could only have been unearthed from one of the murkier upstairs wardrobes. With her long dark hair and unmade-up face she had an old-fashioned appeal, unglamorous, homely, yet somehow reassuring, like comfort food on a cold day. He was very glad to see her.

"You didn't sit up for me, did you?"

"No," she said. "I woke. I was sleeping very lightly. Is one of those for me?"

"Not exactly, but it can be arranged." He tipped whiskey into a third glass. "The alcohol level in this house is plummeting. Are you worried about going to the museum?" She nodded. "Scared?"

"Yes. But I'm still going." She took a mouthful of the neat spirit, making a face as it scalded its way down to her stomach.

They sat for a while in silent companionship. Presently Will lit a candle and switched off the electric light. The sneaking drafts that always permeate old houses set the flame dancing, filling the room with wavering shadows. But gradually the air grew still and the darkness settled into place out of range of the yellow glow that encompassed Will and Gaynor.

"Why did you do that?" she asked.

"Atmosphere."

In one corner the dark seemed to thicken and solidify, acquiring definition. A small shape sidled into existence, a shape that approached the far end of the table in a strange lopsided scuttle, very swift and furtive. There was an empty chair waiting, and Will slid the third tumbler of Scotch toward it. Gaynor was still not quite sure what she had seen when something swarmed monkey-like onto the chair and reached for the glass with long, many-knuckled fingers. As it came within the radius of the candlelight she saw a leather-brown face, squashed against a broad head matted with hair. The features were unnaturally mobile, vividly expressive, though the expression was of a kind she could not read. The tiny flame was reflected twice over in eyes that were neither human nor animal, oblique whiteless eyes bright with their own luster. Gaynor did not move, paralyzed with a kind of awe at seeing such a creature, not in a half dream or nightmare but real and close up—awe touched with a fear that was yet not disagreeable. The goblin drained the whiskey in a single long swallow: the gulp was audible, and the smacking of lips. "A bonny wee dram," he said in a gruff, whiskery voice shaded with an accent assimilated at random over the centuries. "With usquebaugh we'll face the devil!"

"Sounds like Burns," said Will.

"Aye, Burns," said Bradachin. "He stayed at Glen Cracken once, no sae long ago. He wa' the best of poets. He knew mair aboot the worrld than many an auld wizard, Gifted or no. And ye, will ye be facing the devil in the morning?"

"I hope not," Will said. Briefly he explained what they were after: the museum, the clue of the manuscript, Dr. Laye. "If Ragginbone gets back before we do, will you tell him where we've gone?"

"I'm thinking ye'd do better tae wait for the gaberlunzie yoursel'. He's unco wary o' folks like me. He canna believe a boggan's tae be trusted—och, and maybe he's in the right of it, mostly. Seems tae me ye're rushing intae Trouble like a mad cow intae a bog. Ye wilna help the lassie that road."

"We can't wait," said Will. "Ragginbone could be ages."

"Then maybe I shou'd be coming with ye."

"I think we'll take Lougarry. Someone has to stay to report to Ragginbone—whenever he shows up."

"He isna going tae like it," prophesied Bradachin.

Throughout this extraordinary conversation Gaynor had said

nothing, partly from the shock of it, partly because so much of what Bradachin said was virtually unintelligible to her. The goblin had not appeared to look in her direction, addressing himself exclusively to Will, so she was startled and disconcerted when those strange hazel-brown orbs turned abruptly on her. "Ye're nae planning tae tak the hinny with ye?"

"Not exactly," said Will. "Unfortunately, *she's* planning to come. There isn't much I can do about that."

"Havers," Bradachin responded derisively. "I thocht ye had the rummlegumption tae put your foot doon with a wee lass. She's nae Gifted like your sister, only a wee bit thrawn. Ye shoudna be mixed in such a wanchancy business, hin."

Realizing belatedly that she was the object of this advice, Gaynor said: "I have to go. Ancient manuscripts are my specialty. Will needs my—my academic credibility and my know-how. Anyway, I won't stay behind just because I'm a woman. We don't do things like that anymore."

"I'll take care of her," said Will. "Remember: whatever hazards we may come across, Fern's the one who's in real danger." Privately Gaynor suspected him of trying to convince himself.

"Aye, weel," said Bradachin, "I wouldna wish ill tae ony lassie, but I hope ye're right."

Gaynor went to bed exhausted and slept badly, haunted by uncomfortable dreams. Bats pursued her down the endless corridors of crumbling museums, and a man with gray hands reached out toward her, beckoning. "I look forward to eating you," he said, and she saw he had pointed teeth, like a dragon, and his mouth opened wider and wider, and the corridor vanished down the red tunnel of his throat. And then the fragments of nightmare disseminated and she thought she had woken up. She was alone in a large, dark room paneled with wood. Huge mounds of furniture rose around her, monstrous chairs and humpbacked sofas, stiffly cushioned as if stuffed with wire wool, the upholstery intricately patterned in old, dim colors. The paneling seemed to be strangely carved in places, or maybe it was the effect of graining and occasional knots in the wood. She guessed it must be oak; it looked very ancient and hard, so dark in the shadowy corners that it was almost black. Everything was dark. A tall window at one end, heavily curtained, showed a narrow glimpse of a garden in daylight, and she wanted desperately to be out there, but she was trapped in the room. She was very frightened, not the dream panic she had experienced fleeing the bats but a fear that was immediate and real, intense as passion. She knew she was alone but she did not *feel* alone. She felt . . . *watched.* And then she saw the eyes. The first pair caught her off guard, peering from under a cushion; the second emerged slowly from the complex whorls of a design on a piece of brocade, invading her awareness by stealth, fooling her into the belief they had always been there. And there were yet more of them, and more, winking from the knots in the wainscot, lurking in the shadow beneath the mantelpiece, squinnying from among the coals in the chilling fire. Some looked almost human, some animal; others might have been the lidless eyes of insects, the pale discs of an owl, the slanting orbs of a goblin. She knew it was important to keep track of them but they kept disappearing and reappearing elsewhere, moving from shadow to pattern, from pattern to panel. And there were so many of them.

Gradually the feeling grew in her that there was a pair she had missed. She could sense the eyes watching her as a cat watches a mouse, cold, indifferent, faintly intrigued, faintly amused by her antics. She scanned all the others in an attempt to find them, but it was no use: somehow they eluded her. She had all but given up when she finally saw them. They were enormous—so big that the whole room might have been merely a reflection in their depths, and she herself a part of it, enclosed in double images, watched by

eyes within eyes. Her surroundings had become transparent: beyond, she saw gigantic pupils, slitted, feline, black as the abyss, and
slow vapors of thought coiling and uncoiling like oil on water. She
gazed and gazed, no longer afraid, mesmerized and ensnared by
those eyes. "Don't look," said a voice from nowhere. "Never look
into the eyes of a dragon—" and at the word "dragon" her trance was
broken, and she knew everything she saw was a reflection, and the
creature was behind her, *behind* her, and her terror returned with a
vengeance, and her knees were water. She tried to run, but there
was nowhere to run to, and brocade-patterned shrouds impeded
her, sewn with eyes that moved and glittered. Then the fire came,
eating up the paneled walls, encircling and consuming her . . .

She woke to a paler darkness and the unmistakable whiff of
whiskey. "Ye waur having a bad dream, hinny," said the voice of
Bradachin, and though she could not see him, for a moment she
thought she felt a gentle touch on her forehead, smoothing her
hair. She let her eyes close, insensibly comforted, but she did not
sleep again.

Ragginbone came to the house in the afternoon, long after
Will and Gaynor had left. "They went off in t'morning," said Mrs.
Wicklow. "Will said as how they were going to find some kind of
specialist to see Fern—leastways, so I understood, though Mr.
Robin says he has someone coming next week from Edinburgh."
Robin, as the senior Capel, still got the honorific "Mr." "Odd they
took the dog, though."

"Lougarry?" queried Ragginbone.

Mrs. Wicklow nodded. "You don't usually take the dog when
you're off to see a doctor," she asserted unanswerably. "Happen
they think her'll sniff him out."

Frowning, Ragginbone snatched a minute when she was distracted by the washing machine to make his way upstairs, murmuring an excuse about the bathroom. Once in Will's room he

began to chant the Atlantean words of Command, but Bradachin appeared without preamble. "There's nae call for all that," he said dismissively. "I guessed ye'd be asking after Will and the lassie. They wanted me tae tell ye aboot it."

"Where are they?"

"Gone. The lass remembered something aboot an auld book she'd seen on the picture box, and they're gone away noo in search o' the clue. I told them tae wait for ye, but they woudna listen. They went off tae Yorrk the morn, taking the wolf with them."

"York?" Ragginbone's frown deepened, creasing his brow into a concertina of lines. "Why York?"

"The book waur in a museum there, sae she seid."

"Of course. The Museum of Ancient Writings, which has the gray-faced Dr. Laye on its board. How very convenient . . . for somebody."

"It cam' a wee bit timeous for young Will tae swallow, but he said they must gae a-questing, whether or no. He's sae troubled for his sister, his heart's winning over his heid. Ach weel, he's a fine lad. I hanna seen any like him for many a hundert year." In the ensuing silence the late afternoon sun emerged from behind a cloud bank, sending a low ray slanting through the window. The goblin faded in the strong light, remaining visible only as a faint pencil sketch against the solidity of the room. Age sat upon Ragginbone like a veil of dust. "Ye will be following them for sure," murmured the goblin.

"No." The single word was harsh, hiding indecision. "I must go to Fern. Who have they left with her? Her father can't be there all the time."

"The pairrson. They say he's no sae bad—for a man o' the kirk." Habitual contempt for the church and all its works sounded in his voice.

"It won't do. I fear she may need help, more help, perhaps, than I can give. Still, we must do what we can. All of us."

"We must dree our weird," remarked Bradachin without enthusiasm. "The McCrackens were aye for that. It didna bring them much guid."

"By the way—" Ragginbone hesitated, then continued brusquely "—I saw your queen yesterday. She doesn't speak well of you."

The gleam that lit the goblin's face had nothing to do with the sun, a transient flicker that quirked his strange features into what might have been a look of amusement. "She waur aye a contermacious besom. Still, she's only a wee maidie, when all's seid and done. She disna grow aulder like some of us. There's many a lass is ayeways a bairn at heart. She'll forget she's fasht with me any day—unless she's reminded. Forbye, she's all pharisee—she woudna understand men's honor or women's faith."

"And you do?"

"Ye dinna trust me, gaberlunzie? Is that all the trouble?"

"The history of your kind does not inspire trust. House-goblins may feel a passing affection for their human cohabitees, but honor and fidelity do not usually enter into it."

"Yet it was ye put oot the word that brought me here," Bradachin pointed out.

"I thought this place needed an extra pair of eyes. That doesn't mean I have to believe everything they see."

"There's nary a kobold I've kent that I would hae trusted," Bradachin admitted. "Ye must decide for yoursel'."

"I haven't much choice," said Ragginbone.

It was late in the day when he reached the hospital, walking across the moor with a stride so swift that a pair of ramblers sensed his passage only as a draft of air and a flying glimpse of what they thought was an animal. He had worn out his Gift, but the ability to dislocate himself in Time and move to an alternative tempo was a habit that, like so many of his more uncommon traits, he had never lost. At the clinic he found Gus Dinsdale by

Fern's bedside, trying to write his Sunday sermon while plugged into a Walkman playing Jethro Tull. Gus welcomed the newcomer with some relief. "I didn't let Will down," he said, "but I ought to be at home. The boys are up for the weekend—" He had ten-year-old twins, currently at boarding school "—and I don't get many chances to see them. Besides, they're natural vandals—they're at that age, I suppose—a constant flow of uncontrolled energy. They're a bit much for Maggie on her own." He continued, not quite as an afterthought: "Do *you* know what's really going on here? Will seems to think Fern's spirit has been 'driven from her body'—that was the phrase he used. He says she's lost somewhere, in some other dimension. The church doesn't go in for that sort of thing nowadays, but . . . I've always believed in keeping an open mind. And Will's imaginative, but not foolish."

"You should be more careful," Ragginbone said with unusual gravity. "The trouble with keeping an open mind is anything can get in. Or out. Perhaps that is what happened to Fern."

Gus met his gaze with eyes that stared thoughtfully through unsteady spectacles. "This isn't the first time the Capels have been mixed up with something out of the ordinary," he persisted. "There was the death of Alison Redmond and Fern's subsequent disappearance. You and I are barely acquainted, but I've always suspected that you knew more of these matters than any of us. I have even wondered if we are . . . on opposite sides of the fence, so to speak."

Ragginbone's brows went up. "I'm no agent of the devil, if that's what you mean."

"No indeed. I simply felt that you might represent—a more pagan world."

"I was born a Catholic," Ragginbone admitted unexpectedly, "but that was a long time ago. Since then, I've learned to see God through rather different eyes. You could call that pagan. As to what I know about this—" a brief gesture indicated the figure on the bed "—it isn't enough. Even if I were sure where she is, I could not bring her back. I can only watch. That is my fate."

Gus was still hesitating on the verge of departure, his raincoat hanging off one shoulder, the shabby satchel in which he had packed his Walkman dumped back on the floor. "Look, if you need me," he said abruptly, "I can make other arrangements for the boys. This is more important. If there's anything—"

"Do your job," said Ragginbone with a sudden crooked smile. "Pray."

When the vicar had gone Ragginbone bent over Fern for a while, adjusting the wisp of gossamer looped about her neck, lifting a fallen eyelid, studying the frozen features with the passionate absorption of an archaeologist poring over a vintage mummy. As the archaeologist seeks to reconstruct a long-forgotten life from a plethora of tiny clues, so Ragginbone sought to uncover not life but death, to follow the trail of the absent spirit through the gateway of a mind in stasis. It was more than an hour before he straightened up, his back stiff with bending, his face seamed with the lines of vain effort. He had caught only echoes of Fern, glimpses of dream and danger that did nothing to lighten his mood. He had wandered down long, dark tunnels of thought, calling her name, hearing his own voice coming back to him, seeing at rare moments a shadow slipping around a corner or an image of the tunnel's end, too remote for certainty, too fleeting to pin down. Once he might have recalled her, even from the outer reaches of being; but he no longer had the power, and Moonspittle, he knew, would be too ineffectual a tool for such a conjuration. "I can only watch," he repeated, half out loud, and the nurse who had heard the murmur if not the words told a colleague she had always guessed he was a bit mad, dressing like a tramp and muttering to himself: she couldn't understand why they allowed him to be left alone with the patient. But when another nurse went in to check on him, Ragginbone was sitting in silence, his face somber with thought, and she retreated without comment or question, feeling her presence an intrusion.

Robin arrived around three in the morning. "Mrs. Wicklow told me you were here," he said. "Glad to see you. Don't like Fern left alone."

"She mustn't be," Ragginbone impressed on him. "Stay awake. Watch her constantly. I have a feeling something may happen soon." What kind of a feeling it was, hope or fear, he did not specify.

But Robin had gone beyond optimism. "Will and Gaynor haven't come home," he went on. "Don't remember them saying they'd be away for the night. Not too happy about that."

"Lougarry will look after them," said Ragginbone, but the cloud on his brow grew darker, and his eyes were anxious.

Saturday made no difference to the sickroom: here, every day, every hour was the same. Dawn faded the lamplight: in the gray pallor of morning the face on the pillow looked more deathly than ever, and on the heart monitor the pulse beat seemed fainter and slower. Medical staff came and went with disquieting solemnity. Ragginbone snatched a few hours' sleep on the sofa in the waiting area, Robin returned to Dale House for a hasty lunch; but most of the time they were both there, sharing the vigil as if by unspoken accord, one dozing, one waking, making no conversation, finding a meager solace in their tacit companionship. They made a strange couple, the old man and the middle-aged one, the mentor and the father, seated on opposite sides of the bed, and between them under the white coverlet the slight outline of the girl. Once Robin said: "She was never any trouble, you know. No drugs. No undesirable boyfriends. Studied hard at school, did well at college, successful at work. No trouble."

"There are so many kinds of trouble," sighed Ragginbone.

There was no word from Will and Gaynor, no sign of Lougarry. Shortly after five Marcus Greig telephoned at some length; Robin took the call in the nurse's office. "Says he's driving up tomorrow," he reported afterward. "Bit of a token gesture, if you ask me. Gone one moment, back the next, just like a bloody jack-in-the-box. What I mean is, if he'd really cared, he'd have stayed. All along." And, after a pause of several minutes: "He didn't deserve her."

"He didn't get her," said Ragginbone.

"Don't want him here," Robin said with less than his customary tolerance. "Bit of a bugger, having him faffing around all the time. Talks too much." Another long pause. "Still, Abby's coming, too. She'll deal with him. Wanted to come sooner, but I said no. Got her job—house to run—all that. Didn't think it was necessary to have both of us here. Suppose . . . I thought Fern would have come round by now."

"She'll come round soon," said Ragginbone. He had never heard of positive thinking, but he knew when it was important to lie.

The change came suddenly, no slight twitching this time but a violent motion that brought both men to their feet. The body stiffened as if in a convulsion; a flush of scarlet stained the pale cheeks; beads of sweat burst from the skin. The bedding was soaked in seconds. On the monitor, the pulse line shot into overdrive, zigzagging wildly across the screen. Yet the face remained immobile, lifeless, as if Fern were a mere puppet, a thing of wood and string and paint, tormented by the manipulations of an invisible puppeteer. Beside Ragginbone the left hand clenched abruptly into a fist—spasms ran up the arm—there was a smell of singed flesh. Robin thrust his head into the corridor, calling for help, and when he looked back the body was still again, the limbs flaccid, and the pulse had decelerated to an occasional blip, and only the fist was left, knuckles locked into rigidity, to indicate the strength of the seizure. The nurse came running just as the Watcher prized the fingers open. Robin gave a cry of horror and distress; even Ragginbone was unable to check his instinctive recoil. For the exposed palm was burned—burned almost to the bone. Ragged ends of skin peeled away from the underside of the fingers; cracks split the flesh, filling with blood. The nurse went white and bolted in search of a doctor. Robin said: "Dear God. Dear God," over and over again, and: "Water. We should get some water. She must be in agony—"

But Fern's face showed nothing at all.

Part Two

Dragoncraft

◆

✦ X ✦

There is no Time here, beneath the Tree. She has no memory of arriving, or of any journey in between; her memories belong all to that other place, the place where they lived by Time. Dimly she recalls growth, change, constant motion—the wearing out of the body, the swift onset of death. Nothing kills like Time. Here, day and dark are mere simulations, meaningless counterpoints in an endlessly repeated tune, and the many seasons of the Tree go around and around like a carousel, returning always to whence they began. Sysselore tells her you can see the same leaves unfurling, fading, falling, season upon season, to the tiniest detail of the veins. Even some of the heads are the same, ripening only to rot, rotting only to swell and ripen as the wheel comes around again. There is no progress here, only stasis.

It is dark in the cave under the Tree, the cave of roots. Thick tubers form the walls, twisted into pillars, curling overhead to shape the irregular coves and hollows of the roof. In places the stems grope downward like stalactites, tentacles of living fiber, and everywhere they are covered with hair-thin filaments that suck nourishment from their surroundings, bristling if you pass

too close as if sensing the approach of food. In the center is a giant radix, gnarled and convoluted like a fossilized serpent from a
prehistoric age, its lower section split down one side to form a
natural flue. The root is blackened from the spellfire but not damaged: the Tree is impervious to such things. Apart from the wan
glimmer of the fire crystals that smolder almost continuously,
there is little other light. Fluorescent growths cling to some of the
tubers and squirming larvae are suspended in shallow bowls from
hooks on the walls, emitting erratic pulses of greenish wormshine. They are the caterpillars of an indigenous moth: Sysselore
says you must remember to dispose of them at the chrysalis stage,
otherwise the moths hatch out, as big as your hand, and fly into
the spellfire and burn with a black malodorous fume that disrupts
the magic.

Furniture is scanty: there are a few chairs and a table made of
dead wood, their shapes following the original warp of bark and
bough; blankets of coarse-textured cloth; cushions stuffed with
dried grass. Beetles gnaw the wood, mites burrow in the cushions. In a niche between the roots there is a cooking fire of leaf
mold and twigs, all but flameless. In another recess a trickle of
water descends, more a drip than a spring, funneled from somewhere high up on the Tree where the rains can reach, collecting
in a basin-shaped dip below. She washes there, though the others
rarely do so. Their smell merges with the smell of the Tree, becoming a part of it, filling the cave with a dank vegetal fetor; but
she is accustomed to it and hardly notices it anymore.

The gleam of the spellfire oscillates over the roots, folding the
shadows into creases, making the walls writhe with a strange
tuberous animation. A face looms over her, a pale moon face atop
a swollen mound of anatomy, crested with thick clots and tangles
of hair. The flesh has a semiliquid texture, rippling and bulging in
search of a shape to which it can conform; somewhere within,

there must be a substructure of muscle and bone, but the outer mass seems to bear no relation to it, enwrapping the skeleton like a vast unstable blancmange. The features are unfixed: the mouth is stretched into a rapacious hole bordered with lip; the nose is curiously flattened; the nostrils have sunk deep into the face. The thick-lidded eyes have a luminous quality like the eyes of an animal, the whites iridescent, the iris almost as dark as the pupil. The skin is perfectly smooth, pale as milk, glistening here and there with a thin sheen of mucus. Garments once rich and sumptuous billow around the monstrous figure: velvet molted into baldness, fraying clumps of embroidery. Their colors have dimmed to a murky sameness, their outline adapted to their occupant, sagging and shrinking with every movement. She is Morgus, witch queen, self-anointed the greatest of her kind. Power oozes from her pores like perspiration, and the proximity of it is more stifling than any stench. But the girl does not shrink from her. Her hate is a minute red ember deep inside, something she feels but does not know, hiding it in the darkness of her heart, feeding it on morsels, until the moment comes when she is ready to blow it into a flame.

Together they watch the spellfire and study the ancient lore. They see the phantoms dancing in Azmodel; they see potbellied satyrs and fauns with whiteless eyes and nimble feet, winged sylphids clinging mosquitolike to their prey, and other creatures grotesque beyond the design of Nature or werekind. In the Garden of Lost Meanings, plant tendrils hook the ankles of unwary revelers, snapdragons nip their extremities, bee orchids unsheath deadly stings. Above the rainbow lakes a phoenix circles, shedding firedust from its wings; but it does not come down to feed. "See!" says Morgus. "*He* sleeps no longer. He has come back for his revenge: he wants you to die slowly, and suffer long. We were barely able to save you in time."

"I do not fear him," says the girl.

"That is well," says Morgus. "The only person you should fear is me."

His plans are deep laid, his nets spread wide. He has been plotting and weaving for thousands of years, shape-shifting from demon to deity, infusing his strength into a throng of ambulants, whispering his words through empty mouths. Some schemes are abandoned, leaving loose ends to unravel through history, others grow, becoming ever more intricate, meshing strand with strand in tortuous designs of inscrutable complexity. There is a pattern to existence, or so they say, a current of events; but Azmordis aims to direct the current and weave patterns of his own. And somewhere in one of those labyrinthine webs the girl senses there is a single thread that leads to her. It is a thing she feels without knowing, like the hate.

"He has always yearned to control the Lodestone," says Morgus, watching the smoke. "Envy gnaws him, the sharp end of fear. Are we not Prospero's Children, mortals with immortal powers? He shows wisdom in such envy if in nothing else. He sought the key over many centuries, he seeks the other fragments even now. He cannot touch the Stone—it is alien to him—but he sought to dominate it through Alimond, through you. He has never understood its nature. It is a part of us, a force that runs in our *blood*. We do not need to rush around hunting the pieces like beggar brats looking for wishing pebbles."

"Has he found such a piece?" the girl asks. "A wishing pebble to play with?"

"Maybe. But even *he* will have trouble mastering the possessor. Look into the smoke!"

The visions of Azmodel vanish; the smoke spirals into a vortex, thins into clarity. The spellfire cannot be commanded but its shadow show can be nudged in a chosen direction, if you have the skill. Morgus's willpower is a subtle instrument, with the driving force of a battering ram, the flexibility of a bullwhip. The fire quails before her.

Deep in the heart of the smoke they see a man climbing a wall. The wall appears at first sheer, then the improving focus shows it strangely curved, bulging toward them. The fascia is constructed of overlapping slates, irregular oblongs, many of them notched and dented, whose projecting edges offer precarious toeholds to the climber. Seen from the back all they know of him is that he is lean, perhaps tall, agile as a lizard, and the long fingers feeling for purchase on this curious surface are black. Not the chocolate or sable of the African races, which is usually called black, but true black unrelieved by any lightening, untinged by color. The climb is short; at the top, the wall is surmounted by a jagged rampart consisting of flat stone slabs, triangular in shape, each apex terminating in an oblique spike, a couple of which have been broken off. The climber pulls himself up between two of the slabs and sits astride, his legs dangling. The wall moves.

The image is expanding; now it seems to fill half the chamber. A seismic ripple heaves across the fascia; sound impinges, the scraping of slate on slate, a creaking as of some vast arthritic limb. And then they see a crumpled leathern structure, ribbed with slender poles like an enormous tent, unfolding slowly into a sweeping fan. The view broadens, and there is the foreleg, its crooked elbow higher than the rampart of spines, the thick coiling neck, the ridged and battlemented head, sagging beneath its weight of bone. With distance comes a falling into place of details formerly misinterpreted: not slates, but scales, no wall, but the towering flank of the greatest monster of legend. Yet here there is no serpentine speed, no basilisk gaze; the movements are labored, the huge eye closed to a slit, its bloodred deeps glazed as if it is all but blind. The hues of life have faded from the leaden hide: the creature resembles a gigantic hunk of weathered stone, ancient beyond the count of years, crumbling, corroded, brightened only by the occasional patches of lichen that batten on its squamous back. The head swings ponderously from side to side, as if trying to catch a scent long forgotten. It pays no more attention to the invader straggling its spine than to some parasitic insect; possibly it does not even sense he is there. The wings that appear too stiff and venerable for motion, let alone flight, begin to beat, gathering strength from their own momentum, moving faster, faster. And then incredibly, impossibly, the whole massive cumbersome body lifts into the air. The watchers see it not as the dragon rising upward but as the ground falling away beneath: a rocky floor plunging behind obscuring cliffs, the humps and crags of a mountain range heaving in between, then dropping down abruptly to a ragged coastline with white foam frills bordering a cold blue sea. And all the while the stowaway clings on, a dark rider aboard a steed greater and more terrible than any myth could convey.

The picture shifts: they see now with his eyes, the nearest spinal ridge slicing the image in half. Ahead the sun is setting in a yellow smolder between long strips of cloud. Fire sparkles on the sea. They feel the rush of air, hear the booming surge of the wings. Night descends swiftly, and they are soaring higher and higher into a dreamworld of falling stars.

When the sky lightens there are other mountains ahead, the mountains of Elsewhere, snow dabbled, stone shouldered, cloven with hanging valleys, their lower slopes too far below to distinguish clearly, lost in a dizzying vista of height and space. These are the peaks no man has ever climbed, the aeries where no eagle makes its nest. They plummet suddenly into a sickening dive, traversing a natural gateway between two pinnacles of rock, slowing to a drift along the winding passage of a high gorge delved by a torrent long run dry. Short grasses cling to the slopes like sparse hair, thin soil crumbles to show the bony ground beneath. The cleft widens into a valley with many arms branching to either side, a secretive maze of canyons surrounded by steeps that dwarf even the dragon. Animals do not graze here, nor insects breed, nor birds fly: there is only plant life and stone life. But on the floor of these hidden canyons there is death. For this is the dragons' graveyard, the place where the old come to find rest, where the slain who have vanished from the world leave their last remains. No archaeologist ever came here to pick through the bleaching bones; the skeletons lie undisturbed, delicate sculptures of mythical proportions, wind cleansed, sun whitened, the eyeless skulls watchful even in their endless stillness. Here the dragon lands, settling into slumber, and the red fades from his orbs, and the quickened pulse beat of his final flight sinks to a flutter, and is lost. The rider scrambles down from his back and looks around, evidently searching for something. His gaze focuses on what appears to be the entrance to a cave on the far side of the valley. He makes his way toward it, surefooted and nimble as a chamois, ducking beneath a scaffolding of tibia and femur and descending a stepladder of tail vertebrae, leaping from rock to rock across the waterless valley bed, climbing the uneven incline to the cave mouth in hungry strides.

The vision follows him inside, down a narrow defile into absolute darkness. He gropes onward, staying close to the wall—they feel the grainy texture of granite under his hand, hear the soft hiss of his breath. It grows warmer. The dark acquires a rubescent tinge; there is a hot sulphurous smell. The passage debouches into a cavern so large the farther walls are lost to view: the floor immediately below curves around in a broad ledge overhanging an unseen chasm; the air trembles in the updraft of heat; wheezing jets of gas shoot toward the distant roof. The lip of the chasm is silhouetted against a burning glow. The intruder walks to the edge, peers over. They see the lake of magma beneath, its surface crawling with torpid ripples and heaving into bubbles that slowly distend and crack, spitting gobbets of fire. The man leans forward as if fascinated or compelled, apparently indifferent to the furnace heat on his skin. At last he retreats, moving along the ledge to a point where it bulges out into a platform of rock. A giant skeleton is coiled here, the naked fretwork of bones lustered in the flamelight. The passage must have been wider once to admit such a creature, or maybe it found some other way in, now closed. The fragile barrier encircles a shallow depression where a clutch of eggs still remains, their soft shells hardened to porcelain, pristine, undamaged, as if viable life might yet endure within, incubating in the warmth of the earth's fires. The man negotiates the trellis of ribs, slipping easily between curving struts, and crouches down over the hoard. His outstretched hands are black against their gilded pallor. For the first time the watching girl knows him for a thief.

She can see his face now, a concentration of angles focused into a hard, narrow beauty, intent, obsessive, devious; multiple expressions with but a single thought. His mouth is a compressed shadow; his bent gaze is hidden under the curve of lowered eyelids. He resembles a piece of cubist sculpture, the geometric lines of brow and cheekbone, nose and jaw catching the light like polished basalt. She sees his lips part; the background noise recedes and she hears, as if from very close by, the faint sibilance of escaping breath. His hands linger on one of the eggs, sensing by some specialized intuition its differentness from the others. He wraps it in a thick cloth that he has evidently brought for that purpose and places it in a leather pouch hanging from his belt. For a moment his gaze lifts, and she glimpses his savage exultation, and the eyes that burn with a cold blue flame, like crystals in a spellfire. Then he detaches a legbone from the skeleton, leaving the vestigial body to disintegrate in his wake, and with this makeshift weapon he smashes the remaining eggs. His ferocity is terrible to watch: he crushes the shells into fragments, beats each fetus to a bloody pulp. He shows no pity, no hesitation. When the massacre is over there may be a liquid brilliance in his eye, but the tear—if tear it is—is blinked away unshed. He is not a man for tears.

Observing him, the girl is both mesmerized and repelled. His magnetism is real and potent, reaching her from beyond the magic, yet she feels him to be not merely single-minded but controlled by a single passion, amoral, driven, ruthless in the pursuit of his goal. He is a spirit of fire, tempered in the inferno, one of dragonkind made the more monstrous, not less, by his human guise, his mortal cunning. "He was clever," remarks Morgus, as if assimilating her thought. "Clever, beautiful, treacherous. A black ape with a twisted soul and the face of a hero. Do not trust him. He could fool even the spellfire, at need."

"Do you know his name?" she asks.

"Ruvindra Laiï. The family was supposed to be an offshoot of one of the great Houses, the descendants of exiles who fled Atlantis during the Fall. They were the dragon charmers: that was their Gift. Monarchs propitiated them, wizards consulted them. Ruvindra was the greatest of his line, but when he knew the dragons were doomed to extinction he sold himself to the Oldest Spirit, or so it is said, that he might have long life and the opportunity to tame the last dragon on earth. With the Old One's help he stole the egg and placed it somewhere for safekeeping. It did not hatch for many centuries and Ruvindra Laiï slept, waiting, like the princess in the story, for the spell to be broken."

"Did he get a kiss?" the girl asks, but Morgus does not answer.

"In the world of Time," she says, "the egg hatched. It might be recently. The charmer charmed, the dragon grew. But the Oldest One took it for his creature—his pet—and Ruvindra was slain: thus the reward for his perfidy."

"Whom did he betray?"

"Himself. Who knows? Maybe we shall see him here, in next season's crop of heads. Then you may kiss him, if you will."

In the smoke he has emerged from the cave, the grave robber, nest raider, slayer of the unborn. Ruvindra Laiï. He stands on the mountainside, calling in Atlantean. A sudden wind arrives, blowing his long black hair. A vulture comes flying from the deeps of the sky, a night-plumed raptor with a twenty-foot wingspan and a purple nevus on its naked head. It lands in front of him, turning immediately into a small, crooked manikin with the same birthmark disfiguring face and scalp. Words pass between them. Then the shape-shifter resumes his bird form and the thief mounts, bearing his stolen treasure. The vulture gives a harsh croaking scream before rising into the air, cruising the thermals until it is far above the ground, then heading away over the mountains, dwindling rapidly into the blue distance.

The picture changes. Very briefly they make out an old man moving through a vaulted chamber. Perhaps a wine cellar, though they cannot see any wine. His face is invisible in the darkness but the girl knows he is old because she can smell it: the musty, slightly sour smell of an aging body. His flashlight beam roves around, picking out the uneven flags of the floor, the patches of damp on the walls. He locates a cylindrical construction identifiable as a wellhead; it appears far more ancient than the room around it. It is covered with a heavy stone lid. He sets down the flashlight so the beam is pointing his way, though it offers no real illumination. Then he heaves the lid a little to one side, and a red glow spills through the gap, like the glow in the heart of the volcano, and there is a hissing, bubbling noise. For an instant they see him clearly, dyed in the scarlet light, and his face is the face of a corpse. Then the smoke obliterates him, and the images are gone.

The spellfire sinks; Morgus's voice emerges from the gloom. "The dragon is in the egg," she says, "and the Stone paring—the splinter that was an heirloom of the exiles—is in the dragon. In Time, it will grow beyond all other beasts. No prison will contain it. Even *he* will be unable to command its obedience. Only a charmer can speak to a dragon."

But the girl is thinking of the old man, caught briefly in the ruddy glare: the angle of the head, gazing downward; the long-boned skull tapering from hollow temples to angular jaw; the predatory hook of the nose. And the ashen hue of the skin, unwarmed by the fire glow, surely not the result of age but some other factor, perhaps even the diluted effect of a throwback gene . . .

"Of what race was the dragon charmer," she enquires, "to make his skin so black?"

"It was not his race but his fate," replies Morgus. "They say one of his forefathers was burnt by the first of the dragons—burnt but not killed—and the blackened hide of his kindred was fireproof ever after."

"And was it?"

"Maybe," says Morgus.

"Maybe not," counters Sysselore, with a laugh coarsened to a cackle in the vacuum of Time. She passes a thin hand above the spellfire, and the flames shrink from her, until they are almost gone.

Where Morgus is vast and bloated, Sysselore is skeletal. She resembles a mantis, an elongated, insectile creature whose tiny head and attenuated neck appear to have been extruded from her shoulders by a process of enforced growth. The contours of her face recede from the point of her nose toward the furtive chin and pale bulbous eyes. Her hair has thinned to a skein of woolly threads, clinging like a cobweb to anything it touches. Yet at times she retains the vanities of youth and beauty, reddening her lips with cochineal or wearing the rags of diaphanous dresses that reveal her torso: the breasts shriveled into flatness, sunken like empty pouches between ribs and sternum. She often wears two or three garments at once, crisscrossing them with cords and sashes in a far-off caricature of some classical style, braiding the long wisps of her hair and twisting them into haphazard coils on the crown of her head, as if she were a Pre-Raphaelite enchantress.

She should be a figure of pathos, inviting pity; but the insect face is too devoid of humanity to inspire compunction and a degenerate soul looks out of her eyes. She is only less dangerous than Morgus as the viper is less dangerous than the black mamba: the one is large, aggressive, disdaining camouflage, the other may hide in a drift of leaves, and strike at you unawares. And the two are ill at ease together for all their long companionship. Sysselore fawns and needles, flatters and jibes, while Morgus appears virtually indifferent, dominating her coven sister without effort whenever necessary. Yet there is an underlying dependence, the need not merely for a confederate in power but a lesser rival, a cheek-by-jowl comrade, someone to impress, to browbeat, to goad and torment. A witch queen cannot rule in a void: she must have subjects. For time outside Time Sysselore has been courtier and counselor, sidekick and slave.

"But now we have you," says Morgus, drawing the girl to her, and her fat soft hand cups the small face, travels down shoulder and arm, exploring her breast. It feels like the touch of some flabby undersea creature. "So small, so pretty . . . so *young.*" There is a dreadful greed in the way she says "young." "I've waited such a long, long while . . . It should have been my sister Morgun, my twin sister, my soul mate, but she betrayed me. She forfeited the chance of enduring power for the failure of the moment. She was in love with pleasure, with her own body, with a man she could not have. Her head rotted here long ago. There have been others since, but none who could take her place. They were weaklings, afraid of the Gift and all it endowed, or obsessives, chasing after petty revenges, petty desires. There was one you may have known, Alimond—the otherworldly Alimond—but she was haunted by imaginary ghosts. I let her go, and demons of her own creating drove her to her doom. But you . . . I can feel the power in you, like the first green tendrils of some hungry plant. I shall feed it and coax it, and it will grow and bind you to me, and we shall be three at last, the magic number, the coven number. You will be Morgun, my sister, and the name you had before will be as a dream dreamed out, remote as a fantasy."

"No," says the girl, not in defiance but uncertainty, reaching back into the blur of memory for the name they never call her, the identity she left behind. "I am not Morgun. I am Fernanda. Fernanda."

"You are my sister!" orders Morgus, and her mouth writhes around the words. "I shall join you to my kindred, mix you in my blood. Hold her!" Her soft hand tightens, clasping the girl by the forearm; Sysselore seizes her from behind. Her bony grip has a hideous strength. Fern struggles, but it is no use, and now she is still, watching the knife. Morgus releases the slight wrist and pricks her own, pressing deep into the flesh before she draws blood. Then she grips Fern's arm again, though she tries to pull it away. The knife slices across her skin, splitting it open. She experiences no pain, only horror. A ritual is about to be consummated that she senses will contaminate her forever: neither her blood nor her soul will be her own again. She cannot resist, cannot move. Even her mind is numb.

But the cut does not bleed. The wound closes by itself: the flesh around it is white and pinched. Not a drop escapes. "She is protected!" says Sysselore, and Morgus releases her with a curse, sucking thirstily at her own injury. When Sysselore lets her go Fern knows she must not run, must not shrink.

"They cannot protect you always," says Morgus. "You are mine now. My way to reclaim the world."

And then Fern knows what to say. "That world exists in Time. It moves through eternity like a fish through the ocean. Onward, not back. Fernanda is the future; Morgun is the past. Which way do you wish to go?"

Morgus makes no answer, but behind the glutinous mass of her face Fern can see the thought penetrating, traveling through the many recesses of her brain.

Morgus does not try to cut her again.

The dark hours come, the phase of dreams and shadows. They eat, though Fern feels no hunger; sleep, though she is not tired. Morgus's slumbering form is a massive tumulus, quivering with soft, subterranean snores. Sysselore lies under her blanket like a skeleton in a shroud. Sometimes the two of them wake and prowl around, poking the spellfire, muttering to themselves in a thin stream of sound that seems to incorporate many whispers, many tongues. Outside the context of time, Fern finds it difficult to be sure if she herself actually sleeps or how much. Only the dreams divide awareness from oblivion.

She dreams she is *inside* Time. The sensation of movement, growth, vitality fills her with a sudden dizziness, like strong wine on an empty stomach. She can hear clocks ticking, bells calling, the urgent revving of an engine. She is pulled and pushed, tugged and hugged, hurried, harried. The faces around her are anxious, happy, eager—all familiar, familiar and dear, but they come and go too quickly for recognition, and she snatches in vain at name and memory. "Don't be late," they say. "Go—go now—you'll be late—don't be late." She is in what she knows to be a car, a metal cell, leather padded, hurtling forward. And then there is a church, a gray hunched building, towered and gabled, with tombstones crowding at the gate, and the insistent summons of the bells. The faces attach themselves to bodies and go teeming through the doors, and she is left alone; but Time will not let her be. The church clock strikes, and she must go in.

She is walking up the aisle toward an altar decked with flow-ers. The sun pours in through a multicolored window, touching everything with dapples of rainbow light. Petals are falling on her, scattered by a stone angel somewhere up above. Her long dress sweeps the floor; the veil is blown back from her eyes. And there he is, waiting. He turns toward her, holds out his hand. Alone among all the faces, he is a stranger. "No!" she cries. "No! He's not the one. *He's not the one—*" A wind seizes the church and everyone in it, sweeping them like leaves into a heap, whirling them away. There are only the petals falling still, cold and white as snow. She is running through the snow in her long dress, and the skirts billow, lifting her up, and icy hands reach for her, but she slips away, floating skyward, and the bellying skirts have become beating wings, and she is riding the owl, on and on into the dark.

She wakes, remembering a name: not one of her friends but the stranger, the man who awaited her at the end of the aisle. Javier. Javier Holt.

In the waking hours, Fern's education progresses. Morgus is determined to shape her mind, to forge her Gift, to fashion her in her image—as if she has no mind, no will, no image of her own. The witch's knowledge pours into her, flooding every level of her thought, so that sometimes the boundary between experience and learning becomes confused, and Fern fears to lose touch with her Self. But I am Fernanda, she resolves, in the dimness of the cave, in the quiet of her soul. I am Fernanda, not Morgun, and so I will remain. Morgus talks of the Gifted through the ages, both the great and the less: the petty alchemists and street witches whose type still exists, gabbling the future from a pack of cards, chanting spells long impotent in languages long dead, poring over antique grimoires where a grain of truth may hide amid a welter of occult window dressing. Atlantean, she says, is the only language of power, the language that evolved within the aura of the Lodestone, where each word can be a transmitter, controlling and concentrating the Gift of the speaker. She does not know that Fern has visited the past, spoken Atlantean as she might speak in any foreign tongue, before the Stone was broken and the land devoured and the ancient power passed into words and lingered in genes, lest it disseminate forever. She repeats her lessons glibly, and Morgus believes she learns fast. Fern is merely a child to her, a student or disciple: she cannot credit her pupil with a talent for deceit.

"The legacy of the Stone is wayward but enduring," she says. "It is passed from parent to child like eye color or an unusual shade of hair, missing one generation or many, yet recurring constantly. By now, there may be a little of it in most men. The Atlanteans conquered much of the world and spread their seed widely before Zohrâne, the last queen, issued an edict forbidding union with foreigners. Too late! They say my family can trace our ancestry back to a relative of hers, yes, even to the Thirteenth House, the House of Goulabey. We are Gifted indeed. There are many who have an atom or two of power, but few, very few, who can remold their environment, and bind lesser spirits to their will, and outface even the ancient gods. Such are we three, the chosen ones. The immortals have other powers, which the boldest of us may learn to use—if we have the wit and stomach for it—but the Gift is ours alone. Untutored, it may flare in the extremes of emotion, in anger or desperation, blazing out of control: only the words of Atlantis can direct it, shaping it with spells, giving it meaning and purpose. Remember that! It raised us higher than the little gods: it will take us there again. We are the rulers of Earth, the shapers of doom. Think of Pharouq and his daughter, of Merlin and Manannan, Ariadne—Arianrhod—Medea." She thrusts her hand into the springlet and holds it out to Fern with a little water cupped in her palm. The faces slide over the mirror of the meniscus. Dark Merlin, silver-pale Arianrhod, sloe-eyed, sly-eyed Medea . . . "Their power was legend, they might have been all but immortal in their turn—yet they failed in the end. They fell into folly, and their spirits withered, or passed the Gate into eternity."

She lets the water run away; her palm is empty. When she speaks again, her voice is soft and certain. "*We* shall not fail. I have waited as long as need. I will leave my mark upon the world of Time forever."

"What of the Stone splinters?" Fern asks at last, feigning innocence. "Is there power in them still? Or are they truly no more than wishing pebbles—toys for children to play with?"

"Who knows? There was power in the key, perhaps—the kernel of the Lodestone—but it is lost." She does not know that Fern held the key twice, that she touched the Stone in Atlantis long ago. "Something persists, no doubt—a few sparks of magic—but only a few. Had the exiles possessed the powers of yore they would have wielded them and conquered the world anew. Each of the twelve families took a splinter, but only three escaped the Fall; nonetheless, it should have been enough, if the magic was there. Instead the families dwindled into wanderers, rarely outliving their mortal span, passing on the scant relics of their history to their descendants. Now those treasures are mere curiosities with fragments of legend attached. Even their owners have forgotten what they truly mean."

Fern is not convinced, but she keeps her doubts to herself. Maybe the exiles feared to use what remained of the Stone, remembering Atlantis in all its splendor and cruelty, a race of people warped with power, inbred by law, spawning mutants and madmen. But Morgus would not understand such restraint. Any fear she may feel is there to be hidden, overmastered, ignored, a tiny spur pricking her headlong into a ruthless course of action. She would not comprehend that fear can be a manifestation of intelligence. She has lived too long outside Time. But Fern remembers a war that was never fought, a war of weapons unused, horrors undefined: numberless casualties, corrupted earth, unbreathable air. There are times when it is wise to be afraid.

"What of the dragon?" Fern asks her. "Could *we* control it?"

"Only a dragon charmer can charm a dragon," repeats Morgus.

"Find one," mocks Sysselore.

She sees him in the spellfire, the man with the gray face. He looks younger here, but she knows him at once, by his ashen complexion, by the high prow of his nose. He is sitting in a room of books—a room not merely lined but apparently constructed of books. Chinks of bare wall show here and there, but the books are the building blocks: fat books, thin books, ancient calf-bound volumes, gaudy modern hardbacks, their spines crushed together so they can hardly draw breath, jostling and leaning, vertical and horizontal, like bricks stacked at random by a drunken bricklayer. And in the midst of the books the man sits on an upright wooden chair upholstered in studded leather, the light from a desk lamp falling sidelong on his face. The shadow of his own profile stretches across his left cheek, the nose elongated, the thin, pointed lips outthrust in speech, casting a mobile darkness in the hollow above the jaw. As his head moves the beam blinks briefly into his eyes, showing them pale, pale and cold, filled with a desire that is part avarice and part desperation. He might be a caricature of the dragon charmer, aged and flawed, the black purity of his skin dulled, the fine temper of his spirit blunted. Ruvindra Laïï was fearless, reckless, remorseless, a predator without morality or pity, but in this man those strengths appear shriveled, reduced to the littleness of mere evil.

He is talking to a chairback on the other side of the desk. The chair may or may not have an occupant: the spell-watcher cannot see. The back is unusually high, spreading out into a wide oval, the arms curving around to encircle the sitter. There might be a shadowy elbow resting there; it is difficult to be sure. Lower down, the vision blurs into smoke. Sound arrives slowly: the thin mouth tenses into stillness, and she hears the voice of the chairback—a voice from the abyss, deep and cold and familiar. She has heard that voice grating from a throat of stone, dripping like honey from stolen vocal cords; she has heard it harsh with power, cracked with death. But the essence is always the same. "You would not be an ambulant," it is saying. "With an ambulant, the spirit is expelled from the body, to wait in Limbo until that body dies. You would remain in possession: I would lodge in your mind merely as a guest. A visitor. I would be yours to summon whenever you have need of power. Yours to summon, and to dismiss. I would be a djinn at your command." She knows he lies. It is there in the softened tone, in the gentle slither of seductive phrases. She knows it and his auditor knows it: loathing and longing vie for prominence in his gray face. She sees him push knowledge away, sliding toward a willing submission. "Together," says Azmordis, "we can master the last of the dragons, and in so doing we will have mastery of the air, mastery of fire and magic. Forget the crude weapons of the modern age. With a dragon, we have a firebomb that thinks, the ultimate symbol of power. You have dreamed of it, I know you have. I have seen your dreams: the memories of your ancestors passed on in your sleeping thought. The skill is in your blood, too long irrelevant; you have it still, the Gift of the dragon charmers. But your body ages: you need vitality and strength. These things only I can give you. Invite me in!"

Invite me in. The ancient laws forbid anyone to cross a threshold uninvited: the threshold of a house, the threshold of a mind. The door must be opened from within, the words of invitation uttered freely. Who made the laws no one knows: Morgus in all her teaching has not revealed it. Doubtless she is reluctant to admit that there are powers beyond her reach, rules that even she cannot break. The enforcers may be unknown and unseen but they never fail: the Ultimate Laws cannot be gainsaid. Even the weakest individual has this last protection against the invasion of the dark. Your soul is your own: it cannot be stolen from you. But it can be eroded, or sold, or given away.

"Invite me in!" says Azmordis, and in the other man's face there is the dread of creeping age and death, the yearning of dreams unsated. Fern wonders what *he* sees, when she can distinguish nothing beyond the chairback save the impression of an elbow. He wavers, debating within himself—a superfluous exercise: his battle is already lost. *"Invite me in!"* The voice is a dark whisper, less persuasive than hypnotic.

"Very well!" She hears the man speak at last, his tone almost a croak, riven between eagerness and doubt. "With your aid I shall have power beyond imagining. I shall tame the dragon, I shall take what I want from this world and live long enough to enjoy it. We have a bargain." He holds out his hand, but it is not taken.

"Say the words. Invite me into your mind, into your body, into your soul. Say the words!"

There is a hunger behind his insistence, a hunger born of greed. He feeds on swift, perishable lives to swell his one undying life, draining and discarding his human playthings, seeking to refill his immortal emptiness with the brief glimmer of their souls, losing them in the end to the mystery of the Gate. Fern cannot see his face—if there is a face to see—but it is not necessary. All expression is in the voice, in the looming presence of the chairback, grown now to dominate the room, becoming a throne of darkness before which the other cringes like a supplicant. Yet she sees a similar hunger in *his* gray visage, shrunken to mortal dimensions, an object of pathos and contempt, a deadly weakness. He hesitates at the last, unwilling to utter the fearful invocation, but the hunger is too strong for him. They are drawn together in a terrible bond, the greater monster and the less. The man speaks with awful deliberation.

"Come into my mind. Share my body. Infuse my spirit with yours."

"Aaaah!"

The huge sigh of satisfaction changes to a hoarse shriek, like the cry of some long-extinct bird. She has heard such a call once before, in the heart of a tempest long ago: a summons from the world before speech, when the beasts and the elements and the gorge of Earth itself made the only voices to be heard. The impression of an elbow is gone from the arm of the chair. In front, the man stiffens. His eyes widen until the lids all but vanish, staring orbs on which the veins leap to prominence like cracks threading an eggshell. His cheeks are sucked into caverns, his mouth becomes a hole. Ripples tug at his skin. Then with a vast shudder the tension collapses and his features slip back into place. He appears unconscious, breathing through a slackened mouth. His eyes are turned upward in his head and suffused with blood, slits of red wetness in the gray waste of his face. Fern closes her eyes, feeling sick, not only at the physical manifestation of possession but the deeper horror beyond—*someone else* buried in your brain, sifting through your thoughts, sinking into your subconscious. The nausea drains her: she has known no bodily sensation like it in all her measureless hours beneath the Tree.

When she opens her eyes again she notices for the first time that she is alone. Sysselore sleeps in her bower of roots; Morgus must be outside the cave, watching the slow ripening of the heads. (Fern knows there is an exit, though she has never found it.) The spellfire shows its visions only to her. There is the man again, talking with a smooth visible fluency though she hears no sound. He is aged now, perhaps by his tenant, yet he appears imbued with some hidden unnatural strength. The image recedes until he is framed in a black square like a picture, still talking, and his finger comes out of the frame toward her, beckoning, and in the foreground she sees very briefly a back view of a girl with a dark mass of hair. Then the vision is gone, vanishing into smoke. Memories from the world of Time rush into her head. Gaynor— Gaynor and Alison's television set—and the man she had named as Dr. Laye. (Dr. Laye . . . Ruvindra Laïï?) Gaynor her friend— afraid—in danger . . .

Fern reaches into the smoke with mind and will, sensing the power rise in her, feeling it flow through every channel of her body, through the marrow of her bones, through the blood in her veins. She touches the core of the magic, willing it to respond. You cannot force the spellfire, Morgus has said, but Fern is in the grip of a fierce urgency; prudence is overruled; Gift and certainty are strong in her. "Show me Dr. Laye," she demands, her voice suppressed to a hissing whisper in order not to wake Sysselore. "I need to know what he plans. Show me the fate of Ruvindra Laïï. Show me the dragon!" But the fire is no spirit or sibyl whom you can question. The smoke thickens at the pressure, billowing out, swirling around her. Her eyes water. She has a fleeting glimpse of another picture, neither man nor monster, a picture that seems to belong somewhere in her story. A pale figure in a pale bed. White sheets, white pillows, and the still face death-white, cheeks and lips devoid of color. Transparent tubes stream like ribbons from various portions of her anatomy, artificial intestines fueling the machine of the sleeping body. There is something familiar about her, a sense of wrongness . . . But the scene crumples, sucked into a vortex of smoke, and the magic spins out of control, and the cave is filled with a whirlwind of black vapor. Fern crouches down, covering her face. With a sound like a suffocated bomb, the spell-fire implodes.

When the air clears the flames are extinguished, the crystals scattered. Fern's legs, face, torso are blackened. Sysselore rushes over, shrill with fury, scolding like a fishwife. "I wanted to control the spellfire," Fern explains. "I pushed too hard. Sorry."

"What did you see?" And Morgus is behind her, moving silently for all her bulk. "What did you *try* to see?"

"The dragon," Fern answers. "Ruvindra Laii. The man with the gray face." The truth is always safer, as long as it is doled out sparingly.

"And what *did* you see?"

"Nothing."

But she knows now what she saw, and why it felt so wrong. The figure in the bed was her.

Fern lies on her pallet in the darkness, thinking. Nearby Morgus snores with the sound of an earthquake stirring, Sysselore hisses and whistles like an inefficient kettle. They exist here physically, in the flesh; their bodies need sleep. But *her* body is sleeping somewhere else. The person she saw was not the past or the future but the present: a still white figure in a white hospital bed, fed and watered and purged mechanically, a thing, just a thing, tangled in an octopus of tubes, alive on sufferance. She touches her flesh, and knows it for an illusion. Her bodily functions are a mere habit of mind, like the shape she fills. Perhaps that was why she would not bleed when Morgus cut her; she bled elsewhere, in the real world. Yet Morgus knows the truth—of course she does—and she expected blood. What did Sysselore say? "She is protected . . ." There may have been others at her bedside: friends, family, people who care. (Friends like Gaynor, who is in danger.) She knows she must trust them, though they are too distant to picture, memories beyond the reach of thought. If they take care of her body, she must take care of her Self.

She must find the way back.

At least there is no other occupant in her domain. We saved you, said Morgus, meaning from Azmordis, and Fern seems to hear herself in another dimension, calling him, mocking him: *Azmordis! Azmordis! Let him come.* Folly. But if she saved me, Fern concludes, it was for her own purposes, not mine. I will take the ember of my hatred and nurse it carefully, carefully. I need hate, in the dark beneath the Tree where all other emotions are far away. Courage, hope, love are like rainbow-colored ghosts, bright phantoms from the world of warmth and life. Here, only hate is left to me. Hate makes you strong. Hate will find a way.

Now she knows she does not need it she sleeps no longer. She can move about the cave without noise: her spirit-self may appear to have weight and substance but that is an illusion. Her feet touch the earth, but they do not press it. Morgus still does not realize Fern has discovered the true nature of this state of being. She sees Fern always as her pupil, her disciple, too absorbed by her teaching to think for herself, too naïve and too spellmazed to question or speculate. Fern is supposed to soak up her words, follow in her swath. Fern plays her part. In the dark before dawn Morgus wakes alone and moves about the cave, strangely light on her feet for all her size, as if her body floats on a cushion of air, gliding just above the ground. The spellfire is unlit and the erratic wormshine makes her shadow dance in her wake, breaking up over the uneven floor and walls into separate shadow flecks that seem to caper with a brief life of their own. The whispers as she talks to herself trail after her, hissing echoes finding their way between the crannied roots, where they are trapped a moment or two, stifling. Fern hears her name, suddenly clear among the shapeless murmurs, uttered with a kind of deadly lust. Morgus moves away into one of the cave's many corners, where the tubers form a twisted arch filled with darkness. Another word emerges, a command: *"Inyé!"* Her hand describes a gesture and a light appears, a candleflame without a candle, hovering at her side. Under the arch, the darkness withdraws, receding into a tunnel that appears to slope upward. Morgus must surely be too large to enter such a narrow space, but the fluid mass of her flesh ripples and changes, pouring through the gap, and in a moment she is gone.

Fern follows her, without light, touching earth and root for guidance in the gloom. And then she is *outside*.

The tunnel issues through a slot beneath a huge root limb,
buckled and sinewy, like the outflung arm of a felled giant
scrunching at the ground. Here the darkness is several shades
paler, suggesting the imminence of dawn, or what passes for dawn
in this place. All around Fern can see similar limbs, the smallest
thread-fine, the largest many feet in diameter, crushing the land
into a bizarre rootscape of humps and hollows, ridges and clefts.
Somewhere above looms the bole, half-veiled in mist, like a curving gray wall, many-ribbed, crusted with flaking slabs of bark, immense and ghostly in the dusklight. For the first time she begins to
appreciate the true vastness of the Tree. Sysselore has told her
that beyond there are shadow forests that you cannot pass, where
the stray wanderer will become lost or sicken: offshoots of the
Tree's imagining, manifestations of its dreams. Only the great
birds may come and go. But such boundaries are not necessary:
the Tree fills the world, it *is* the world. It stands outside reality, between the dimensions; its roots drink from the depths of being, its
upper branches out-top the stars. The cave itself is a mere niche
scooped out among the labyrinth of its lesser tubers. She feels as
insignificant as an aphid crawling over its feet.

Morgus is visible some way off, a dark blot against the grayness. The outline of her many-robed figure waxes and wanes like
a monstrous amoeba as she moves swiftly over the uneven
ground. Fern sets off after her, halting abruptly on a sudden terrible realization—looking back to impress on her mind the exact
pattern of the roots around the exit, so she can find it again. It
would be too easy to become lost in such a place. Then she hurries in pursuit of Morgus, clambering, sometimes on all fours,
over the hunches and hummocks of the Tree's nether limbs, ascending gradually on an oblique route toward the bole. The witch
is well ahead of her now, often concealed by a dip in the terrain.

When she vanishes from sight Fern finds herself hastening instinctively, afraid Morgus will elude her altogether; on one occasion, Morgus emerges much too close, and her pursuer drops down into a hollow, melting herself into the gloaming. Morgus has evidently slowed her pace, stopping frequently to examine the lower branches, which hang down here within easy reach. Fern can distinguish the leaves, shaped like those of an oak only far larger, gathered into dim masses that rustle softly together although there is no wind. There are globes depending below the foliage, apple-sized, each at some distance from its neighbor: it is these that interest Morgus. And suddenly Fern realizes what they are. The fruit of the Tree, which will swell and ripen into form and feature, character and speech. The heads of the dead.

She peers closer at some of them, although she does not touch, whatever horror she may feel mitigated by a kind of detached curiosity. Horror is out of place here: the Tree cannot comprehend it. The fruit are still small and hard, a slight irregularity of shape being the only indication of eye sockets and developing nose. On the more advanced, petal-fine lines show where lids and lips will open, shallow depressions mark the nostrils, sprouting protuberances the beginnings of ears. The hair will come last. Morgus has told her that many may grow the preliminary stages of a neck, but it will always peter out, dangling like a starved shoot beneath the jaw. It is as if the Tree tries to generate a whole body but lacks the will or the sap, losing momentum after the head. The light is still too poor to define color, but the fruit appear mostly pale, with darker veins spreading out from the stalk. Some have a faint blush that might be brown or bronze, rose or gold. Gradually Fern intimates that Morgus is looking for one in particular, one she will recognize, even this early on, by some stigma that will mark it out from the rest; but if so, she does not find it. Intrigued by the strange seeds, Fern is inattentive: the witch is almost on her before it becomes clear she is returning on her tracks. Slipping out of sight behind a double-jointed root twist, Fern finds herself sliding backward into a dip. Morgus passes by, and as Fern goes to scramble out she sees it. A thin branch swooping so low that it is screened by root and ridge, a solitary fruit ripening in secrecy, hidden from casual search. And the fruit is black.

Initially, she suspects some disease, but there is no scent of rottenness, the skin is hard and glossy. And then she knows what it must be. After a long hesitation she departs reluctantly on the witch's trail, impressing the place on her memory so she can find it again.

The light is growing now, not with the sparkle and freshness of a true dawn but with a slow paling of the world, a gradual transition from the gray twilight to the normal hues of day. After the gloom of the cave the colors appear overbright even without the dazzle of sunshine, stinging her eyes. Different browns shade earth and bark; the leaves are the deep green of late summer, threaded with crimson veins, for the sap of the Tree is red. Bronze drifts lie in many hollows, the leaf fall of countless seasons, harboring tiny clusters of cloche-hatted toadstools, one among the many fungi whose use Morgus teaches. Grasses cushion every bank, mosses pad every root. Flowers are few and furtive. The air is filled with the morning small talk of birds, though Fern can see none. She feels very exposed, caught in the daylight, no longer a shadow among shadows but a displaced being, standing out against the groundscape like an alien. She follows in the direction Morgus has gone, but cautiously, taking care to remain well behind. When Morgus finally disappears from view altogether Fern has a moment's panic before she identifies the giant's arm tree root and the entrance to the tunnel. Color changes everything. She plunges into the narrow darkness, debouching with a strange sense of relief into the retreat of the cave.

Morgus is there, waiting. Her fat soft hands seize her victim, their flabby grip thewed with hidden strength. Fern is pressed against the wall: the huge body envelops her, overwhelming her slight figure so her very bones are crushed and her ribs squeeze at her heart. She can barely draw breath into constricted lungs. "What were you doing?" The words writhe from ragged lips; the hot red hole of the mouth is close to her face. "Creeping around outside like a spy on my heels. Why did you follow me? *Why did you follow me?*"

Struggle is pointless. Fern blinks at her like someone emerging from sleep or trance. "You called me," she says, her voice cramped into hoarseness. "You called me . . . and I came . . . but I couldn't catch up with you. I was lost in a world of roots—you were always ahead of me, but I never seemed to get any nearer. Like a dream . . ."

Her expression remains blank, tinged with the bewilderment of a sleepwalker too roughly awakened. Morgus knows well that the Gifted experience many things in dreams or dreamlike states; she must recall that she spoke Fern's name. Fern sees the realization sinking in, permeating the many layers of her mind; she is sifting it, checking for any possible mendacity. But Morgus can perceive no slyness in her pupil, no deceit. She is flattered to believe that a name uttered in private musing could act as a summons, that the captive spirit is so well attuned to her command. She surveys the girl with a kind of drooling exultation. "So," she says, "you belong to me completely now. You come at a murmur, trailing my footsteps even in sleep. It is well. It is very well. I shall give you a new name, neither Fernanda nor Morgun: a name for the future. Morcadis. You are my coven sister, my brood child, my handmaiden. Body and soul, you are mine. All mine." The heel of her hand grinds into Fern's breast; then the hand moves down, groping her abdomen, parting her clothes. She reaches for her sex, penetrating her with a bloated finger. Excitement heightens the sweat sheen on Morgus's face; her irregular panting sends the breath blasting through her lips. Fern can feel no details of the vast anatomy pressed against her, only a surging tidal wave of flesh. She is helpless, powerless, smothered into submission. But the rape cannot touch her: it is only an illusion of her being that is invaded and mangled, her shape, not her Self. Her body is far away, lying in a pristine white bed under white sheets. Clean. Protected.

When it is over she sinks to the floor, unable to speak.

"Get to your bed," says Morgus, and Fern obeys.

Back on her pallet, she feigns sleep. Inside her there is a great stillness. Hate burns there with a bright, steady flame, filling her with a strange calm where her thoughts can evolve undisturbed, clear and sharp as steel. She needs Morgus. She must learn all her teachings, suck her dry of skill and knowledge. She must find out more about the dragon, the gray-faced Dr. Laye, the danger that threatens her friends and kindred in the world of Time. And then she must go back—back to reality, to life, to Self. I will take the name Morgus has chosen for me, Fern vows, and when my power waxes she will know what she has made. With all her wisdom, she is not wise. Blinded by ambition and pride, trapped within the confines of her own ego, she thinks to develop my Gift and use it for her own ends. But I will grow beyond her reach and when I am indeed Morcadis, Morcadis the witch, I will challenge her, and she will be destroyed. Fern has never thought of killing another human creature in all her life. Yet the decision is made, without effort or vacillation, as certain as fate. It is written, so they say, and that is how she feels. One day, she will kill Morgus. *It is written.*

✦ XI ✦

Fern sits alone, watching the spellfire. She sees visions too numerous to record, scenes from an age long gone: jousts, tourneys, ogres slain, knights triumphant. Then two sisters, perhaps thirteen or fourteen, playing with their newfound powers—plucking stars from the twilight, shedding leaves into a cauldron. One of them takes a live frog and drops it distastefully into a liquid that seethes and bubbles in its wake. Fern glimpses them romping together, exploring each other's young breasts. They are twins, but not quite identical: one is thinner and sharper of feature, the other more rounded, more beautiful, but not more gentle. Their skin is milk-pale, their hair coal-black. "They are the witchkind," says a female voice, and a serving woman in a wimple obliterates the picture, casting a nervous glance over her shoulder. "They had a nursemaid, but she scolded them, and then she died, though there was nothing amiss with her . . ." More images come and go. Fern sees one of the twins, older now, on a white horse. She rides astride, her skirt kilted, her black hair streaming out behind her. There is something in the hungry parting of her lips that is familiar. Her face comes closer, closer, filling the smoke, blurring until only the mouth and eyes remain, floating alone in a haze of vapor.

The scene changes. Fern sees an island, bleached gold by the sun, cloud wreathing the summit of its single mountain like a whorl of whipped cream. There is a boat drawn up on the beach, a boat whose sail is patched and tattered, whose timbers are weather stained. Many footprints lead away from it across the sand. The eye of vision travels up the mountain to a pillared house overgrown with strange flowers, blood-orange trumpets from which stamens protrude like tongues. There are pigs in an adjacent pen, shaggy wild pigs with angry eyes. Unlike normal animals they stand very still, watching the man who has come for one of them. The picture changes: it is evening now, and in a lamplit kitchen there is a woman bending. Her hair is long and fine and greenish-fair, hanging down so straight it looks almost wet; her eyes are large under smooth eyelids. Although not dressed for cooking she is tending a spit that turns in the wide fireplace, licking a dainty fingertip where the juices have scalded her. A whole hog revolves over the fire. The flavor of the meat seeps into Fern's mouth: not quite pork, something stronger . . . Then both taste and vision are gone; the smoke fades as she opens the flue. From somewhere up above she hears a pig snorting, rooting under the Tree for windfalls.

Fern has heard about the pig from Sysselore. Both she and Morgus seem to be wary of it, perhaps because they do not know exactly what it is, or where it comes from. There is only one. It must live somewhere around the Tree—every creature here lives somewhere on or around the Tree—but it is usually seen only during the season of the heads. Even this early on fruit may fall, still unripe and shapeless, the stem pecked by birds or gnawed by insects. "They will come again," says Sysselore. "Each head must ripen, and open its eyes, ere its time here is done with." The pig, she relates, is very large, black bristled, double tusked, grown

strong and fierce on its strange diet. "People eat pigs," says Sysselore, "and pigs eat people. But there is always a way to vary the
cycle." And in her mind Fern sees again the young woman with
green-gold hair, sucking the gravy from her finger.

Sysselore is with her now, laying a hand on her shoulder. Her
fingers are all bones; if you sucked them, you would taste marrow.
"Did you see what you sought?" she asks.

"No. It was just a jumble of images. None of them meant anything to me."

"You must use your power, but gently. It is like blowing on a
small flame to fan it into fire. If you blow too hard, you will extinguish it. Watch. We will look for the dragon charmer, you and I.
We will see how he died." And a sudden lust flickers over her
face, illuminating it with brief color. For an instant Fern glimpses
in the flesh the far-off enchantress, her perfect cheek flushed
from the fire glow. In front of them, the smoke re-forms. As before, phantom pictures come and go—tournaments and pageants,
queens, vagabonds, assassins—but nowhere is the dark face of
Ruvindra Laï. Sysselore's thin mouth curls into a snarl of vexa-
tion. "The magic is wayward," she mutters. "Sometimes it runs
like meltwater down a mountain: the torrent is too swift to be
nudged into an eddy." It is an excuse, and she knows it, moving
away in a flounce of moth-eaten rags, exuding ill temper.

Fern says nothing. For reasons that she cannot explain, she
feels Ruvindra's death is her business and hers alone, a dark secret to be shared only between herself and him. When Sysselore
is gone Fern releases her tenuous hold on the spellfire. The
quick-change tableaux decelerate, dissolving into vague shapes
and hues that reassemble into a new scene, clear-cut and still. A
scene of fantastic rocks, time-sculpted into a multiface of planes
and ridges, pockmarked, scooped, jagged. On either side they rise
into topless cliffs; ahead, they hold mirror-smooth waters, broken
into a chain of pools and dyed with hot, vivid colors, bright as

stained glass against a rockscape achromatized by the descending sun. Fern knows this scene; she feels she has known it agelong. This is Azmodel, sometimes called the Beautiful Valley, the Valley of the Damned, the Valley at the Bottom of the World. But now she recognizes that, like the Tree, its very nature is unnatural, the time-sculpture is an illusion, the rocks are the rocks of dreams— the dreams of Azmordis, Oldest of Spirits, who has molded this place from his own thoughts and desires. And he is there: she feels the presence that she cannot see. He fills the valley like the sunlight; the indentations in the rocks are his fingerprints; every shadow is a sigil of one of his many names.

The man begins as a black dot, the only moving thing in that petrified scene. Azmordis's awareness surrounds him, at once focusing on him and enclosing him in menace, yet he is not a part of it, his blackness is alone and separate. He is climbing toward Fern, springing light-footed over the crooked rocks. The very way he moves is instantly familiar. He is predatory and solitary, unquestionably more evil than good, yet she is drawn to him, as if they are two points linked by the invisible leyline of their Gift. His clothing is tattered, too dark to show color, yet less dark than his skin. He halts on the edge of a pool whose emerald depths shade to shallows of acid-green. "Call it," says the voice of one she cannot see. There may be a physical manifestation, perhaps human or humanoid, an image of the omnipresent Spirit, but all she can distinguish is a shadow on the border of the picture that might be the outline of a shoulder, the musculature of an upper arm. As in the room of books with Dr. Laye, the spell-scene avoids him. "Call it," the voice repeats, and the cliffs give back the command in echoes and whispers. "It is time. It has played here too long. Summon your servant."

The dark face hardens, misliking either the tenor of the voice or the word "servant." Nonetheless, he seems to acquiesce, bending over the pool, his eyes lowered. Fern can only guess at the intensity

of his gaze. "Angharial!" he calls softly. "Inferneling! Little crocodile!" Fern guesses these must be pet names: the beast he coaxes is
still young and nameless. For a while nothing happens, but he
shows no impatience, though she can sense Azmordis's frustration.
Then something breaks the surface; a V-shaped ripple travels
smoothly toward the bank. The creature emerges, half opening
fragile wings to fan its lithe body, shaking the water from its scales
in a storm of glittering droplets. It is perhaps twelve or fourteen feet
long but serpent slender: at its broadest the trunk could be
spanned by two hands. It still has the snub nose and overlarge eyes
of the hatchling; its scales are shiny with newness, green-tinged
with first youth; the skin of its unused pinions is barely thicker than
tissue paper. It approaches the man with evident pleasure, as a
beloved master long missed. Its forked tongue licks his outstretched hand, the twin prongs moving individually, twining his
fingers like tentacles. The dragon charmer caresses its crested head
with great gentleness, but the hardness of his face does not change.

"Is it ready?" asks the voice of Azmordis.

"*He* is ready," says the dragon charmer. He begins to stroke its
neck with slow rhythmical movements, and the beast rears up,
arching its head back, a strange rippling motion appearing beneath the supple covering of throat and belly. Its tail lashes; the
wings unfurl to their full extent and beat the air, sending the rock
dust whirling. Its mouth gapes wide: needle fangs glint in the
sunlight. Its gorge swells. And then with the cry of a thunderclap
the firstfire comes, a bolt of flame shooting up fifty feet or more,
flaming, fading, sucked back into the dragon's body. The inner
furnace flushes every scale so that its whole being becomes in-
candescent, gleaming red-hot, and the thrashing of its wings lifts
it from the ground, its hind claws striking out in confusion. The
eyes, formerly dark, fill with light like giant rubies. Then it subsides back to earth and begins to cool, its flanks dimming to
bronze, much of the greenish luster of immaturity already gone.

Its throat now pulses with a throbbing sound somewhere between a growl and a purr.

"It is well," says Ruvindra, looking at the dragon, not the demon.

"Name him!" orders Azmordis.

"This is not the time."

"Name him, and bind him to me. It was for this purpose only that I gave you deep sleep and long life. Fulfill your part of the bargain!"

Ruvindra wheels to confront him with disconcerting speed. "I have more than done my part. I stole the egg for you and destroyed the rest, all the clutch of Senecxys save this one, the last of dragonkind. I found the monastery where I knew the egg might remain unsuspected and undisturbed. I was there for the hatching, and I took the infant and cared for him until—on your orders—I brought him here. He has breathed his firstfire at my touch, risen briefly in flight. All for you. It is enough. My debt is paid."

"Only I can declare when your debt is paid." Azmordis's voice grates with a stony dryness deadlier than any anger.

"You cannot threaten me—no, not even you. You need me too much." Ruvindra's face is proud and impudent and cold. His boldness before this most powerful of adversaries is reckless to the point of madness, terrifying, wonderful. In this moment, Fern knows that she loves him, and her heart shrinks with the fear he does not feel. "The dragon cannot be bound. He is not a slave or a familiar: dragons are the freest of the free creatures. Only a true charmer may talk with them. And thanks to you I, too, am the last of my kin. I have outlived my descendants, and the blood of my family is muddied with lesser blends. You will not find another with my complexion and my skill. Slay me, and you will lose your mind link with the dragon, and all your scheming over the empty centuries will be in vain."

"Our bargain was that *I* should control the dragon," says Azmordis, very softly. "Do you wish to . . . renege?"

"You can control him—if that is the word—only through me. His name will be of my choosing, and the hour in which it is given." And he reiterates, dispassionate even in defiance, hot blooded, cold tempered: "Our bargain is voided. I have paid my dues."

"So be it." The huge whisper is bone deep, rock deep; the air shudders with it. "You made the covenant that cannot be broken, signed in your own blood, yet you would break it. Despite your Gift, you are as lesser mortals. You think to take and take and never pay the price. Be sure, in time I will claim all that is due to me. For now, the dragon shall remain unnamed, a hatchling still. Dismiss it."

"He is not a pet to be so lightly dismissed, as you will learn," says Ruvindra. But he speaks to the dragon, and it stretches up to nuzzle his cheek before moving away, lifting now on a double wingbeat, hovering an instant as if in glee at its newfound ability, and then plunging into a lake of scarlet. The ripples hiss into steam at its entry, then the water smooths over it into immobility.

"So be it!" says Azmordis, and his voice expands with the words, making the mountains resonate. The outline of arm and shoulder blurs, soaring upward into a cusp of darkness that leans over the recusant. The sun, sinking toward the pith of the valley, turns red; shadows reach out like spears from every jut of rock. "Our covenant is ended. The payment is all that you have, and all that you are. For I have found another of your kith to serve me in your stead: a degenerate whose blood is impure, yet his skill will suffice to finish what you began. His hunger is strong but his spirit is weak. He will open his mind to me, and I will bend his little will like pliant wood. The dragon will be his, and through him, mine. My weapon and my plaything. You will never give it a name or send it forth to ravage the world. Think on that, while thought endures. You broke a compact with Azmordis: your life is forfeit. All that you sought to gain I will take, and you will die in pain, knowing that where you sowed, your enemy will reap. That is my price for oath-breaking."

The black figure stands motionless. "I could recall the dragon."

"It is young and still vulnerable, its flame uncertain. It would die with you—and believe me, I would rather see it dead than beyond my power. Recall it!"

Laïï does not answer. His silhouette is straight and tall against the red sunlight. "So be it."

Then: "Come to me!" cries Azmordis. "Creatures of Azmodel! Come to me and FEED!"

Out of every shadow, every hollow, every wormhole they come, out of stillness and emptiness, wriggling and writhing into a multitude of unnatural forms. They are blotched and piebald, maggot white, scarlet speckled, slime green. Some are earless, some bat eared, eyeless or many eyed, some with rat's whiskers, beetle's antennae, the warts of a toad. They pour over the ground in a slow tide, skimming on lizard feet or pattering on cloven hooves, groping with fingers, talons, claws. They are too many and too diverse to identify species or similarity, creatures of drugged delusion or fevered fancy, but each has at least one mouth, and all are open, and the whole horde flickers with the darting of wet red tongues, and strands of saliva drool from every lip.

Still Ruvindra Laïï does not move. He has drawn a knife from his belt, his only weapon: the naked blade is as black as the hand that wields it, and so held that it seems to be an extension of his arm. But it means less than nothing against the swarm now converging on him. The spell-scene closes in, until he is staring directly at Fern, his blue eyes burning all the more fiercely on the edge of despair. And in that instant she knows he sees through Time and Reality, past danger and death, across the dimensions— he sees *her*. She glimpses something in his gaze that is almost recognition. In that meeting of eyes there is a bond, like a sudden cord drawn tight around her heart, a bond stronger than all loves, deep as the roots of the Tree. *I will know you again,* says that look, though his final moment is come. And then the horde engulfs him like a wave, and the dance of the knife is black lightning, and grotesque fragments of anatomy are sent spinning through the air.

But he is overwhelmed in seconds, and the lightning is quenched. She hears not a cry, not a scream, only the sucking, swilling, rending noises of gluttons at a feast. Spatters of blood fly upward, organs discarded by one feeder only to be fought over by two more. Faces, claws, arms emerge smeared red. Teeth crunch on bone. She watches because she cannot turn away: she must watch and go on watching until the very last instant. Morgus, Sysselore, the Tree, personal peril, and peril of friends are all forgotten. "What do you think of your bargain now, Ruvindra?" murmurs Azmordis, and the shadow of his being is withdrawn, and the sun is swallowed up in the jaws of the valley. The dark flows down over the grisly banquet, and the smoke enfolds it all. Fern is released, and she steals softly to her pallet, and lies down, curled like a fetus, shivering as if with an ague.

When day returns she resolves to find the black fruit, and see if it is ripening.

Fern can come and go now without hindrance: Morgus does not stop or question her anymore. She believes Fern has accepted her fate, and thus she is accepted in her turn. Sysselore follows her sometimes, dogging her steps like a furtive shadow, not because she thinks their apprentice capable of secret rebellion but because such is her nature, or so her nature has become. It gives her pleasure to take Fern unawares, sidling softly to her shoulder to whisper in her ear, or reaching out to touch her unexpectedly with her choppy fingers. But Fern learns to sense when she is near: she feels that prickle on the nape that betrays a watcher. When she goes to visit that one special fruit, she is careful to remain unobserved.

Morgus still hunts for it, roaming the root maze, examining the heads at every stage of their early growth, probing half-formed features or the swelling hump of a nose. She pays particular attention to those whose color appears darker or to be darkening; imagination cheats her, as she revisits this fruit or that, fancying it is the one she seeks. The crop hangs only on the lower branches; maybe the Tree bears other fruit higher up. If there are any she cannot reach she sends her magpies to look at them. Many of the smaller birds dislike and fear her, chattering spitefully at her approach, but the magpies come at her command, bringing her the larvae that light the cave, performing nameless errands for her. They are bigger than they should be, bullying gangsters with stabbing beaks, their customary black-and-white marking enhanced with bands of blue on the wing. They are not her only allies among the avian population. Once Fern sees her with a kind of hawk that hovers and screeches at her; another time with a gigantic owl, white masked and sloe eyed. There is something familiar about it, and something frightening, but she cannot remember why.

But Morgus does not find the black fruit.

It is changing now, lengthening into narrow shapeliness, the definition of the nose increasing, the ridges of cheekbone and brow bone beginning to swell. The first hairs sprout prematurely around the stem, ears start to uncurl. The closed eyelids bulge like buds. Fern does not touch it: she feels to do so would be an intrusion, like caressing a sleeping stranger. In the night, the hog has been here. There are the prints of trotters in the earth, nearly a foot long, and deep furrows made by tusks, raw wounds in the grass. So far she has hidden the fruit with a wish, a thought, nudging the search always in another direction, keeping the pressure so gentle that Morgus does not feel it—even as they have taught her to do with the spellfire. They little suspect how well she has learned her lessons. Now a stronger protection is needed, a deeper and more subtle concealment. She must weave a net to hide this hollow not merely from the witches but from the marauding pig. She visualizes it suddenly very clearly, stamping the ground until the fruit shakes on its stem, lifting its snout to catch the scent of ripening. Fern knows the words for the spell but fears that Morgus may hear it, sense it, brush its outer strands in passing, and then she is lost. But the risk must be taken. This fruit above all others matters to her, though she cannot explain exactly why. And so she concentrates all her thought, reaching for the power within, channeling it through the Atlantean phrases—the language of the Gift, the words of the Stone—binding, hiding. A spell to cloak a spell, a deception of leaves and shadows, of turning away and leaving alone. She seals it with a Command, though she dreads the mind of Morgus may be sharper than her ears. She can feel the danger, watching her back. Yet when she turns around no one is there.

The spell hangs fire, visible to seeing eyes, a cat's cradle of spider lines that glitter faintly before fading into air. Fern withdraws slowly, watching the fruit disappear into a maze of foliage, climbing out of the hollow, which seems to close behind her, lost beneath a plaited mass of root and earth. Then she lets herself succumb to a trickle of relief, a release of tension that might be premature.

"You go to a great deal of trouble," says a voice, "to hide one unripe plum."

It is a dark, ugly, feral voice, thick as a bear's growl. Fern starts abruptly, turns to stare—yet still sees nothing. And then gradually a shape develops, as if it has been there all the while, like a secret image in a puzzle picture, twisted horn and knotted muscle emerging from the twists and knots of the roots, the shag-haired lower limbs from grasses and leaf mold. The hues of skin and pelt seem to take color from their background, camouflaged chameleon style against bark and blade. But the eyes, set aslant in the deep cleft between cheekbone and brow, have a darkness all their own. Apart from the hog and the denizens of the Tree itself, she believed Morgus and Sysselore to be the only living beings here. They have never mentioned any other, resident or visitant. And he has seen her bind her spell, he knows what she wishes to protect. She inches cautiously into speech, picking her words. "What is it to you, if I wish my plum to ripen unharmed? The pig has been here . . ."

"I can smell it." His wide nostrils flare, as if savoring every tincture of the air. Fern can smell only him. He has the warm, rank odor of a hot animal and the fresh-sweat smell of a hot human.

"Anyway, why are you spying on me?"

"I had heard Morgus had a new toy. I wanted to take a look at you. Maybe she will let me play with you, one day."

"You can try," she says with an edge of contempt, confident in the reflexes of power. It is a long time since she feared any male. "What is Morgus to you?"

His laugh is arid, as if starved of merriment.

"She's my mother."

For a moment Fern says nothing, struck dumb at the thought. That Morgus could mother anything seems incredible, that a child of hers might be freak or monster all too likely, but this is no victim of birth defects: he is a creature of an older kind. She senses his nature, alien and inimical to Man, yet with a suggestion of warped humanity. His very hostility reminds her of something she cannot quite place. She speaks without reflection or dissimulation, asking the question in her mind. "Who was your father?"

"Can't you guess? He is an Old Spirit: Cerne they call him in one form, Pan in another. He is the Hunter, the Wild Man of the Woods. Such a union should produce no offspring, since the immortals live forever and have no need to reproduce. But my mother-to-be planned to outwit fate: by her arts she conceived, and summoned an elemental to inhabit her unborn fetus. She hoped to bear a child of exceptional powers; instead, she got me.

A mongrel, a hybrid, a sport. Half-human, but without a soul; half-spirit, but alienated by a vestigial humanity. My mother hates me, since I remind her of failure. I am her punishment for transgressing the Ultimate Laws, but for what am I being punished? Are you clever enough to tell me that, little witch?"

The elusive familiarity crystallizes: she remembers a young man in Atlantis long ago—a young man beautiful as a god—talking with derision of his own mixed blood, part highborn Atlantean, part plebian mainlander. Rafarl Dev, whom she loved once and always, or so she thought—the man she unwittingly sent to his death. His face seems dim now, but she can still hear the self-mockery in his voice, masking pain. The one before her is almost ludicrously different, a face of lumpy bones with a cruel, sardonic mouth, deep-delved eyes and a cunning, secret intelligence, yet the same pain might be hidden there, buried far down where its owner cannot touch it. She says: "You may be more human than you know."

"If that is meant for reassurance or compliment, I require neither."

"It is neither. I spoke my thought, that's all. Your—attitude—reminded me of someone I once knew."

"Mortal or otherwise?"

"He was a man I loved."

"So you are drawn to misfits and monsters, creatures of crooked make. That is the witch in you. What unnatural seed will you grow in your little belly? Will you swallow that black plum you protect so carefully, and sprout a baby plum tree of your own?" He is standing very close to her now. His loins and chest are hung about with rags of leather and skins, but much of his torso is bare. The giant muscles appear to wind his limbs like cables imprisoning him within the bondage of his own body. He seems more primate than man, more demon than spirit.

"What I do with my black plum," says Fern, "is my own affair."

"And if I tell Morgus?"

"She will be pleased. She has been looking for it."

"So if I leave you to your spells, what will you do for *me*?"

"Nothing." She will ask no favors from him. Instinct tells her he will batten onto weakness like a vampire onto an open vein.

"I thought we might make a bargain."

"No. Tell Morgus, and she will pat your head, and call you her good dog. This is a bone she has been seeking for a little while. Also, she will be angry with me, she may punish me. Tell her, or don't tell her. It's your choice. I do not bargain."

"You are a proud little witch, aren't you?" he says sourly. "So it's to be my choice. How do you think I will choose?"

"I won't play that game," Fern says, "so don't try it."

"What games *do* you play?"

"None that you know."

There is a red glint in the darkness of his eyes, but he laughs unexpectedly, this time with genuine amusement, and it fades. He moves away suddenly and swiftly on clawed feet, padded like the paws of a lion: a fantastic conglomerate of beasts, like the mythical monsters of old, parts of this animal or that tacked together to create an improbable whole. Lion's feet and ram's horns, human skin and matted pelt. Briefly he pauses to look back, dropping to a crouch on a shoulder of root, balancing with his tail. "I go to Morgus," he taunts, "like a good dog. I will see you there."

"What should I call you?" she asks.

"Kal."

And on the name he is gone, vanishing into the environs of the Tree as if it was his native habitat. Fern follows more slowly, picking her way by the marks she has trained herself to recognize. She hopes or hazards that he will tell Morgus nothing, but nonetheless she reenters the cave of roots with a certain trepidation. But for once Morgus pays her no attention. "What are *you* doing here?" she is saying, and the scorn in her tone is blatant. In front of her Kal stands at a little distance: he is so much the shorter he appears to be cowering. "Filial duty? Affection? I hardly think so. We know each other too well for that. Your loathing for me can only begin to match mine for you. The first of my sons, for all his failings and failures, had beauty if not charm; the second—"

"Mordraid was a monster under the skin; I show it. I am as you made me, mother dear. The fruit of your womb."

"The heads are the fruit of the Tree, but it lets them fall and the wild hog eats their brains. Don't dabble in sentiment: it doesn't become you. Stick to your jeers and gibes: they are pinpricks I cannot feel, and as long as I ignore you, you are safe from me. What brings you here?"

"I met someone who was asking after you. It inspired me with a curious urge to pay a visit."

"It inspired you with curiosity, no doubt. Who was it? I am not one to be casually spoken of. *Who was it?*"

"An ancient spider—a negligible creature—setting his nets for a fly too big for him." He speaks in riddles, or so it seems to Fern. "But there was another in the background, one far more skilled, a tarantula who has lost his venom but not his bite. *He* was telling the first little spinner how to weave his silken traps. I wondered who—or what—he was hoping to catch. So I came here, to consult the Greek oracle."

"*Syrcé!*" The S sounds hiss like snakes.

"I told him only what he could learn for himself," says Sysselore defensively.

"You have a pretty new toy, Mother. *Such* a pretty thing. May I play with it?"

Still Fern says nothing, and Morgus does not spare her a look, though she must sense the girl's presence.

"Don't touch her," Morgus says, bored, "or you may live to regret it"—but whether the threat is personal or an expression of her confidence in her apprentice is unclear. "Who was this tarantula who impressed you so much?"

"I didn't say he impressed me."

"You didn't need to. Who was he?"

"You knew him of old. I thought you would remember."

"Him." Derision warps her face, tugging her thick mouth off center. "He's no tarantula. A legless crawler who champs his hollow fangs because he can no longer dance. What does *he* want in all this?"

As she speaks, Fern has a sudden mind picture of a weather-brown face, creviced and cragged, lurking in the shadow of a pointed hood, of green-gold eyes bright as sunlight on spring leaves. She sees him in the fire circle, shaking the sparks of were-glow like water drops from his coat. And she sees him beside a clean white bed, watching over the sleeper who lies there. Cara-candal. Ragginbone. Once her ally, if sometimes unreliable, always her friend, though it is long since they have exchanged a word. The awareness that he might be searching for her, shielding her unoccupied body, is like a hand reaching out when she had believed herself entirely alone. But she keeps her face immobile: even in the uncertain wormshine Morgus can read the slightest change of expression, and the thought behind the change. Fern moves toward them, letting her gaze fall coldly on Kal. Morgus's luminous black stare flickers over her—flickers and passes on.

"Maybe," Kal is saying, "he too is driven by . . . curiosity."

"He is driven by the urge to spy and pry. He is the sort who minds other people's business, and calls it *responsibility.* He does nothing, neither evil nor good, and makes a virtue of it. He will spend ten years watching a pebble, waiting for it to hatch. He was a charlatan, a poison peddler who tried to turn himself into a magus and sickened of his own failure. And now he is a snooper who, without reason or power, lays claim to some kind of mandate from an unknown Authority. Senile delusions. His mind is as calcified as his body."

"All the same," Sysselore interjects, perhaps for provocation, "he lives in the world beyond—the world of Time. He moves around. He meets people. He knows things. His presence—his interest—always means something. You have said so yourself."

No one likes having their own words used against them. Morgus rounds on her, spitting vituperation. As her attention shifts Kal looks sidelong at Fern, a sly sardonic smile on his misshapen face. "It is good to know that the coven sisters still exude so much sisterly love," he remarks. Morgus turns back with a word, a gesture, so swift that there is barely a break in her tirade. The sudden whiplash of power knocks him down like a blow: he sprawls on the ground, helpless and ungainly, before snapping his body into a huddle from which he glowers, red eyed, rubbing a mark like a burn on his chest. Fern has never seen Morgus use her strength in such a way before and the ease, the carelessness of it is terrifying. She recalls lashing out herself once, at the house-goblin—a reflex of anger without thought—but she made no contact, caused no pain. She finds herself clutching right hand in left as if to keep it under control.

Sysselore cowers under the diatribe with the resentful cringing of a subordinate who feigns submission while plotting a petty revenge. The long habit of sisterhood has engendered certain rules between them: conflict is only ever verbal. Morgus stops as abruptly as she began; her black gaze veers, finding the girl. "Are you enjoying the spectacle, Fernanda?" she asks.

Fern shrugs. "A family squabble."

Morgus laughs—her mouth splits and widens, the soft flesh shifts and re-forms itself around the red hole of her mirth. "Do you see this?" she says at last, indicating the hunched figure on the ground. "This was a mistake. Learn from it. I had a son once, when I was young: his father was a king whose legend they still remember."

"He was your half brother," mutters Sysselore.

"Irrelevant. My son was handsome and proud, though with little Gift, but he was also impatient and greedy. Ambition and rancor destroyed him. When I saw he was flawed I set out to make myself a better child. I took the seed of a god and warmed it into mortal life, I infused it with a phantom drawn from the ether. It was a magic like no other—"

"Galatæa," murmurs Sysselore. "The flower bride of Llew Llaw Gyffes."

"Galatæa was a statue, a receptor put to a different use. Blodeuwedd was a doll made of forget-me-nots and love-in-idleness. My experiment was with flesh and blood—my flesh, my blood. I nursed it like a fragile plant and it grew in my belly like a tumor. When it emerged I saw—this. Neither Man nor Spirit, a monster from infancy, crawling in his own dirt. I gave him to a peasant half-wit and he drank in stupidity with her breast milk. When he was older, he used what little power he had to sneak and steal, growing only in vice—the crude vices that spring from a mean imagination, from brute sensuality and bile. I had named him after Caliburn, the sword of fame and fable. Now he is Kaliban, a byword for a beast. I let him live as a reminder. The Ultimate Laws can be bent but not broken. Look at him and learn."

You let him live to torment him, Fern says, but only to herself. You take vengeance on him for your own aberration.

"Did you ever try to love him?" she asks, as if in a spirit of scientific enquiry.

"Love!" Morgus laughs again, but without sound. "What do you know of such things, beyond poetic sentiment and story? Listen: I will tell you of love. Love is a phantom of the mind, a famine in a hungry heart. To love is to go forever yearning and empty. It is a gift that cannot be given, a stone that weighs you down, incapacitating instead of conferring power. It was spawned as part of the machinery of nature, a wayward link in the reproductive chain; but we live outside the natural world, we do not need such bonds. Had this creature here fulfilled my hopes I would have used him and gloried in him, but never loved him. Why should I waste emotion on him now?"

Kal gets to his feet, looking at Fern, addressing his mother. "I know many secrets," he says. "Secrets you would give much to share."

"Droppings from a feast table where you will never have a seat," retorts Morgus. "Keep them to yourself. I do not pick over other men's crumbs."

He moves away from her crabwise, vanishing into the shadows around the exit, but for a long while Fern seems to feel his eyes, watching her from the dark.

Fern does not sleep anymore, but sometimes she dreams. The same dream as before: a gray church, full of turning heads. From somewhere, there comes the boom of solemn music. This time she is watching, not taking part. There is a long white dress moving slowly up the aisle. It seems to have no occupant. The man is waiting for it beside a fountain of flowers: he is dark, stocky, slightly balding, with a clever, not-quite-handsome face, amusing and amused. She sees him vividly, and he is vividly familiar, spearing her with a strange kind of pain. She even knows his name: Marcus Greig. The dress places an invisible hand in his. "I'm not there!" Fern screams in a sudden panic. "Can't you see I'm not there?" But the ceremony proceeds, and she wrenches herself back to consciousness, sweating as if from a fever, forgetful that her body's trembling and the perspiration that soaks her are mere illusion. As she grows calmer, memories trickle back, details she has not thought of before, insignificant beside the greater priorities that burden her. She is supposed to marry Marcus; he may even be waiting at her bedside. Dimly she recalls that this was something she wanted, though her reasons for so doing have evaporated like raindrops in the sun. She knows now that she can take no such empty vows, that even to have considered it was a kind of madness that had nothing to do with either Morcadis or Fernanda. She reaches for another, older memory, a memory that has lain untouched at the back of her thought for what seems like aeons—a beach in Atlantis, golden with sunset, and waves breaking, and a man rising up out of the water to meet her like a sea god. But even as the image surfaces, it has changed. He is dark against the sea's glitter, too dark, and as he comes toward her she sees his face is the face of Ruvindra Laiï.

The fruit is ripening.

Fern wanders beneath the laden branches with Sysselore observing the swelling globes, seeing the strands of hair dripping with moisture, the burgeoning of new colors beneath the skin. Already some of the faces begin to look faintly recognizable, as if she has seen them in the other world, on a square screen or a printed page. Once in a rare while there will be one that does reappear, season after season, fading a little with every fruiting. "Whatever the reason," Sysselore says, "they cannot pass the Gate. Their soul may be eroded, or their will. They may be trapped by vain emotion, residue of a lost life—caught in a rut until their flame withers and vanishes utterly. Here is one." The head hangs low, within easy reach. The cheeks have an unhealthy pallor, blotched here and there with red; greasy threads of hair slip forward across the brow; more hair sprouts over the upper lip. Eyes and forehead are scrunched together in a blind scowl, savage and meaningless. As they watch, the eyelids split, bursting open, the mouth begins to jabber. But the light-blue stare is unfocused, the voice curiously remote, like a radio with the volume turned down. The words pour out in an unceasing stream, vehement, passionate, raucous, with now and then the echo of an identifiable language, but for the most part incomprehensible, all gibberish. "In the first couple of seasons he was much louder," says Sysselore. "He used to harangue us—Morgus understood him; she speaks many tongues. He doesn't see us now. In a day or two his eyes will become bloodshot and he'll start to rot from within." It is a face Fern knows, though she cannot recall the name; names are unimportant here, except in conjuration. Yet somehow she remembers the face as fuller, stronger, more solid, whereas the fruit, though barely mature, seems already shriveled, decayed before its time. It has become a weak, pathetic, shrunken object, where the last flicker of a soul is imprisoned, gleaming fitfully ere it expires. The eyes shine with a dreadful ferocity of spirit, but they are the eyes of a madman, expending his enmity on monsters that only he can see.

Most of the heads appear young, though they may have died old. "The sap of the Tree is strong," says Sysselore. "Morgus believes it was a Spirit once, old as the Oldest: immortal ichor runs in every bough. At the very least it is—an entity, something with a power all its own. Many of the fruit will wither into age before they fall."

"There was a tree in Paradise," Fern says. "Maybe this is the Tree of Purgatory."

"Paradise! Purgatory!" scoffs Sysselore. "You talk in clichés, like the old priests. Apples grew here once, so Morgus says, apples of gold whose juices were the nectar of the gods, conferring wisdom and youth. A serpent was coiled about the trunk to protect them, greater than all other serpents save only the Nenheedra; his venom was as deadly as the juice of the apples was sweet. Now—now the heads of the dead grow where golden apples once ripened, and a wild pig devours what the serpent used to protect. When the nature of Man changes, there may be apples here again. But I think you will wait a long time for another such harvest."

When she returns to the cave Fern remains, sitting astride a thick twist of root close to the bole. A part of the trunk is visible looming above her, like a tiny glimpse at the base of a gigantic tower—a construction of many towers welded together, living towers sprouting around a single core, curve melding with curve, growth with growth, to create a Babel among trees, clamorous with the din of birds and the gibbering of the heads. And all she sees are the lowest branches and the ground beneath; who knows what creatures may breed in the long, long journey toward the crown? It is a cold thought, like looking into eternity. She flinches away from it, shivering.

No sun penetrates this close to the bole. Farther away there are hollows full of dancing light, green-gold flecks that have filtered through the endless leaves to make their way to the ground, where they cavort like fireflies in the strange breezes that circle the outer reaches of the Tree. Where such breezes come from even Morgus does not know; perhaps from the Tree itself, breathing to its own rhythm, swaying to some secret music in its dark heart. The very sun that shines on the upper branches may be an emanation of the Tree's own thought, as unreal as the timeless pulse beat of day and night. Here below the bole, however, the hollows are forever sunless, overhung by shadowy clouds of foliage, encased in a permanent green twilight. She feels the Tree's power not only in the groping tanglewood of roots but in the crumbling soil beneath her feet, in the leaf mulch of innumerable seasons, in the ripening and rotting of the heads. It is a gluttony that feeds on itself, a greed that has outgrown its reach and is now condemned to ingrowing. And Morgus has drawn on that power, nourishing her Gift from an alien source, fattening her spirit on the Tree that harbors her like a gross parasite engorged with the blood of its host. It is a thing Fern has long sensed, without understanding, but now at last it becomes clear to her. Morgus and the Tree are bound together in an unholy union: her vast storehouse of flesh is merely the physical manifestation of her leechdom. Her mind, too, must have absorbed its great appetite with its strength: in the horror of her embrace Fern felt its smothering hunger, and the lust for absolute dominion looks out of the witch's eyes. But the Tree is fixed in a dimension of its own, outside reality, between worlds. Morgus is mortal, and mobile, and she would take her appetite into other realms, and feed there unsated, and spread the tendrils of her power through wider pastures. The Tree may be a monstrosity, but the thought of Morgus rampaging through Time and reality stabs Fern with a new and deeper dread. While the evil of Azmordis is a part of the world's evil, something to be fought and resisted in an unending conflict on the edge of defeat that can never be won and must never be lost, Morgus would be a bane outside such reckoning, capable of tipping the balance into darkness. And Fern is the mechanism she needs for her return, completing the coven of three, connecting her with the long-lost thread of the present. The flame of Fern's hatred chills inside her, becoming cold and hard as resolution. She has too many battles to fight and too little to fight them with. Morgus has taught her the ways of power; with her help Fern could forestall Azmordis. But she must do without help. She is trapped within the influence of the Tree, her body sleeps, and far away the dragon is stirring unrestrained, and there is danger to those she left behind. Faced with such need, her inadequacies no longer matter. She must elude Morgus, and find the way back, before the current of Time runs away from her forever.

In its hidden dell, safe in a cocoon of spells, the black fruit is almost mature.

In the dark time Fern lies with her eyes closed, simulating sleep. But the lids have become almost transparent: she can still dimly perceive the root tracery of walls and roof, the erratic pulse of the wormshine, the bluish glow of the spellfire reflected on the glistening moon of Morgus's face. Sysselore is at her shoulder, her long neck thrust forward, bulbous eyes agleam; Kal is nowhere to be seen. Fern can distinguish too much, and instinct or some deeper knowledge tells her why. Her spirit-body has been too long out of touch with its fleshly home; it is beginning to lose its shape, forgetting the precepts of physical incarnation. If she is not restored very soon she may become only an amorphous blob of ectoplasm, a phantom of half-remembered anatomy, unable to resume a garment that does not fit her degenerate form. But surely Morgus must have reckoned with such a possibility. Fern would be no use to her as a permanent ghost.

"When? When?" It is Sysselore who speaks, eagerness and fear commingling in her voice.

"When she is ready. When I am sure of her." The pictures in the smoke are invisible, only a light that is not that of the fire passes over Morgus's features, changing them. "Then I will pour her back into her mortal body and possess her utterly. But we must be diligent: she has more power than Alimond, perhaps more power than I have seen in any individual in a hundred centuries. Her Gift has been so long suppressed it is hard to measure, but I know it is strong. The spellfire has shown us none like her since I was last in the world. Small wonder the Old One seeks to destroy or ensnare her. When I can wield her Gift unhindered, I will know its limits."

"Alimond was obsessive—dangerous. How do we know this one is not the same?"

"Alimond was a fool, blinkered by her own obduracy. Impetuosity and clumsiness hampered what Gift she had. She was not destined for us; indeed, I saw nothing in her future but futility and death: that was why I let her go. Fernanda is far more intelligent but she is still pliable, untried, untempered. The beggar Gabbandolfo has made no imprint on her soul. She is mine to shape: my creature, my creation. Her very destiny is mine, to rough-hew as I wish. Soon, the hour will come—the hour when Time begins again. The life of the Tree runs in us both: the changeless cycles without spring or winter, the leaves forever green, forever rotting. So will it be with us. We will slough off these worn-out chrysalids and appear as once we were, strong in youth and beauty. Through her, we will go back. I tell you, I have watched this modern world, and we will not need to rule by seducing kings or bewitching lost sailors. There are other ways now. There are crystal balls that operate without magic, visions without a spellfire, ships that fly, wires that speak. There are weapons our heroes never dreamed of, steel tubes that spit death, fireballs that could engulf a whole city. The human race has invented a thousand new forms of torment, a thousand new fashions on the road to suffering. Through Morcadis, we will learn them all—we will use them—we will reenter the world—taste it—dominate—*live*. The Unnamed has reigned many ages without rival. In any case, what has *he* ever been but a shadow in men's minds, one who bargains for souls that we could reach out and take? We will be *real*. I will take back my island, the green island of Britain, and this time no one shall wrest it from me. *No one.*" Fern cannot see Morgus's expression clearly through her eyelids but Fern can hear the relentless steamroller of Morgus's voice, the insatiable lust, the implacable will.

"We must hurry," says Sysselore, injecting a tiny needle of doubt, maybe for provocation, maybe because of Morgus's use of the final "me," excluding her partner. "Sometimes I think she is starting to fade."

"She cannot," says Morgus. "She does not appreciate her own condition. While she believes in her body, it will endure."

"Kal might have told her."

"If he did . . . I will fill his entrails with liquid fire. I will boil the blood in his veins. He will know what it is to burn from within. I do not tolerate treachery."

A red gleam strafes her face, coming from nothing in the cave. "So," she murmurs, concentrating on images Fern cannot see, "the Old One has found another to charm his winged snakeling. Look at him!—a dotard, gray as dirt, a bastard unworthy of his forefathers. Laïï is dead indeed."

"Yet you have not found it."

"His season will come; it comes for them all. He is dead a week—a year—a day: what is Time to us? It was written in the ashes, whispered in the rainsong. Such a one cannot die unremarked. He must ripen here soon. And then—he will tell me his secrets. All his secrets. I shall suck the truth from him like juice, squeeze out his thoughts like seeds, till there is only the husk of his skull for the pig to chew on."

"All this for a wishing pebble!" Sysselore derides.

"Imbecile. Your brain has rotted like the fruit. I should feed you to the pig—there would be a sweet justice in that—but I fear there is too little meat on your bones to interest him. I have no need of the *Stone*. But the dragon—that is another matter. The Old One knows the value of such a weapon, in any age. A flying steed that can outpace the wind, a firestorm with mind and magic. A dragon is not simply the manifestation of might but its living symbol: who since the dragon charmers has ever controlled one? Yet through this gray half-caste *he* seeks just such control. We have taken the girl from him; it would be more than satisfying to take the dragon, too. I will show him who is the true power on earth. When I find the head—"

"Only a dragon charmer can talk to a dragon," says Sysselore.

"Do you dare to doubt me? Now, when we are so close?"

Sysselore flinches from her, squeaking and chittering in protest, and Morgus quenches the fire with a gesture. The smoke swirls in between them, and when Fern opens her eyes they are gone. She sees the witch dispassionately now, without hate, as a growing tumor that must be cut out to save existence itself. Not an enemy to be killed but a disease to eradicate. She lies there, between thought and oblivion, rerunning Morgus's speech, dreaming of terminal surgery.

It is time to plan. Fern watches the spellfire herself now, sewing with big, ragged stitches at a few scraps of old cloth. "I want another pillow," she tells Sysselore, and the hag laughs as Fern knew she would, mocking her love of comfort, but she provides a needle made from the bone of a bird, unused pieces of clothing, unraveled strands of silk. But it is not a pillow that Fern is making. In the fire, she lets the images show what they will. The smoke fades into dust devils dancing across the surface of a desert. One of them assumes a specific shape, impossibly tall, manlike yet not a man, pacing the sand with a strange flowing motion. The face is a study in vapor, the features blurring and re-forming, unable to maintain fixity, but the eyes gaze steadily out, narrowed against the sun, long slits too bright to look at. The smoky figure fills her with a grayness of fear, a sudden chill that stills her working hands. As it moves across the empty waste it grows in height and substance, drawing the dust into itself; its questing gaze mirrors the flames of sunset. Dusk steals like a cloud over the land, and in the distance there are campfires twinkling, and tethered animals, and the conical shapes of tents. The pacing figure halts, grown now to monstrous size. The stars shine through the shadow pattern of its ribs. It stretches out its arm, spreading wavering fingers, and the remote fires sink beneath the pressure of its hand. And far away Fern hears the voices of the nomads, calling on the God of the Dark in terror and worship. "*Azmordias! Azmordias!*"

Night merges into night. The vast spaces of the desert close in; the dust whorls pale into snowflakes, whisked into a blizzard by a yowling wind. Beyond, she sees two—no, three—slots of yellow light, windows in a sheer wall. The shape of a roof looms above, with pointed gables and a shaggy outline suggesting thatch. The blizzard prowls around the building, plucking straw from the eaves and probing the unglazed window slots. Shutters slam against it. Within, there is the sound of carousing, of songs defying the winter cold. But outside the snowflakes are sucked into a column of storm and darkness, and a glance like white lightning flickers over gable and wall. The shutters are flung back, lamps and songs extinguished, and from those who cower at the invasion comes a single cry of fear and prayer: "Utzmord!"

It was easy to be a god, in the days of magic and superstition, when the immortals, greedy for power, fed on belief and grew strong, and only the Gifted gainsaid them. Now Science has reduced the world to a whirligig of molecules, and magic is driven into corners and over the edge of reality to the borderland of Being. But Azmordis—Azmordis thrives forever, changing with mankind, learning new ways to replace the old. Maybe it is harder for him, and the world's weariness corrodes his dark heart, and a creeping despair contaminates all that he does, but if so, that will only make him the more vengeful and bitter—he who knows no pity, least of all for himself. And very briefly—in a vision, in a nightmare—Fern seems to glimpse the abyss of his spirit: an existence without fear of death or hope of life, aeons of nothingness to fill, every emotion, every passion turned to a bile that chokes him even as he spews it out. Envy consumes him—for the brevity of mortal lives, their freshness, their endless renewal. In the death of others he seeks his own. But the aftertaste of sweetness fades all too quickly, and there is only the void. In the spellfire, Fern sees idols and temples, ritual and sacrifice. Perhaps she is watching not fragments of the past but the memories of Azmordis, scenes from the days when his hunger was a new-kindled flame and his power over the early races still aroused him—the days before all was drowned in the dreariness of unending hate.

She touches his unwary mind—and flinches away, lest he should feel her there. His souvenirs are too long ago and far removed for him to sense her gaze, but she knows now why the spell-scene shrinks from closer encounters. Like Ruvindra Laï, he might be aware of the watcher, and seek her out. And suddenly she remembers how sometimes, in the world beyond, she felt herself observed, and how once she saw the eyes of Morgus staring at her from the depths of a mirror.

She should have learned and been more vigilant. Too late now.

The images grow smaller and are lost in smoke. The flames wither.

"So what are you stitching, little witch? Simple Susan sewing samplers . . . What kind of a spell is this?"

Kal.

"There are many kinds of spells," Fern says, ignoring sarcasm. "You might say this was a part of one."

"And does my dear mother know that you are embroidering a veil for her sight—or a net to snare her?"

"Neither," she retorts. "This is hardly embroidery. I am setting crooked stitches in old rags of material. I told Sysselore it was for an extra pillow. She laughed at me for needing to sleep soft."

"You always go softly, don't you? Soft-footed, soft-voiced, weaving your enchanted webs so quietly that none will know they are there." He crouches close to her, his breath warm against her cheek and sharp as the breath of a fox, his splayed hand beside her thigh, the long fingers probing the ground. "Come. What will you give me for my discretion? I see you clearer than Morgus, for all her power and her knowledge."

"What could you tell her?" Fern holds up her crude handiwork. "I have nothing to hide."

"Except a certain black plum that must be almost ripe now. Is it fat and sweet? Is it juicy? Would it tempt my appetite?"

"It is food for pigs," she says with a shrug, "if that is to your taste."

He draws back, his feral odor changing with anger. "You go too far, little witch," he rasps.

For the first time Fern turns to meet his eyes. "We play with words," she says. "A game of insult and insinuation. What is there in a *game* to sting your pride? You wanted to bargain with me, or so you said: very well, we will bargain. But not in a game, not for trivia. We will bargain for life and death, for friendship in danger, for all things lasting and true. We will make a pact, you and I. Fernanda and Kaliban. Is that what you wish?"

"Fernanda and Kaliban. Beauty and the beast." He savors the words with a curious mixture of satisfaction and derision. "And what would my part be in this pact?"

"To stand my friend, and aid me, even against Morgus."

"And yours?"

"I would be your debtor, to pay however and whenever you choose, so long as it does not dishonor me, or cause me injury."

"A clever proviso!" The wolf's smile splits his face. "You are indeed among the Crooked Ones, Simple Susan. No doubt you have a fine sense of dishonor."

"We bargain for your friendship. A friend would not injure or shame me. If you fulfill your part, there should be no qualification required."

"Cleverer and cleverer. You are far neater with words than with stitches."

"You can refuse," says Fern.

The ruby gleam flickers in his slanting orbs—flickers and dims, leaving pupil and iris altogether dark. Only the whites shine in the velvet shadows beneath his heavy brow. In the uncertain glimmer of the cave he seems a creature all darkness, an overpowering physical presence more sensed than seen, malicious, unchancy, but not treacherous. Fern gambles on that. Not treacherous. In the gloom she feels his festering unhappiness as a tangible thing, a rawness that must not be touched, a hidden wound, bleeding internally. Yet the night-black stare conceals all suffering, challenges, taunts.

"No one has ever made me an offer so noble," he drawls at last. "So high sounding! So gallant! So generous and so proud! We might be back in the days of chivalry."

"Were there any?"

"So they say. All I remember of those knights and heroes was that they hunted me through the woods like the beast I resemble. They hunted me with hounds, and my scent drove them mad; with horses, and I dragged them into bogs; with men, and . . . I bit out their throats. But armored collars are hard on the teeth." He grins a jagged grin. "So much for chivalry. And now you offer me not a thieves' bargain, but a pact of honor. I give, you take, and we call it friendship. Some honor. Still, it might be sweet to have you in my debt, little witch. To hold you in the palm of my hand, to claim my price at my pleasure—at my leisure. What particular aid do you want, Fernanda?"

"First, you must agree."

"Very well. It is agreed."

She extends her hand; he grips it lightly, withholding his strength. She feels the calluses on his fingers.

"And now," he says, "what *do* you want, Fernanda my friend?"

"I have to return to the real world, the world of Time. You come and go without Morgus's permission: you must know the way. Take me with you."

Her sewing is finished, her plan almost complete. She sits beneath the boughs in her secretive hollow, waiting. The black fruit is ripe now; the long hair hangs down, veiling the ugly neck stump, the features are full-grown, the ebony skin gleams as if it has been waxed. Under oblique brows the eyes appear but lightly closed, as if in sleep. The mouth, too, slumbers, its subtlety and tension gone with the waking mind. She waits long, disciplining herself to patience; the Tree cannot be hurried. Sometimes a faint quiver contracts the muscles, and she starts up in eagerness, but always the dark face remains immobile, that flicker of motion merely an illusion, a trick of the light, at most a reflex of the growing process. Then at last, after too many disappointments to mention, a spasm comes that is more prolonged, and the eyes open. They are blue as the sky and crackling with a cold brilliance, like crystals of ice. Even though she has seen them in the spellfire, nothing has prepared her for their intensity, for the savage vital force that neither death nor the Tree can diminish. The mouth hardens into character, parts on a word.

"You."

Not an accusation: an acknowledgment.

"Yes," she says. "I watched you in the spellfire. I have been a long time watching and waiting."

"I caught the old hags at it, once or twice," he says, "peering through the smoke, spying out my ways. But you are young for a hag."

"I will grow older. One day I will be a hag in my turn."

"I think not. A hag is a predatory creature: a harpy without wings, a succubus without sex appeal. There is that in you that will never be predatory."

"You saw so much, in one look?"

"In the moment before death your vision is very clear," he responds. "And now—now I am dead, and I must hang here till I rot. I have to pay the price for my life. It was not a life of virtue or principle, but I enjoyed it; so the price is high. Did you come to ease my purgatory?"

"Not exactly. Before you pass the Gate, you have some unfinished business in the world. I . . . . could help you finish it."

"What business is that?" asks the head, and the expression shifts into skepticism, becoming at once guileful and discerning.

"With the dragon."

"I am dead. I am sterile fruit on a fruitless tree. I am a voice without a throat, a mind without a heart. Hunger without a belly. Perhaps this is not really death but a state in between, unalive and undead. Mortification of the flesh. Refinement of the soul. Who knows? Anyway, the dragon is the business of others now. My connection with the world has been permanently severed. And why should you help me, witch-girl? Are you sure it isn't *my* help that *you* need?"

"Both," Fern admits. She knows she cannot handle him as she handled Kaliban, hiding deviousness with candor, using another's unhappiness and resentment for her own ends. Where Kal is cunning, mocking, suspicious, Ruvindra is acute, disconcerting, dangerously perceptive. For him, truth alone will serve. "We need each other. The dragon is in the power of the Oldest Spirit—"

"That is impossible."

"A descendant of your kin has the dragon penned in a well—or at least in a pit or cave beneath a well. He calls himself Laye, Jerrold Laye. His heritage is corrupted, like his name. Whether he has any love for dragonkind I do not know, but he is greedy, greedy for power and life and the opportunities he thinks have passed him by. He has invited the Unnamed into his body, into his *mind*; I don't believe he could eject him now even if he would. Through him, the Oldest has immediate contact with the dragon. He will use the dragon without regard for his true nature; you know that. He may slay him, or arrange for him to be slain, in order to obtain the splinter of Lodestone within. He has always lusted after it, though he cannot touch it or use it himself. You let this happen, Ruvindra Laï. It is your business. You alone can put it right."

"That is fighting talk," says the head, "from a stray spirit who has not even given me her name."

The blue of his gaze seems to enter her like a probing ray, penetrating to the back of her thought, to the nucleus of her soul, seeing what she is, and the truth in her heart. And Fern stares back, eye to eye, soul to soul, and in that mutual seeing she senses once more the link between them, the bond that is beyond mere understanding, beyond love. She needs no persuasion for Ruvindra, no bargaining. The necessity is enough.

"I am called Fernanda," she responds.

"And your Gift name?"

"I will be Morcadis, when I am ready."

"And did the old hag choose that?" he asks shrewdly. "The fat hag Morgus, who crowns herself a queen."

"Even she makes mistakes," Fern says. "She has taught me how to use my Gift—given her slayer a name to live up to."

"So you hate her?"

"Hate burns the heart away, leaving you with ashes. I will keep mine cold, until I want it."

For a minute he is silent, and the many angles of his face seem to tighten, concentrating on a focal thought, an instant of dark revelation. "Why do we meet now, who might have met in life? It is too late for me, witch-girl, too late for us both. My hour—if I had an hour—is long past. Go back to your spellfire and look for someone else to help you."

"There is no one else," she retorts bleakly. "I will come again."

"You waste your breath."

"I am a spirit. I have no breath to waste."

He laughs a sudden harsh laugh, making the leaves dance. "Then we are two!"

"Do not laugh so loud," says Fern, "or you may shake loose from your anchorage, and the wild pig will find you, when next he roots here. Or Morgus may hear you. My spells divert her from this place, but they cannot make you either invisible or inaudible. She, too, wants your aid, and she is less patient than me."

The head does not answer, merely gazing at her through narrowed eyes. Unwillingly she moves away, and sets off back to the cave.

In that timeless place, Fern senses that somewhere her Time is running out. The spellfire shows her an old house, grim visaged, hooded with roofs of stone, and at a casement she sees a pale face heavily curtained with hair. But the casement is barred, and the face alone and desperate. "Who is that?" asks Sysselore, leaning over her shoulder, cobweb tresses brushing her cheek.

"I do not know. The magic is willful; it reveals nothing to the purpose."

But she knows.

Now the fruit is ripe she fears to leave it, lest her fragile protection prove inadequate and the hog strays there, pounding at the Tree roots till it falls from the bough, or Morgus discovers it in her absence. Yet she is equally afraid to visit it too often, to arouse suspicion, to be followed unawares. She ventures out when the witches sleep, in the half-light before dawn, collecting fungi and wild herbs to excuse her roaming. Morgus has taught her much plant lore and she finds a use for some of her harvest beyond that of study. Outside the cave she wanders as if at random, watching and listening with all her senses, approaching the hollow only when she is confident of being unobserved. "We must go soon," she tells the head.

"I am going nowhere. I have finished with my life; only the Gate awaits me. Besides, this fruit would not last long in the real world. Two days at most."

"We don't need long," says Fern. "Here you may last awhile, but to what end? Morgus will suck out the pips of your thought and burrow like a worm into all your secrets. She, too, wants to harness the dragon's power."

"Whatever she does, it will avail her nothing. That Gift is mine alone."

"Yours and your descendant's," Fern reminds him. "Do not forget Jerrold Laye."

"A degenerate. You said so yourself. No other could understand dragonkind as I did. To touch the mind of a spirit all fire, to experience passion in the raw, hunger, rage, love—yes, love—uncomplicated by the mazes of human thought, unchecked by meaningless scruples—only the strongest could survive such a contact. A weaker man would be driven mad."

"Maybe Laye *is* mad," says Fern, "but he is still a vehicle for the Old One. *He* has no regard for the mental condition of his instruments."

The dark mouth twists in contempt. "Such a one as this Laye—corruptible and possessed—could never hold any true communion with a dragon. They perceive human reactions with an enhanced intensity, almost as if in color. A lie is dull, tainted, *dis*colored. They see all the affectations of man, our morality, hypocrisy, deceit, as inhibiting the vital elements of nature—a wanton folly that is beyond their comprehension. To communicate, the dragon charmer must set aside all barriers, he must open his mind to that of the dragon. They do not speak as we do but their thought takes shape in your head, there is an intuitive understanding, a joining of two spirits. Once that bond is made, you are changed forever. The fire has entered you, and it will burn until you die." He fixes her with the blue lance of his gaze, but she does not turn away. "It burns in me still, even here, but this is the last smolder. Soon it will be ashes."

"If you were so close to the dragons," Fern asks hesitantly, "how could you have destroyed the other eggs? When you went to the dragons' graveyard and robbed the nest, why not leave the ones you did not want?"

"You don't understand," he says, and there is an edge in his voice sharper than a naked blade. "I left no rival, no possible threat for the future. *I did as dragons do.*"

Fern absorbs this in silence. "This opening of the mind," she says at last, "this conjunction of two spirits . . . did you try that with me, when our eyes met in the spellfire?"

"No," he answers. "But perhaps *you* did."

Later on, in the daylight period, Fern watches Morgus. She is searching with increased determination, covering ground already explored, peering under every leaf, into every knothole. Soon she will pass close to the dell where only a thin film of magic and the convoluted ground hide the black fruit. She may sense the perimeter of the spell brushing her thought with an unfamiliar bewilderment. Fern, knowing her own inexperience, fears a possible clumsiness may betray her: Morgus's perceptions are too acute to be easily bemazed. Fern observes the witch through a slit between root and earth, seeing her draw nearer to the hollow, moving slower with every step, as though conscious that somewhere close by there are shadows that have eluded her. Now she has almost reached the penumbra of the spell. Fern thrusts down panic, stretching out with her mind, probing the labyrinthine branches far overhead for inspiration—for a creature she can use, a brain simple enough to be malleable. Somewhere above she senses a clot of matter sagging from a bough, a whining buzz of sound—the drone of busy wings, the many-celled awareness of the swarm. Her thought quickens into recklessness, pushing self-doubt aside. Softly, softly the power flows from her, murmured words giving it direction and purpose. A hundred feet above, the swarm feels the menace.

They swoop down on Morgus in a wedge-shaped arrow of rage, a multiple mind with but a single thought. Not bees, as Fern expected—though the vicinity of the Tree is almost flowerless

and she has only ever seen one, a cuckoo bee that hives alone—
but wasps. Fat black wasps with scarlet stings, zooming in on their
target like a dive-bomber, whirling, darting, stabbing. Taken off
guard, it is a moment before Morgus can protect herself—before
the crack of Command that has her tormentors frying in midair,
sizzling into cinerous particles that fall harmlessly to the ground.
But she has been stung: there are pinpoints of red on her cheek
and the flesh roll of her neck. Fern, sinking deep into the dead
leaves, sees her turn toward the cave. She will be back, wanting
to explore the reason for such an attack—knowing there may be
no reason, since the denizens of the Tree are often wayward and
savage—coldly curious, nursing, perhaps, a burgeoning suspicion.
She will be back very soon. Even here, there is no Time left.

When the witch has gone Fern clambers down into the hollow.

The head is waiting, watching her with its hawk's stare, dark
lips slightly parted to show the glint of teeth, a trace of sap dripping redly from its neck stump. It greets her with a challenge, and
the sharp edge of a smile. "What now, sorceress? What witch
games have you been playing up there?"

"I was saving your rind," says Fern, choosing the noun with
deliberation. "Morgus was close by: she knows she has missed
something near here. I called up a swarm of wasps to distract
her."

"I heard them," says the head. "Also her curses. You are
skilled for your years."

"Not skilled enough. She didn't curse: that was a Command.
My champions burned in midflight. It was a temporary measure
only; she will return, and shortly. I must leave when it is dark,
with or without you. The choice is yours."

"Can you give me a choice?" sneers Ruvindra. "I am an apple
ripe for plucking, by you or by her. I am a dainty for your delecta-
tion. Would you offer me a *real* choice? Would you destroy me
with your witch-fire, even as Morgus destroyed those wasps?

Would you set me free—free of this shape, this punishment, free to pass the Gate into eternity?"

Fern hesitates, trembling suddenly, though she does not know why. "You are bigger than a wasp," she says. "I am not sure—I am not sure if the heat would be enough. A strong fire needs more fuel than a little spell. I could steal some fire crystals, I suppose . . . Yes, I would do it. If that is what you wish."

"Won't you set conditions? That is the way of witchkind. Nothing for nothing."

"No," says Fern, with a touch of pride. "That is not *my* way. I offered you a choice. Choose freely."

"Very well," says the head. "I will hold you to your promise. I choose the completion of my death—a swift passage through the Gate instead of a slow lingering in between. Do not forget. But first I will go with you as you asked, back to the world of Life, to forestall the Oldest of liars, the Stealer of Souls—if we can."

Fern smiles—a great warmth rushes through her, so her spirit-body becomes suddenly radiant, though she does not know it. She stretches out one bright finger, stroking the black hair. The dark face seems to soften. "It will be hard," he says, "returning to a dimension of strength and vitality, in this form. When I lived, I lived as dragons do, with every fiber of my being, every nerve. Now I am a stunted misshapen thing—a gargoyle—emasculated—helpless. A fruit without seed—a head without body or limbs."

"I will be your limbs," says Fern.

Her tone is very serious, as in a vow, and quiet falls between them.

"Do you seek to touch my heart?" mocks Ruvindra at last. "I have no heart. The Tree does not provide such inessentials."

"I will be your heart," says Fern.

· XII ·

On the day Ragginbone returned to Yorkshire, Will and Gaynor had left Dale House shortly after breakfast. They took the aging Ford Fiesta in which Will paid his occasional visits to the university or went on exploratory drives in search of scenery to distort in his pictures. There were sketch pads and canvases in the back, the seats were daubed with random smears of paint, and the external bodywork had been enlivened with representations of holes from which various insect and animal heads peeked out. "Fern won't go in this car," Will remarked. "She says it's embarrassing. I hope you don't mind too much?"

"I don't mind at all." Privately Gaynor wondered if Fern's objections were actually founded on the stuttering condition of the engine and the delayed reaction time of the brakes, but she did not say so. "Do we know how to find this museum?" she asked.

"Not offhand," said Will, "but I know York pretty well. Anyway, we can always ask."

They asked several times before they happened on the museum, more or less by chance. Gaynor found her confidence restored in the familiar ambience of unlived-in rooms, of bleared glass display cases, of the carefully conserved scribblings of history. This was her normal work environment, a haunt little frequented by visitors, where fragments of the past were studied, restored, illuminated, giving brief glimpses of light in the darkness of lost ages. There was a smell of dust hovering, awaiting only the departure of a wandering vacuum cleaner before settling comfortably back into place. The rooms must once have been heavy with late-Victorian gloom, overfurnished, somberly curtained, but now naked windows let in the gray daylight, and neutral paintwork reduced everything to a background. The exhibits had taken over. In her own workplace Gaynor often felt the books had both presence and personality: the aloof superiority of priceless tomes, the secrets reaching out to her from half-obliterated pages, the arcane wisdom groping for new expression. They were awakened by her touch, alive and curious. Here, however, the books seemed crippled with age and intellectual neglect, collector's items, preserved, imprisoned, unread. She could almost hear the creaking of arthritic spines, the crackle of desiccated paper. Occasional patches of color stood out, vivid as if new-painted, a stylized illustration or elaborately decorated capital; but they were few and far between. It was the gleam of gold leaf that drew her to the dragons.

The book was the centerpiece of one of the smaller showcases, open at the section Gaynor had seen fleetingly on the television. "A grate dragon, grater than anye other lyving beaste, ravaged the kyngdom, devouring anye who stood in yts way. Onlie one Knyghte was found brave enough to stande against yt . . ."

"It does sound like your dream," Gaynor said.

"Described by someone who wasn't there. Still, frontline journalism was in its infancy in the Middle Ages—and anyone who *was* there wouldn't have lived to tell the tale. How about asking for the curator, and seeing if we can get a proper look at this?"

The curator—the elderly young man Gaynor remembered from the television program—was stirred almost to enthusiasm by

Gaynor's interest and her credentials. "We have so few visitors," he
explained. "I had thought, after the TV publicity . . . but no. People don't want *books*, you see. They don't want *knowledge*. They
want to gawp at the assassin's knife, the courtesan's jewelry, the
collar of the royal lapdog. We get the odd American, of course, researching a thesis, or someone writing a book, but they tend to be
more crank than scholar. Chasing the Grail legend, or one of those
conspiracy theories, Freemasons and stuff. Not *genuine* study, just
some hypothesis they've got hold of, and they think they can attach the evidence to it afterward, like hanging bells on a Christmas tree. Usually they want to spend more time talking about how
clever they are than actually looking at the exhibits."

"We're interested in dragons," Gaynor said a little nervously,
aware that this, too, might be labeled cranky.

The curator, however, seemed pleasantly surprised. "Dragons," he murmured. "Well, that's different. No one's interested in
dragons. They believe in secret societies and magical artifacts,
but a dragon is just a crocodile story that got out of hand. Still,
I've always thought the symbolism might reward analysis. Is that
what you're studying?"

"More or less," said Will.

"I'm his supervisor," Gaynor explained, giving Will a minatory
look. "He's doing a doctorate, but he's quite sensible about it. He
doesn't have any weird ideas, honestly." With his connections, she
amended privately, he doesn't need them. "He's working on the 'Origins of the Dragon in British Mythology.' "

"Strictly speaking," the curator pointed out with what might
have been suspicion, "there's no such concept as British mythology."

"Celtic, Norse, Greco-Roman . . ."

"Oh, all right . . ."

The curator removed the book from the display case and carried it to an upstairs room where an untidy desk was cramped between filing cabinets under the slope of the roof. "You'll be

careful, of course," he adjured. "It's from Dr. Laye's collection; we have a number of his things on loan at the moment. You may know of him: he's on the board here."

"I saw him on the television," said Gaynor, trying to sound natural.

"An extraordinary man," the curator said, with a nuance in his manner that Will could not quite clarify. It might have been merely the resentment of a weaker character outweighed by one more forceful, or it might have been something else. Apprehension, uncertainty, *fear* . . . "Curiously enough, he, too, has an interest— almost an obsession—with dragons. Perhaps you ought to . . . speak to him."

Gaynor missed the hesitation, but Will didn't. "I don't think so," she said. "I mean, we won't trouble him. He isn't here, is he?"

"Not today."

"Do you know of any other documents we ought to be studying?"

"I'll have a look for you."

With the departure of the curator she turned to the book, her nervousness vanishing in professional absorption. "It's vellum," she informed Will. "The condition is almost perfect. I've never seen one more beautiful. It really should be in a major museum, not an obscure place like this. Don't touch it! I'll turn the pages." It began with an account of how Shaitan, presumably the Devil, made the first dragons out of stone and fire, inhabiting their bodies with hungry spirits from below the nethermost regions of Hell. "And those elementals, being born of the grate heate of the Inferno, took fire even in lyfe, and breathed flames of Hell, and poysonous fumes; but their spirits were tempered with the cunnynge of Shaitan, and they spoke with tongues, and there was sorcerie in the glaunce of their eyes. And he sente them forthe into the world, to be a plague on beastes and menne." Various accounts followed, some familiar, some new or strangely altered, of dragons

and their activities. The story of St. George was set in Egypt; another tale featured the Leviathan sleeping beneath the ocean's
floor until the end of the world, when it would awake to swallow
the sun. ("Not a dragon, a serpent," said Will. "The Sea Serpent,
Jiormungund, the Nenheedra. Fern saw it once.") There were few
details, however, to flesh out the substance of Will's dream. The
dragon who had swallowed "a thyng of grate power and magicke"
was described as growing to enormous size and finally being consumed in its own fires, while the warrior who had confronted it
joined the ranks of other heroes, lost in the realm of mystery and
myth. In due course the curator returned with a stack of manuscripts and a couple of more recent books bound in calf and printed
on paper. A plunge into the filing cabinets offered the opportunity
to trace related material.

"This is going to take ages," said Will. "I hadn't realized."

"It's called work," Gaynor said with a rueful smile.

"Somehow, I don't really believe we'll find anything of use."

"We won't know till we've finished."

Around three o'clock Will departed to take Lougarry for a
walk, though they had left the car window open and she was
quite capable of taking herself. Gaynor remained at the desk, im-
mersed in a welter of arcana, turning from manuscript to file and
back again, scrawling notes on a piece of scrap. The habit of
study cocooned her, shutting out darkness and danger, numbing
anxiety. She found herself hoping against hope that this would all
prove useful, searching for something that constantly eluded
her—something hiding between the words, behind the tales. But
whatever it was, she could not find it. One manuscript in particular held her attention: the story of "a Tamer of dragons, who could
speke with them, and they would answere, and their fire did not
burn him, for he had the countenaunce of his House. His ancestor was blackened in the flames of Taebor Infernes, father of
dragons, and lyved, and no other flame could burn him, nor anye

of his kyn." But later pages were missing, and what the Tamer did was unrevealed. Gaynor sensed the story was important, but she did not know why, and wondered if the pricking of instinct was merely unsatisfied curiosity. She pushed both manuscript and file away, assailed by the recurring image of Fern's still face, feeling ineffectual and frustrated.

And then it happened. The room around her—the sloping planes of ceiling and skylight, the narrow rhomboids of wall, the many corners of cabinet and desk—seemed to shift very slightly, as if adjusting to another dimension. One moment she felt secure, unthinking, fretting only at her problem; the next she was being crowded, crushed, folded away between hard, flat surfaces, boxed into a tiny cube of existence where no one would ever find her. She tried to scream, but the constricted air squeezed the voice from her throat. She struggled to get up, and the chair tumbled, and the desk seemed to tilt, spilling its clutter on the floor. And from the crack between the dimensions—the splinter of nothing between time and Time, somewhere and elsewhere— eyes watched her, flickering and vanishing as the door opened and the room jolted abruptly back into place.

"Are you all right?" asked the curator. "What has happened here?"

"I—I'm sorry," stammered Gaynor. "I must have fallen asleep."

The curator may have believed her, but she knew better now than to believe herself.

"Well?" she said to Will, over a beer in a dim corner of a student pub. "What do we do next?"

"You know the answer to that one," he retorted. "I've been thinking about it all afternoon. I don't like it, but we've no alternative. It's been obvious all along. You needn't come if you don't want to."

"I'm coming," Gaynor whispered.

"Fine," said Will. "I'll go and call a mate, fix up a sofa for the night—or a sofa and a floor, since I expect that's what you'll prefer. Then we'll go out for a really good meal—French, I think, with Italian undertones—and you can tell me the story of your life. Afterward—some time afterward—I'll kiss you. Things may even go further, though not too far. You're not the sort of girl to be hurried, and this is the wrong moment for hurrying."

Gaynor gaped at him. "You're not serious," she said, pulling herself together. "We're supposed to be helping Fern—"

"And tomorrow," Will persisted, "we'll pay a call on Dr. Jerrold Laye."

Gaynor's indignation stopped in midflow. "I see," she said.

"Do you?" he responded. Her face showed sudden doubt. "I remember the first time I saw you. I was sixteen, so you must have been about twenty. You'd come to the house with Fern on your way to a Christmas party. It was somewhere outside London, and you were driving. Fern looked immaculate the way she always does, sort of perfectly finished, red spangly dress, high-heeled shoes. You wore black, which doesn't suit you, something with lots of tatty lace, and you'd tied your hair back but it had burst the elastic, and you had flat squashy boots for driving. You didn't look pretty, or glamorous, but I thought you so bloody sexy. *A sweet disorder in the dress* . . . I said to myself: 'One day, I'm going to have that girl.' I don't know that I meant it seriously, not then. But I could have picked your face out in a crowd any time after that night. Any time."

"It wasn't *tatty* lace," Gaynor muttered. "It was antique."

"Same difference."

"And Fern's dress was burgundy, not red. I've never seen her wear red. It's a bit flamboyant for her."

"Anything else you'd like to correct? I must point out it's *my* memory. If I want to remember a red dress and tatty lace, I bloody well will. I suppose all you noticed of me was a grubby schoolboy who leered at you from the stairs?"

"Actually," said Gaynor, carefully noncommittal, "I told Fern I thought you'd be causing a lot of trouble in a few years' time."

Will gave her an impish grin. "I already was."

"That's what Fern said."

He went to telephone, and she sat finishing her drink. All my life, she thought, I'm going to remember this. Not just the horror and the magic—the phantom in the snow, the gray beckoning finger of Dr. Jerrold Laye—but this moment, this dark, crowded, beery interior, and waiting for Will to come back from the telephone. All my life . . . A wave of feeling washed over her, so violent that she shook from the impact of it, a mixture of shock and revelation, of wonder and happiness and terror. She thought of her previous encounters with that feeling, of the giddying highs and lows of her six-year relationship with a married man who had ultimately left his wife, but not for her. It would be so easy to tell herself, in hope, in fear: *This is different.* She mustn't dare to think such thoughts, not of Will, who was her best friend's brother, who had more than his fair share of charm, who took nothing seriously, not even the Dark. Fern's spirit was lost, and a shadow lay beyond the next dawn, and all she had was this one evening, to live in it with all her senses, saving it for memory, expecting no more. But treacherous longing and inevitable doubt would not be so lightly thrust aside, and when Will returned he found her pale and quiet, her drink undrunk, her responses monosyllabic.

"Come on," he said, and they went. Afterward—long afterward—Gaynor realized she had never even noticed what that forever-to-be-remembered pub was called.

The restaurant, as Will had promised, offered a Mediterranean menu, a French wine list, Italian waiters. It was cramped, busy, and noisy, but they did not notice, too absorbed in each other to be distracted by extraneous details. For an hour or two they set aside their current preoccupations to explore each other's lives, exchange ideas and hopes, to luxuriate in the enchantment of mutual understanding. It's just a game, Gaynor told herself, it's always just a game, but she had never really grasped the rules, so she always staked too much, lost too much, and was left in the end impoverished and alone. But for this time—this little time—she would pretend the game was for real, and abandon herself to the illusion of a perfect companionship. Will's smile teased her but his eyes were serious, or so she fancied, and in their steady gaze she felt her heart shiver. "Fern once told me you're the sort of exceptionally nice girl who always falls for a bad lot," he said as she concluded the saga of her past affair.

"Did she?" Gaynor's flicker of indignation died swiftly, giving way to a resigned weariness. "Anyway, I thought I was supposed to be falling for you. Isn't that supposed to be the idea?"

"Touché," said Will. "I'm not exactly a bad lot—neither black sheep nor whiter than white. More sort of—piebald. Or white with black spots."

"Gray?" suggested Gaynor.

"Thanks. Maybe we could move into a wider color spectrum? For instance, how purple do you feel? Gaynor—"

"Wait!" Her expression had changed to one of anguished concentration; she was clutching her temples in furious thought. "White—black—gray—that reminds me—that *connects* . . . I'll have it in a second." Her hands dropped: she looked at him with the clarity of dawning realization. "Listen. There was this story I found this afternoon—I was sure it was important but I couldn't think why. It was about this ancient family who had a special gift of being able to talk to dragons, and tame them. One of their ancestors had been burnt in dragonfire and had lived, and his skin was black ever after, and fireproof, and so was the skin of his descendants. Supposing . . . supposing the family heritage got so dissipated over the centuries that the black faded, and became *gray?* Didn't Ragginbone say something—about a certain family? I *wish* I could remember . . . Our Dr. Laye—"

"—could be a tamer of dragons," Will agreed. "Hell. Hell and bugger."

"This is another clue," said Gaynor, "and it's leading somewhere."

"That's what I don't like," Will said. "I don't imagine I could assert my macho authority and make you stay behind tomorrow?"

"No," said Gaynor. "You need me. I'm the expert on old books and manuscripts. He won't talk to you unless I'm there. Anyhow, it's become something I have to do. Fate. Also, I'm older than you. If you get assertive, I can claim seniority. And it isn't as if there were dragons anymore. And—"

"Coffee?" said Will.

Gaynor shook her head. Their stolen interlude was over, aborted long before midnight. Fears for the morrow had invaded, destroying their brief indulgence in romance. When Will kissed her good night before settling on his friend's sofa, the sudden flare of passion seemed less sexual than desperate, a commitment to each other not as lovers but as partners, setting out together on a dark road. His lips felt hard and his mouth tasted of wine and peppered steak. She found herself thinking she would never be able to eat it again without remembering that kiss. It was swift and hungry and soon over, but afterward, lying alone in the spare bed, she relived it and savored it, sensing it would be their first and last, knowing a chance had passed her by that she might regret and she might not, but it would not come again.

She fell asleep with the throb of that brief passion running in her blood and disturbing her dreams.

The following morning did not dawn bright and fair. It just dawned, night paling slowly into the grayness of day. Will's friends left early, one for part-time computer programming to supplement her student grant, the other for a full-time job as a garbage man that appeared to be the only thing for which his philosophy degree had fitted him. Gaynor heard the belch and gurgle of water in the pipes, indistinct voices from the kitchen downstairs. Eventually the front door banged, and there was silence. If Will had been woken, he must have gone straight back to sleep. Gaynor knew she should get up but a huge reluctance seemed to be weighing her down, a feeling that once she left her bed the wheels of fate would start to turn, and she would be carried forward inexorably into the shadows of the immediate future. She tried to recapture the sweetness of last night's intimacy, the pepper-and-wine aftertaste of that kiss, but only gray thoughts came with the gray daylight, deepening her premonition of an unspecified doom. In the end she forced herself to get up and, finding the shower little more than a trickle, ran herself a bath. Scrubbing at her limbs with a coarse loofah, she was visited by the fancy that her actions were those of a soldier purifying herself before the battle—or a victim before sacrifice. It was not a pleasant thought.

The morning was well advanced before they got on the road, armed with their maps and Dr. Laye's West Riding address, courtesy of the museum curator. It was a long drive from York to the Dales and the house proved elusive, or maybe they were unwilling to find it too easily, so they halted at a pub for lunch. The conversation steered clear of emotional entanglement and the potential for passion; instead Will related more details of his and Fern's previous connection with Ragginbone and Lougarry, Alison Redmond, the Old Spirit, and the otherworld they represented. Gaynor asked so many questions that it was late when they returned to their search, later still when they finally saw the place they sought, a silhouette of steepled roofs and knobbled chimneys against a sky dark with cloud. It had been built on a ridge just below the crest, so that its ragged gables topped the hillside; the millstone grit façade was cloven with tall windows that seemed to be narrowed against the wind. "Wuthering Heights," said Gaynor. She thought it looked like the kind of house where there always *would* be a wind, moaning in the chimneys, creeling under the eaves, making doors rattle and fires smoke. The somber afternoon seemed to provide its natural background.

The road swooped below it, and they pulled up beside the single entrance in the high stone wall. Their way was barred by a black ironwork gate crowned with spikes; the gateposts on either side were surmounted by statuary that might once have been heraldic, but endless cycles of wind and rain had eroded them into shapelessness. However, there was a modern intercom inset on the right, complete with microphone and overlooked by a video camera. "If his collection is so valuable," said Gaynor, "he must be afraid of burglars."

"Maybe," said Will.

The name of the house was on a panel in the gate: Drakemyre Hall. "No sign of a mire," Will remarked, "and no ducks either."

"Myre may be a corruption of moor," Gaynor explained. "And drake usually means dragon."

After a short argument, she was the one who rang the bell. Her recollection of the television program was imperfect but she was almost sure the voice that responded was not that of Dr. Laye. She gave her name and professional status and enquired for him, feeling gauche and uncomfortable, thinking: He knows already. He knows who I am. He's expecting me. The gate opened automatically and they got into the car and drove up to the house. In the backseat Gaynor saw Lougarry's hackles lifting; her eyes shone yellow in the dingy afternoon. "Stay out of sight," Will told her. "We'll leave the window open. Come if we call." He parked in the lee of a wall where a silver Mercedes lurked incongruously, gleaming like a giant pike in the shadows of a murky pond. In front of the house, someone had attempted to create a formal garden, their efforts long defeated by bleak climate and poor soil. The wind had twisted the topiary into strange, unshapely forms; a few predatory shrubs and spiny weeds sprawled over the flowerless beds; moss encroached on the pathways. Two or three holly trees huddled close to the building, weather-warped into an arthritic crooked-ness, seeking shelter under the man-made walls. The Hall itself loomed over its unpromising surroundings, grimly solid, a bulwark against long winters and bitter springs, sprouting into irregular wings on either side, capped with many roofs. The front door stood open, showing an arch of light that looked unexpectedly warm and welcoming. Will took Gaynor's arm and they stepped across the threshold.

The door swung shut to reveal a man standing behind it—a short, gnomelike man, with a lumpy face that appeared to have been made of dough, a tight mouth, jutting ears, and eyes so deeply shadowed he might have been wearing a mask. But his dark suit was immaculate, his manner that of the perfect butler. "I have reported your arrival to Dr. Laye," he said. "I am afraid he cannot be with you just yet: he is on the telephone to Kuala Lumpur. A manuscript has come on the market that he has been seeking for some time. However, if you will follow me . . ." He led them down a corridor that branched left and through another door into a large drawing room. In contrast to its exterior, inside the house everything was warmth and luxury. The room was partly paneled in some mellow wood; the flicker of a fire—real or fake, it was impossible to tell—picked out glints of gold in its graining. Central heating engulfed them, Oriental carpets deadened their footsteps. They sank into the depths of a sumptuous modern sofa as into a soft clinging bog. Most of the furniture looked antique: heavy oak sideboards, unvarnished and ostentatiously venerable, elegant little tables poised on twiglet legs, a baby grand piano, an-other instrument that Gaynor thought might be a spinet. Will, scanning the pictures, noted something that could have been a Paul Klee and a pseudo-mythical scene of rural frolics that might have been painted by Poussin on LSD. "Dragons are good business," he murmured for Gaynor's private ear.

"I will bring you some tea," said the butler. "Indian or China?"

"China," said Gaynor, and: "PG Tips," from Will.

"The lady has the preference," the manservant declared, and retreated with the soundless tread of butlers long extinct—or of gnomes.

"The butler did it," said Will when he had gone.

"He looks like Goebbels." Gaynor shuddered. "All the same, this isn't what I—"

"Nor me. I wonder if that Paul Klee really *is* a Paul Klee?"

"I was wondering if this really is a good time to phone Kuala Lumpur." She paused, fiddling with a stray lock of hair, braiding the ends into a plait. "Will—what exactly are we looking for?"

"I don't know," he admitted. "A dragon's tale—a broken spear—a piece of stone. I ought to try to case the joint while our host is occupied elsewhere. When the butler comes back I'll say I need a piss. Going in search of the bathroom should give me a chance to see a bit more of this place: it's bound to be miles away."

"You won't leave me?"

"Not for long." He appeared slightly startled at the note of panic in her voice.

"It's an awfully well-worn ploy," she explained, pulling herself together, fighting an irrational upsurge of fear. "Do you think he'll believe you? The butler, I mean."

"Nothing succeeds like an old trick," said Will optimistically. "Anyway, why shouldn't he? I can—if necessary—prove my point."

But Gaynor did not smile. "The thing is," she pursued, "we didn't really come here to follow a clue, or trace a long-dead dragon or a magic spear. We came . . . because this is a trap, just like you said, and you want to find out who set it and why, and the only way to do that is to walk right into it. But . . ."

"Whatever the reason," said Will, "we're here now, and we may as well get on with the job."

Presently the butler returned bearing a tray laden with crockery and a teapot from which wafted the scent of Lapsang Soochong. Gaynor struggled to rise and failed as a table was whisked in front of her and the tray set down on it. Will scrambled to his feet, hampered by the cushions, requesting a bathroom. "Of course," the butler said. "I will show you the way."

"I won't be a minute," Will said to Gaynor by way of reassurance, and left in the wake of the gnome, following him back into the corridor, past numerous doors, and through what seemed to be a breakfast parlor to the farthest reaches of the house. Here he was shown a room with a lavatory and basin and left to his own devices. "I can find my own way back," he assured his escort, and when he reemerged, he was alone.

Adjacent to the parlor was a kitchen and a storeroom, both unoccupied. Back in the passageway, he approached the first of the doors with caution, listening at the panels before venturing to turn the handle and push it a little way open, his excuse—"I'm afraid I missed my way"—on the tip of his tongue. Instead he found himself staring into a broom closet. The second door admitted him to a small bare room that seemed at a quick glance unremarkable. Then he tripped over a footstool that he was almost sure hadn't been there a moment earlier, picked himself up, and was immediately confronted by a picture so unpleasant, so seething with subliminal motion, that the ill-formed patches of color appeared to be actually heaving off the canvas toward him. He retreated shaken, trying to shrug off what he hoped was just fancy, approaching the next door with trepidation. It opened into a kind of gallery, with glass cabinets against the walls and a display case in the center similar to the type used in the museum. Forgetful of Gaynor waiting nervously in the drawing room, Will closed the door behind him and gazed and gazed.

The room was full of weapons. There were pikes, halberds, longbows, claymores, a broadsword whose blade was notched and misshapen, a ten-foot spear that looked too heavy for a normal man to lift. A ragged banner adorned the far wall showing a dragon rampant, rouge on sable. In the cabinets were helmets, many of them battered and blackened, reduced to mere lumps of metal, breastplates scored as if by giant claws, the tattered shreds of mail coats. The display case showed a single huge glaive, engraved with words in a language Will did not understand; red jewels shone in the hilt. The sight of it sent a strange shiver down his spine. He thought: Those stones must be worth a fortune; but it was the words that drew him, though their meaning could not be guessed. He pored over them, peering closer and closer, and when he finally wrenched himself away he seemed to have lost track of time. The room appeared to have both grown and shrunk, its proportions distorted, and the dragon banner rippled as if with hidden life, and he was staring at a hanging shield that he thought he had seen before, in a dream long ago. Realization dawned; he said to himself: These are the weapons of the dragonslayers, and for an instant he smelled fire, and there was blood running down the walls. The room shivered with the potency of what it contained.

He was horribly afraid, but he knew he had to stay, to look at every spearhead, every fragment of arrow or blade: the thing he sought might be here. But the shafts were tipped only with iron and steel, stone and bronze, all scorched and chipped and scarred; the splinter of Lodestone would be unmarked and unmistakable. At the far end on a small table he came across a knife that looked different from the rest. It was entirely black, without scratch or ornament, gleaming as if new: when he touched it the hilt seemed to nestle into his hand. It felt like something that belonged to him, that had been made for him, for this contact, for his grip. A leather sheath lay beside it. He slid the knife into the sheath and then, with a cursory glance over his shoulder, tucked it into his jeans, dismissing a minor qualm of conscience: he might have need of a weapon. It occurred to him that he had been absent for too long; Gaynor must be frantic. He hurried to the door, opened it without precaution, stepped into the corridor.

The blow fell dully on the back of his head.

Gaynor waited. She had poured a cup of tea, but she did not drink it. He wouldn't leave me, she told herself. He wouldn't leave me here. Nearby, a clock ticked. And slowly, very slowly, the light changed. The fire sank and guttered, the gold flecks faded from the paneling, the electric lamps seemed to blear. The gray daylight retreated beyond the half-curtained window, leaving the room dim and unfriendly. Shadows gathered behind the furniture. A disquieting sense of déjà vu assailed her. And then she remembered: It's my dream . . . The room there had been darker, the woodwork more somber, the details exaggerated, but surely, surely it was the same. Soon she would see the eyes . . . She got to her feet, stumbled over a rug, but even as she reached the door it opened. "I am sorry to have kept you waiting," said Dr. Laye.

In the flesh, his grayness was shocking, a hideous abnormality. The insides of his eyelids remained pink, making his eyes look bloodshot, the irises luridly blue. As he spoke, yellow-ivory teeth flickered between colorless lips. His suit was almost as immaculate as that of his servant, but Gaynor could not help shrinking at the proffered handshake, her gaze averted from the remembered horrors of finger and nail. Yet his voice was not quite the one that had summoned her nearly two weeks ago. It was somehow lighter, single toned, more . . . human. "I see my complexion disturbs you," he said, withdrawing the gesture. "Many people react that way. It is a hereditary peculiarity: I assure you not contagious. Do sit down. I trust Harbeak has made you comfortable."

And she was plunged back into the sofa, stammering something incoherent, while he added with a thin smile: "I have been so looking forward to meeting you." For a moment her head spun: she thought he might actually allude to the nightmare incident of the television screen. Then: "I have acquaintances among your colleagues," he went on, and named a couple of people she hardly knew. "I understand you are interested in dragons."

She had not said so, but perhaps the curator had telephoned him. How else would he know? "Will," she interrupted. "My friend. He's the one who—I mean, I think we should wait for him."

"We'll let him take his time," said Dr. Laye. "I expect he's having a look around. There are many interesting things in this house."

"Maybe he's lost," said Gaynor, braving raised eyebrows. "I ought to go and find him."

"Then you might become lost, too," Laye responded. "Much wiser to stay here." She did not like his choice of adjective. "Shall I order fresh tea? Brandy, perhaps? No? Very well then. We will talk. You are interested, as I said, in dragons." It was a statement, not a question. Gaynor did her best to assume an academic mien. She could think of no alternative. "Dragons have always fascinated me," he continued. "Did they ever exist? If not, why did we have to invent them? Of all the monsters of mythology, they are the most charismatic, the most enduring. And yet, what are they? Lizards with wings—magical cousins of the dinosaur, breathing flames, endowed with a hypnotic eye and a human intelligence. According to legend—and we have few other sources—they eat virgins and hoard gold, undoubtedly human traits. Such creatures can only be demons born of the wishful thinking of mortal men. Yet I used to dream that in the dawn of history there were true dragons, spirits of fire, dreadful and irresistible, soaring beyond the imaginings of minstrels into a wider world. There was a tradition in my family that our ancestors were once dragonslayers, their skin not gray but black, dragon burned, dragonproof." And, as Gaynor started: "Perhaps you have heard that tale?"

"Yes," she said, "Yes, I . . . It was in a manuscript in the museum."

"I lent them that manuscript. From my earliest youth, I wanted to learn the truth behind the story, the real cause of a pigmentation that no dermatologist could explain. Was it a genetic freak, a rare illness, the mark of Cain—or of a hero? Surely you can appreciate my obsession."

Gaynor nodded. For all her repulsion, she felt a stab of sympathy for this man disfigured from birth, marked out by he knew not what. He had slipped under her guard, stirring both her compassion and her curiosity. She found herself urging him to go on.

"I spent my life searching. There were no fossilized bones, no remains preserved in glacier or bog. Only written accounts, thirdhand, secondhand, a very few by genuine witnesses. I became a collector, a scholar with an established reputation. Yet the more I learned, the less I knew. My dreams told me more than any document—dreams of fire and combat, of desperate valor culminating at last in a mind link with the monster itself. I *was* the dragon, I clove the skies in flight, I controlled its thoughts, wielded its power. For, as that manuscript you read had told me— and it took me thirty years to procure it—my ancestors were not slayers but tamers, the dragon charmers whose inherited talent set them above lords and kings, uniting them with the immortals. The discoloration of my skin, so often abhorred, was not a deformity but a gift, the greatest Gift of all." Gaynor's eyes widened at the word. "Yet there seemed to be no dragons left for me to charm. My search had become a quest doomed to unfulfillment."

He paused as if awaiting comment or commiseration, but Gaynor's momentary sympathy had dried up. Beyond the highflown language she glimpsed an ego swollen with the lust of power and the cult of Self. She said, trying for a note of pragmatism: "If there ever *were* any dragons, there are none now."

"So I thought." He licked his lips. "So I feared. Yet the dreams still haunted me. I saw a dragon hatched in a high lonely place among men too simple and too foolish to do more than marvel at it; but the hands that held it were black. I knew this must be long ago, yet my heart swelled with hope. I saw the dragon grow in a hidden valley far from the farthest outposts of civilization. I saw it dance on the air above lakes of green and scarlet. I dreamed it was alone, the last of dragons, living while I lived yet forever beyond my reach, and I woke to disillusionment and an empty existence." He paused once again, but this time Gaynor said nothing at all. "And then I had a visitor. He came in the night, nearly a year ago. He said he had felt me calling. He was—not like us." The tongue reemerged, circling the moistureless mouth, a gross red thing against the monochrome flesh. "Would you like to meet him?"

"No!" Suddenly Gaynor noticed that the daylight had drained from the window. Jerked back to the terrors of the moment, she cried: "Will! Where's Will? *What have you done with him?*"

But the face of Dr. Jerrold Laye had changed. His eyes were infused with a baleful phosphorescence; the voice that issued from his mouth was deeper, colder, and familiar. "We meet again, Gaynor Mobberley."

"No," she reiterated, but her tone had shrunk to a whisper. She tried to stand but her knees gave, and the quagmire of the cushions reclaimed her.

"You are not like your friend," the voice continued. "Fernanda is Gifted, and strong; you are powerless, weak, afraid. Yet you came to me. I called you, and you came." I chose to come, thought Gaynor; but she wasn't sure. "And Fernanda will come for you, you and her brother. She will come to me at last."

"She c-can't," Gaynor managed, though her lips shook. "She's in a coma—in hospital. Her spirit is lost—"

"Fool! Do I not know her better than you—better than that beggar Brokenwand whose wisdom has gone with his Gift? She is strong: strong and cunning. She will find a way back, no matter how perilous or how far. Danger draws her. Power guides her. She does not need your feeble assistance, or that of the vagabond who seeks to be her mentor. I understand her mind—her spirit—as no other can. I have cast the augury, and seen her. She will come to me, and submit to me, or die, knowing that both you and the boy will perish with her. To lose all, or to gain all: there is but one choice. Love will betray her, and in my service she will be loveless forever."

Gaynor wanted to cry out in defiance—She will fight you! You cannot win—but her vocal cords were numb. The gray hand reached out toward her, the arm extended over an impossible distance; dust-dry fingers wound around her throat. Horror filled her, paralyzing struggle; but only for an instant. The strength of that hand was beyond Nature, and in seconds the room darkened, and went out.

"**H**arbeak!" The man's voice had returned to its usual timbre, but his face was drawn as if in the aftermath of pain and his breathing came short and fast. The servant entered, saw the girl crumpled on the sofa. "What have you done with the other?"

"In the cellar, master."

"Was that wise? He may be inquisitive."

"That would be unfortunate." The pallid features twitched involuntarily. "However, the cellar is secure. You wanted the special room for the girl; in one of the others, he might climb down from the window or break inadequate locks. Unless we put them together . . ."

"Apart. Together, they might encourage each other, console each other. Apart, they will have nothing but fear. By the time the witch arrives, *he* wants them—I want them—to be very afraid. I want them begging her for mercy. She will never be able to refuse. We will have to risk the cellar. I thought this one would come alone. The boy was not called."

"I could give him another dose of the soporific. The longer he sleeps, the less able he is to cause us any trouble."

"It is well thought of. Do it. The girl, too."

"Perhaps I should feed your little pet?"

"Not tonight. Tomorrow you may go hunting; it may need fresh meat. The witch will come after midnight. *He* has seen her. If she submits, it will be hungry still. If not . . ."

The butler responded with a gargoyle smile.

Jerrold Laye pointed to the unconscious figure. "Take that away. You know what to do with her. She will be watched."

Harbeak lifted Gaynor without effort and carried her from the room. Behind him, the brief werelight flickered in Dr. Laye's eyes, the other voice spoke through his stiffened lips. "I have you now, Fernanda. You can choose: the slow torment of a gradual enslavement or the swift anguish of a triple death. Either way, you cannot escape me. You will belong to me, or I will destroy you. Vengeance is mine, saith the lord, and what other lord is there for men to worship, save me?"

✦ XIII ✦

"It is a dark road for a mortal," says Kal. "Dark and still deadly. Are you sure you wish to venture it?"

"I thought you said it was abandoned," says Fern.

"The gods went away long ago. But a few spirits linger there, unable to move on, phantoms without shape or name craving anything that reminds them of the life they have lost. If you look back, they will seize on you."

"I won't look back."

"It will be harder than you think. There may be pursuit. Morgus will not release you so easily and Sysselore, for all her gibes, will go where Morgus leads. A fat woman with a thin shadow. You must cross the river before you can turn to face them."

"They cannot follow me," she says, "if they do not wake." And she crumbles the pale toadstools between her fingers, catching a whiff of their faint drowsy scent, the scent of moonbeams on a warm night. The silvery powder sifts into the mud-green depths of the brew that Sysselore always keeps at a simmer over the cooking fire.

"Is that poison?" There is doubt in Kal's voice.

"No. These are slumbertops: they bring sleep, not death. I will not kill wantonly."

Hatred can wait. That is not the way.

"They will suspect something if you don't drink it," Kal points out.

"I never drink it," Fern replies. "Morgus would suspect something if I did. It tastes vile; I always tip mine away."

The potion bubbles up, absorbing the powder: the stink of pungent herbs boiled to liquefaction eclipses the aroma of moonbeams.

"How fast does it take effect?"

"Slowly," she says. "Like natural sleep, only deeper. They say it brings sweet dreams to the weary."

"Beware," says Kal. "My mother distrusts sweet dreams. In any case, her mountain of flesh is too vast to succumb to the influence of any drug. Are you sure it will work?"

"No," answers Fern.

She knows Morgus can see beyond the veil of expression, picking the thoughts from her mind. To deceive her, she must lie not only with her face but with every nuance of emotion: Morgus must detect no unnatural excitement in her apprentice, no hint of concealment. Fern creates an image in her head of the black fruit, not as it is now but unripe, a lumpen thing of half-formed features and petaled eyes—something new-discovered, still mysterious, hanging high in the leaves. She intends to give Morgus a distraction, a focus for her plans other than Fern herself. Above all, she must not think of *wasps*. But when the witch queen appears the angry stings seem to have already faded, as if no poison can penetrate far into that swollen flesh, so imbued with its own power that it has no space to absorb an alien substance. As the light fails they sit by the spellfire while the crystals crack in cooling, spitting blue sparks, and Fern accepts Sysselore's herbal infusion out of custom, unwilling to offend, and she catches Morgus's sly sideways glance as she pours it unobtrusively away. The liquid

sinks into the earth, leaving a faint residue on the surface, the betraying glitter of powdered toadstool. She quells a sudden leap of
panic, making herself ignore it, trusting that what she overlooks,
Morgus, too, will not see. Fortunately, Morgus's attention has
shifted. Kal enters, taunting Sysselore for her witch's brew, dis-
tracting both with an exchange of insults until the potion is drunk
and he is driven back outside to sleep where he can. His mood is
reckless; he seems wilder than usual, somehow less human, carrying with him an aura of primeval dark, the red smell of blood,
the black smell of midnight. His ugliness is exaggerated by the
wavering shadows, turning him into a being all monster, without
hidden grief or sworn allegiance. Yet his arrival is well-timed, his
departure prearranged. When he has gone, Morgus asks: "So
what have you learned of late, little apprentice, and where did
you learn it?" Fern answers lightly, letting the recollection of the
black fruit slide through her mind, resolving to visit it by daylight,
knowing Morgus will follow. Morgus does not catechize her further. Fern yawns her way to her pallet and watches Morgus's toying with the spellfire, whispering to Sysselore so that the cave is
filled with furtive echoes. The fire is extinguished; the flickering
wormshine dapples the walls with will-o'-the-wisps of light. The
whispers merge into the roving shadows. The witches appear to
be melded into a single figure, huge, distorted, many-limbed, the
head dividing into two and then rejoining as more confidences
pass between them. At last the amorphous blob separates into
one thin shade and one bloated one, and they go to their beds.
Presently, Morgus's snore begins to rumble through the cave like
a restless volcano.

Fern waits a long time before she moves.

As always, she is sleeping in her underwear; it takes her only a
few moments to dress. Tight sweater, loose trousers, trainers: the
clothes she has been wearing all along. Such garments are a
habit, like her physical form, and in the borderland of reality that

is enough to give them substance. Her head has been resting on the result of her sewing: she empties out the temporary stuffing of grass and dry leaves and hooks the strap diagonally across her chest so the pouch hangs on her hip. Belatedly she looks around for a weapon, but the cave offers little choice. The knives they use for eating are sharp but small, the blade barely a finger length, no more than a pinprick to Morgus, whose vital organs must be buried far beyond the reach of any dagger. Fern takes one for other purposes, slipping it into her bag, and, remembering her promise to Ruvindra, she snatches a handful of fire crystals and thrusts them into her left-hand pocket. Then she steals toward the exit, passing close to Sysselore, who moans as Fern's shadow touches her face, moving as if to brush it away, relapsing into slumber. For an instant Fern freezes, tension seizing every muscle; then the dread releases her, and she is able to creep into the passage, feeling her way between the roots. Only the sudden sense of space and a thin drift of cooler air tell her when she is outside.

It is utterly dark. She has never ventured abroad before at this hour, the lightless time, when the Tree itself sleeps. The heads are silent, the birds roost; the very process of growing seems to stop. With a word and gesture she conjures a tiny ball of wereglow that hovers just ahead of her, its diminutive glimmer showing few details of her surroundings: a groping leaf, a shadow rearing behind a twisted root. She steps forward cautiously, still bruising herself against unseen hazards. The ground dips and rises, folds and writhes. Every so often a low-slung branch intrudes into the circle of light, a swath of foliage, the distorted globe of a head with closed eyes and slackened mouth. Once fraying hair strokes her brow like the strands of a spider's web. She begins to feel imprisoned between the ceiling of leaves and the convoluted earthen floor. The darkness seems to be compressed into a greater density in that narrow space, crushing out any breathable air. Then: "Take my hand," says a voice beside her, and Kal's arm emerges into the light—the arm of a lycanthrope, thick with sinew, crackling with hair—and she puts her hand in his, warily reassured. With his help she travels faster: his eyes can see shadows at midnight, differentiating between dark and dark. His mockery is gone; he speaks only to guide her. "This is the place," he says at last. "I cannot see the hollow: you must unbind the spell." And, with a hint of his usual manner: "No doubt your black plum ripens best at midnight."

The air glistens briefly as the magic dissolves. Fern descends into the dell, taking the knife from her pouch. The head sleeps. She reaches up to touch it, but the eyes open before she makes contact, blinking once in the wereglow, then becoming fixed and steady. "It is time," she tells him. She cuts the stem at its junction with the main branch: it comes away easily, and the head is light in her grasp. She places it carefully in the pouch, pulling the ragged flap over the top. Then she turns to climb out of the dell. The noise behind her is very slight—a rustle in the leaf mold, a snuffling intake of breath. There is nothing to prepare her for what she sees.

The hog. Standing on the lip of the hollow, glaring down not at her but at the bag on her hip and the bulge within it. Food. The fruit that is nourishment for the hog alone, its rightful diet. The wavering light shows it is far bigger than a pig should be: warty, many-jowled, covered in coarse bristles as thick as spines. Its up-turned snout is squashed into a quivering oval of pinkish skin; the nostrils twitch and flex at every atom of scent. Fern can see the double tusks protruding on either side, discolored with the red-brown stains of dried sap, and the small round eyes like bloodshot beads. Rage emanates from it—rage at the theft and the thief and the fruit itself, a reasonless rage that turns its gut to acid and its brain to madness. It snorts, an ominous adenoidal rumble, and paws the ground with a trotter the size of a dinner plate. Kal has vanished. Shock holds Fern petrified, blanking out her knowledge of Atlantean. She stands rigid, helpless. Stupid. Her brain stalls. The hog charges.

Hands reach down from above, seizing her under the arms, swinging her clear of the ground. The hog hurtles beneath her; bristles brush her feet. And then she is lifted into the branches, the werelight soaring in her wake, and Kal is steadying her, and she finds herself sitting on a forked limb while her legs unstiffen into the inevitable trembling of reaction. Kal balances on a neighboring bough that is still vibrating from his acrobatics: he seems as much at home in the Tree as on the ground, with the agility and muscle power of a giant ape. Below, the pig rushes to and fro in fury and frustration, scouring the dell, too unintelligent to register bafflement, following the scent that is all that remains of its quarry in blind obsession. Presently the snout lifts, locating their perch; Fern can see the red pinpricks of its eyes. Kal curses under his breath. "It won't go away," he says. "It smells the head. It will wait till we climb down. You'll have to abandon your prize."

"No." Her nerve steadies. She struggles to marshall her thoughts, and her power.

"Your skills won't help you here. It's too late to conceal us, even if it were possible, and the pig is impervious to attack by magic. Spells bounce off it, like potting peanuts at an elephant. Throw down your black fruit."

"No."

Kal hears the finality in her voice, and says no more. They wait. The pig grunts and whiffles, churning up the earth, sucking at the air. "We can't stay here indefinitely," Fern says, and a picture rises in her mind of Morgus, her vast form heaving and tossing on her straw bed as she wrestles against clinging dreams of an unfamiliar sweetness. "Perhaps we could jump down and run for it . . ."

"Over this terrain?" He moves away without waiting for an answer, springing from branch to branch, setting the massed leaves shuddering and rustling in his wake. Fern looks down, but the hog does not stir. It is squatting on its haunches now, staring upward, the tiny mind in its huge body knuckled into a tight little knot of purpose. There is no way into that mind. It is too small, too limited, too clenched in upon itself to leave any chinks where she might insert a distraction. She murmurs a spell, hurling darts of fire that singe its bristles, but they cannot penetrate the thick hide. It squirms and bucks, yowling with pain, but it does not run away.

Kal returns just as she remembers the fire crystals. He is carrying another head. It is large, white-haired, the massive brow crushing the eyes deep into their sockets, the outthrust jaw set for ram. Once it must have been forceful and angry, someone of power and consequence; now, it is just a head among a hundred others, a fruit that ripens only to decay. Like so many of them, it talks incessantly, ranting at Kal in the language of arrogance and petty tyranny; but he ignores it. He leaps for the strongest of the low boughs, swinging down close to the hog with his legs twined around the branch. The head dangles just above the questing snout. The pig, diverted, veers toward it in a sudden rush, then circles below at manic speed, until vertigo brings it to a staggering halt. The tusked muzzle sways and jabs at the ground. Kal begins to rock to and fro, gaining momentum; the snout lifts again, swiveling to follow his movements. At the extreme point of the arc he releases the head, hurling it through the air. Fern hears the swish of leaves skimmed in its flight, the fading bellow of its voice. The pig races after it, squealing. The sound of its charge merges with the thuds as the head bounces over the ground. There is a screech, too deep to have come from the hog. From the subsequent crashing noises she deduces that the beast is wheeling again, bumping into protruding roots. The screams continue. In her mind's eye Fern sees the head spitted on a single tusk, while the pig rampages around trying to shake it loose . . .

"Now." Kal reappears beside her. "Come on." He jumps down, assisting her to follow. They scramble out of the dell and progress as fast as they can over the twisted network of roots. Behind them, the screaming of the head and the pig's raging gradually die away. Beyond the narrow range of the werelight the dark encircles them, impenetrable as a wall. Kal is surefooted but Fern stumbles frequently. As they circumnavigate the bole she is increasingly aware of the Tree's dimensions; occasional glimpses show the bastion of the trunk to her left, like the foundations of a giant fortress whose higher towers are swagged in shadow. Kal has told her they are aiming for a point on the far side, but the route seems interminable, the trunk boundless, a pillar mighty enough to uphold the cosmos.

Then Kal turns aside into a deep cleft; the earth closes in and they are in a passage between matted webs of root. The walls shoulder inward, forcing Kal to move crabwise. For a while Fern proceeds more easily, being smaller, but the wereglow dims, its light greening to sallow, shrinking into a spark and vanishing, slowly. "Don't make another," says Kal, taking her hand again. "Save your strength. We may need it." The passage plunges steeply downhill. Underfoot, soil and plant sinew give way to rock. Fern's free hand skims the wall, touching the chill hardness of stone, ribbed and sculpted by runnels of moisture long dried up. The atmosphere grows colder, but she *knows* rather than senses the change; a warmth flows into her from Kal's grip that staves off trembling—Kal the half-breed, the botched man-beast whom she trusts only because of his hatred for his mother. There are some things that are beyond explaining. To her eyes, the dark is absolute, but Kal's guidance does not falter, and the susurration of his breath, the very rankness of his odor have become her one link with existence and vitality in the dead blackness. She clutches his unseen fingers like a talisman.

The tunnel widens slightly, descending ever deeper, but be-

neath what earth, or where, Fern cannot guess. The presence of
the Tree is lost; she is in a realm where nothing lives, even to stag-
nate. She seems to be in suspension, trapped indefinitely in the
moment between one frozen hour and the next. She finds herself
imagining that the ridges on the walls were made by the melting
seconds, trickling down from some loophole in reality far above.
Her head is filled with the silent drip-drip of the ages . . .

The change is so subtle that at first she distrusts it. The
diminution in the dark might be only in her mind; but no, she can
make out the shaggy mound of Kal's mane, the hump of a shoulder, the coil of a horn. She sees veins of faint glitter rippling
through the rock, and rough encrustations of quartz or crystal
touched with a ghost sparkle that disappears even as she looks at
it. Below, the light increases, still little more than a dimness, a
gray shade softer and blander than the dusk of the outer world,
but dazzling to the dark-adapted eye. The tunnel opens abruptly
into a cavern.

It is immense. Behind them, the walls soar beyond sight, the
roof is lost; ahead is only distance. This is no subterranean hollow
but a whole new region, a different layer of being. It is filled with a
twilight that comes from nowhere, diffuse and shadowless, muting
the hard edges of things, softening perspective. The space is dizzying after the narrow confines of the passage, but the sensation
fades quickly. Immediately in front of them is the lip of a chasm
that stretches away to right and left, spanned by a solitary bridge.
It seems to be made of natural rock, irregular in shape, cracked
and eroded so that in places it is less than a yard wide, less than a
foot. Evidently there was once a rail, but the remaining posts lean
drunkenly, and whatever joined them is gone. "This is the ancient
Underworld," says Kal. "When we have crossed the bridge, we will
be within its borders. Remember, whatever happens, *you must not
look back.* Long ago, so they say, when the Tree bore apples and
not heads, it was here that the spirits of the dead waited, ere they

could pass the Gate. That was in the days when men still worshiped the immortals, before they started to look for their gods higher than heaven—or closer to earth. There are old memories clinging on here—phantoms—poor weak things for the most part, but you are mortal and vulnerable, and they will yearn for you."

"And you?" she asks. "Can you pass with impunity?"

"It is your soul that draws them, little witch," he says, and his grin is ugly. "I have none. Does your nerve fail?"

"I have no nerves," Fern retorts.

She lies. The phantoms do not trouble her—not yet—but she shrinks from the bridge. A great cold emanates from the chasm, the chill she sensed in the passage; but here nothing can warm it, and it eats into her bones. In the depths there is a flow of white vapor, like the ghost of a river long gone. Air currents move over it in waves, ruffling it into peaks and hollowing out troughs that collapse slowly, one into the other. "Yes, there was a river," says Kal. "One of the great rivers of legend. There were many others, with many names, but they are dry and nameless now. All save one." He steps lightly onto the bridge, pausing a moment to mock her, waiting for her to reach for the assistance of his hand. But she knows she must cross alone, unaided, showing no fear. Morgus is in him, and the legacy of spirits old and wild: his instinct is to prey on weakness. She spreads her arms for balance, steadying her gaze on his face. He moves backward, indifferent to the drop, and she follows, step by careful step, not looking down. Never looking down. Her features are expressionless, still as a mask. It is only when she reaches the other side, and begins to relax, that she realizes her breath was pent and her jaw muscles clamped with the effort of self-control.

And now they are in the Underworld. A path winds ahead of them across what seems to be a vast plain, a gray impression of meadow whose dim grasses are stirred by winds they cannot feel.

At times a flicker of white snatches at the tail of Fern's eye, tempting her to turn, a trick of the light perhaps, if light is wily, and knows such tricks. Then she sees one more clearly, close by the path, a pale star shape like a flower . . . and another, and another. The petals are ephemeral as mist, holding only loosely to the calyx; the long stems toss and bend. Now there is a whole cluster approaching, five or six of them, but a zephyr plucks the blossoms from their tenuous anchorage and spins them away, scattering them over the waste like spectral butterflies. At the same instant she catches on the perimeter of hearing a faint surge of sound, music without a tune, singing without words, a faerie summons from somewhere far behind her. "There are no flowers here," says Kal. "Like me, flowers have no souls."

"Did you hear something?" she asks.

"No. Shut your ears. There is nothing for you to listen to."

She sees no more flowers. There is only the rolling emptiness of shivering grass and flaccid air. Once or twice she glimpses lone trees in the distance, but they are half-formed and shadowy, phantom growths that have forgotten how they ought to appear, and they are blown away into nothingness more swiftly than the blossoms. The music does not recur, but sometimes she hears a few silvery notes, like the tinkle of wind chimes or tiny bells, always behind her.

The horn comes later. She hears it winding across the plains, the sound traveling from somewhere very far away, more echo than horn call. It is audible even to Kal; his face is blank, frozen on a memory—he who once was hunted, hunted like a beast, reacting instinctively to the message in that swelling peal. Other sounds come after, faint as a rumor: the belling of hounds, and the hoofbeats of horses, and the eager cries of many riders. Then Fern sees the stag, white as virgin snow, swift as a forest fire, racing over the meadow. A clot of darkness streams in its wake, many-limbed, studded with pale eyes and red tongues, breaking into separate shadow flecks that spread out to surround their prey. She knows them of old, the hounds of Arawn, and she does not want to encounter them again. But as the chase draws nearer she sees the stag is transparent, a drawing in mist that fades even as it passes by, and the hounds are mere shades, bodiless and flimsy; the grass shows through their eyes. Behind them come ethereal horses, unfinished shapes wayward as smoke, their riders still more insubstantial. Fern sees blowing hair leaf-crowned, the shimmer of a diadem, phantom spears glittering like frost. They sweep by with a rushing noise like the wind in the trees, and the hounds' braying and the horn calls carry far behind her; yet the air that touches her cheek is still.

"Illusion," says Kal, and a shiver crawls over his skin. "The Wild Hunt has not been seen for many centuries, and never on the Gray Plains. What would they have found to chase, in the Land of the Dead? The hounds may have kenneled here, but they preferred to pursue living quarry."

"I know," Fern murmurs. "I've seen them."

"Have you run from them?" demands Kal, and there is no mistaking the bitter edge in his tone. "Have you run and run—until your mouth is dry and your muscles scream and the breath gripes in your lungs?" Fern says nothing, only taking his hand, and his fingers crush hers till she winces, but she does not draw them away. "Those who dwell here are playing out memories," he resumes eventually, "clutching at the tag ends of forgotten tales. They cannot even complete the images they call up; their minds are withered like winter leaves, but their famine is evergreen. Beware, little witch. They lust after you: your youth, and your life, and your soul. No mortal has come this way for ages beyond count."

"They must be lonely," she says.

"You are too easy with your pity." His grip releases her. "They will twist it into a thread to bind you here. If you are going to waste your heart on *pity*, I may as well leave you now."

"Pity is never wasted," says Fern.

They go on. The meads seem limitless, stretching into vacancy on every hand, but at last they come to an end of them. Fern has forgotten that they are underground, until she sees the cavern walls drawing in once more. Another river curves to meet them, cutting a great swath across the plain; no mist flows in its arid bed, but at intervals the depths gleam into pools, and reflections flicker there of scenes long past. The grasses cease, ebbing from the rock like a tide. Ahead, the wall is riven with many openings through which the light flows like vapor, penetrating subterranean cathedrals pillared with slow-growing stone, sacrificial altars whose blood has hardened to porphyry. Beyond, there are shadows that must have lain undisturbed since before the advent of Man. "Who made this place?" Fern asks, but Kal does not know.

"Maybe it was the first Spirits," he says, "in the days when they were gods. Maybe the men who worshiped them. There are many such realms, though most are deserted now. Once people needed heaven and hell, Elysium and Faerie. They *believed*. Belief is the great creative force, the faith that moves mountains. If Someone had not believed in us, so they say, we would never have been born. I have spent my darkest hours wondering what kind of a Creator would have believed in me."

"I believe in you," says Fern. "I have to, or I would be lost here."

"So it's your fault," Kal retorts. "Go carefully, little witch, lest I take you at your word. I have often dreamed of strangling my Creator."

She laughs at him, not to hurt but to shake his mood, to send her laughter into his darkness. And for a moment, she feels the Underworld itself shaken, as if that little quiver of sound has pierced its deepest foundations. None other has ever laughed here, since the halls were made. Perhaps none ever will. And so she laughs again, lighthearted with her own sacrilege, and the ghosts watch her from their holes, starving and afraid, stabbed by the echo of something whose meaning they have long mislaid.

"You are one alone," says Kal, "even among witches."

He moves on, following the river cleft through the widest of the apertures. The path shrinks to a ledge; above, the overhang is fringed with stalactites forming a frozen curtain that screens the space beyond from view. The ravine below them becomes narrow and deep. Formerly the river here must have been a torrent, seething and foaming between constricting cliffs, making the caves resonate to the roar of its waters; now the crevasse yawns like a parched mouth and a great hush lies over all. The noise of their footsteps is deadened; not an echo follows on their heels. The ledge hugs ever closer to the wall and is cloven in several places from rockfalls; Fern is grateful for the proximity of the sta-lactites that provide her with much-needed handholds. The path clings on by its teeth. On one occasion, circumventing a particu-larly awkward gap, her foot slips and she starts to fall. She hears *them* again close behind, reduced to a shapeless whispering with-out music or tone: the threadlike remnant of voices probing the silence. But Kal is ready, seizing her arms, pulling her up again, and the whispers sink reluctantly out of sound.

At last they enter a large grotto where the river cleft broadens to form what must have been a pool. Fountains of petrified car-bonate spill over the rim; the walls are ribbed with cascades of thick pale stone. Above the center of the pool, the roof swoops downward into a single massive stalactite, many-tiered and gleam-ing like a huge natural chandelier. And there is sound—real sound, not the subsilent mutterings of voices long stilled. Soft but very clear, filling the endless quiet of the Underworld. The sound of water.

On the farther side of the pool a small spring bubbles out of the rock, spilling into a basin hollowed out over the ages from which it must formerly have overflowed into pool and river. Now there must be a fissure in the basin through which it drains away, for little collects there although the flow appears constant. Its few pellucid notes seem to Fern, in that place where Death himself has moved out, to be the most beautiful sound she has ever heard.

They skirt the pool, drawing nearer. The water is unclouded, pure and clear as liquid light. "May we drink?" she asks Kal.

His dark ugliness softens briefly with a kind of saturnine amusement. "No! Have you forgotten all you ever knew? You should neither drink nor eat here, if you would leave. Next you will be demanding a pomegranate to nibble. But in any case, this is no ordinary spring. It is the Well of Lethe, the waters of Oblivion. One drink, and your spirit will be cleansed of care and sorrow, love and hatred and pain. A second, and all memory will be drained; a third, and your soul is suspended in nirvana. Long ago, many drank deep from the spring and bathed in the pool, washing away the burdens of the past, and their vacant minds were filled with the gentleness of death. Only so could they pass the Gate, and hope for rebirth, or so I was told."

"*Is* there rebirth?"

His face twists into a scowl. "Who knows? Ask of the Ultimate Powers, not of me. If they exist. Mortals have hope. I—do not." He pauses beside the spring, turns toward her with a sudden change of mood. "One drink to erase all griefs, to ease heartache, and loneliness, and loss. Does it tempt you, Fernanda? Has grief ever marked that cold little face? Do you indeed have no heart to ache?"

"Grief is easy to recall," she answers. "Is there a drink to blot out the memory of happiness? The human heart is strong to bear all things, save only that."

Kal stares at her, baffled, but says no more. They enter a crooked passage leading out of the cave, and the music of Lethe fades behind them.

The passage descends in an erratic series of inclines, awkward and hazardous. The light has been squeezed out and only its dregs remain, insufficient to show the fluctuations in the slope. Fern misses her footing often, blundering against the walls. She may be spirit, not substance; yet she still seems to feel the bruises. Beyond the tunnel there is another cavern, another ravine. Already she is disorientated by the vastness of the place—by the sourceless light that blurs outlines and confounds distance, by the quiet, more a lull than a silence, pregnant with the unheard voices of the dead. She peers into the ravine, expecting another dry riverbed, but instead there is a black torrent of rock, its surface swollen with misshapen waves, seamed with the cracks of long cooling. Rags of vapor issue from these cracks, white foggy wisps that hang motionless on the air or are tugged hither and thither by intangible drafts. Some begin to assume forms that are blown away before they come to completion, not horses or trees but other things less pleasant. The chasm is bridged by a single arch, apparently manmade, its stonework inset with carvings that echo the unfinished shapes in the mist, grasping hands and half-formed faces whose lineaments are twisted with pain. The bridge is broad and easily crossed, though there are gaps among the stones where fragments of masonry have broken away. On the far side two tall pillars stand sentinel, black and ominous against the paler gloom beyond. They resemble the trunkless limbs of some vanished colossus. The ruins of what might have been a wall extend along the border of the ravine; between the pillars, the remnants of great gates sag from their hinges, shrunken to calcined panels, warped in fires now withered to ash. Strands of mist vacillate toward the columns and spiral around them.

"This was the River of Fire," says Kal. "It has been cold now for many ages, though somewhere far below, maybe, you might still feel the heat of the ancient world. The bridge leads to the Region of Hel, by some called Tartarus, the Dungeons of Death. The wall is fallen now, the gates rusted. Only the ghosts remain. Be wary, little witch. They are strongest here, strong with remembered pain. Most of the spirits have departed from the Gray Plains, but few of those who were bound in the pits of Hel could ever leave. Their souls are rotted with evil: the phantoms that endure are empty of all but hunger and the memory of torment. Close your ears and your heart against them; this is no place for pity."

They pass between the twisted gates; ahead, the way lies through a complex warren of caves. The light is diminished here, as though shrinking from sights it has no wish to illuminate, and shadows cluster thickly on either side. The roof is obscured; the occasional stalactite extruding from the darkness like an accusing finger. As they approach one of them it writhes into serpentine life, rearing its head and hissing; but Kal ignores it and Fern follows his example, walking on by with only a sidelong glance. The whispers have started again, nudging at the outer limits of hearing. And gradually she begins to fancy she hears footsteps, hurrying, hurrying on their trail. She is seized with a desperate urge to turn, neither a reflex nor the prompting of her own will but a feeling that seems to come from outside, insinuating itself into her brain, pulling her like compulsion. She thrusts it away, using her Gift, forcing it to relinquish its grip on her thought. For a brief space the tongueless voices dwindle as if disheartened; but the footsteps do not relent. She says nothing to Kal, trying to convince herself they are an illusion that only she can hear.

Now they are traversing one of the larger caverns. Mist devils chase after them, hovering beside their path, and there is a sound of sighing, a thin gray noise somewhere between a breath and a moan, inexplicably malevolent. "Look!" says Kal. "This was the chamber of punishment. There is the Chair, the Well of Thirst, the Wheel." Fern sees them indistinctly among a bewilderment of shadows: the looming contours of an empty seat, the mouth of a pit, the wheel's giant arc. The sighing intensifies, becoming a mournful buzz that bores inside her head, and suddenly she can make out the torn flesh and bone adhering to the arms of the Chair, the glint of undrinkable water in the Well, the blood dripping down the spokes of the Wheel. "There's nothing here now," Kal says, and she rubs her eyes to dispel the fantasy, and when she looks again there is only a crumbling stone slab, a primitive hub ringed with broken prongs, a hole in the ground. As they move on the footsteps resume, nearer now and louder, almost as if they were in the next cave. Fern can distinguish two different sets: a light, uneven pattering and a smoother, more regular pace, swift as the wingbeats of a bird. A picture comes into her mind, unwanted and disturbing: Morgus, striding along with her rapid, gliding motion, and the mantislike figure of Sysselore following at her heels. "Kal," she murmurs hesitantly, "can *you* hear footsteps?"

"I heard them a way back, when they left the first passage. My ears are sharper than yours, and I haven't let them become clogged with sounds that aren't there. I didn't think sweet dreams would hold my mother long. They have already crossed the Gray Plains; they are gaining on us." His tone is flat, devoid of expression, but the set of his mouth is taut.

"They sound so *near*," Fern says, wishing she hadn't. More than ever she needs to turn, and see . . .

"The acoustics are strange here. Don't let them deceive you." He adds, with what might be incredulity: "Morgus heard you laughing. I think—it *hurt* her. It really hurt."

They leave the cave via an archway partially blocked by a rockfall. Kal slides like a snake through the narrow gap; Fern wriggles after him. "Morgus will never get through there," she says.

"Don't believe it," Kal responds. "She could pour herself through a keyhole, if she wished."

The footsteps are always with them now.

The path ascends steeply until it becomes an actual stair, winding upward. On either side infrequent apertures reveal slender vistas of the caves beyond, clumps of stalagmites like sprouting forests, the dried-up cavities of long-lost pools. Once, near at hand, the furtive light touches a hook embedded in the rock above a curved recess. "A cauldron hung there," Kal says, following the direction of Fern's gaze, "but it was stolen many ages ago. All stories meet here. This is the realm of Annwn, Hades, Osiris, Iutharn. You find here the myths you expect, or so it used to be."

"So why do we find—all this?" Fern enquires.

"These are the relics of other people's dreams," Kal answers. "The dreams of the dead."

They enter another cavern, vaulted like a great hall, lofty and long. At the far end the floor rises into a curiously shaped outcrop: as they advance Fern sees steps etched deep in the rock, and above them a structure that appears to be made of four or five huge slabs, piled together in the form of a throne. The slabs resemble rough-hewn sarsens; the throne itself is massive, crude, like something not carved but riven from the earth's core, ancient beyond the annals of history, impregnated with forgotten potency. Rock dust sifts across the pedestal; mist ghosts drift around the high back, avoiding the emptiness that sits between its stony arms. It generates an awe that even abandonment cannot disperse. In its vicinity the whispers die away, and despite the pursuing footfalls Fern halts and gazes, half in fear, half in wonder, until Kal's impatience drives her onward. "We cannot linger," he says. "The dark king is long gone; he has not been worshiped for a thousand generations. Come!"

"Ah, but we remember," she says. "Not all immortals were like Azmordis. Legend says he weighed the truth of the soul on his enchanted scales."

"He is gone," Kal reiterates, "and so must we, if you would live. Morgus is on the bridge over the Fiery River; I hear the echo of her footfalls in the ravine. Hurry!"

They hurry. Cavern leads into cave, passage into passageway. The following steps grow ever closer; now it seems to Fern they are only yards behind. It requires a constant effort of will not to turn and look. At last they emerge from a broad tunnel into a space without visible roof or farther wall. The last of the light is spread thinly through its vastness. Below them stretches the still expanse of a river—the boundary of the Underworld, the final barrier on their journey to reality. The watermark on the rocks shows the level has sunk, but it remains wide and deep, colder than ice, though Kal says it never freezes, with a cold that bites not merely to the bone but to the heart. The surface is the color of iron; ponderous ripples travel slowly downstream, barely touching the nearer bank.

But immediately before them the darkness lies across their path in a solid bar. Haste makes Fern incautious: she brushes against it, and feels coarse fur; belatedly she recognizes an outstretched forelimb, thick as a young tree, a giant paw with claws twisted from the creeping growth of centuries in hibernation. To the right she can distinguish a looming mass the size of an elephant: the mound of a head, the slumped ridge of a body. It might be one of the hounds of Arawn, grown to impossible proportions, bound forever in enchanted sleep. But as she touches it she seems to hear a sudden intake of breath, the mound shifts a fraction of an inch, a faint muscular spasm quickens the extended leg . . .

"Don't do that!" hisses Kal. "This is the Guardian. Time was, not an ant might have passed him by. Walk softly; he may hear you in his dreams."

They steal around him, down to the river. There is no bridge, but a narrow boat is drawn up in the lee of the rock. The footsteps accelerate: Fern hears the scratching of cloth on stone, the whisper of gossamer. An eager panting is hot on the nape of her neck. Involuntarily, she starts to turn . . .

But Kal holds her, hands clamped around her skull, his eyes red with a dull anger.

"She's there! She's behind me! I can feel her!" I can *feel* her, very close to me, a dreadful gloating presence, fat slug fingers reaching toward me. She's there. *She's there.* I *know* it—

"They're in the last tunnel. Get in the boat, and don't look back. Not now, when we've come so far. Not till the other side. *Don't look back!*"

He jumps down into the boat, half lifting, half pulling her in after him. She folds up in the bow, weak and stupid with panic, keeping her gaze fixed desperately on the farther bank. She hears the creak and splash of the pole, senses the drag of the current against the prow. The chill off the water makes her muscles ache. As they move forward, the footsteps recede a little. Ripple by ripple, the bank draws nearer.

And then at last the boat is nudging against rock, and she is scrambling ashore, but the low overhang defeats her, and her knees give. She can see her hands, clutching safety, but they have not the strength to draw her body after them. Then Kal is there, seizing her by the arms, swinging her onto the bank, and for a moment she is pressed close to his chest, feeling matted hair and knotted sinew, inhaling the animal odor that was stifled in the Underworld, the smell of sweat and life and warmth. "I'm sorry," she murmurs. "I lost my head."

"Morgus got inside it."

Morgus . . .

Now Fern can turn and look, and there she is, poised at the river's edge, her figure diminished with distance but no less

grotesque, her robes molting embroidery, her black hair raveled
into a corona. Even at that range Fern can see the wet glistening
of her skin, like the sheen on an oyster. Her lower lip moves
though the upper is frozen in a snarl; one outflung hand points to
the river just below the bank in a gesture that is vaguely familiar.
Sysselore crouches at her side, like a bundle of twigs wrapped in
cobwebs. Fern's start of warning comes too late: the painter un-
winds from the rock where Kal had looped it and slips like an eel
into the stream, and the boat retreats steadily away from them.
The pole is still shipped; the leaden waters divide reluctantly in
its wake. There is a long moment while they stand as though mesmerized. Already Sysselore is reaching for the prow. Fern thinks: I
am Morcadis, Morcadis the witch, but all her witchcraft is
drained from her, and she searches in vain for the inspiration of
power, for a spell, a word . . .

They are getting into the boat, pushing off from the bank.
Sysselore poles with unexpected vigor, her thin arms moving like
wires.

"You'll have to run for it." Kal grasps Fern by the elbow, pointing her to the farther limits of the cave where a faint leakage of
light shows the mouth of a tunnel yawning in the distant wall.
"That's the way out. Just follow it up and up till you get where you
want to be. Go now! I can't hold her."

"But you—"

"She won't harm me: I am her son. Go!"

Fern takes a few steps, falters, spins at a cry. Kal is doubled
over as if with a sudden cramp; in midstream, Morgus sways in
the boat, words bubbling from her mouth, soft, ugly words, shaping pain. Even as Fern reaches him he falls, writhing. His body
jerks and arches out of control; violent shudders batter him
against the rock. "Run!" he gasps through a rictus of agony. "She
can't—reach *you*. Run!"

But she pledged friendship, though not from the heart, manipulating him, seducing him to her will . . .

She says in a shaken voice: "I won't leave you."

She struggles to focus her mind, to locate the nucleus of pain and fight it. The distraction is fatal. A moment slips away and Morgus is on her.

There is a hand around her throat: its boneless grip has the strength of an octopus. Her lungs tighten, the voice is squeezed from her mouth. As she looks into those luminous eyes she knows it will not be quick. Morgus wants to kill slowly, slowly, savoring every second, every tiny increase of torment, aroused to the verge of ecstasy, until her whole vast bulk is vibrating with pleasure and she is filled and sated and glutted with death. Her other hand caresses Fern's face, fumbling for a nostril to rip open, an eyeball to pluck out. At her side, Sysselore clings like a leech, throbbing with shared rapture. And in a cold small corner of her brain Fern registers the weight of the head, bounced against her hip, and on the left side, forgotten throughout the journey, the contents of her pocket, pressed into her thigh. Morgus has left Fern's arms free, enjoying her ineffectual scrabbling at that deadly grip. Fern reaches into the pocket, closes her fist tight on the fire crystals. Then she withdraws it, and thrusts it deep into the quagmire of the witch's bosom. Fern's voice is gone but her lips move and her mind speaks, her will speaks, and the buried hatred rises, transmuted into raw power. *"Fiumé! Cirrach fiumé!"* Her hand bursts into flame.

There is an instant of hideous anguish—then Fern stumbles backward, suddenly released, and the pain is gone. In front of her, Morgus begins to scream. Her mouth opens into a gaping red pit, her teeth rattle like pebbles in the wind of her shrieks. Those tentacle fingers wrench at her clothing and tear her own skin, but the crystals cling, eating into her breast, and the dry garments blaze like tinder. Sysselore pulls back quickly, but not quick enough:

she is engulfed in flame like a sapling in the path of a firestorm, bucking and twisting with the force of the conflagration. She seems to be trying to reach the river, but there is no time, no time at all. Paper skin and cotton-wool hair crumple into ash, and the charred sticks of her bones fold up and disintegrate, broken into fragments that scatter as they hit the rock. Morgus is still moving, a blackened formless mass crawling in a pool of molten fat toward the bank. Crisped flakes peel away from her, lumps that might be cloth or hide or flesh. She has no face left, no hands, only a blind groping of fingerless stumps, the slow agonized heaving of what was once a body. Fern watches in a sort of petrified horror, wanting it over. Convulsions rack her that must surely end it, but somehow Morgus impels herself forward, covering the ground in millimeters, until at last she reaches the edge, and very gradually topples down into the water. The river swallows her, hissing. Icy steams rise into the air.

"Quickly!" Kal urges, on his feet beside her, his pain gone even as Morgus's agony began. "Put your burned hand in."

"But I can't feel anything—"

"You will, if you don't treat it now. This is the Styx: it may heal you. But don't leave it there more than a second or two—"

She needs no such admonition. The cold sears; a moment longer, and it might have taken her hand off at the wrist. As she withdraws she looks for Morgus's body, but it does not reappear.

"When you came back for me," Kal says abruptly, "did you plan this?"

"No."

He scans her face, looking for truth, unsure of what he finds. "You still owe me. Remember that, little witch. I'll collect one day."

"I know." She reaches up to kiss his cheek, unnerving him. "Thank you."

"Now *go*. Follow the tunnel. Uphill, always uphill . . ."

And now she is running, over the rocks, up the slope, pouring out the dregs of her energy in one final spurt. There is a stitch in her chest crushing the breath from her lungs, and the light is growing, brighter and brighter, until she can no longer see the ground beneath her feet, but still she goes on, dazzled, sightless, until the ground vanishes altogether, and she is falling, falling, into the light.

⬧ XIV ⬧

Fern dragged herself laboriously from a sleep so deep it
was bottomless. Even as she struggled toward consciousness the thought reached her that never before had she
slept so profoundly; trying to reawaken was like swimming
through treacle, a desperate floundering in clinging blackness. In
that last, interminable second before she opened her eyes it occurred to her that she had had too much to drink, and this must
be a hangover—the hangover to end all hangovers. She couldn't
remember what had happened, but Gaynor must have taken care
of her. Then Fern lifted her eyelids. She was in a room she had
never seen before, in a white clinical bed with a rail across the
bottom. There were soothing blue walls, dawn light streaming
through the window, an unnatural quantity of flowers. Hospital.
The shock was so great her stomach jolted. She tried to sit up, but
her limbs felt weighted and she could barely raise her head. She
saw the tubes surrounding her, invading her, the plastic chrysalis
of the drip, the dancing line on the monitor. And lastly, to her
overwhelming relief, Ragginbone. His hood was pushed back and
he was surveying her with an expression she had never seen before, a strange softening that made him appear old like any other

old man, tired and weak and human. His scarecrow hair stood up
as if it had been kneaded, and there were more lines on his face
than a thousand-piece jigsaw.

"I must have been *awfully* drunk," she said. Her voice sounded
very faint, hardly more than a whisper.

"Awfully," echoed Ragginbone.

After a minute, she asked: "What am I doing here? Was there
a car accident?"

"You've been ill," said the Watcher.

"Ill? But—" memory returned, in fragments "—I'm supposed
to be getting married. I'm getting married today."

"That was last week."

"Oh." She digested this. "Did I get married?"

"No."

For no reason that she could analyze, she felt comforted. Her
brain tried to grapple with the situation, but it was too much for
her, and she lay inert, letting her thoughts float where they would.
Ragginbone knew he ought to call a nurse, but he saw no immediate
need, and his instinct told him she was best left to herself. The
green line on the heart monitor had accelerated to normal, causing the machine no particular concern. He was a little surprised
she seemed to feel no pain from her burnt hand; however, the doctor said the nerve endings had been destroyed, and presumably it
was still numb.

Some time later, she said: "What a mess."

"I shouldn't worry about it."

She turned her head on the pillow, looking toward him.
"Where is everyone?"

"Well, your father was here last night, but he went home for a
few hours' sleep. He'll be back soon. I believe Miss Markham is at
Dale House now, Will and Gaynor are . . . somewhere, and Marcus Greig is in London, though he's due here later today."

"Marcus?"

"Your groom-to-be," Ragginbone supplied.

"Of course," Fern murmured. "I'd forgotten . . . How dreadful."

He wasn't sure if her last comment referred to her forgetfulness or Marcus's absence, but on the whole he favored the former.

Presently a nurse came in, white capped and bustling. "She's conscious," said Ragginbone.

The nurse said: "My God!" and bent over the bed, her features melting into an expression of professional satisfaction. "How are you feeling?" she beamed, and, without waiting for a response: "I'd better get you some painkillers. Your hand must be hurting." As she spoke she looked slightly uncomfortable, evidently embarrassed at the existence of first-degree burns for which there was no logical explanation.

"*Pain*killers . . . ?" Fern thought about that, and concluded the nurse must be mildly insane. "No, thank you. Could you get rid of all this stuff, please?" She indicated with a twist of her head the drip and the leads connecting her to the heart monitor.

"I'm afraid I can't do that. When the doctor comes—"

"Get rid of it. *Please*."

"You just lie there and rest, and as soon as the doctor—"

"If you don't get rid of it," Fern said, the feebleness of her voice belied by the determination underneath, "I'll pull out the needle and those electrodes and the bloody catheter myself. Now. So just—do it."

"You'll do yourself an injury!"

"I don't care. Anyway, if I do . . . you can bring me those painkillers you're so keen on. *Do it!*"

"I think you'd better," Ragginbone said gently, trying not to smile.

With a nervous glance around for absent superiors, the nurse complied, whisking a curtain around the bed to conceal her activities. As Ragginbone shifted his chair aside to avoid obstructing her his feet touched something partially concealed under the bed. A quick look showed him a patchwork bag made of soiled scraps of material untidily cobbled together, evidently containing a fair-sized object, vaguely spherical in shape. He frowned, moving it behind the cabinet, out of the nurse's way. He knew it had not been there when he came in.

Freed from her medical trappings, Fern noticed something else. "Why is my hand bandaged?" she said accusingly. (Hadn't the nurse mentioned something about her hand?)

"You—you burnt it . . ."

Fern tried to take this in, and failed. The bandages annoyed her—the hand felt perfectly all right—but she was too worn out for a further tussle with authority. The nurse, grateful for the respite, checked pulse and temperature, administered a few sips of water, and scurried off to write a report for her ward nurse. Ragginbone moved the patchwork bag farther out of sight and waited.

"Caracandal," Fern said at last—he started to hear her use his Gift name, something she had never done before—"what's been happening to me?"

"You went out with Gaynor for your hen night, had too much to drink—"

"I knew drink came into it somewhere."

"—and passed out. We got you home, in the end, but you wouldn't wake. You've been here for a week, in deep coma. Yesterday evening severe burns appeared on your left hand."

"How?"

"I was hoping," said the Watcher, "that you would tell me."

"I had dreams," she said, groping in the recesses of her mind. "Very *complicated* dreams. There was a Tree . . . and a witch—two witches . . . and a man with a black face . . . smoke, and—yes—*fire* . . ."

After that, she did not speak for a long time.

Robin arrived simultaneously with the doctor, hugged his daughter, damp eyed, and murmured repeatedly: "You should have phoned," thus impeding the process of medical examination.

"I knew you were coming shortly," Ragginbone said, but Robin plainly did not expect a response, merely gazing at his daughter with an expression compounded of besottedness and relief.

Fern, who had insisted on sitting up, submitted patiently to the doctor's explorations. "She *seems* to be making a good recovery," he told Robin with an air of disapproval. "Of course, it'll be several days before we can be certain. I'll change the dressing later, when I've had a chat with the ward nurse." He turned back to his patient. "You just relax, young lady, get lots of sleep, and we'll have you up and about again in no time."

"I've *had* lots of sleep," Fern pointed out to his departing back. Her right hand tightened on the veil that was still draped around her shoulders. "Who brought me this?"

"I think it was Gaynor," Robin said. "Pretty, isn't it? Can't say I've seen it before."

"Have I any other clothes here?"

"No," said her father. "Took them home for the wash."

"Daddy, would you mind very much going back and getting me some? I know it's a chore, but I don't want to walk out of here in a dressing gown."

"Don't think they're going to let you come home just yet, old girl," Robin said. Already the habitual look of nebulous anxiety was creeping back onto his face.

"Did you hear that doctor?" Fern said. "He called me *young lady*. He can't be more than a couple of years older than I am. Anyway, there's nothing wrong with me. I'm just a bit floppy from being in bed too long. All I need is exercise and decent food, and I won't get either of those here. Please, Daddy."

"That hand of yours is pretty bad," Robin said awkwardly. "I know it doesn't seem to hurt right now, but—well, they say you may need a skin graft."

"I can be an outpatient at a burns unit," Fern said. "Anyway, it's my left, and I'm right-handed. I can manage with one. It's doing me no good, lying here." In fact, she was still sitting, but Robin did not quibble. "I just want to get up, get dressed, feel like myself again . . . If I find I'm not up to it, I'll stay a bit longer."

Liar, thought Ragginbone.

Eventually Robin gave in, preparing to depart with a list of her requirements. "Don't know what Abby'll say," he mumbled. "Maybe Marcus can make you change your mind . . ." The prospect did not appear to fill him with enthusiasm.

As soon as he had gone Fern began to tug at the bandage.

"I don't think you should do that," said Ragginbone.

"I want to *see*," she persisted. "Everyone says I have these awful burns, but my hand feels fine except that I can't move it properly because the bandage is too tight. Have you any scissors?"

Their eyes met in something that was part mutual comprehension, part conflict of will. He thought that hers were deeper and brighter than before, their veining of color more pronounced, green within the gray: they shone with a steady brilliance against the anemic pallor of her face. "I have a knife," he said at last. Not defeat, concession. He produced a penknife from an inner pocket and unclipped a narrow blade. Carefully he slit the bandage up the back of her hand. Fern tugged it off, pulling with her teeth at the bindings on her fingers.

"I feel like a mummy," she complained.

She extended her palm. It was smooth and unmarked, the palm of a career woman who never does housework, crisscrossed only lightly with the lines of her destiny. A gypsy would have found little there to read. Her fingertips had a bluish tinge; perhaps the bandaging had restricted her blood supply. When Ragginbone touched them, they felt very cold. "Last night," he said evenly, "your skin was burnt off, your tendons so badly damaged that the doctor said you might never recover the use of the hand. Your Gift would not mend that. Only the ancient druids had such power, at least according to legend."

"Last night . . ." Fern's brow contracted. "Yes, I suppose so. Time must move differently when you're outside it. A week might feel like a year, a night . . . only a few moments."

She looked up as the doctor returned, with the ward nurse in his train pushing a hostess trolley of sterilized dishes. "Out of the way," she told Ragginbone briskly. She still suspected him of Munchausen, and had an unacknowledged yearning to be the one responsible for its diagnosis. Ragginbone, with a slight, ironic bow, moved aside. "Miss Capel! *What* have you done with your bandage?"

Wordlessly Fern proffered her hand. The nurse turned red, the doctor pale. "This is impossible!" he said after a lengthy pause. "I examined the injuries myself; there can be no question of a mistake." He fixed Fern with a rather wild stare. "You have some explanation?"

"Me?" Fern responded with just the right degree of emphasis.

The doctor, aware he had sounded accusatory, floundered into apology.

"All this has caused my family considerable distress," Fern said blandly, seizing her chance. "Of course, this is clearly a very exclusive clinic, and I would not wish to impugn your reputation . . ."

The doctor took a grip on himself and retired to consider his position. He was among those who had classified Fern as an "interesting case"—at least until she woke up. He might have reflected, had he been given to reflection, that one of the many advantages of treating coma patients is that they cannot make

themselves awkward. Ragginbone, watching Fern's performance
with deep appreciation, estimated that by the time Robin returned the medical staff would probably be only too happy to permit her departure. Her voice had strengthened dramatically since
she first awoke, and the physical debility that would normally
succeed a prolonged period in bed seemed to have dissipated
with unnatural speed. He guessed she was using her Gift to accelerate her recovery, transforming power into raw energy, pump-
ing blood into muscle with the force of her will; but whether she
realized what she was doing or was acting solely on instinct he did
not know. He thought: She's having to expend too much power
just to keep going. If a crisis occurs, she'll have very little left.

The ward nurse was still hovering, covertly watching Ragginbone. Miracle cures were out of place in a modern hospital, and
intuition told her this was all an elaborate confidence trick, with
him as the undoubted mastermind. She busied herself with the
flowers overloading Fern's bedside cabinet, remarking as she did
so: "You really have too many bouquets here, Miss Capel. They
get in everyone's way. It would have been nice if you had suggested giving some of them to other, less fortunate, patients."

"No doubt I would have done," said Fern, with an air of faint
hauteur, "if I talked in my sleep."

"You shouldn't have taken that bandage off," the nurse pursued, ignoring the implied rebuke. "You could have done yourself
a great deal of harm. Burns have to be treated very carefully." The
inference was that if the bandage had remained in its place, so
would the injury.

"I knew there was nothing wrong with my hand," said Fern. "I
could feel it."

"Doctors don't make mistakes."

"Everyone makes mistakes," her patient retorted unanswerably.

Balked, the nurse moved toward the door. It was then that her glance fell on the patchwork bag shoved behind the cabinet away from the general view. "What is this?" she said. "I suppose *you* brought it—" to Ragginbone. "It looks extremely dirty. We do like to maintain standards of basic hygiene here." She bent over it and, being the sort of person who believed she had the right to pry into anything that impinged on her territory, she lifted the flap and peered at the contents.

The angry red that was still in her face drained away, leaving her cheeks sallow pale, brackish with the frayed ends of blood vessels. Her mouth dropped open, but only a sort of gasp emerged, like a soundless scream. Then gradually, as if in slow motion, she buckled, crumpled, and subsided into a heap on the floor. Fern, unable to see what it was she had been looking at, craned over the edge of the bed—and shot backward, round-eyed with horror.

"I don't know what it is you've got in there," Ragginbone said, his tone perilously close to a drawl, "but I think it might be a good idea if you made it resemble something different . . . before anybody else takes a look."

"Something—different?" Fern repeated stupidly.

"Similar in shape and size, perhaps. Something . . . likely. Not a bunch of grapes, but along those lines. If you have the power left—?"

But Fern, hands pressed against her forehead, was already muttering in Atlantean. Satisfied, Ragginbone picked his way around the unconscious ward nurse in a leisurely manner and leaned into the corridor to summon assistance.

Eventually a pair of muscular porters removed the body for revival elsewhere, and in due course the doctor returned. He appeared harassed and increasingly ill at ease. The recollection of the ward nurse's stone-faced assertions, when she recovered from her faint, had shaken his remaining confidence. She had always been so practical, so down-to-earth, so reliably unimaginative . . . "I looked in the bag," she had said, "and there was a head. A severed head. It was alive. Its eyes rolled. It *smiled* at me." She was currently being dosed with tranquilizers while the doctor, feeling foolish, found himself asking Fern what was in the patchwork bag.

"Someone brought me a watermelon," said Fern. "I'm very fond of them. I can't think why it should have upset her so much. Unless she has a phobia of watermelons?"

The bag did look as if it contained a severed head, the doctor thought, but when he opened it, in a would-be careless manner, all it contained was watermelon. Only watermelon. He apologized yet again, and retreated to suspend the ward nurse from duty and recommend her for an intensive course of psychoanalysis. Ragginbone, who had found the accusation of Munchausen both stupid and distasteful, tried not to feel avenged. It was only several days later, describing the incident to a friend over a game of golf, that it occurred to the doctor to wonder, with a twinge of sudden doubt, why anyone should bring fruit for a patient in deep coma.

Marcus Greig arrived around lunchtime to find Fern fully dressed, sitting on the edge of the bed. She was barefoot, since she had forgotten, in the aftermath of her awakening, to request any shoes, and neither Robin nor Abby had thought to repair the omission. She had already tried standing up, fighting the onset of giddiness and the weakness of her legs, forcing her head to clear and her limbs to support her. She knew she was drawing too heavily on her resources, leaving herself almost empty of power, but a sense of urgency gripped her, left over from her escape through the Underworld, and she longed above all to get home. Her surroundings in the clinic felt less a trap than a hindrance; at Dale House she would be free to think, to talk to Ragginbone, to plan. She had had time to coax from the Watcher a brief account of Will and Gaynor's disappearance, two days earlier, but she wanted more details. She had a feeling of imminent danger, of the need for desperate action. Weakness, weariness, hospital confinement all got in the way. When Marcus walked in, primed by one of the staff and aglow with appropriate happiness, she felt only guilt and a shameful pang of irritation, because here was yet another delay. The pleasure she must once have felt on seeing him seemed an emotion as unreal as a daydream. She struggled to thrust urgency aside, to respond suitably to his warmth. Then she asked her family—and Ragginbone—to wait outside.

She knew of no way to mitigate the blow—if it was a blow. She half thought he might be secretly relieved. Desirable brides do not lapse into unexplained comas on the eve of the wedding. "I can't marry you," she said bluntly, and then cursed herself for sounding ridiculously melodramatic.

"We can discuss it when you're feeling better," Marcus said, remarkably unperturbed. "The doctors said your condition might be psychosomatic—"

"I *am* feeling better."

"—a childhood trauma resulting in a secret horror of commitment, some connection with your mother's death maybe. Alternatively, you could have an abnormal reaction to certain forms of alcohol. Gaynor told me you'd had several brandies that night. You don't usually drink much, and I've never seen you touch brandy. If a postprandial cognac is always going to have this effect, we ought to be forewarned. These days, you hear of people *dying* of peanut allergy, and someone I know had to have his stomach pumped after a bad reaction to a couple of aspirin. Anyway, we don't have to rush into marriage. We'll talk about it when you're ready."

"I'm ready now," sighed Fern. "You don't understand. I'm not—I'm not in love with you. I never was. I'm so sorry, Marcus. I've behaved very badly. I *wanted* to be in love with you: you have all the qualities which . . . The problem is, I'm not sure I could ever really love anyone. Perhaps I'm just too cold . . ."

"Nonsense," said Marcus with uncomfortable enthusiasm. "I *know* that's not true."

"Well . . . maybe the trouble is that I've always been in love with—someone imaginary. An unattainable ideal . . ."

"We all do that," Marcus responded to Fern's surprise. "I remember there was a painting I saw once in an exhibition, when I was in my teens: it haunted me for years. I bought a postcard of it and pinned it up in my room. I might still have it somewhere. It was by one of the lesser Pre-Raphaelites, nobody distinguished, I can't even recall his name. It wasn't really all that good. Just a picture of a woman—well, a girl—Circe, or Morgan Le Fay, someone like that. She had that crinkly hair that all the Pre-Raphaelites went in for, done up in a sort of Bacchanalian disorder, all loops and tendrils and bits of ivy leaf, but it was her face that got to me. One of those wistful, Burne-Jones faces with a drooping mouth, but the eyes—the eyes were different. Slanting and sly and wild. An improbable shade of green. I used to fantasize that one day I would meet a woman with eyes like that, a witch woman with an untamed soul looking out from behind a sweet, solemn façade." He smiled at her with a tenderness that she had forgotten. "I settled for sweet and solemn. When you're a teenager you read Yeets and Keats—" he mispronounced deliberately "—you dream of a Belle Dame Sans Merci, of Bridget with her long, dim hair. It's a phase. A germ of it stays with you and recurs from time to time. First dreams are like first love: best in souvenir. That sort of thing isn't real."

"I never knew," she whispered, confused and distracted by the strangeness of it, by a kind of bittersweet irony, an insight that was both pointless and too late. "I never knew you wanted—*magic*."

He did not notice the special emphasis she gave the word. "It passes," he said. "Romance—dreams—they don't matter. What matters is liking, companionship, affection, respect. Even sex. That's the sort of love that works."

"Not for me," she said, horrified to find herself on the verge of tears. "Maybe I'm too young for you. Or you're too old for me. Too wise, too worldly, too—I'm sorry, I'm sorry, that sounds cruel. I didn't mean it so. I think something got lost, in the eighteen years between us. There was a level where we might have met, a different plane which . . . But it's gone, it's gone for good, we won't find it now. I'm so *sorry*, Marcus . . ."

"Leave it," he insisted. "You're not in a state to make decisions. We'll talk again in a week or so."

"I need to be on my own . . ."

He grimaced. "I've just driven up. I was planning to stay over—leave around six in the morning. I've got a lecture tomorrow. No, don't worry. It's probably easiest if I head back now. I'll call you."

"All right," Fern said, seizing control of herself. He would accept it, she thought, given time. Liking, affection, respect—he could find those with someone else. With any number of someone elses.

"Good-bye, Marcus."

"Bye, darling."

And so he went, leaving her alone. Presently Robin and Abby assisted her out to the car. Ragginbone followed, with the patchwork bag.

"**I**'m not going to marry Marcus," Fern told her relatives, back at Dale House. "I know you've both gone to a lot of trouble, spent serious money—I'll pay you back, Dad, I've got plenty of savings—"

"No, no." Robin waved away the offer with genuine revulsion. "Just want you to be happy, that's all. Not a bad chap, Marcus, but I never thought he was the one for you. Didn't stick around long when you were in hospital. So much for that 'in sickness and in health' bit."

"He couldn't help it," Fern said. "He's fond of me—he really is—but he's not good at sitting still." She went on, rather wearily: "We'll have to return the presents. Oh lord, all that packing . . . I'll make a start soon."

"I've done it," Abby said. "They're all ready to go."

Fern squeezed her hand and looked at her long and silently, and Abby, like Ragginbone, thought: She's different. Something about the eyes . . .

Yoda attempted to jump on Fern's lap, falling well short of his goal. Absentmindedly Fern picked him up and stroked his head.

"Where's Lougarry?" she asked.

"I think Will took her," Robin said. "Odd, that. He and Gaynor went off to find a specialist; can't think where they've got to. Not necessary now, I'm glad to say. Bit worrying, though. They haven't phoned, not while I've been here. They're adults, they can take care of themselves. All the same . . ."

"Perhaps they've gone for a romantic weekend," said Abby, "though it seems a strange time to choose."

"I doubt it," said Ragginbone, entering with tea and Mrs. Wicklow, who, in an unusual excess of sentiment, was dabbing her cheeks with a skein of toilet paper. "They were both far too concerned about Fern to think of something like that. They'll turn up."

"If it's not one thing it's another," said Mrs. Wicklow, pulling herself together. "It's that Redmond woman, I'm sure of it. Saw her in t'mirror, I did. You want to get the vicar round to do an exorcism. I don't hold with that sort of thing mostly, but I reckon it's needed here."

"Oh, no, we can't do that," said Fern. "It would upset the house-goblin."

It was some time before she found herself alone with Ragginbone.

"Well?" she said. She was still idly caressing Yoda, the gentleness of her hands at variance with the edge in her voice. "You must have some idea where they've gone."

"I fear," said the Watcher, "they may have gone to look for a dragon—or someone who knows about dragons. There is a story—a rumor—that the last of dragonkind still lives, with a splinter of the Lodestone lodged in his heart. Will's theory was that the touch of the Stone might help to bring you back. I didn't have a chance to speak to them, but Gaynor seems to have remembered seeing a manuscript that might be relevant. Unfortunately, it's in a museum with one Dr. Laye on the board—"

"They've gone to meet Dr. Laye?"

"I doubt if I could have dissuaded them, even if I'd had the opportunity. Will was very determined."

"He would be," Fern said bitterly. "I have to find them. Dr. Laye sold himself to the Oldest Spirit. He's like an ambulant, only worse. They're both in there, sharing his body, sharing his *mind*. He's a descendant of the dragon charmers, and the Oldest One is feeding off him, using his skill. He's got the dragon imprisoned somewhere, beneath a well . . ."

"You know a lot," said Ragginbone. "More than I." There was a hint of enquiry in his tone.

"I haven't time to explain," said Fern. "Where's this museum?"

"You can do nothing till tomorrow," Ragginbone said sternly. "You've exhausted your power simply getting out of bed. You must rest. Without your Gift, you'll be no use to Will and Gaynor, whatever trouble they're in. We have to trust them."

"And the dragon?" said Fern.

"Let's hope it stays where it's penned. None of us can do much against a dragon." He went on, perhaps with the object of diverting her. "Tell me about the Tree. And Morgus. It was Morgus, wasn't it?"

"How did you know?"

"A long shot. A lucky guess. Go on."

So she told him. About the two hags hovering around the

spellfire, the visions she had seen there, her lessons in witchcraft, Kal. She told him everything, or almost everything.

"What," he said at last, "is in the bag?"

"A watermelon," said Fern, and she did not smile.

She went to bed early, pleading fatigue. Robin and Abby followed suit; Ragginbone had already left. She needs to recoup her strength, he told himself. She would never be so foolish as to face Azmordis in her present condition. Tomorrow . . .

"Tomorrow will be too late," Fern said to the darkness. Beneath the duvet she was still in underwear and tight-fitting sweater. Jeans, jacket, and trainers lay ready to hand. The curtains were not completely drawn and the glimmer of the paler gloom outside showed in the gap. Presently the moon peered through, a gibbous moon, old and pockmarked, its stunted profile blurred by a nimbus of milky light. Its groping gaze reached toward the bed but fell short, cut off by the shadow of the pelmet. A night bird passed by, unusually close, calling out in a croaking scream that Fern could not identify. She was glad of the dark that hid her, wary even of the moon. She listened for the telltale grumble of the plumbing, the final shutting of the other bedroom door. Perhaps as a result of her recent experiences, perhaps because she was surviving on adrenaline shots of raw power, she found that now her vision had adjusted she could see in the dark far better than ever before, distinguishing outlines formerly hidden in the dimness of the room. At last Robin's door closed and the house subsided gradually into silence. "Bradachin!" Fern called. Her voice was a whisper without softness, hissing like a knife blade. He took shape reluctantly, one shade among many, but she saw him. "I need you."

"Ye woudna speak tae me for many a year, yet now ye're ordering me like a servant—"

"This is no time to stand on your dignity. I had my reasons; you

know that, if you know anything. I was fond of your predecessor—
or at least I pitied him. He was weak. Will says you're strong,
brave and strong. He and Gaynor are in trouble. I'm going after
them. I'll need your help."

"Ye're meaning tae gae after them tonight?"

"Yes. Now. Tonight."

"I'm thinking ye shoudna be doing that, hinny. Ye've slept tae
long tae gae running aboot the noo; ye maun be puggled."

"Probably," said Fern, in too much haste to attempt to decipher his dialect. "I'm going anyway. Can you see to it that my father and Abby don't wake? I might do it, but it would exhaust
whatever I've got left—and that isn't much."

"I can do a pickle charming, aye, but if ye would be saving
your brother ye'll need your cantrips. Ye canna gae after Trouble
withoot them."

"I'll be all right. Stop fussing: it wastes time. While you're in
the other room, can you get my father's car keys? My car's at the
garage, and Will's taken his, so the Volvo's my only option. The keys
will be on the dressing table. Will you recognize them?"

"Aye, but—"

"Good," said Fern. "Hurry."

When she was sure he had gone she slid her legs over the
edge of the bed and stood up. There was a millisecond of dizziness, of knees folding, muscles failing; but she forced a surge of
energy through every artery, every junction of bone and sinew, and
the weakness passed. The patchwork bag lay where Ragginbone
had left it, on the floor by her bed. She squatted down beside it
and reached for the flap—then hesitated, taken with a sudden
trembling, a nascent horror of the thing inside. Beyond reality, in
the dimension of the Tree, she had accepted every aspect of her
strange environment without qualm or question, existing in a
dream state where the bizarre became the norm. But here, beset

by Time, pressured by the fears and feelings of the everyday world, she could not suppress her loathing at the thought of the object she had brought with her. It took all her self-control to open the bag and seize the severed stem, flinching from the touch of hair. Averting her eyes, she lifted it out, propped it up on her pillow. It seemed to her a dreadful unnatural thing, a form of obscenity, this head without body or limb. She must not look at the squirming neck stump, leaking sap; she must concentrate on the features—the dark familiar features of the dragon charmer. Ruvindra Laïï, her partner, her ally. She focused her gaze on his face, only his face, murmuring his name. In this ordinary bedroom the black geometry of his bones seemed somehow more rarefied, more dauntingly beautiful, arrogant as an antique prince, ominous as a malediction; his eyes opened onto a glimmer of blue, like witch-fires seen from far off. With that wakening, his personality dominated the night.

"We have little time," he said, and the soft dark voice was somehow shocking, against nature, coming from undeveloped vocal cords, from lips without lungs. "The fruit of the Eternal Tree was not meant for this world. This head will rot quickly in the clear air and the hasty hours. We must move now, before it is too late. Do you know where we can find this recreant offspring of my house?"

"No," said Fern. "But I can find out." She withdrew her gaze from him, still shaking with latent horror, and began to pull on her jeans.

"The old man," the head remarked, "he whom you spoke with earlier—he reminded me of one I knew, though that was long ago."

"He's been around quite a while."

"What of the goblin? They say malmorths make mischievous enemies and treacherous friends. They are little in all things: they will stab you in the back with a silver pin, and desert you for a bowl of broth."

"I expect so," Fern said indifferently, lacing up her trainers. Suddenly she looked straight at him. "What do *they* say of a dragon charmer who broke faith with the creatures he loved—an oath breaker who sold his soul and cheated on the bargain—an apple that talks, pilfered from the Tree of Life and Death?"

"They say the thief must be fearless, to pluck such deadly fruit. There is a secret hardness in you, Fernanda, like a single thread of steel in a knot of silk. For that alone, I would trust you—if we had not come so far that trust is no longer relevant."

"*You* aren't particularly trustworthy," said Fern. "But I never doubted you." She picked up the patchwork bag and squinted closely at it: the tattered fragments of cloth were already pulling away from the stitching. She dropped it again and rifled briskly in the wardrobe, emerging with a small carpetbag on a shoulder strap. "I'm sure Perseus never had this trouble," she remarked.

"I brought ye the keys," said a voice behind her. Bradachin had reappeared, carrying not only the car keys but an ancient spear nearly twice his own height. He was staring fixedly at the head.

"What's that for?" asked Fern.

"I thought I might be needing it."

She frowned, but let it go. "Are the others sleeping?"

"Aye. I ken a lullaby or two for the likes o' they. If ye dinna make a noise, they won't be waking long awhile. Cailin . . ."

"Well done," said Fern. "Thanks. Could you—would you tell Ragginbone where I've gone? Tell him I'm sorry. I ought to write a note but I haven't time."

"I'm thinking he'll know weel enough. Cailin, I dinna ken what ye want with yon, but . . . ye're mixing in devil's magic here. Ye shoudna gae meddling in necromancy—"

"I know what I'm doing," Fern said. "I think." She picked up

the head again and placed it carefully in the new bag, this time
without a shudder, if only because Bradachin was watching. "If I
don't come back, tell them . . . Oh, never mind. I can't bother
about that now."

"Ye must tell them yourself," said Bradachin, "if ye can. I'm
coming wi' ye."

"You can't do that." Fern paused, disconcerted. "You're a
house-goblin."

"Ye'll need me. How waur ye planning tae enter the museum,
in the midst o' the night? There'll be alarums and such, nae doot.
Ye woudna be much guid as a lock picker, Gifted or no."

"*Can* you break in? If you're not invited . . ."

"It's no a hoose. Any road, when there's kidnapping and worse
afoot, the laws don't hold. Dinna fret, cailin. I'm coming wi' ye.
I'm nae afeard o' Trouble. And I ha' the spear. This is the Sleer
Bronaw, the war spear o' the McCrackens. When their sons' sons
turned tae drinkers o' milk and takers o' daily baths, it came tae
me. There's nae man can stand agin this spear."

It looked far too large and unwieldy for the goblin to use, but
Fern refrained from comment. "And this?" she said, touching the
bag at her side.

"Aye," said Bradachin after a pause. "I fear yon heid. I fear all
black sortilege. But . . ."

"But?"

"I'm coming wi' ye."

Fern said no more. They stole softly down the stairs into the
hall. She switched on a light to consult the telephone directory,
found the two addresses she wanted, and went outside to the car.
Bradachin and his antique weapon disappeared somehow into the
back. In the driver's seat, she searched the side pockets for the
necessary maps; Robin, trained by his daughter, always traveled
in a welter of cartography. Although Gaynor had taken the main

ordinance survey map from the study, years of driving around Yorkshire meant the car was well stocked with alternatives. "I don't know the area at all well," Fern told Bradachin. "Can you direct me?" A grunt answered her. Then she turned the key in the ignition and the engine purred into unobtrusive life. As they swept out of the drive and onto the open road, she put her foot down on the throttle, and began to drive much too fast southwest toward York.

It was nearly midnight when they reached the suburbs. The dingy aureole of the city was reflected off a low-slung cloud canopy, not illuminating the sky but merely smudging it with a kind of dirty glimmer. In the country the clouds had form and depth, moon-edged or rent into pale tatters across a gap of stars, but here they were shapeless, a vast, lowering gloom. With the aid of a street map they found the road they wanted. Fern parked awkwardly with her nearside wheels on the sidewalk, unaccustomed to handling so large a vehicle. Bradachin faded from the interior of the car without using the door; Fern got out in a more mundane fashion. There was a strange, stifled silence over this part of the city, as if the sagging cloud cover was crushing the air against the earth, muffling noise. The sound of nearby footsteps, a burst of laughter, a sudden shout, carried as though in a long, low room rather than outdoors. The museum was an old house among other old houses, with little to distinguish it save the plaque on the door. It was ugly with the ponderous, labored ugliness of the late Victorians, weather grimed, its black windows uncurtained and unforthcoming. On one side there was a gate in a high wall overhung with some dark shrub; Fern tried the latch and it opened easily, admitting her to a shabby strip of garden tangled with plant shadows. There was a smell of dank vegetation, of last year's leaves rotting unswept on pathway and lawn, of new growth choked with old. It reminded her of the Tree, and with that memory a subtle change came over her, though she herself was not aware of it. She had been moving like any ordinary person who is trying to be quiet; now, her whole body became more fluid, noiseless and circumspect as a wild creature. Her senses strained; her dilating eyes soaked up every atom of light. She could see a bent twig, a broken paving. Around the back of the building she went to a window and peered in, making out an empty office, an open door, a glimpse of the passage beyond. She felt Bradachin materialize close by her.

"I assume there's no one there."

"No a body in the place. I coudna find ought but books, many books, and parchments and scribblings. Men will iver be scribbling and scribbling o' something. There's alarums tae protect them, with beams crissing and crossing, like all yon books waur a treasure o' gold. I could fix them for ye, if ye waur wishing tae gae in, but it would tak' a while."

"We haven't got a while," said Fern. "It isn't necessary." She turned back to the garden, conscious of a sudden prickling down her spine, an inexplicable disquiet. Here at the back the shrubs had run wild, clotted into thickets black with something more than ordinary darkness. There was no coherent form, no discernible movement, but she saw the eyes for a moment before they winked out: the narrow, whiteless eyes of something that watches from under a stone.

"Did you see it?"

"Aye," said Bradachin, and there was a note in his voice she had not heard before, a change of timbre that was close to fear.

"What was it?"

"I'm no sure . . . If it wa' what I thought, he shouldna be here. He's muckle far from home. The pugwidgies are no meant for our world."

"What's a pugwidgie?" asked Fern.

"Ye dinna want tae find oot," said Bradachin. "They're *his* creatures, from *his* place. They come from Azmodel."

Fern remembered the things she had seen in the spellfire,

crawling from every rock and shadow to devour Ruvindra Laï.
Her skin chilled.

All she said was: "There's nothing more for us here. Let's get
back to the car."

They drove off, heading out of the city, into a night as black as
the abyss.

◆ XV ◆

Lougarry sat on the backseat of the car, listening with straining ears and all six senses on alert for the call that did not come. At one point a man came around the corner of the house, a man with a pale face and eyes sunken in a mask of shadow. He approached the car and even peered inside, but the wolf had dropped to the floor and in the poor light he did not see her. When he was gone she resumed her vigil. Afternoon sombered into a premature evening; dim swirls of cloud rolled down from the Pennines like a hangover from the preceding winter, darkening the belated spring. A few birds passed overhead, flying home to roost, but none sought shelter at Drakemyre Hall. There is some evil here that the birds avoid, thought Lougarry, and her ears flattened and her eyes gleamed brighter in the dusk. All living creatures coexisted naturally alongside both werefolk and witchkind: the animal kingdom made no moral judgments. There would have to be something very wrong for even the rooks and jackdaws to leave twisted tree and crooked chimney stack untenanted. An abnormal disturbance in the earth's magnetic field— a place where the shadow world had encroached too far on reality.

Or the presence of a predator so deadly that neither bird nor beast would venture into its vicinity . . .

When the night was as black as an unopened tomb, she slipped through the window. She sensed the wrongness as soon as her paws touched the ground: it was there in the deep vibrations of earth, in the invisible ripples that irradiated from Hall and hillside, from the flight of a moth to the fall of a tree. Her skin prickled; the fur on her nape stood on end. The normal darkness of a country night seemed to have been invaded by something deeper and older, the Dark that was before any dawn. And the ground itself transmitted the beat of a gigantic heart, and the savagery of some subterranean beast, hungry and desperate, caged against its will. Lougarry always trod lightly, but here she moved with a kind of wary delicacy, as if walking on broken glass. She skirted the house: no lights showed from within and every window was closed. She found a back door that her nose told her led to the kitchen but it was locked, not latched, and there was no way of opening it. Close by was a coal bunker, now empty and unused, with a chute that might, she thought, lead somewhere. She was about to investigate when intuition told her she was being watched. She hackled and turned.

To the wolf's eyes, the night was less dark than monochrome. And among the black shapes of tree and scrub was a shape that did not belong. It was too indistinct for her to make out the fine details, but it appeared to have long ears, splayed feet, and arms of unequal length . . . She lowered her muzzle, questing for its scent, and froze. The smell that reached her was one no animal could mistake. Carrion . . .

With extraordinary speed it leapt away, running on its longer arm as well as the flapping feet, vanishing around the corner of the house. Lougarry sprang after it, following the scent. Unlike ordinary wolves, lycanthropes do not eat carrion unless they are starving, and her upper lip was lifted in what might have been a snarl of distaste. But the thing had fled and her reflex was to pursue, to catch if possible and kill if necessary. She saw it skittering ahead of her down one of the paths into the formal garden: it disappeared into a net of shadows, reemerging a moment later looking somehow altered. Its ears were shorter, its legs longer, the feet taloned—but it moved too fast for her to be sure. The smell of dead flesh tugged her on like a gleaming thread in a labyrinth, over barren flower beds, under tangled shrubs, crisscrossing from path to path. In front of her she saw what must be a sundial on a squat plinth, and *there* it was, the thing, clearly visible at last, leaping up and down as though taunting her. Only now it had a huge warty head like a toad, a toad with fangs, and its hind feet were webbed, but its forepaws looked like goblin hands. Gathering all her strength she hurled herself over the leaf-mottled paving toward it. She never saw the trap, hidden in the shadows, half-buried between broken stones. She never saw it, until her flying step released the spring, and the iron jaws closed with a crunch on her foreleg.

She did not yelp, nor howl. Werewolves are forever silent. The sundial was empty now but the smell remained, imprinted in the ground, in the very air around her. She explored the injury with her tongue, tasting blood; she knew the bone was broken, she had heard it go. The human part of her mind raged at her own stupidity, but the wolf was already scanning the darkness, summarizing her situation. She realized immediately that she could not open the trap: the mechanism needed the cunning of dexterous fingers, and its grip was too strong for her to force the jaws apart. The shock had caused a temporary numbness but she knew that soon the pain would begin, draining her energy, blinding her senses. And it—they—were out there, not very far away, slipping from shadow to shadow, circling. Soon they would start to creep nearer. Stunted, malformed things, goblin-sized but not goblin-scented, smelling *dead* . . .

A memory floated to the surface of her thought: Caracandal,

leaning against a rock on a warm southern evening long ago, describing his one visit to Azmodel. His words had taken the warmth from the evening and the smile from the face of the moon. He had told her of the poisonous vapors that hovered over the rainbow lakes, and fauns and sylphids dancing in the Garden of Lost Meanings, and sacrifices screaming in the temple. And other beings who dwelt there, neither human nor animal, botched creations from the leftovers of the dead, possessed by the lowest form of elementals, mindless and ravenous. "Many centuries before I was born there was a wizard called Morloch who was thought to be the greatest magician of his day. *He* thought so, anyway. I believe he was an ancestor of Morgus, who had similar delusions: evidently a family trait. He became obsessed with the Cauldron of Rebirth—the Cauldron of Hell, as it was later known, stolen from the ancient Underworld in a time before history, misused and ultimately shattered. Legend said that if, after a battle, the dead bodies and body parts were placed in it and heated, with the correct incantation spoken, they would coalesce and spring forth again in a terrible semblance of life renewed, possessed by demons, voiceless killers of unbelievable ferocity. Morloch, no doubt, hoped the Cauldron would make him a true creator, a father of armies. He spent half his life searching for the fragments, taking those he could find and welding them together in a patchwork reincarnation of the dread crucible. Then he instructed his servants to bring him carcasses for experiment: beast, man, goblin, whatever. Presumably he saw his first spellbinding as a mere trial. He heated the Cauldron, spoke the liturgy—but the Cauldron burst asunder, and the deformities that leapt forth were not warriors but only mouths, forever hungry. It is said, if they do not eat their famine will abate, but once they have tasted blood, unless prevented, they will feed and feed until they burst. They are supposed to have devoured Morloch himself first: he could not control them. The Old Spirits might have destroyed them, horrified by such monstrosities, but the Oldest took them, and hid them in Azmodel, calling them his pets, making them subservient only to him. He has used them ever since. They have no name, no kind, but sometimes they are called after their maker . . ."

Morlochs.

Caracandal had said they were bound to Azmodel, but her nose could not deceive her. They smelled of the carrion from which they were made. Somehow the denizens of the Beautiful Valley were here, in this corner of the real world, part of the wrongness that made up Drakemyre Hall. She was certain now that Will and Gaynor were imprisoned, maybe slain. As for her, she knew there was no chance. Her bared teeth and claws might hold the morlochs back for a while—a little while—but no help would come, because she was the help. She licked the fresh blood from her leg, that they might not catch the scent. Already the pain was beginning. She crouched with burning eyes, watching every shadow. Her last resolve was that she would make them pay dearly for their feast.

The night wore on. She began to catch glimpses of them, skimming the cracked pavings, skulking behind bush or plinth. Initially she thought there were three or four, later six, ten, maybe a dozen. They started to throw things at her—gravel chips, bits of twig—making her twist from side to side in a futile attempt to seize her tormentors. Eventually one of them ventured too close: a bulbous, vaguely arachnoid creature that approached with a swift scuttling motion. It was fast, but she was faster: her teeth met in its body. She ate it, though her stomach turned at the meal. It was all the sustenance she would get. She was thirsty from loss of blood and the thing had a high fluid content. She could sense the others watching as she ate; after that, they were more wary. They knew she would weaken soon.

A pale, windy dawn blew in from the east; leaves stirred on the pathways. No one came from the house to gloat or administer the final blow. The morlochs had no speech to pass on messages, no capacity to plan, only appetite and instinct. By day they grew more furtive, shrinking into the scenery, the poisonous hues of skin and fur, scale and slime dimming to blend with a background of gnarled stems, faded soil, lichened stone. She might almost have thought they were gone, if their distinctive odor had not been so pervasive. The pain swelled, battering her in waves, traveling in spasms up the injured leg and racking her whole body. Her thirst returned with a vengeance: the watchers saw her furred tongue lolling between parched lips, the droop of her head, the gradual closing of her fierce eyes. A couple slithered from the spaces between leaves, from a snarl of matted stems. Cautiously they crawled nearer. The day was pale and shadowless; the sun gleamed intermittently far away, never reaching Drakemyre Hall. Yet Lougarry, her mind a still, cold place in the midst of a spinning maelstrom of agony, felt the glare of another sun on her back, and saw the neglected garden melt into an alternative Eden, with improbable fountains and weedy grottoes and dim green shade. She could hear an eldritch piping, and the thrum of cat gut, and the patter of finger drums. This is Yorkshire, she told herself. It's spring—a chilly gray day such as you only get in an English spring. There is no music, no fountains . . . A wolf is without imagination to exploit, without a vision beyond reality. The fantasy receded. Her narrowed gaze measured the distance to the nearest morloch. It was the one with the toad's head, its wide maw snake fanged, its flickering tongue already tasting her savor on the air. More reckless than its fellows, it drew nearer, nearer. Lougarry let her eyes close completely; smell pinpointed its position. When it was within touch she pounced. Her jaws scrunched the thin skull; the warty hide excreted a sour mucus, but she ignored it. She ate quickly, trying not to gag, her yellow stare once more bright and deadly. Warning. Challenging.

She thought: I won't get away with that again.

The day changed. Gradually, inexorably, her lupine reflexes dimmed with pain; her injured leg had swollen into stiffness; her strength lessened. Ears that could hear an ant in the grass were deafened with the beat of her own heart; eyes that could see the night wind misted into a blur. More than once she felt the stabbing rays of a merciless sun, caught the elusive strains of goblin music. Only her nose did not fail or lie, telling her the morlochs were growing bolder. They stalked from bush to scrub, from leaf shadow to stone shadow, making quick darting rushes toward her, testing her defenses. There were more of them now, she was sure: she saw stubby horns, grasping hands, claws, hooves. And mouths opening like red gashes, with broken teeth and questing tongues. She wanted to kill and kill before she died, but she sensed that they were waiting till her vigor and her resistance were gone. They wanted an easy meal.

It would not be long now.

Will awoke slowly and unpleasantly to find he was lying on cold stone with the scratch of sacking against his cheek. A pneumatic drill appeared to be boring into his skull and the dryness in his mouth had shriveled his palate. When he tried to move a wave of nausea rolled over him, and he lay still for some time, closing his eyes against the gyrations of his surroundings. He had no idea where he was or how he had got there. Recollection trickled back piecemeal. Gaynor . . . he had left her for too long, much too long; she would think he had abandoned her. He tried to call her name, but it emerged as a groan and there was no answer. He thought he was in a sepulchre, with his head on a shroud. The ceiling seemed to be vaulted, and the only light came from a single naked bulb, swaying slightly from side to side although there was no draft: the shadows around him stretched and shrank, stretched and shrank, reviving his sickness. A muted tremor reached him from the stone itself, but he dismissed the sensation

as a hallucination born of his condition. He found himself remembering other things: a sword whose hilt was set with red
stones, a faded banner, stepping out too hastily into an empty corridor. And then—nothing. Realization stabbed him: he had been
careless, careless and stupid, and now he was a prisoner, and
Gaynor—God knew what had happened to Gaynor. He struggled
to sit up, and retched violently. When the paroxysm subsided he
crawled to a nearby wall and propped his back against it. He was
in what appeared to be a large cellar divided into separate units
by stone arches: the few windows were sealed and set high out of
reach, and a flight of steps straddled one wall, climbing to a door
that looked as solid and immovable as the exit from a dungeon.
His previous experience of cellars had included racks of wine,
beer barrels, chest freezers, root vegetables stored in the cool; but
there was nothing here except a couple of broken crates and an
ancient wellhead covered by a stone slab. His captors had not left
him either food or drink, and he was very thirsty. When he could
stand, he went to take a piss against a wall in one of the more distant corners. As he unzipped his jeans he found the knife, still
wedged against his hip: it made him feel slightly better, but it was
of no immediate use. Feeling wobbly in both legs and stomach,
he mounted the steps to examine the door.

It was old and heavy, made of oak probably three or four inches
thick; even if he had been possessed of his normal strength, he
could not have smashed his way through it. He thrust his shoulder
against the panels with what force he could muster, but it barely
shuddered. The lock looked recent, a businesslike specimen of
steely efficiency. Will studied it for several minutes, principally to
convince himself he was covering all the angles. Even if he had
known how to pick locks, this one did not appear easily picked. He
staggered back down the steps and collapsed shakily onto the floor.
Since there was no possibility of instant action he rested the di-
minuendo of his headache against the wall and tried to think. His

watch told him it was half past six but there was no daylight to clarify if this was morning or evening. He feared it must be morning, guessing he had been unconscious for a long time. His arms felt stiff and sore: rolling up the sleeves of his sweatshirt, he found black bruises and the marks of clumsy injections. The discovery both disturbed and frightened him, pushing him further into disorientation. With artificial sedation, he might have slept not merely hours but days: Gaynor could have been spirited half a world away, Fern been drawn deeper and deeper into oblivion. He tried to rationalize, to hold on to his sanity, inadvertently touching the hilt of the knife that protruded from his waistband. It felt inexplicably reassuring, as if it were not stolen from his enemy but the gift of an unknown ally, the weapon of a dragonslayer endowed, perhaps, with some special power. He could not imagine a dagger being much use against a dragon, but he had an idea warriors used to cut out the tongue in proof of victory, as if dragon carcasses did not remain lying around in evidence. He pulled the knife out and tested the blade with a cautious fingertip. A tiny red line opened on his skin, and he sucked it almost with relish, feeling a sudden tingle of excitement. This, he thought, is a blade that would split a candle flame, or slice the shadow from your heel. The knife of a hero or a villain, maybe tempered in dragonfire, touched with magic. With such a knife, he was neither alone nor helpless. He surveyed his surroundings with different eyes, looking for weaknesses.

But the walls were solid, the windows bricked up and inaccessible. The door he knew was impassable, with its gleaming steel lock. His headache was clearing and he found himself wondering *why* the lock had been installed, when there was no valuable wine to protect, nothing in the vault but rubbish. It could hardly have been for his benefit: he could not believe Dr. Laye made a habit of keeping prisoners here. Yet the lock was new, it was here for a purpose, shutting something in, keeping people out. And inevitably his eye was drawn to the wellhead. Wells were often dug in the cellars of old houses, he remembered; when you might have to dig a long way down, it was logical to start as low as possible. It did not seem a likely object for so much security, but there was nothing else. He got up, still feeling rather unsteady about the knees, and went over for a better look.

The stone lid fitted very closely to the rim and it took him a while to find a crack where he could insert his fingers and get a grip. When he tried to lift it the weight was too much for his drained physique: he raised it an inch or so and then dropped it, almost catching his hand in the gap. The thud of its fall carried far down into the ground, the echoes coming back to him, making the floor shiver. Imagination, he told himself, cursing his own feebleness and the stone that defied him. Next time he concentrated on shifting it sideways, though it took considerable effort before he could open up even a narrow space. He leaned over, staring down into a crescent of absolute blackness. He had been half expecting some gruesome secret, a putrefying corpse or an antique skeleton; but there was no glimmer of bones, no stench of decay. The draft that issued from below was warm, very warm, and there was a faint sulfurous smell, an elusive hint of burning. He could not tell how deep the well was. Will took a coin from his pocket and tossed it into the shaft, hearing it ricochet off the wall and the fluting echo of a clink as it struck bottom a couple of heartbeats later. And gradually, as he peered into the darkness, he began to distinguish a disc of murky red far beneath at what must be the base of the shaft. *It opens out into somewhere else*, he thought, with a sudden surge of optimism. *Maybe a cave* . . . Grasping the lip of the well, he poked his head under the cover in order to see better. The circle of red seemed to brighten, the air grew hot. Belatedly Will's brain made the missing connection.

He sprang back, tugging furiously at the unwieldy slab. Adrenaline pumped into dehydrated muscle: the stone creaked over just in time. Even so, there was still a sliver of space remaining as he threw himself to the ground. A thin jet of flame shot through the crack with the force of a blowtorch, reaching the high ceiling and hissing against the vault. After a moment or two it sank to a flicker and retreated back into the well. Will saw the stonework blackened, noticing other evidence of charring in the vicinity. He found he was shaking and a sweat had broken out all over his body. He sat for a long while until the tremors abated, cursing himself for his weakness.

"At least I know why the lock is there," he reflected aloud, striving for a pragmatic approach, for a note of bravado or flippancy, though there was no one else to hear. "All I have to do is open it."

Since there was no other way out, he climbed back up the steps to the door.

Once before he had lifted a window latch with the aid of a kitchen knife. Will knew this lock was too sophisticated for similar manipulation, but he drew out the dagger for an exploratory probe, attempting to insert the tip of the blade into the threadlike chink between door and frame. To his astonishment, it slid in smoothly, without effort; when he withdrew it a slender wood shaving fell out onto the top step. He looked at it for a minute, then at the crack, which seemed a millimeter wider. He discovered he was holding his breath, and released it in a long sweet sigh. Then he stood up, and plunged the knife into the door above the lock. The hard, seasoned wood parted at its touch as if it were chipboard. Sawing it to and fro, he cut his way around the mortise. A little sawdust sifted out: otherwise, the line was as neat as a surgical incision. When he had finished he slipped the dagger into the crack and levered the door toward him. Exercising far more caution than on previous occasions, he snaked his body through the gap into the passageway beyond.

He had been hoping for daylight, but it was dark. His watch

showed nearly nine, but whether it was the same evening, or a day later, or more, he had no way of telling. Through an adjacent doorway he saw the kitchen, with unwashed plates and crockery stacked in the sink. The lights were on, but he could hear no one. Physical need took over: he nipped inside, switched on the tap, grabbed a nearby cup—and drank, and drank, and drank. He thought he could feel the water flooding through him like a spring tide, swelling shrunken muscles, lubricating, revitalizing. He glanced around for something to eat, lifted the lid on what proved to be a cheese dish, and cut himself a hunk of cheddar. His hand hovered over an apple in the fruit bowl, but there was little other fruit and he knew its absence might be noticed. He must not lapse into carelessness again. He had closed the cellar door, slotting the lock section into place like a piece in a jigsaw puzzle. He took another long drink of water, then replaced the cup where he had found it.

There were other doors from the kitchen leading variously to a coal cellar, a breakfast parlor, and a storeroom; he remembered from his earlier exploration that beyond the parlor was the long corridor that led back to the heart of the house. His first priority was to find Gaynor, but he had no wish to run into the manservant, or the as yet unknown figure of Dr. Laye. He returned to the short passage outside the main cellar. A narrow stair ascended from it to an upper floor and at one end was a back door opening on the garden. Will hesitated. The stair was tempting, but outside was the car, where Lougarry might still be waiting. He could enlist her support, or send her for assistance. Use your head, he told himself, just for once. He opened the door and stepped out into the night.

It was very dark. The hunchback ridge loomed over him, close against a low sky: he could see dim shapes of rolling cloud, hear the fretful wind whining among the chimney pots. It had been warm in the house (not surprising, he reflected, in view of the underfloor heating) but out here it was cold, and he shivered automatically. Guessing he was around the back, he skirted the building until he could see the gnarled topiary of the formal garden and the approach to the main entrance. There was a light behind shrouded windows on the ground floor, possibly the drawing room, and another light on an upper story showing a striped pattern against the curtains that might have been bars. Will stared at it with fierce concentration, fixing its location in his mind. Then he made his way to where the car was still parked, peered inside while fumbling for his keys. But Lougarry was gone.

She's gone for help, he thought. That's it. She would never have waited this long. (How long *had* it been?) Nothing could have happened to her. He had known her to stop a speeding motorbike, confront both witch and demon, outrun the hounds of the Underworld. Nothing could happen to Lougarry. But it was unlike her to go straight for Ragginbone, instead of searching for Will and Gaynor first . . . He began to call her, softly, uncertainly, more with mind than voice, accustomed over the years to hearing the werewolf without the interruption of ears, touching thought to thought. And almost immediately the call came back to him, urgent to the point of desperation, but faint and growing fainter. *Run* . . . run . . . *too dangerous . . . Azmodel . . . this is Azmodel . . .*

"Where are you?" Will whispered; but his voice was loud in his head.

Don't come . . . don't look . . . run . . .

She was near, he was sure: he could feel her urgency, her danger, somewhere very close by. He drew out the black knife. It looked like a splinter of the abyss in his hand. He grasped the hilt firmly: it seemed to convey to him the strength of an owner long dead, someone nightwise, dauntless, reckless, as sharp and deadly as the blade he wielded. The warning in his mind had dwindled to a whisper—*run*—but he knew now where it came from. He padded softly across the weed-grown drive and into the formal garden.

Fading paths crossed one another, trickling away into unkempt flower beds or vanishing under roving shrubs. Will trampled the beds, thrust a passage between impeding bushes. He was vaguely aware of thorny stems plucking his jeans, the scratching fingers of twigs, but Lougarry's despair filled his thought to the exclusion of all else. Behind him, the house was lost: the garden appeared far larger than he had realized, a sprawling maze where everything was crippled, eroded, diseased, and nothing grew but the hardiest of weeds. He saw the sundial first, like the stump of a pillar, significant and ominous. Then he perceived movement, right in front of him—indistinct shapes circling something that did not move, darting, pouncing—the snapping of feeble jaws, the moonglow of eyes once bright and fierce. He was so close, he had almost stumbled straight into it. He took a second—less than a second—to absorb what was happening. Then he attacked.

The black knife arced to and fro, singing as it cut the air. He felt its hatred for these creatures that he could not see, the dreadful eagerness with which it sliced through flesh and limb. Some of them tried to turn on him—talons scored his leg, flabby hands seized him—but the knife was too quick for them. In moments, all lay dying, dismembered on the ground, or fled into the night. Yet when Will came to step over the bodies there was nothing there. Only Lougarry. He knelt down beside her, took her head in his hands.

That is a good knife, she said, in the silence of his mind.

"I stole it," said Will. "Crime pays. Are you badly hurt?"

She indicated the trap. He cleaned the dagger on a clump of moss, sheathed it, and crouched down to release the mechanism. It took him a little while, groping in the dark, unable to see either trap or wolf clearly. When she was free he ran a hand over the injured leg, saw the dark ooze of fresh blood on his palm. "I'll try and carry you to the car," he said. "I've got some rags in there; they'll do for a bandage. Temporarily. I'll have to leave you there for a bit. I must find Gaynor."

She was heavy but he managed, arms linked under her belly, holding her close to his chest. When they reached the car he set her down, unlocked it, and lifted her onto the backseat, glancing around every other second, thankful that the automatic light did not work. He explored the side pockets by feel, unwilling to switch on any illumination, finding some old paint rags that he trusted were not too unhygienic. "I'm sorry," he murmured, as he bound them inexpertly round the wound. "These'll have to do. I think the leg's broken—"

Yes.

Her mental response sounded weak, the whisper of a thought, but he assimilated it with relief. "We'll get it set as soon as we can," he said, struggling with the knot.

Tighter.

"What were those . . . things that attacked you? Where did they go?"

Morlochs. (The name took shape in his head.) *They did not go anywhere. We . . . went.*

"*We* went?" Will echoed.

This place is in two dimensions. They are . . . they should be . . . there. We were there, and here.

She added: *We were lucky they were so few. In numbers, they are deadly.*

"By there," said Will, "do you mean . . . Azmodel? That's what you told me. *This is Azmodel.*"

You should have run, said the thought in his mind.

He had tied the makeshift bandage as tightly as he dared. Now he stroked her neck, both giving reassurance and seeking it. Her fur felt rough and sticky with sweat.

She requested: *Water.*

"I don't think I—"

When I drink, I am strong. You need help. I will fetch someone.

"You can't," said Will. "Your leg is broken."

Lougarry showed her teeth. *I have three more.*

Will thought of his own tormenting thirst in the cellar, and the perils of the kitchen. He said: "I won't be long."

He was gone over half an hour.

The manservant was there, washing the dishes; Will heard him in time, retreating back outside. Ear to the door panel, he caught the sound of footsteps approaching the little passageway, but if Harbeak glanced toward the cellar he must have seen nothing amiss. Feet returned to the kitchen, cupboards opened and shut, crockery chinked. When silence ensued, Will waited several minutes before he dared to venture indoors. He found a large jug, filled it, and made his way back to the car.

Lougarry was waiting, without impatience or complaint. She drank half the water fast, the rest more slowly, pacing herself, knowing both her own capacity and her need. "You can't walk," Will reiterated. "You were half-dead earlier. I had to carry you."

I have rested, she responded, *and I have drunk. Now I am strong again. But you must come with me to the gate. I do not know how to work it, and I cannot jump the wall.*

They stole down the driveway, keeping to the deepest shadows. The clouds opened briefly overhead, showing a sly glimpse of moon, and they shrank from its probing beam, but it was quickly obscured. Lougarry hobbled on three legs, ungainly but apparently restored to part of her strength. When they reached the gate it was some time before Will located the button to open it; he had been secretly afraid it might be operated only by remote control. Lougarry slipped through as soon as there was space, glanced back once—an untypical gesture—then limped off into the night. Will found a stone fallen from the coping and wedged it against the post so the gate could not be properly closed, hoping this would not set off any alarms. If someone comes, he thought, at least they'll be able to get in. *If . . .*

He stared back up the drive at the dark huddle of the Hall. *This is Azmodel . . .* He thought of the monster beneath the cellar, and the loathing that infused the she-wolf's mind when she uttered *Morlochs,* and the unseen hand of Dr. Jerrold Laye. He could go now, follow Lougarry, find backup. It would be the sensible thing to do. He was exhausted and half-starved; he had no Gift to aid him, no plan to follow. Fear loomed in front of him like a vast insurmountable barrier. He tried to picture Gaynor, desperate and terrified, needing him; he touched the knife for courage or luck. But in that moment he knew only that it was dark and cold, and he was terribly alone, and as frightened as a child.

Eventually he began to walk back toward the house.

Gaynor lay in a crimson nightmare struggling to draw breath. Fluorescent amoebas drifted across her vision, subdividing and rejoining. Presently they began to cohere into strange aberrant forms, unshapes cobbled together from a range of ill-assorted body parts, sprouting like fungi all around her. She did not want to look at them, so she opened her eyes, but they were still there. They seemed to be watching her, not with their eyes but with their mouths. Random incisors extruded over spotted lip or curved inward to hook their prey; tongues slithered into view like eels. She wanted to scream but her throat closed and the sound was stifled inside her. Darkness surged upward, smothering her, and when she woke again it was day.

She was in bed, but not her bed at Dale House. For a minute she wondered if she might be back in London—the window was in the right place for London—but the room was utterly unfamiliar. Heavy beams spanned the high ceiling; the curtains were of some old-fashioned brocade; beyond, shadow bars striped the daylight. She thought: Bars? I'm in a room with *bars* on the window? It seemed not merely worrying, but preposterous. In real life people did not wake up in unfamiliar rooms with barred windows. She tried to turn her head in order to see more of her surroundings but her neck felt painful and very stiff. And then memory returned, not in a trickle but a flood, and she knew where she was, and why, and fear filled her. Fear for herself, for Will, for Fern, who, if Dr. Laye was right, was walking into a trap. (But he wasn't Dr. Laye: he was the Spirit they had spoken of, Azmordis.) A trap, and she was the bait. She tried to sit up, and nausea rippled through her in waves, too gentle for actual vomiting but more than enough to send her reeling back onto the pillow.

A preliminary check revealed that she was still more or less fully dressed, except for her jacket and shoes. She undid the zip in her trousers in order to remove the pressure on her stomach and eventually her insides relaxed into their normal patterns of behavior. Bodily concerns took priority; she got up carefully, determined not to relapse, and surveyed the amenities. There was a modern washstand, a couple of vintage armchairs, an oval mirror in a carved frame. That was all. In the end, she was forced to improvise with a porcelain basin possibly intended for fruit, a disagreeable proceeding that made her conclude that the real issue behind penis envy is accuracy of aim. Then she washed her face and hands with the soap provided, and felt her skin crinkling for lack of moisturizer. She tried the door, a forlorn hope: it was locked. She was reluctant to draw the curtains, wanting neither to see the bars in all their grim reality nor make herself visible to whatever unfriendly eyes might be waiting outside. But she had no watch, and although she sensed it was morning she needed to be sure. She pulled the drapes back a little way.

Gaynor could make out the formal garden that she had noticed on arrival, looking, from above, as if a part of the design had slipped sideways: paths and flower beds failed to interconnect, shrubs huddled together in thickets and then trailed away into a bristle of barren twigs. There was something moving down there, close to an object that might have been a sundial, but the neglected topiary intervened, blotting most of whatever it was from view, and her long-range vision was not good, though she wore glasses only to drive. She squinted at it for a while, but it seemed to be motionless now, or had disappeared. The garden was bordered by a hedge; beyond, the land fell away into a deep fold of the valley, only the high stone wall marking the boundary of the property. Clouds shaped like the underside of huge boats paddled across the sky. The colors were gray-brown, gray-green, gray-white, a hundred aquatints of gray. A brisk wind was hurrying the cloud boats, breaking their trails into scuds of cirrus foam. In between, isolated sunbeams stalked the remote landscape, touching the earth with fleeting tracks of brilliance. Gaynor recollected from the previous day that the house faced roughly southeast, so it seemed safe to deduce that it was still morning, though whether early or late she could not tell. Now she had summoned the nerve to look out she could not look away; she drew a chair up to the window and sat there, elbows on the sill, gazing down the long hillside into a blur of distance.

She was interrupted by a sound behind her: the click of a lock, and the door opening. She started and turned.

"Good morning," said Harbeak. His manner, as always, was that of the ideal servant but his voice was a dead monotone, and in the stronger light she could see the dough of his face pinched and kneaded into tiny peaks and troughs that somehow gave him less expression, not more. "I'm afraid you missed breakfast: I looked in on you at half past nine, but you were sleeping. However, I will bring you some lunch presently. First, I expect you would like to use the toilet."

Gaynor reddened, remembering the fruit bowl. She said: "Yes, please," and then wished she hadn't put in the *please*, sensing that on some deeper level, far below his outward impassivity, he was taking pleasure in her subjection, her embarrassment, her exposure to petty indignity. She wondered suddenly if it was he who had carried her to bed, he who had removed her jacket and shoes, perhaps searching her, touching her, exploring the secret niches of her body. She shuddered, and knew that the shudder reached him, and thrilled through him in a spasm of unholy satisfaction.

"Follow me," he said. "Remember you are watched. All the time."

The nightmare creatures with their oozing mouths . . . eyes, eyes in a paneled room . . .

She pushed the fantasies away, looking for security cameras, though she saw none. She had horrors enough without imagining more.

"I won't try to escape," she said. For the present, it was true. She felt too physically weak, too unsure of her ground.

"You won't succeed," he retorted. Or maybe it wasn't a retort, just an affirmation. His tone provided no clue.

The lavatory had a lock on the door, giving her a few minutes of privacy, but no window. Even if there had been, she knew she would have been unable to clamber out. At a guess they were on the third floor, and it was a long way down.

Back in her room Harbeak brought her lunch consisting of thick vegetable soup, brown bread, cheese. "I want to see Will," she said, as he set down the tray. "Where is he?"

"Somewhere less comfortable than here," Harbeak responded, ignoring her request.

The day passed with horrible slowness. Prison must be like this, Gaynor decided, dull, dull, dull, but without the edge of fear to sharpen the tedium into regular bouts of panic. She had no television, no book, nothing to do but think, nothing to think about but her current predicament. Thinking sent her pulse into a crescendo and drove her to beat on the door, crying to be let out, finally controlling herself with an effort that seemed to drain all her willpower. But no one answered, no one came. At other times she stood by the window, trying to bend or dislodge the bars, but they were cemented in, and the iron was rigid and immovable. And if I *could* shift them, she thought, how would I get down? In stories, heroines made use of knotted sheets; but although sheets were available they were too strong to tear, and she had neither knife nor scissors to help her out. In any case, she had never been any good at rope climbing when she was at school, and she saw no likelihood of dramatic improvement now. But I suppose it would be worse, she concluded, if I made the rope, and knew how to climb, and still couldn't get between the bars.

Periodically she checked the mirror, made wary by experience, looking for reflections that should not have been there, lifting it clear of the wall to search for technological devices. But it remained just a mirror, glossy, limpid, as if any memories it might have retained had been polished out of existence. *You are watched,* Harbeak had said, and she went frantic investigating portraits for eyeholes, examining light fittings and the knobs on drawer and cabinet for miniaturized cameras. He said it to frighten me, she decided, as if that were necessary. He was probably watching her now, enjoying her fear, savoring it—but from where? She had turned over every wood louse. She tried hate instead of fear—not for Dr. Laye, who was too potent, too awesome a figure, far beyond any passion of hers—but for Harbeak, Harbeak with his impeccable suit and his façade of courtesy and his elusive resemblance to Goebbels. But she was no better at hating than she was at rope climbing. Her enmity was a poor, weak thing, an ember that never grew into a flame, and the thought of what Harbeak might have done to her in her sleep—what he might yet do—only filled her with horror and disgust. Disgust not only at him but at herself: her fear, her vulnerability, her helplessness, her sheer imbecility for being here. We should never have come, she thought. Fern will return to her body without our help. What did the Spirit say? *I have cast the augury, and seen her.* She will awaken, and come here to find us, and it would be better if she had stayed in a coma forever.

A depression crept over her that was worse than panic, gray and hopeless. In the late afternoon Harbeak brought her a cup of tea and a plate of cookies. She looked at him with dull eyes. "Your friend will be here soon," he said, not to encourage her but to goad. "She will want you to live. The master is sure of it."

"Which master?" said Gaynor, and for a moment he looked afraid. He withdrew without further comment.

After dark he brought her supper, and took her for the obligatory visit to the toilet. There was an air of repressed excitement about him, like a habitual wife killer who plans to spend the evening sawing up the corpse. Gaynor thought: I must do something. I must do *something*. A different kind of fever gripped her; she had passed through despair into desperation.

Left alone, her vague resolution crystallized. Fortunately, she had read plenty of the right sort of books—not "serious" literary fiction where the heroines have single-parent status and unsuccessful love affairs and Angst, but the kind where they have to escape from locked rooms on ropes of knotted sheets, or by hitting an unwary jailer over the head with a convenient blunt instrument. When Fern arrives, Gaynor reasoned, he'll come to escort me downstairs. He won't expect an attack: he believes me too cowed, too terrified, incapable of action. And he was shorter than her; the blow would be easy. She could hide behind the door and he would walk into the room . . . She needed something to lull him, to draw him in and keep him off guard. If she plumped up the duvet, bunched her sweater on the pillow—it was maroon, and a smooth knit, but in a bad light it might pass for brown, and hair. She would have to wait in the dark—but no, that wouldn't do, he would switch on the main light. Better to leave the lamp on beside the washstand: that cast a restricted glow floorward that did not reach the bed. She took off her sweater, began to arrange the bedding. All she needed now was a blunt instrument.

But there were few to choose from. She considered unscrewing a leg from the bedside table, but the legs were fixed in place and a lopsided table would have looked suspicious. Pictures, she knew, were only used in comedy: you can't knock someone out with a sheet of canvas. Finally she settled on her old friend the china bowl. It was large, and should be heavy enough, even if it broke. Besides, she felt it was somehow appropriate. She sat on the nearest chair, clutching the bowl, listening for an approaching footstep, the rattle of a key. She was trembling, but she told herself it didn't matter. You don't need a steady hand to hit a man on the head.

She sat there for what seemed like hours. Her trembling increased to teeth-chattering spasms and then diminished to a gentle shiver as the tension mounted and ebbed inside her. At long last, when she had almost gone beyond anticipation, she heard footsteps in the passageway. She darted behind the door, gripping the bowl in both hands. He took a long time with the key and she began to tremble again: when she glanced down she saw her arms shaking like jelly in an earthquake. The door opened; she lifted the bowl. A dark figure strode toward the bed—

A tall dark figure, in jeans. The bowl dropped from Gaynor's slackened fingers and spun on the carpet.

"Will!" she cried. "Oh, *Will!*" And even as he turned she grasped his sweatshirt, tears starting in her eyes, and buried her face in his chest.

· XVI ·

The wolf appeared very suddenly in the middle of the road. Fern saw the flash of its eyes in the headlights and swerved violently, ending up on the opposite verge. Bradachin was flung across the passenger seat clutching the bag with the head; from within it came a muffled oath. Fern did not stop to apologize. She jerked on the hand brake and shot out of the door in a single movement. She was almost certain she had missed it but the wolf was lying on the tarmac: the light from the interior of the car was just sufficient to show the pattern of ribs in its panting flank, the clumsy bandage that bound one leg. "Lougarry?" Fern gasped. "What's *happened* to you?" The she-wolf half raised her head, then let it fall back on the ground. But Fern felt the heartbeat in her side, saw the straining breath come and go. Carefully she lifted the injured leg, made out the blood on the cotton, and other stains, not darkly red but blue and yellow. Paint. "Will did this," she said. "Only Will would use paint rags . . . I've got to get you into the car. Bradachin! Can you open the back door? Leave—*that*. Is he all right?"

"He's a mickle bruised and no very blithe, but—aye, we're

338

baith right enough. I didna ken ye would drive the carriage in sae hellirackit—"

"Never mind all that. Get the door open and help me."

Between them, they managed to lift Lougarry into the back of the car. "I think that leg's broken," said Fern. She heard the faint confirmation in her mind. "Try not to jolt it. We need to get her to a vet—"

"I'm no sae partial tae werebeasties," Bradachin was muttering. "Even if they canna change themselves. She and I, we've always walked round one another. It would be mair healthsome if we didna get too close. That road, we've rested friendly . . ."

Trapped, said the whisper in Fern's head. *Will released me. Went back—for Gaynor. The leg . . . will keep.* Caracandal . . .

"No time," said Fern. "Where are they? At—what's the name of it?—Drakemyre Hall?"

She sensed rather than heard the warning. *Danger. Azmodel.*

"*Azmodel?*"

What is here, is also there. The power of the Old One . . .

"You mean—" Fern struggled for comprehension "—the dimensions overlap? The world we know, and—the world beyond?"

Azmodel is his place. *His lair. Wherever he is, it is. The house. Maybe—the museum. He is there. He must be.*

"Dr. Laye," said Fern. "I know."

As he can possess the human mind, so Azmodel . . . can possess the place. There is . . . great danger. The she-wolf's unheard voice was getting weaker and weaker. *Morlochs . . .*

"What are morlochs?" asked Fern.

It was Bradachin who answered, his grumbles forgotten. "Pugwidgies."

As she drove away it took an effort of self-discipline for Fern to keep her speed down. She found her pressure on the accelerator pedal was increasing almost in spite of herself and her lips clenched as she eased her foot upward; minutes later a police car passed her, traveling in the other direction. She allowed herself a fleeting vision of what might happen if she was stopped, with all her Gift channeled into maintaining her own strength. Bradachin would be able to fade from the picture, but that would still leave an injured wolf on the backseat and a disembodied head in front. For a moment, the specter of a smile relaxed her taut mouth.

"What amuses you, Fernanda?" asked the head. Bradachin had left the bag open and the ice-blue eyes watched her as she drove.

"Nothing," she answered. "Nothing I can explain, anyway."

"I heard you laughing in the Underworld," he said, "down among the ghosts where no laughter has sounded since time began. And now—now you are heading for a confrontation with powers far beyond your scope, and your own life and the lives of those you love are at stake, yet you smile. But I do not believe you smile carelessly or laugh lightly, witch-maiden."

"Maybe not," said Fern. "But when everything is dark it is important to smile, or to laugh, if you can. Laughter has a power of its own. It's a human thing—or have you forgotten so soon?"

"Dragons do not laugh," the head replied. "That was the only power I knew. It is late to learn of laughter, when you are dead."

"It's just—unusual," said Fern.

She pulled over briefly to consult her map of the Dales, on which Drakemyre Hall featured by name. The road was empty now and when she calculated they were drawing near she switched off the headlights. The crest of the ridge became visible, black against the pale underbelly of the clouds. Farther on, she made out the pointed spines of rooftops, the spiky silhouettes of clustered bushes and trees. Still some way from the entrance she stopped and began to reverse, maneuvering the car until it was right on the verge. "Stay here," she told Bradachin, and, with a glance at the wolf: "Look after her."

"I'm coming wi' ye—"

"No. You know what she said. You wouldn't stand a chance against these . . . pugwidgies. Wait here."

"And who will be protecting ye? Yon heid?"

"I'm a witch," Fern said. "I can take care of myself." She picked up the bag. "Ready?"

"Yes," said the head.

She hooked the strap over her shoulder and slid out of the car, closing the door as softly as she could. The automatic light was extinguished and the night enveloped her, a huge night of empty hillside and silent road and broken clouds chasing across a star-ridden sky. Her eyesight adjusted, absorbing details no ordinary human would have seen, shadows within shadows, tiny crawlings and creepings in the darkness of the grass. She followed the road to the gate, saw the tracery of ironwork athwart her path and the paler line of the driveway beyond, curving up toward the irregular outline of the house. The stone was still in place, wedging the gate open: Fern squeezed through the gap. Immediately her witch senses prickled at the change. She felt displaced, as if she had crossed an invisible threshold into a dimension that, though it might appear the same, was altogether different. Here, the night was not merely alive but aware, sapient, an entity made of the dark itself. She felt it watching, perhaps for her, though it had not yet seen the slight intruder flitting from bush to bush. The very ground seemed sensitive, like skin, and she trod lightly, trying not to bend a single blade of grass, merging herself into the quiet and the gloom more by instinct than power. And there were moments when the actual stuff of the land became insubstantial, and she felt rock beneath her feet, and the crest of the ridge soared into a measureless cliff, imprisoning her in a valley crack too deep for normal reckoning. She fought against the incursion of that other place, pushing it away, focusing on the uncertain reality all around her. And somewhere below the thin crust of solid ground she detected a faint seismic stirring, and a pulse beat that was not that of the earth.

As she approached the house she saw the steely glimmer of the Mercedes, and another vehicle drawn up beside it. Coming nearer, she made out something that had once been a car. But the doors had been wrenched and twisted from their hinges, the hood buckled, disemboweled ends of piping protruded from the engine. Inside, she registered pale stuffing leaking from ripped seats, ragged wires sprouting where the dashboard had been. Even so, she did not need to see the paintings on the residual bodywork to recognize it. For a second, her control failed: she was on the edge of screaming challenge and defiance. The soft tones of the head checked her.

"Morlochs' work," it said. "What was it?"

"My brother's car."

"I smell blood."

With her heightened sensitivity, Fern, too, could smell it—a hot, sharp, angry smell that sent the adrenaline pounding through her veins and made the tiny hairs rise on her neck. She had never been able to *smell* blood before, yet she recognized it at once. She had hoped to get Will and Gaynor away from the house before any confrontation, but she realized now there was no chance. They were prisoners still, or worse. She was too late for a rescue, too late, perhaps, for anything, except a last stand, a final gamble. Further caution was futile; she could feel the watching eyes. "Stay quiet," she admonished the head, and pulled the flap down to cover it. Then she walked up to the front door and pressed the bell. Within the house, she heard it echo through the hallway like a gong. There was no sound of any approach, only the soft click as the handle turned, and the noiseless opening of the door.

It was like being trapped in a dream, Gaynor thought, one of those dreams where, just when you hope everything is going to work out well, the old familiar nightmare intrudes, and you are sucked back into darkness. With the advent of Will she experienced an illusory return to normality, a feeling that it would be all right, they would come through, the horrors of her captivity would fade into unreality; but it could not last. They compared notes, speaking softly and urgently. Gaynor knew she must be terrified at the idea of the dragon, seething like a potted volcano beneath the house; yet it seemed all a part of the inevitable, another aspect of delirium. "They can't have checked the cellar," Will said. "At a guess, they won't go near it unless they have to, so they don't know I've escaped. I'm not important; you are. You're the hostage they wanted. This room must've been prepared for you. I was just rubbish to be dumped out of the way."

"But how did you get in *here*?"

"Keys." Will patted his pocket. "After I left Lougarry I sneaked back in past the kitchen. The butler—what's his name? Harbeak?— was in there. It must be his domain. I'm not sure what he was doing—preparing meat, I suppose; I could see blood on his arms—but he'd taken his jacket off to do it. It was hung up by the door. While his back was turned I went through the pockets. Then he washed his hands and started moving about the place. I waited ages before I could get upstairs." He took her arm. "Come on. It's time to leave."

The room felt suddenly very safe, a refuge rather than a prison cell. When they stepped out into the corridor its emptiness seemed somehow threatening, pregnant with the possibility of unseen watchers. Gaynor considered mentioning that she was scared and then decided it was unnecessary. "Where's this knife you found?" she asked.

"To hand," said Will.

He led her to the top of the stairwell. There was plenty of light here, not wavering, sinister light from an era of gas lamps and candles, which Gaynor felt would be more appropriate, but the kind of light that had welcomed them on the afternoon of their arrival, with lavish wattage and a mellow tinge. Modern light in an old house, pushing the dark behind the window curtains, and sweeping it under the carpet. And there was a good deal of carpet, lapping at the walls, muffling the stairs, hiding the loose board that creaked treacherously at their descent. Will whisked Gaynor out of sight on the second-floor landing. They sensed rather than heard someone approaching below, the X-ray gaze upturned toward them, the listening of hypersensitive ears. "Harbeak?" Will held his breath. "Harbeak!" No answer. But the man below evidently did not feel the silence merited investigation. His departure was as noiseless as a cat, but they caught the sound of a closing door, sensed the withdrawal of his presence. Even so, Will waited for more than a minute before he would allow them to move.

They hurried down the last flight of stairs, headed for the front door. A clock began to strike, making them jump almost out of their skins. Midnight, thought Gaynor, glancing at the clock face. This was the hour when spells ran out, when rats left their holes, when graveyards disgorged their dead. The clock continued striking, loud and imperative as a summons. Any second, she expected someone to come running in response. She shivered with sudden cold.

Will was standing by the open door. "Hurry—"

And then they were outside.

Will shut the door as quietly as he could, closing off the light. They held hands, stumbling around the corner of the house, colliding with the parked car in a mess of shadows. Will found his key by feel, tugged at the handle. Moments later they were inside the car, looking out at the alien night, encased in a shell of metal, an illusion of security. There was no sound but the panting of the wind and clearer still, the scratching of an ivy tendril on the rear windshield. "I wedged the gate," said Will. "When we get there, you'll have to jump out and pull it open. It shouldn't be a problem."

"All right."

"I won't put the headlights on till we're out of here." He

turned the key in the ignition. The car shuddered but the engine did not respond.

Gaynor thought: There's no ivy nearby . . .

Will tried again.

"Switch on the light!" cried Gaynor. "I can't see!"

"Of course you can't. It's dark."

"No—I *really* can't see. Something's blocking the windows—"

She flicked the switch for the interior light, and saw.

They were all around, piled on top of the hood, clinging to the bodywork, their mouths pressed hungrily against the glass. Like her dream—the too-familiar nightmare—of hidden watchers now made visible, of mouths that clung like polyps, red holes full of tongues and teeth. "Morlochs!" cried Will, rattling the key in the ignition, but already they heard the sound of tearing metal as the hood was ripped away, glimpsed segments of internal tubing tossed into the air. Gaynor's window broke first, and there were arms reaching in, prehensile hands, lizard claws. Will drew the knife and hacked at them, spattering blood over Gaynor, the dashboard, the seating, but there were too many, too many, and his window splintered, and the door was torn from its hinges, and he was rolling on the ground, stabbing at creatures he could hardly see. Gaynor had given only one short scream, and that frightened him most of all, because as long as he could hear her scream he knew she was alive.

"Enough!" It was the voice of Azmordis. Will had heard it just once, in a fantasy, in a trance, when he was a boy, but he knew it immediately. It was a voice of adamant, dark as dark matter, and as empty as space. "It is not yet time to feed. Bring them back into the house."

Will managed to slide the knife out of sight before both his arms were seized in a dozen different grips. He felt the blood soaking through his jeans, and hoped it wasn't his. The sound of sobbing nearby must be Gaynor. He could not see Dr. Laye save as a deeper blackness against the night, but he appeared taller than any ordinary man and the aura of his occupant was as tangible as a smell.

Behind, they heard the clamor of destruction as the morlochs invaded the car, unraveling the wiring, rending both plastic and steel. My car, thought Will, and he felt as if they were wrecking one of his paintings, something intrinsic to himself, but there was no time for anger, no time for trauma. Their last chance was gone and he must think to save his life, because that was all he had left . . .

Harbeak was waiting for them in the entrance hall. The morlochs fell back from the light, becoming a part of their surroundings: an ornament with eyes, a pattern that moved. "Don't try to run," said Dr. Laye, his voice his own once more. "They're still there." And, to Harbeak, in a snarl: "How did this boy get out of the cellar?"

"He cut his way around the lock. It can't have been done with a standard knife: he must have used a machine."

"And where is this machine?"

"I don't—"

Jerrold Laye rounded on Will, and he saw for the first time the gray face and the eyes that seemed to bleed around the rim. "How did you do it?"

"The Gift is hereditary," said Will. "What makes you so sure it is only my sister who has it?"

"The Gift cannot cut through a solid door."

"Have it your own way." In one of his pockets he had a small penknife that he used occasionally for the application of oil paint. He took it out and tossed it on the carpet. It was an idiotic gamble, a preposterous bluff; but he did not want them to search him, and find the dagger. "You try hacking through a door with that," he said with what he hoped would pass for scorn.

"Take it," ordered Dr. Laye.

Harbeak picked it up and unclipped the blade. It was short,

and blunt, and red with paint, not blood. "This wouldn't cut through paper!"

"Yet he got out . . . The Gift takes many forms. There are those who could make a sword out of such a knife, and pierce a man's heart with it. He has no aura of magic, but power can be hidden: I gather his sister has always hidden hers. Perhaps it would be prudent to kill him now . . ."

"Fern will never bargain with her brother's murderer," Will said.

Laye studied him for a long minute with baleful eyes. "Lock them both up! And try not to lose the key. As for you, boy, remember: the morlochs will be watching you every moment. They will be in the room with you, under the bed, behind the pictures, on the wrong side of the mirror. One stupid move, and they will be on you—and then there will be nothing left for even a witch to find."

"She will find *you*," said Will, "wherever you run to." But his defiance was meaningless, and they both knew it. He was counting his survival by the minute; every breath, every heartbeat was a minor achievement.

Harbeak led them back to the upstairs room where Gaynor had been imprisoned before. Behind them, the walls rippled, the carpet crawled. The morlochs were following.

There was no sound of any approach. Only the soft click as the handle turned, and the noiseless opening of the door.

Somewhere at the back of her mind Fern registered the warm electric light, the densely carpeted floor and picture-hung walls, but without surprise or interest. All her attention was focused elsewhere. She said: "I've come to see Dr. Laye."

And: "I think he's expecting me."

It was Harbeak who betrayed surprise, a gleam of derision brightening the shadow band over his eyes. Perhaps, having been permitted a glimpse of his master's schemes, he had been expecting a cliché of a witch, endowed with height and arrogance and a wild mane of hair. Not this waiflike creature, hardly more than a girl, with her straight bob and serious features in a small pale face. The contempt showed in his voice. "I'll ask if he'll see you."

"He'll see me," she said, and stepped uninvited inside. Here the rules had already been broken, and she could trespass. Harbeak drew back from her, feeling a sudden cold: the cold of the Underworld where she had walked, of the River of Death where she had dipped her hand. The chill of indrawn power, the ice in icy control.

"Take me to him." Her eyes, too, were cold, green in the mellow light.

He gave a quick jerk of the head by way of assent, his customary façade of the perfect butler discarded or forgotten. Like Will and Gaynor before her, she followed him along the corridor and into the drawing room.

Dr. Laye was waiting for her. Dr. Laye, not Azmordis. She had seen the Oldest of Spirits before, across a restaurant table behind the face of Javier Holt, and in the dead blind gaze of Ixavo, ten thousand years ago in the ruin of Atlantis. But she knew more of him now: she had gazed into the spellfire and seen him worshiped, both as god and demon; she had glimpsed the void of his unsoul, and the horror of that void, *his* horror, and all the bitterness and cruelty and evil that it engendered. Hell is not other people, she thought. Hell is always and only yourself. And Azmodel was his vision of that Hell, a place of beauty and dread, where all color was poison, and every flower was deformed, and nothing grew save by enchantment; nothing was real, nothing died, nothing lived. His Eden, his nightmare concept of Paradise, not an embellishment of truth but a distortion, an illusion whose roots went deep in Time. He had grown for her, grown in stature and in terror, but her resolution, too, had grown. She looked into the gray countenance of Jerrold Laye and saw a pinpoint glimmer of a mind huge beyond imagining, an endless depth of evil, an unrelenting dark. It occurred to her that somewhere within himself Laye's own mind and soul must be warped into madness from the sheer pressure of such an invader—even more than from contact with the dragon—and the man who spoke to her was a being from whom all normal human reactions had long been eradicated.

He said: "Welcome," and smiled, a thin gray smile, red on the inside. "We have waited many years for you. It is good to see you come as a supplicant at last."

Fern made no comment. Her right hand rested lightly on her bag but her thoughts steered away from it, lest he, or his cohabitant, should be able to read them.

"Take a seat." He indicated a chair, and she sat down. "May I offer you a drink?"

"No."

"I see. No doubt you would not touch my food either. How very *careful* of you, my dear. However, I trust you will overcome these prejudices in the—immediate—future. Once we have come to an agreement . . ."

"Where are my brother and my friend?"

"We will come to that in time. Try to cultivate patience. Firstly, we have important matters to discuss—"

"Where are they?" She was on her feet again, but he loomed over her, and the mellow light could not warm his ashen face. "Are they all right?"

"They are alive. For the moment, that will have to content you. Sit down."

"Azmordis!" She gazed up into his eyes, saw the slow pale glimmer that suffused the blue, the gradual apparition of his other, his hidden partner, his master.

He repeated: "We have important matters to discuss," but his voice had changed. A lean gray hand thrust her back into the chair with more-than-human strength. "You have come a long way since we last met. The power has grown in you: I can feel it. Your body is weary but the Gift is all you need—it is the river in your veins, the engine of your spirit. Your so-called friends doubted you, did you know that? They thought you were lost forever. But I knew you would find a way back. I know you better than kith or kin—certainly better than Caracandal Brokenwand, who would be your mentor. You have learned a great deal, I think, but not from him."

"I learned from Morgus," she said.

"So the old hag lingers still! It was she then who stole your spirit, that night in the snow . . . and now you are her pupil, her messenger perhaps. Running errands for a mad crone whose ambitions stretch no farther than the coastline of this petty isle. A waste of your talents, a misuse of your power. My vassalage would serve you otherwise."

Fern said: "I am no one's vassal." She looked away from the baleful stare that sought to hold and mesmerize her, fixing her gaze stonily on chair, lamp, wall. "I came here to find Will and Gaynor. I know you have them. I saw the wrecked car. I smelled the blood. Are they hurt?"

"You shall see them." He went to the door, called for Harbeak. "Bring our guests."

There was a wait that seemed interminable, though in reality it was only a minute or two, and then Harbeak, still in derisive parody of the perfect butler, ushered them in. Their clothes were torn, their exposed limbs marked with scratches and dried blood. Gaynor looked both desperate and wretched, Will warily alert. But their hands were not tied and they appeared to have suffered no serious injury. Fern fought the upsurge of relief and anger, hope and fear, keeping her expression still if not calm, showing nothing. She knew Azmordis would leave no obvious loopholes.

"Release them," she said. "They have no part in this. Your business is with me."

"You gave them their part," he responded. She thought he was gloating; she felt he was implacable. "It is for you to release them."

"How?"

She had spoken too quickly: her eagerness betrayed her.

He smiled, sure of victory.

"Ally yourself with me. Morgus, no doubt, has taught you much—and demanded a high price. Only through me can you be free of her, for all your proud words. You need my power, as I need yours. The Brokenwand cannot aid you. He has nothing to offer but a cheap philosophy and the ethics of a hypocrite. His hands are empty. Without me, you are lost. Bind yourself to me: you have no choice. Once before we talked of these things, when you were too young to understand; you are wiser now. Give me your Gift, and I will restore it to you a hundredfold, I will set you among the great, the rare, the few. You will be more than Merlin or Nimuë, more than Zohrâne, the queen of Atlantis—"

"No!" The whispered protest came from Gaynor. "Don't listen to him! He will cheat you—"

"I know," mouthed Fern. Harbeak seized Gaynor's wrist, twisting it; her warning was cut off in a gasp of pain.

"Leave her!" cried Will, and "Leave her," said Fern. Dr. Laye made a curt gesture, and Harbeak let her go.

"If I refuse?" Fern asked.

"Look around you." The paneled walls dissolved into a raw light; the expensive furnishings and antique ornaments were gone. There was rock beneath their feet. The prisoners stared about them, blank with shock, seeing the lakes of vermilion and scarlet and green, the cliffs on either side rising to immeasurable heights, the sky crack in between. The sun, as always, appeared to be caught in the gap, sinking slowly toward the valley's throat. Heat shimmered from the many faces of stone. But Fern barely glanced at the scene: she knew it too well. In front of her, Dr. Laye seemed to have grown, towering against the sunlight like a shadow made flesh, his features dimmed save for the livid glitter in his eyes. This was his place, his lair, and he drew strength from it, waxing in might, becoming visibly less and less a man. "Do you know where you are?"

"I am in Drakemyre Hall," said Fern doggedly. "We are in Yorkshire. Outside, it is dark."

"Don't try to resist. You are too small, too weak. Your power is already strained keeping you on your feet. This is Azmodel. *These* are its creatures. Look well, Fernanda."

And so they came, the morlochs, as in the spellfire, from cranny and crevice, from shade and sunshimmer, closing on Will and Gaynor, slowly, slowly. Fern saw without looking the slaver of their mouths, the light that slimed over mottled skin and scabrous paw.

The voice of Azmordis said: "These are the locusts of Azmodel. They are made of hunger. Deny me, and you will see your brother and your friend devoured before your eyes, knowing that with a word you could have saved them."

Fern thought: I didn't plan for this. I didn't plan at all. I don't know what to do. Ragginbone was right: I should have waited. *I don't know what to do . . .*

She said, through rigid lips: "We're in Yorkshire," but the scene did not change. Will's left hand found Gaynor's, his right moved toward the hidden knife. Beside them, Harbeak looked no longer like a butler: his short legs had bowed, his hair writhed into curls around thrusting horns. His face glistened with anticipation.

The morlochs slunk nearer.

"Choose, Fernanda," said Azmordis.

The thought raced around and around in her head, leafing at light speed through everything she had learnt, from the spellfire, from Caracandal, from Morgus. The head could not help her, her Gift was all but drained: she had nothing with which to fight . . .

I don't know what to do . . .

And then she knew. One choice remained. One move.

She said: "I must submit." And hesitantly, as if in doubt, she extended her hand. Dr. Laye responded, the man, not the master, a mortal reflex. Palm touched palm, Fern's small fingers were caught in its gray bony grasp—but it was she who held on, her grip tightening on his while she reached out with mind and will, drawing on *his* power, *his* Gift . . . She had seen Caracandal borrow from Alimond, Morgus bloated with the power of the Tree. Hand-locked, she sucked his vigor into her body, into her spirit, like the desperate inhalation that revives a drowning man—

But the power that rushed into her was not from Jerrold Laye. It was from Azmordis.

It swept through her like a vast black surge, lifting her on the crest of a tsunami, so she felt herself growing, swelling, while the world shrank, and the tide of morlochs was a crawling of ants, and their prey dwindled into insignificance. Azmordis was taken by surprise, even he, and his fleshly home sagged and crumpled, and his shriek of startled fury was abruptly curtailed. The morlochs, freed from restraint, sprang toward their feast—Will's knife gleamed black in the sunset—Harbeak crouched on goat legs, and leapt. But a spear hurled from behind a stone took him in the chest, splitting him from rib to spine. Gaynor cried: "Fern! *Help us!*", and she fought to regain her Self, loosing her hold on Dr. Laye; the power crackled from her outflung arm in a current of dark lightning, and the foremost morlochs fell like swatted flies. There was an instant when room and valley overlapped, the walls closed on sunlight, and the carrion dead were scattered on sofa and carpet. Then there were only the three of them, and the slumped figure of Jerrold Laye, and Bradachin cleaning his spear on a cushion.

"Quick!" panted Fern. "The window! He'll recover any minute—"

They scrambled over the sill; the ground was only a little way below. After the sunglare of Azmodel the darkness blinded them, but still they ran, guided by the night-eyed goblin, down the drive, toward the gate. Above, the clouds reeled, the stars screamed in their tracks. Fern had no breath either to thank Bradachin or to scold him for disobeying her order; she could feel the energy ebbing from muscle and sinew, the dragging of limbs suddenly weighted. The bag bounced at her side, hampering her movements. She hoped the head was not too bruised by such a battering. The gate was near but behind she heard Azmordis, his voice grown to a gigantic boom, summoning his remaining creatures to the chase. In the garden the shadows sprang to life, skimming over the earth with flab foot and claw foot, reaching out with a hundred hands—

Too late. The fugitives were through the gap, staggering onto the road, and the gate to Drakemyre Hall swung shut behind them.

"They can't cross the boundary," Fern was saying; she clutched her brother to steady herself. "We must get to the car. This way."

"Listen." Will, too, was fighting for breath. "There's a *dragon*— a bloody *dragon*—in a cave—under the cellar. If he lets it loose— we won't have a prayer."

"He will," said Fern. "Come on."

"You're hurt." Gaynor wrapped an arm around her.

"Just—puggled," Fern managed, with half a smile. They could make out the car now, an inky shape against the verge. "I'll keep going . . . as long as I need to." She hoped she was right. "You get in. I have something to do. If I fail—drive like hell."

"We can't *leave* you—"

"The Gift will protect me," Fern prevaricated, pushing them toward the car. "Bradachin?"

"Aye?"

"Take care of them. And thanks."

"Aye."

She stepped back into the road, pouring the last of her power in a flood tide through her body. She was suddenly aware of her physical being as a mass of living cells, pulsing, growing, of the torrent of her blood, the piston thump of her heart. She breathed, and the night flowed into her like an elixir. Behind her Will, Gaynor, and Bradachin stood beside the car. Will had taken the keys and unlocked, but by some unspoken concensus none of them made any move to get in. Bradachin held his spear at the ready, the butt end resting lightly on the ground. Twenty yards away, beyond the gate, they saw Dr. Laye appear. In Azmodel he had seemed to be made of shadow, but now he shone with a dim phosphorescence, as if the wereglow that filled his eyes with the invasion of Azmordis had infected skin, hair, even clothing. Fern thought he did not walk but glided over the ground. He passed through the gate and moved out into the middle of the road. "Did you think the boundary would hold *me*?" he said, and Gaynor started, for though he spoke very softly the sound seemed to come from close by. "Fool! *This* is not the gate through which you can escape me. You have been very clever, Fernanda, too clever for your own good. To steal power from an immortal—to grab at my spirit like a pickpocket—that is blasphemy, and blasphemy merits the ultimate punishment. You have thrown away all your choices, all your chances. You—and your companions—are doomed."

Bradachin readied his spear, but Fern did not answer. Her earlier impatience had gone. Her heartbeat sounded like a great drum in the stillness of the night.

"How did it feel," taunted Azmordis, "to taste—just for a few seconds—the power that might have been yours all your life? Was it not sweet, to ride the darkness, to touch godhood? Then die regretting, and may your bitterness endure even beyond the world!"

"I have no regrets," said Fern, and her voice was clear and cold against his giant whisper.

"You will!" he retorted, and now his words were loud with the anticipation of triumph. "Did you imagine the morlochs were my only servants? Run, Fernanda, ere I call on one who is not bound in Azmodel—one against whom your feeble Gift is meaningless. Run while you can!"

He lifted his hand, and from his mouth came a noise that no human throat should be able to achieve, the bellow of tearing rock, of wounded earth. Power stabbed from his fingers and lanced toward the house, searing through the solid stonework, splitting it from gable to cellar. Windows shattered, floors crumbled, foundations groaned. Chimneys teetered and fell. As if in slow motion the two halves of the building pulled apart; floorboards, furniture, vases, paintings crashed into the new-made chasm. A pale glimmer of dust rose into the dark. "The time has come!" said Jerrold Laye. "Arise, Tenegrys! Arise, and come to me!"

A red light sprang from the depths of the house, showing the raw edges of torn plaster and paneling, the black gape of exposed rooms. At its source, Fern thought she could see a minute dart of flame.

Will said to Gaynor: *"Get in the car."*

She opened the door but stayed where she was, held by a fascination beyond fear, unable to wrench her gaze from the Hall.

Stubbornly, knowing it would be futile, Bradachin hefted the spear.

And then the dragon came.

It burst from its prison like an erupting volcano, rearing skyward on the jet thrust of its own rage—no longer the snake-slender creature Fern had seen in the spellfire but a titan among reptiles. It rose twice as high as the house—three times—four—shaking huge chunks of debris from its sides as if they were crumbs. Vast umbrella pinions opened out, fanning the flames exploring the lower stories into a conflagration; the uncoiling of its whiplash tail flattened the residual walls in its swath. On the giant S-bend of throat and belly, chinks of heat flickered between the scales like the fire cracks in a lava flow. It was greater and more terrible than anything they had imagined, yet an awe filled them that was stronger than terror, so that for a moment even Gaynor felt that such a sight surpassed all self-concern, erasing the prospect of imminent death. This was the epitome of dream and nightmare, of aspiration and fantasy, and it was *there*, it was real—its fury made the air throb— and the beauty and the dread and the splendor of it engulfed their hearts. It threw back its head and roared with the exultation of sudden freedom, belching a fire column that reached the underside of the lowest cloud and sent a hundred tentacles of flame coruscating across the canopy. Then it was airborne, its wingbeats quickening to a gale that drove blazing embers like leaves. In the garden, pieces of topiary ignited and misshapen shadows fled along the broken paths, trailing sparks. The dragon swooped low over the hillside, landing by the gate, a snap of its jaws mashing the iron fretwork like a bundle of twigs. Will drew his knife—a pointless reflex—and Bradachin poised his spear for the throw. Fern did not move.

The flamelight played over Dr. Laye, emphasizing his corpse color so he resembled Death himself, stalking the brimstone pits of Hell. "Tenegrys!" he ordered, and in his voice were two voices, echo within echo, invader and invaded, "here is meat for you, after your long fasting! These are my enemies: I give them to you. Hunt and feed!"

The dragon arched its spine, the great head swung around. Fern stood right in its path, silhouetted against the glare. She looked very small and helpless, clutching her bag. (Will thought in sudden pain: *How like a girl* . . . His Fern, who had never been like other girls.) One hand slipped under the flap, seized a hunk of stem and hair . . .

The dragon lunged—

—and stopped, halfway to the kill, abruptly immobilized, suspended in midspring on the tremor of its wings.

"Look well, Tenegrys!" Fern cried, lifting the fruit of the Tree as high as she could. "Behold the head of Ruvindra Laiï!"

Bradachin lowered his spear, but his grip did not slacken. Will and Gaynor stared in incredulous horror at the object Fern held, at its stunted gorge and tangle of hair . . .

Dr. Laye was motionless, momentarily dumbfounded. "It's an illusion," he croaked. "Fakery—a charlatan's trick . . . Take her! I *command* you!"

But the dragon stooped until its muzzle was on a level with the head, and the forked tongue extruded, investigating remembered features. Fern sensed the ebbing of its rage, touched a void of old sorrow, and long loneliness. "You have grown great, Angharial," said the head—and to Will and Gaynor, looking for the speaker, realization was perhaps more shocking than the advent of the dragon. "I can call you little crocodile no longer. Indeed you are the Infernest, like your father, Pharaïzon, lord of dragonkind." The rumble in the monster's throat was almost a purr. "I betrayed you," Ruvindra continued, and his voice was double-edged. "Before you were born, I enslaved you to Azmordis, the ancient Spirit who slew me in reward. But I kept faith with you in death, as I could not in life. Take heed! The one who seeks to command you now—to control you—is altogether faithless. That same Spirit has his soul in its claws—his very words are not his own."

"Lies!" shrieked Dr. Laye. "That *thing* is a cheat—a chimera—it is the girl talking! Kill her! Kill her *now*!"

Clouds moved across the dragon's eyes; doubt struggled with comprehension in the primitive simplicities of its brain. Fern felt its thought as something huge and tangible, an elemental intelligence all passion and hunger.

"He will use you," Ruvindra persisted, "and ultimately destroy you. He lusts for the Stone splinter that lies beneath your heart, last relic of a power he cannot hold. She whom he would have you kill is the witch-maiden whose art brought me here, even from beyond the world—from the Eternal Tree where I hung in purgatory with other such fruit. I would have you befriend her, Angharial, as she has befriended me. Will you do this?"

"She is no charmer!" raged Dr. Laye. "Don't you see? She is using that grotesque puppet to turn you against me—"

He stretched out his arm, impossibly far, snatching at the head with distended fingers—but the dragon wheeled, snake swift for all its size, and a hissing javelin of flame barred his way.

"Azmordis reveals himself!" said Ruvindra. "Has any normal man such a reach?"

Tenegrys swung back toward him: gaze met gaze.

The charmer said softly: "Trust me, Angharial—if you can. I returned only for that."

At the periphery of her vision Fern saw Dr. Laye move—not a natural movement but a sudden spasm, jerking at his body. His eyes widened—and widened—the lids peeled back from bulging eyeballs; his teeth rattled; foam bubbled from the corner of his mouth. He seemed to be trying to speak, to plead, but the only sounds that escaped from his contorted throat were shapeless and unintelligible. His joints twisted until the ligaments snapped; at one point his head appeared to be wrenched around until it was all but back to front . . . And behind him, his shadow rose upward, expanding and thickening, a separate entity, darker than the darkness against which it stood. The flamelight could not touch it; it extended a monstrous hand—

But the dragon bellowed, and a tongue of fire seared its very core, blasting it into tiny darknesses that fled away over hill and hollow to re-form on some other horizon, in some other place, and only the man remained, crawling on crippled limbs, whimpering. For an instant, a heartbeat, Fern saw into the dregs of his soul, deprived of dreams, of certainty, of power, a shrunken, cowering thing. He whispered: "Mercy! I beg you . . . All I wanted was the dragon—to rule it, to be one with it, like my ancestors long ago . . ."

"Be merciful," said Ruvindra.

The flame that hit Jerrold Laye must have been hotter than the surface of the sun. In a millisecond he was gone, reduced to a puff of ash, a smear on the road . . .

Gaynor murmured: "Dear God."

"It is well," said Ruvindra.

Fern's arm was beginning to tremble from the strain of holding him aloft, but she dared not relax. The dragon's maw was very near: she could see the wisps of smoke threading between its teeth, the blackened chasm of its nostril. Its breath smelled like an infernal ventilator and the heat of it was beginning to shrivel her cheek.

"And now," said the head, "I, too, have need of your mercy. I am trapped in this—vessel—this unholy apple—until it perishes. Only then may I pass Death's portal. Set me free."

The dragon made a strange noise somewhere between a snarl and a yammer.

"I do not command you," Ruvindra said. "Neither I nor any man has that right. Give me a quick road to eternity, or let me rot." Tenegrys dropped its head in submission: its grief and anguish invaded the mind of every watcher, eclipsing lesser emotion. The dragon could not weep, but Gaynor, forgetful of danger, felt the tears start in her eyes. "It is well," repeated the dragon charmer. "Afterward, if you will, give your allegiance to the witch, in gratitude for us both. And when I am indeed no more, remember that I loved thee, and I did not fail thee in the end."

The great head descended still lower, the double-pronged tongue flickered out as in a kiss. The last words were spoken so quietly that only Fern could hear them. "Farewell, Fernanda Morcadis. If I had a heart, it would go with thee." And then came a single shaft of concentrated flame—Fern felt her arm scorched, though somehow the skin was unmarked—and the black fruit was consumed, and all that remained was a lock of hair, clasped in her hand.

She stood silent, so full of loss that she was oblivious to exhaustion and peril, to the proximity of the dragon, to the others waiting beside the car. It seemed to her that the night grew still in that moment, and the wind held its breath, the clouds halted in their pathways through the upper air, the stars froze. But it was only her fancy. Her right hand fell to her side. She looked up, and saw the dragon's jaws barely a yard away, still slightly parted, and a red glimmer of flame receding down the tunnel of its throat. She knew she should be afraid, but she had no emotion left. The dragon watched her with eyes like globes of blood.

And then she realized that the last move was for her. She held out the lock of hair. "I will keep this," she said, "as a—as a token, a pledge between us. Now go . . ." She bit her lip at the phrase: it was as if she were driving it away. "Go where you will, Angharial Tenegrys. Fly free. Find the mountains at the edge of being—the deserted kingdoms of the otherworld. There is no place for you here. They say you are the last of the dragons, but . . . who knows? I wish you well. Fly free!"

There was a pause that seemed to Will and Gaynor to stretch out indefinitely. Then the dragon rose, and the tempest of its wings warped hedge and tree, and sent the flames streaming through the burning house so they flew like banners in the night. Higher it soared and higher, and the clouds whirled into a vortex around it, and its fires were drawn up into a spinning funnel of cumulus, and the dragon followed. For one instant more they saw it, far above the cloud cover, a star among stars; then it twinkled, faded, and was lost to view. The bonfire of Drakemyre Hall burned on merrily; below, the hillside was dark and empty.

Epilogue

Morgus

The morning was far advanced when they finally returned to Dale House. Will drove; Fern curled up on the back-seat with Lougarry, barely able to sit up unaided, let alone stand. They stopped at a vet's surgery that Will knew of on the way and the she-wolf's leg was set and splinted, though they had some trouble persuading the vet that an overnight stay was undesirable.

"What breed of dog is she?" he asked with burgeoning suspicion.

"Mongrel," suggested Gaynor.

"Cousin to White Fang," said Will.

Fern had stayed in the car, sleeping.

As they drove, there was little conversation: they were all tired and overburdened with their own thoughts. Tomorrow would be time enough to talk things through.

Dawn had come and gone behind a bank of cloud, but when they crossed the high moor the sun broke cover, illuminating the green of spring on plateau and in hollow. As they drew up in front of the house, its dour façade looked mellowed and welcoming to their eyes; Bradachin vanished, and Robin and Abby rushed out to meet them, and Mrs. Wicklow stood in the doorway, and on the slope beyond Ragginbone watched and waited, patient as a stone. It's over, thought Gaynor, and thought became a murmur, uttered under her breath, as she walked beside Will carrying his sister into the hall.

"No," muttered Fern, and her eyes half-opened, gleaming blearily through her lashes. "It has begun."

Two days later, when they had talked themselves out—when Will had claimed his stolen knife as a personal bequest from the dragon charmer, and Robin and Abby were puzzling over the explanations they had been offered—when Lougarry was hobbling from room to room snarling soundlessly at Yoda—when the faint and far-off moan of the bagpipes enlivened the slumbering house—Gaynor rose before the others and tapped on Fern's bedroom door.

She went in without waiting for an answer. Fern rolled over, brushing aside the clinging strands of sleep. "Gaynor," she said. And then: "You're going."

It was not a question.

"What about you and Will?"

Gaynor did not ask her how she knew. "That's why I'm going. I've ordered a taxi. Would you say good-bye to him for me?"

"If that's what you want."

"It has to be." She sat down on the bed, twisting and untwisting the long tendrils of her hair. "He's too young."

"Don't be ridiculous."

"I mean, too young for commitment. He likes me, but he doesn't love me—not yet, not enough, maybe not ever. He's got— oh, so many fields to play, so many wild oats to sow. And he's your brother. I couldn't bear for it to happen, and then to go wrong. Not when we've all been through so much, grown so close . . ."

"Coward," said Fern.

"Yes," said Gaynor.

Presently the taxi came. She kissed her friend, and went downstairs and out of the door, closing it softly behind her, and got in the car and was driven away, up over the moors into the April morning.

I burn, I burn.

The fire is within me and without . . . it eats into a thousand years of flesh, seeking my very core. The pain is beyond bearing. Hearing, sight, smell are all destroyed—I crawl toward the water, guided by some faculty beyond the senses. Every inch is an increase of agony. And then I reach the river—the River of Death, of healing, of renewal, the river where the gods plunged the Cauldron of Rebirth to be cooled after its forging, in an age before recorded history, before it was stolen and broken and abused. They say something of its power still flows in the ancient stream. The cold swallows me, quenching flame, freezing me to the heart. My blackened skin hardens to a chrysalis in which all that remains of my swollen body coils like a blind white larva in a red pulp of blood. The chrysalis fastens itself to the rock beneath the surface: inside, I am nourished by the old spell, the maggot spell, the spell of all naked, wormlike creatures who must turn to stone ere they can be transformed and hatch anew. Here in the dark I can feel my substance changing, growing, unfolding into pale soft limbs and wisps of swimming hair. The shell that protects me is sealed and set hard, stronger than obsidian. I am warm and moist in my strange new womb, a thing half-embryo, half-adult, carrying memory, knowledge, power in the nucleus of my being. I can feel my toes sprouting, the uncurling of my fingers . . . Above me the Styx flows on untroubled.

When I am full-made, the chrysalis will float to the surface, and crack, and I shall rise like a new Aphrodite from the leaden waves . . .

Glossary

Names

Angharial (Ang-har-ee-al) A pet name for the young Tenegrys, its origins are obscure, but there may be some connection with *gharial*, a type of small, very slender crocodile.

Azmordis (Az-moor-diss) The name generally used in these accounts for the Oldest Spirit. As stated in *Prospero's Children*, it is probably a corruption of Asmodeus, a malignant spirit or senior demon in the hierarchy of Hell. The Spirit uses many such names, of both gods and devils (Shaitan, mentioned in the manuscript Gaynor studies, is a well-known variant of Satan, but may also refer to the same being).

Agamo (Ag-ar-moh), the toad god of the swamp, is an identity lost in obscurity.

Bethesne (Beth-ez-nee) The name sounds biblical, but the character relates more to the Greek mythos, in which Perseus consults three witches who pass a single eye from hand to hand. There may also be some connection with the Nordic Volas: Skaetha (Skay-tha), the seeress who saw the future, probably derives from Skuld, who rose from the grave to foretell the battle of Ragnarok for Odin.

Bradachin   (Bra-da-chin, with the "ch" pronounced as in loch)
    From the old Scottish Gaelic, meaning "little thief."

Caracandal   (Ca-ra-can-dal) For sources see *Prospero's Children*.
    Other names mentioned in this book for Ragginbone include
    Elvincape, a reference to his customary coatlike garment with
    its pointed hood, and Gabbandoflo, an Italian version with the
    same meaning (literally, *gabbano d'elfo*).

Elivayzar   (El-ee-vay-zar) A variant of the biblical Eleazar. Moon-
    spittle, as explained in the text, is a mistranslation of Mond-
    spitzl, German for Moonpoint, with the suffix "l" signifying
    small. This might be an ancient term for the pointed crescent
    of the new moon.

Infernest   A courtesy title habitually given by dragon charmers
    to the greatest of dragons. It derives from Taebor Infernes
    (Tay-boor In-fur-nees), largest and most intelligent of the
    early dragons, the obvious origin being the Latin *inferno*.
    When Ruvindra Laiï calls the dragon "inferneling" (in-fur-nel-
    ing), this is clearly a diminutive of the same.

Kaliban   As stated in the text, this comes from Caliburn, also
    known as Excalibur, King Arthur's famous sword. Morgus's
    choice of this as a name for her son could be an early mani-
    festation of the same trend that leads rock and film stars to
    christen their children Moon, Heaven, and so on. Shake-
    speare may well have borrowed the name for use in *The Tem-
    pest* after hearing some legend about the monstrous son of an
    ancient witch.

Laiï   (Ly-ee) The family name of the dragon charmers was for-
    merly Ylai: they were an offshoot of the Atlantean House of
    Ghond, one of the twelve Ruling Families. Fleeing the fall of
    Atlantis, they spent some time in the vicinity of India and Ti-
    bet, which would account for the orientalization of their sur-
    name. Ruvindra has an Indian sound, and it was, of course, in
    this area that he chose to conceal the dragon's egg.

It is worth noting that in all worlds great mountains have a special power, and many in this world are linked to their otherworldly counterparts. In the Himalayas there are secret ways leading to the dimension of myth and magic, to hidden valleys beyond reality, eternal gardens among the snows. Some say the route to Azmodel is there, a tunnel plunging down and down to the poisoned anti-Paradise of the Oldest of Evils.

Lougarry   From the French *loup garou* (werewolf). See *Prospero's Children*.

Mabb   Sometimes romanticized as the Faery Queen, Mabb's true nature is the essence of all that made goblinkind both inimical to us and a caricature of so many of our less attractive traits. She is vain, mischievous, capricious, egotistical, given to petty cruelty, incapable of profound thought. The concept of kings and queens is a mortal idea that goblins have assimilated for reasons of their own, perhaps because of their long association with Man. In general, werefolk live in an otherworld without social order, where the weak avoid the strong, and do not serve them. However, there are a few exceptions among the Old Spirits, most notably Azmordis, who has the human need to dominate, and who enlarges his own power spectrum by controlling many lesser beings.

Morgus   Legend tells of Morgause or Morgawze, sister of Morgana Le Fay and half sister of Arthur, though little is known of her in comparison to her more famous siblings. Here we learn the sisters are twins, Morgus and Morgun, born of a line long celebrated for their Gifting. Mordraid is mentioned as an older son of Morgus, although stories differ as to which of them was the mother of Arthur's incestuous child.

The prefix Mor- was a feature of naming in this family, designating someone who was exceptionally Gifted. Since the Gift rarely shows till adolescence, it is likely that the name was acquired then, and with an arrogance that seems to be a characteristic of the line, the birth name was dropped altogether. The meaning may derive from various words for "dark," notably the Swedish *mörk* or the Spanish *morcillo*. In giving Fernanda the Gift name of Morcadis, Morgus was evidently attempting to establish a kinship with her by means more subtle than mixing blood. What significance there may be in Fern's acceptance of the name is not yet clear.

morloch   (moor-loch, with the "ch" pronounced as in Scots) The story of the wizard Morloch appears in the text and there is little to add. Once again, the prefix Mor- indicates a relationship to the same family. As with certain of the Old Spirits, we see in his tale a desire to create life by magical means, the normal human methods evidently proving unsatisfactory. The morlochs, however, like the creatures made by the spirits (reputedly including mermaids, goblins, and other werefolk) are merely things of flesh and clay animated by elementals, who already existed on a low plane in the cosmos. In theory, magical beings can have no souls—hence Kaliban's obsession with the subject. Morgus experimented with her own body to conceive her second son; otherwise the child of an Old Spirit would be stillborn. Immortals do not need to reproduce. Whether any living creature, mortal or otherwise, has a soul is, of course, a matter for debate and currently beyond scientific proof.

Pharaïzon   (Fah-ry-ee-zon) The greatest of the dragons. Dragon names are usually given by humans: this one may come from the same stem as the Egyptian *pharaoh*.

pugwidgie   This term was originally applied to a particularly mischievous goblin, but was transposed as a common name for the morlochs, since the lesser werefolk are superstitious about using their mastername. The source is probably Puck-wight.

Senecxys   (Seh-nek-siss) The mate of Pharaïzon. Origin unknown.

Sysselore   (Siss-se-loor) This could be a complex play on words, from sister-in-lore (i.e., coven sister), but is more likely to be a variant of the medieval name Sisley, or a derivative of the witch's former name Syrcé, from Seersay, meaning sibyl or pythoness. This, in its turn, is clearly related to the Greek Circe.

tannasgeal   Direct from Scots Gaelic, this combines the elements *tannasg*, ghost, and *geal*, white.

Tenegrys   (Teh-ne-griss) This could be a derivative of the Latin *tenebra*, *tenebrae* (pl.), shadow(s). Alternatively it might come from the Gaelic *tannasg*, as above, and *greis*, time. The name was given by Dr. Laye, but almost certainly suggested by Azmordis.

On Dragons

Very little is known about when and how dragons originated. The manuscript Gaynor discovered stated that they were made by Shaitan, one of several names for the devil and a possible identity of Azmordis, but this may have been poetic license on the part of the writer. It is true that long ago many of the Old Spirits manifested themselves as pagan gods and demons, trying thus to gain ascendancy over Man or Nature, and in the earliest days "creating" beings of their own—bodies of spell and substance, often combining anatomical details from several creatures, inhabited by primitive elementals. As mentioned above, this was how many of the werefolk came into existence. Others were self-created, crude spirits strong enough to make themselves a physical image that expressed their essence. Windhorses, which occasionally metamorphose into unicorns, are among this latter group—sprites of the moving air who have acquired a suitable form in which they can appear and fade at will. Most werefolk are far from solid, their shapes flickering in and out of reality according to the eye of the observer or their own uncertain moods.

Dragons, however, seem to be both more "real" and more potent, with a power that even the Oldest cannot control. If they
were made by Azmordis or one of his ilk, then the fire-spirits summoned to possess them must have proved impossible to manipulate, and the creation escaped the yoke of the creator. Their
curious affinity with humans—with all that is most cruel and savage in our nature, yet also all that is most passionate and free—is
well documented. Whether we invented dragons ourselves, calling them into being to fulfill some deep and dreadful need, we
can only speculate.

There seem to be many kinds of dragons, with differing tem-
peraments and anatomical features—winged or wingless, some
with feathery manes, others with many variations of color, horn,
and scale. Not all breathe fire. Oriental dragons are frequently
beneficent, while their northern kin are associated with hoarded
treasure and appear to epitomize mortal greed. It is a significant
fact that in our modern, high-tech world dragons have become
the ultimate symbol of freedom—freedom not only from the laws
of science but also from the laws of Man, a fierce amorality that
recognizes no check or hindrance. In Tenegrys we are reminded
that although dragons are beautiful and awesome, beyond the
reach of the everyday world they are deadly, and without the skills
of a dragon charmer would kill and burn without compunction.

How the line of dragon charmers acquired their extraordinary
relationship with these monsters is a tale told elsewhere.

On the Gift

At this point it may be helpful to add a word or two about the
power known as the Gift. Of its origins much is said in *Prospero's
Children*: how it was caused by the Lodestone, a ball of matter
the size of a serpent's egg coming from, or even composed of, another universe, a whole cosmos with different rules, different sci-

ence. It was kept in Atlantis and those born in its immediate vicinity were genetically altered, giving them the ability to break the physical laws of this world. The Lodestone was destroyed, as was Atlantis and almost all its people, but the mutant genes had already been passed on and they spread throughout the human race, recurring down the centuries, often ignored or unused by the possessor, but never weakening or dying out.

Various powers can be produced by the Gift. The most common is the so-called sixth sense: telepathy, precognition, telegnosis— "the ability to know that which cannot be ascertained by normal means." Gaynor, we are told, is a "sensitive": she can see ghosts, and is peculiarly susceptible to atmosphere, another variant of the same. Most of us have a little of this talent, and it manifests itself in symbolic dreams, in a heightened awareness of the emotions and feelings of others, in instinct and intuition. The whole of our mystic self, though not dependent on the Gift, is strengthened and empowered by it. In its most potent form, as in Fern's case, it gives you the capacity to influence both people and objects without physical contact, to create true-seeming illusions, to change your own shape or that of others—in short, to break the rules. It can be transmitted as raw energy: light, heat, force. But without discipline it becomes as wayward and perilous as weather. Only through the ancient spell patterns and the Atlantean language can it be shaped and directed, given meaning and purpose. Atlantean is an ancestor language of many European tongues, but it evolved within the Lodestone's force field, attuned to its rhythms, and when the Stone was broken it is thought the power thus released passed into the speech to which it had given birth. Perhaps the energy it engendered was transmuted into sound and tone, a music from beyond the spheres. Whatever the truth, without Atlantean the most extreme form of the Gift, if used, will be out of control, and may be deadly both to the user and to anyone against whom they may lash out.

JAN SIEGEL has already lived one lifetime—during which she traveled the world and supported herself through a variety of professions, including that of actress, barmaid, garage hand, laboratory assistant, journalist, and model. Her new life is devoted to her writing, but she also finds time to ride, ski, and attend the opera.